Sophie Kinsella is the author of the best-selling 'Shopaholic' series: *The Secret Dreamworld of a Shopaholic*, *Shopaholic Abroad*, *Shopaholic Ties the Knot* and *Shopaholic & Sister* as well as the best-selling *Can You Keep a Secret?*.

Also by Sophie Kinsella

THE SECRET DREAMWORLD OF A SHOPAHOLIC
SHOPAHOLIC ABROAD
SHOPAHOLIC TIES THE KNOT

and published by Black Swan

Can You Keep A Secret?

Sophie Kinsella

BLACK SWAN

CAN YOU KEEP A SECRET
A BLACK SWAN BOOK : 9780552771108

First publication in Great Britain

PRINTING HISTORY
Black Swan edition published 2003

13 15 17 19 20 18 16 14 12

Set in 11/13pt Melior by
Phoenix Typesetting, Burley-in-Wharfedale, West Yorkshire.

Black Swan Books are published by Transworld Publishers,
61–63 Uxbridge Road, London W5 5SA,
a division of The Random House Group Ltd.

Addresses for Random House Group Ltd companies outside the UK
can be found at: www.randomhouse.co.uk

The Random House Group Ltd Reg. No. 954009.

Printed and bound in Great Britain by
Cox & Wyman Ltd, Reading, Berkshire

The Random House Group Limited makes every effort to ensure
that the papers used in its books are made from trees that have
been legally sourced from well-managed and credibly certified
forests. Our paper procurement policy can be found at:
www.randomhouse.co.uk/paper.htm.

To H, from whom I have no secrets.
Well, not many, anyway.

Acknowledgements

A big thank you to Mark Hedley, Jenny Bond, Rosie Andrews and Olivia Heywood for all their generous advice.

And hugest gratitude as always to Linda Evans, Patrick Plonkington-Smythe, Araminta Whitley and Celia Hayley, my boys and the board.

ONE

Of course I have secrets.

Of course I do. Everyone has a few secrets. It's completely normal. I'm sure I don't have any more than anybody else.

I'm not talking about big, earth-shattering secrets. Not the-president-is-planning-to-bomb-Japan-and-only-Will-Smith-can-save-the-world type secrets. Just normal, everyday little secrets.

Like for example, here are a few random secrets of mine, off the top of my head:

1. My Kate Spade bag is a fake.
2. I love sweet sherry, the least cool drink in the universe.
3. I have no idea what NATO stands for. Or even what it is.
4. I weigh 9 stone 3. Not 8 stone 3, like my boyfriend Connor thinks. (Although in my defence, I was planning to go on a diet when I told him that. And to be fair, it is only one number different.)
5 I've always thought Connor looks a bit like Ken. As in Barbie and Ken.
6. Sometimes, when we're right in the middle of passionate sex, I suddenly want to laugh.
7. I lost my virginity in the spare bedroom with Danny Nussbaum, while Mum and Dad were downstairs watching *Ben Hur*.

8. I've already drunk the wine that Dad told me to lay down for twenty years.

9. Sammy the goldfish at home isn't the same goldfish that Mum and Dad gave me to look after when they went to Egypt.

10. When my colleague Artemis really annoys me, I feed her plant orange juice. (Which is pretty much every day.)

11. I once had this weird lesbian dream about my flatmate Lissy.

12. My G-string is hurting me.

13. I've always had this deep down conviction that I'm not like everybody else, and there's an amazingly exciting new life waiting for me just around the corner.

14. I have no idea what this guy in the grey suit is going on about.

15. Plus I've already forgotten his name.

And I only met him ten minutes ago.

'We believe in logistical formative alliances,' he's saying in a nasal, droning voice, 'both above and below the line.'

'Absolutely!' I reply brightly, as though to say: Doesn't everybody?

Logistical. What does that mean, again?

Oh God. What if they ask me?

Don't be stupid, Emma. They won't suddenly demand, 'What does logistical mean?' I'm a fellow marketing professional, aren't I? Obviously I know these things.

And anyway, if they mention it again I'll change the subject. Or I'll say I'm post-logistical or something.

The important thing is to keep confident and businesslike. I can do this. This is my big chance and I'm not going to screw it up.

I'm sitting in the offices of Glen Oil's headquarters in Glasgow, and as I glance at my reflection in the window, I look just like a top businesswoman. My hair is straightened, I'm wearing discreet earrings like they tell you to in How-to-win-that-job articles, and I've got on my smart new Jigsaw suit. (At least, it's practically new. I got it from the Cancer Research shop and sewed on a button to replace the missing one, and you can hardly tell.)

I'm here representing the Panther Corporation, which is where I work. The meeting is to finalize a promotional arrangement between the new cranberry-flavoured Panther Prime sports drink and Glen Oil, and I flew up this morning from London, especially. (The company paid, and everything!)

When I arrived, the Glen Oil marketing guys started on this long, show-offy 'who's-travelled-the-most?' conversation about airmiles and the red-eye to Washington – and I think I bluffed pretty convincingly. (Except when I said I'd flown Concorde to Ottawa, and it turns out Concorde doesn't go to Ottawa.) But the truth is, this is the first time I've ever had to travel for a deal.

OK. The *real* truth is, this is the first deal I've ever done, full stop. I've been at the Panther Corporation for eleven months as a marketing assistant, and until now all I've been allowed to do is type out copy, arrange meetings for other people, get the sandwiches and pick up my boss's dry-cleaning.

So this is kind of my big break. And I've got this secret little hope that if I do this well, maybe I'll get promoted. The ad for my job said 'possibility of promotion after a year', and on Monday I'm having my yearly appraisal meeting with my boss, Paul. I looked up 'Appraisals' in the staff induction book, and it said

11

they are 'an ideal opportunity to discuss possibilities for career advancement'.

Career advancement! At the thought, I feel a familiar stab of longing in my chest. It would just show Dad I'm not a complete loser. And Mum. And Kerry. If I could go home and casually say, 'By the way, I've been promoted to Marketing Executive.'

Emma Corrigan, Marketing Executive.

Emma Corrigan, Senior Vice-President (Marketing.)

As long as everything goes well today. Paul said the deal was done and dusted and all I had to do was nod and shake their hands, and even I should be able to manage that. And so far, I reckon it's going really well.

OK, so I don't understand about 90 per cent of what they're saying. But then I didn't understand much of my GCSE French Oral either, and I still got a B.

'Rebranding . . . analysis . . . cost-effective . . .'

The man in the grey suit is still droning on about something or other. As casually as possible, I extend my hand and inch his business card towards me so I can read it.

Doug Hamilton. That's right. OK, I can remember this. Doug. Dug. Easy. I'll picture a shovel. Together with a *ham*. Which . . . which looks *ill* . . . and . . .

OK, forget this. I'll just write it down.

I write down 'rebranding' and 'Doug Hamilton' on my notepad and give an awkward little wriggle. God, my knickers really are uncomfortable. I mean, G-strings are never that comfortable at the best of times, in my opinion, but these are particularly bad. Which could be because they're two sizes too small.

Which could possibly be because Connor bought them for me, and told the lingerie assistant I weighed eight stone three. Whereupon she told him I must be size eight. Size eight!

(Frankly, I think she was just being mean. She *must* have known I was fibbing.)

So it's Christmas Eve, and we're exchanging presents, and I unwrap this pair of gorgeous pale pink silk knickers. Size eight. And I basically have two options.

A: Confess the truth: 'Actually these are too small, I'm more of a 12, and by the way, I don't really weigh eight stone three.' Or . . .

B: Shoe-horn myself into them.

Actually, it was fine. You could hardly see the red lines on my skin afterwards. And all it meant was that I had to quickly cut all the labels out of my clothes so Connor would never realize.

Since then, I've hardly ever worn this particular set of underwear, needless to say. But every so often I see them looking all nice and expensive in the drawer and think, Oh come on, they can't be *that* tight, and somehow squeeze into them. Which is what I did this morning. I even decided I must have lost weight, because they didn't feel too bad.

I am such a deluded moron.

'. . . unfortunately since rebranding . . . major rethink . . . feel we need to be considering alternative synergies . . .'

Up to now I've just been sitting and nodding, thinking this business meeting lark is really easy. But now Doug Hamilton's voice starts to impinge on my consciousness. What's he saying?

'. . . two products diverging . . . becoming incompatible . . .'

What was that about incompatible? What was that about a major rethink? I feel a jolt of alarm. Maybe this isn't just waffle. Maybe he's actually *saying* something. Quick, listen.

'We appreciate the functional and synergetic

partnership that Panther and Glen Oil have enjoyed in the past,' Doug Hamilton is saying. 'But you'll agree that clearly we're going in different directions.'

Different directions?

Is *that* what he's been talking about all this time?

My stomach gives an anxious lurch.

He can't be—

Is he trying to pull out of the deal?

'Excuse me, Doug,' I say, in my most relaxed voice. 'Obviously I was closely following what you were saying earlier.' I give a friendly, we're-all-professionals-together smile. 'But if you could just . . . um, recap the situation for all our benefits . . .'

In plain English, I beg silently.

Doug Hamilton and the other guy exchange glances.

'We're a little unhappy about your brand values,' says Doug Hamilton.

'My brand values?' I echo in panic.

'The brand values of the *product*,' he says, giving me an odd look. 'As I've been explaining, we here at Glen Oil are going through a rebranding process at the moment, and we see our new image very much as a *caring* petrol, as our new daffodil logo demonstrates. And we feel Panther Prime, with its emphasis on sport and competition, is simply too aggressive.'

'Aggressive?' I stare at him, bewildered. 'But . . . it's a fruit drink.'

This makes no sense. Glen Oil is fume-making, world-ruining petrol. Panther Prime is an innocent cranberry-flavoured drink. How can it be too aggressive?

'The values it espouses.' He gestures to the marketing brochures on the table. 'Drive. Elitism. Masculinity. The very slogan, "Don't Pause". Frankly, it seems a little dated.' He shrugs. 'We just don't think a joint initiative will be possible.'

14

No. No. This can't be happening. He can't be pulling out.

Everyone at the office will think it was my fault. They'll think I cocked it up and I'm completely crap.

My heart is thumping. My face is hot. I can't let this happen. But what do I say? I haven't prepared anything. Paul said it was all set up and all I had to do was shake their hands.

'We'll certainly discuss it again before we make a decision,' Doug's saying. He gives me a brief smile. 'And as I say, we would like to continue links with the Panther Corporation, so this has been a useful meeting in any case.'

He's pushing back his chair.

I can't let this slip away! I have to try to win them round. I have to try and shut the deal.

Close the deal. That's what I meant.

'Wait!' I hear myself say. 'Just . . . wait a moment! I have a few points to make.'

What am I talking about? I have no points to make.

There's a can of Panther Prime sitting on the desk, and I grab it for inspiration. Playing for time, I stand up, walk to the centre of the room and raise the can high into the air where we can all see it.

'Panther Prime is . . . a sports drink.'

I stop, and there's a polite silence. My face is prickling.

'It . . . um . . . it is very . . .'

Oh God. What am I doing?

Come *on*, Emma. *Think*. Think Panther Prime . . . think Panther Cola . . . think . . . think . . .

Yes! Of course!

OK, start again.

'Since the launch of Panther Cola in the late 1980s, Panther drinks have been a byword for energy, excitement and excellence,' I say fluently.

Thank God. This is the standard marketing blurb for Panther Cola. I've typed it out so many zillions of times, I could recite it in my sleep.

'Panther drinks are a marketing phenomenon,' I continue. 'The Panther character is one of the most widely recognized in the world, while the classic slogan "Don't Pause" has made it into dictionaries. We are now offering Glen Oil an exclusive opportunity to join with this premium, world-famous brand.'

My confidence growing, I start to stride around the room, gesturing with the can.

'By buying a Panther health drink, the consumer is signalling that he will settle for nothing but the best.' I hit the can sharply with my other hand. 'He expects the best from his energy drink, he expects the best from his petrol, he expects the best from himself.'

I'm flying! I'm fantastic! If Paul could see me now, he'd give me a promotion on the spot!

I come over to the desk and look Doug Hamilton right in the eye. 'When the Panther consumer opens that can, he is making a choice which tells the world who he is. I'm asking Glen Oil to make the same choice.'

As I finish speaking I plant the can firmly in the middle of the desk, reach for the ring pull and, with a cool smile, snap it back.

It's like a volcano erupting.

Fizzy cranberry-flavoured drink explodes in a whoosh out of the can, landing on the desk, drenching the papers and blotters in lurid red liquid . . . and oh no, please no . . . spattering all over Doug Hamilton's shirt.

'Fuck!' I gasp. 'I mean, I'm really sorry . . .'

'Jesus Christ,' says Doug Hamilton irritably, standing up and getting a handkerchief out of his pocket. 'Does this stuff stain?'

'Er . . .' I grab the can helplessly. 'I don't know.'

'I'll get a cloth,' says the other guy, and leaps to his feet.

The door closes behind him and there's silence, apart from the sound of cranberry drink dripping slowly onto the floor.

I stare at Doug Hamilton, my face hot and blood throbbing through my ears.

'Please . . .' I say, and clear my husky throat. 'Don't tell my boss.'

After all that. I screwed it up.

As I drag my heels across the concourse at Glasgow Airport, I feel completely dejected. Doug Hamilton was quite sweet in the end. He said he was sure the stain would come out, and promised he wouldn't tell Paul what happened. But he didn't change his mind about the deal.

My first big meeting. My first big chance – and this is what happens. I feel like giving up on the whole thing. I feel like phoning the office and saying 'That's it, I'm never coming back again, and by the way, it was me who jammed the photocopier that time.'

But I can't. This is my third career in four years. It *has* to work. For my own self-worth. For my own self-esteem. And also because I owe my dad four thousand quid.

'So what can I get you?' says an Australian guy, and I look up dazedly. I've arrived at the airport with an hour to go, and have headed straight for the bar.

'Erm . . .' My mind is blank. 'Er . . . white wine. No, actually, a vodka and tonic. Thanks.'

As he moves away, I slump down again in my stool. An air hostess with a French plait comes and sits down, two bar stools away. She smiles at me, and I smile weakly in return.

I don't know how other people manage their careers, I really don't. Like my oldest friend Lissy. She's always known she wanted to be a lawyer – and now, ta-daah! She's a fraud barrister. But I left college with absolutely no clue. My first job was in estate agency, and I only went into it because I've always quite liked looking round houses, plus I met this woman with amazing red lacquered nails at a career fair who told me she made so much money, she'd be able to retire when she was forty.

But the minute I started, I hated it. I hated all the other trainee estate agents. I hated saying things like 'a lovely aspect'. And I hated the way if someone said they could afford £300,000 we were supposed to give them details of houses costing at least £400,000, and then kind of look down our noses, like, 'You only have £300,000? God, you complete loser.'

So after six months I announced I was changing career and was going to be a photographer instead. It was *such* a fantastic moment, like in a film or something. My dad lent me the money for a photography course and camera, and I was going to launch this amazing new creative career, and it was going to be the start of my new life . . .

Except it didn't quite happen like that.

I mean, for a start, do you have any idea how much a photographer's assistant gets paid?

Nothing. It's nothing.

Which, you know, I wouldn't have minded if anyone had actually *offered* me a photographer's assistant's job.

I heave a heavy sigh, and gaze at my doleful expression in the mirror behind the bar. As well as everything else, my hair, which I carefully straightened with serum this morning, has gone all frizzy. Typical.

At least I wasn't the only one who didn't get anywhere. Out of the eight people on my course, one became instantly successful and now takes photos for *Vogue* and stuff, one became a wedding photographer, one had an affair with the tutor, one went travelling, one had a baby, one works at Snappy Snaps and one is now at Morgan Stanley.

Meanwhile I got more and more into debt, and started temping and applying for jobs which actually paid money. And eventually, eleven months ago, I started as a marketing assistant at the Panther Corporation.

The barman places a vodka and tonic in front of me, and gives me a quizzical look. 'Cheer up!' he says. 'It can't be that bad!'

'Thanks,' I say gratefully, and take a sip. That feels a bit better. I'm just taking a second sip when my mobile starts to ring.

My stomach gives a nervous flip. If it's the office, I'll just pretend I didn't hear.

But it's not, it's our home number flashing on the little screen.

'Hi,' I say, pressing green.

'Hiya!' comes Lissy's voice. 'Only me! So how did it go?'

Lissy is my flatmate and my oldest friend in the world. She has tufty dark hair and an IQ of about 600 and is the sweetest person I know.

'It was a disaster,' I say miserably.

'What happened? Didn't you get the deal?'

'Not only did I not get the deal, I drenched the marketing director of Glen Oil in cranberry drink.'

Along the bar, I can see the air hostess hiding a smile, and I feel myself flush. Great. Now the whole world knows.

'Oh dear.' I can almost *feel* Lissy trying to think of

19

something positive to say. 'Well, at least you got their attention,' she says at last. 'At least they won't forget you in a hurry.'

'I suppose,' I say morosely. 'So, did I have any messages?'

'Oh! Erm . . . no. I mean, your dad did phone, but . . . um . . . you know . . . it wasn't . . .' She tails off evasively.

'Lissy. What did he want?'

There's a pause.

'Apparently your cousin's won some industry award,' she says apologetically. 'They're going to be celebrating it on Saturday as well as your mum's birthday.'

'Oh. Great.'

I slump deeper in my chair. That's all I need. My cousin Kerry triumphantly clutching some silver Best-travel-agent-in-the-world-no-make-that-universe trophy.

'And Connor rang, too, to see how you got on,' adds Lissy quickly. 'He was really sweet, he said he didn't want to ring your mobile during your meeting in case it disturbed you.'

'Really?'

For the first time today, I feel a lift in spirits.

Connor. My boyfriend. My lovely, thoughtful boyfriend.

'He's such a sweetheart!' Lissy is saying. 'He said he's tied up in a big meeting all afternoon but he's cancelled his squash game especially, so do you want to go out to supper tonight?'

'Oh,' I say, with a flicker of pleasure. 'Oh well, that'll be nice. Thanks, Lissy.'

I click off and take another sip of vodka, feeling much more cheerful.

My boyfriend.

It's just like Julie Andrews said. When the dog bites, when the bee stings . . . I simply remember I have a boyfriend – and suddenly things don't seem quite so completely shit.

Or however she put it.

And not just any boyfriend. A tall, handsome, clever boyfriend, whom *Marketing Week* called 'one of the brightest sparks in marketing research today'.

I sit nursing my vodka, allowing thoughts of Connor to roll round my brain and comfort me. The way his blond hair shines in the sunshine, and the way he's always smiling. And the way he upgraded all the software on my computer the other day without me even asking, and the way he . . . he . . .

My mind's gone blank. This is ridiculous. I mean, there's so much that is wonderful about Connor. From his . . . his long legs. Yes. And his broad shoulders. To the time he looked after me when I had the flu. I mean, how many boyfriends do that? Exactly.

I'm so lucky, I really am.

I put the phone away, run my fingers through my hair, and glance at the clock behind the bar. Forty minutes to go before the flight. Not long now. Nerves are starting to creep over me like little insects, and I take a deep gulp of vodka, draining my glass.

It'll be fine, I tell myself for the zillionth time. It'll be absolutely fine.

I'm not frightened. I'm just . . . I'm just . . .

OK. I am frightened.

16. I'm scared of flying.

I've never told anyone I'm scared of flying. It just sounds so lame. And I mean, it's not like I'm phobic or anything. It's not like I can't *get* on a plane. It's just . . . all things being equal, I would prefer to be on the ground.

I never used to be scared. But over the last few years, I've gradually got more and more nervous. I know it's completely irrational. I know thousands of people fly every day and it's practically safer than lying in bed. You have less chance of being in a plane crash than . . . than finding a man in London, or something.

But still. I just don't like it.

Maybe I'll have another quick vodka.

By the time my flight is called, I've drunk two more vodkas and am feeling a lot more positive. I mean, Lissy's right. At least I made an impression, didn't I? At least they'll remember who I am. As I stride towards the gate, clutching my briefcase, I almost start to feel like a confident businesswoman again. A couple of people smile at me as they pass, and I smile broadly back, feeling a warm glow of friendliness. You see. The world's not so bad after all. It's all just a question of being positive. Anything can happen in life, can't it? You never know what's round the next corner.

I reach the entrance to the plane, and there at the door, taking boarding passes, is the air hostess with the French plait who was sitting at the bar earlier.

'Hi again,' I say smiling. 'This is a coincidence!'

The air hostess stares at me.

'Hi. Erm . . .'

'What?'

Why does she look embarrassed?

'Sorry. It's just . . . did you know that . . .' She gestures awkwardly to my front.

'What is it?' I say, pleasantly. I look down, and freeze, aghast.

Somehow my silky shirt has been unbuttoning itself

22

while I've been walking along. Three buttons have come undone and it's gaping at the front.

My bra shows. My pink lacy bra. The one that went a bit blobby in the wash.

That's why those people were smiling at me. Not because the world is a nice place, but because I'm Pink-Blobby-Bra-Woman.

'Thanks,' I mutter, and do up the buttons with fumbling fingers, my face hot with humiliation.

'It hasn't been your day, has it?' says the air hostess sympathetically, holding out a hand for my boarding pass. 'Sorry, I couldn't help overhearing, earlier.'

'That's all right.' I raise a half-smile. 'No, it hasn't been the best day of my life.' There's a short silence as she studies my boarding pass.

'Tell you what,' she says in a low voice. 'Would you like an on-board upgrade?'

'A what?' I stare at her blankly.

'Come on. You deserve a break.'

'Really? But . . . can you just upgrade people like that?'

'If there are spare seats, we can. We use our discretion. And this flight is so short.' She gives me a conspiratorial smile. 'Just don't tell everyone, OK?'

She leads me into the front section of the plane and gestures to a big, wide, comfortable seat. I've never been upgraded before in my life! I can't quite believe she's really letting me do this.

'Is this first class?' I whisper, taking in the hushed, luxury atmosphere. A man in a smart suit is tapping at a laptop to my right, and two elderly women in the corner are plugging themselves into headsets.

'Business class. There's no first class on this flight.' She lifts her voice to a normal volume. 'Is everything OK for you?'

'It's perfect! Thanks very much.'

'No problem.' She smiles again and walks away, and I push my briefcase under the seat in front.

Wow. This really is lovely. Big wide seats, and footrests, and everything. This is going to be a completely pleasurable experience from start to finish, I tell myself firmly. I reach for my seatbelt and buckle it up nonchalantly, trying to ignore the flutters of apprehension in my stomach.

'Would you like some champagne?'

It's my friend the air hostess, beaming down at me.

'That would be great,' I say. 'Thanks!'

Champagne!

'And for you, sir? Some champagne?'

The man in the seat next to mine hasn't even looked up yet. He's wearing jeans and an old sweatshirt and is staring out of the window. As he turns to answer I catch a glimpse of dark eyes, stubble; a deep frown etched on his forehead.

'No thanks. Just a brandy. Thanks.'

His voice is dry and has an American accent. I'm about to ask him politely where he's from, but he immediately turns back and stares out of the window again.

Which is fine, because to be honest, I'm not much in the mood for talking either.

TWO

OK. The truth is, I don't like this.

I know it's business class, I know it's all lovely luxury. But my stomach is still a tight knot of fear.

While we were taking off I counted very slowly with my eyes closed, and that kind of worked. But I ran out of steam at about 350. So now I'm just sitting, sipping champagne, reading an article on '30 Things To Do Before You're 30' in *Cosmo*. I'm trying very hard to look like a relaxed business-class top marketing executive. But oh God. Every tiny sound makes me start; every judder makes me catch my breath.

With an outward veneer of calm I reach for the laminated safety instructions and run my eyes over them. Safety exits. Brace position. If life jackets are required, please assist the elderly and children first. Oh God—

Why am I even *looking* at this? How will it help me to gaze at pictures of little stick people jumping into the ocean while their plane explodes behind them? I stuff the safety instructions quickly back in their pocket and take a gulp of champagne.

'Excuse me, madam.' An air hostess with red curls has appeared by my side. 'Are you travelling on business?'

'Yes,' I say, smoothing down my hair with a prickle of pride. 'Yes I am.'

She hands me a leaflet entitled 'Executive

Facilities', on which there's a photo of businesspeople talking animatedly in front of a clipboard with a wavy graph on it.

'This is some information about our new business class lounge at Gatwick. We provide full conference call facilities, and meeting rooms, should you require them. Would you be interested?'

OK. I am a top businesswoman. I am a top high-flying business executive.

'Quite possibly,' I say, looking nonchalantly at the leaflet. 'Yes, I may well use one of these rooms to . . . brief my team. I have a large team, and obviously they need a lot of briefing. On business matters.' I clear my throat. 'Mostly . . . logistical.'

'Would you like me to book you a room now?' says the hostess helpfully.

'Er, no thanks,' I say after a pause, 'My team is currently . . . at home. I gave them all the day off.'

'Right.' The hostess looks a little puzzled.

'But another time, maybe,' I say quickly. 'And while you're here – I was just wondering. Is that sound normal?'

'What sound?' The air hostess cocks her head.

'That sound. That kind of whining, coming from the wing?'

'I can't hear anything.' She looks at me sympathetically. 'Are you a nervous flyer?'

'No!' I say at once, and give a little laugh. 'No, I'm not *nervous*! I just . . . was wondering. Just out of interest.'

'I'll see if I can find out for you,' she says kindly. 'Here you are, sir. Some information about our executive facilities at Gatwick.'

The American man takes his leaflet wordlessly and puts it down without even looking at it, and the hostess moves on, staggering a little as the plane gives a bump.

Why is the plane bumping?

Oh God. A sudden rush of fear hits me with no warning. This is madness. Madness! Sitting in this big heavy box, with no way of escape, thousands and thousands of feet above the ground . . .

I can't do this on my own. I have an overpowering need to talk to someone. Someone reassuring. Someone safe.

Connor.

Instinctively I fish out my mobile phone, but immediately the air hostess swoops down on me.

'I'm afraid you can't use that on board the plane,' she says with a bright smile. 'Could you please ensure that it's switched off?'

'Oh. Er . . . sorry.'

Of course I can't use my mobile. They've only said it about fifty-five zillion times. I am such a durr-brain. Anyway, never mind. It doesn't matter. I'm fine. I put the phone away in my bag, and try to concentrate on an old episode of *Fawlty Towers* which is showing on the screen.

Maybe I'll start counting again. Three hundred and forty-nine. Three hundred and fifty. Three hundred and—

Fuck. My head jerks up. What was that bump? Did we just get *hit*?

OK, don't panic. It was just a bump. I'm sure everything's fine. We probably just flew into a pigeon or something. Where was I?

Three hundred and fifty-one. Three hundred and fifty-two. Three hundred and fifty—

And that's it.

That's the moment.

Everything seems to fragment.

I hear the screams like a wave over my head, almost before I realize what's happening.

Oh God. Oh God Oh God Oh God Oh . . . OH . . . NO. NO. NO.

We're falling. Oh God, we're falling.

We're plummeting downwards. The plane's dropping through the air like a stone. A man over there has just shot up through the air and banged his head on the ceiling. He's bleeding. I'm gasping, clutching onto my seat, trying not to do the same thing, but I can feel myself being wrenched upwards, it's like someone's tugging me, like gravity's suddenly switched the other way. There's no time to think. My mind can't . . . Bags are flying around, drinks are spilling, one of the cabin crew has fallen over, she's clutching at a seat . . .

Oh God. Oh God. OK, it's slowing down now. It's . . . it's better.

Fuck. I just . . . I just can't . . . I . . .

I look at the American man, and he's grasping his seat as tightly as I am.

I feel sick. I think I might be sick. Oh God.

OK. It's . . . it's kind of . . . back to normal.

'Ladies and gentlemen,' comes a voice over the intercom, and everyone's heads jerk up. 'This is your captain speaking.'

My heart's juddering in my chest. I can't listen. I can't think.

'We're currently hitting some clear-air turbulence, and things may be unsteady for a while. I have switched on the seatbelt signs and would ask that you all return to your seats as quickly as—'

There's another huge lurch, and his voice is drowned by screams and cries all round the plane.

It's like a bad dream. A bad rollercoaster dream.

The cabin crew are all strapping themselves into their seats. One of the hostesses is mopping blood on her face. A minute ago they were happily doling out honey-roast peanuts.

This is what happens to other people in other planes. People on safety videos. Not me.

'Please keep calm,' the captain is saying. 'As soon as we have more information . . .'

Keep *calm*? I can't breathe, let alone keep calm. What are we going to do? Are we all supposed to just *sit* here while the plane bucks like an out-of-control horse?

I can hear someone behind me reciting 'Hail Mary, full of grace . . .' and a fresh, choking panic sweeps through me. People are praying. This is real.

We're going to die.

We're going to die.

'I'm sorry?' The American man in the next seat looks at me, his face tense and white.

Did I just say that aloud?

'We're going to die.' I stare into his face. This could be the last person I ever see alive. I take in the lines etched around his dark eyes; his strong jaw, shaded with stubble.

The plane suddenly drops down again, and I give an involuntary shriek.

'I don't think we're going to die,' he says. But he's gripping his seat-arms, too. 'They said it was just turbulence—'

'Of course they did!' I can hear the hysteria in my voice. 'They wouldn't exactly say, "OK folks, that's it, you're all goners"!' The plane gives another terrifying swoop and I find myself clutching the man's hand in panic. 'We're not going to make it. I know we're not. This is it. I'm twenty-five years old, for God's sake. I'm not ready. I haven't achieved anything. I've never had

29

children, I've never saved a life . . .' My eyes fall randomly on the '30 Things To Do Before You're 30' article. 'I haven't ever climbed a mountain, I haven't got a tattoo, I don't even *know* if I've got a G spot . . .'

'I'm sorry?' says the man, sounding taken aback, but I barely hear him.

'My career's a complete joke. I'm not a top businesswoman at all.' I gesture half-tearfully to my suit. 'I haven't got a team! I'm just a crappy assistant and I just had my first ever big meeting and it was a complete disaster. Half the time I haven't got a clue what people are talking about, I don't know what logistical means, I'm never going to get promoted, and I owe my dad four thousand quid, and I've never really been in love . . .'

I draw myself up short with a jolt. 'I'm sorry,' I say, and exhale sharply. 'You don't want to hear all this.'

'That's quite all right,' says the man.

God. I'm completely losing it.

And anyway, what I just said wasn't true. Because I am in love with Connor. It must be the altitude or something, confusing my mind.

Flustered, I push the hair off my face and try to get a hold of myself. OK, let's try counting again. Three hundred and fifty . . . six. Three hundred and—

Oh God. Oh God. No. Please. The plane's lurching again. We're plummeting.

'I've never done anything to make my parents proud of me.' The words come spilling out of my mouth before I can stop them. 'Never.'

'I'm sure that's not true,' says the man nicely.

'It's true. Maybe they used to be proud of me. But then my cousin Kerry came to live with us and all at once it was like my parents couldn't see me any more. All they could see was her. She was fourteen when she arrived, and I was ten, and I thought it was going to be great, you know. Like having an older sister. But it didn't work out like that . . .'

I can't stop talking. I just can't stop.

Every time the plane bumps or jolts, another torrent of words pours randomly out of my mouth, like water gushing over a waterfall.

It's either talk or scream.

'. . . she was a swimming champion, and an everything champion, and I was just . . . nothing in comparison . . .'

'. . . photography course and I honestly thought it was going to change my life . . .'

'. . . eight stone three. But I was planning to go on a diet . . .'

'I applied for every single job in the world. I was so desperate, I even applied to . . .'

'. . . awful girl called Artemis. This new desk arrived the other day, and she just took it, even though I've got this really grotty little desk . . .'

'. . . sometimes I water her stupid spider plant with orange juice, just to serve her right . . .'

'. . . sweet girl Katie, who works in Personnel. We have this secret code where she comes in and says, "Can I go through some numbers with you, Emma?" and it really means "Shall we nip out to Starbucks . . ."'

'. . . awful presents, and I have to pretend I like them . . .'

'. . . coffee at work is the most disgusting stuff you've ever drunk, absolute poison . . .'

'. . . put "Maths GCSE grade A" on my CV, when I really only got C. I know it was dishonest. I know I shouldn't have done it, but I *so* wanted to get the job . . .'

What's happened to me? Normally there's a kind of filter which stops me blurting out everything I'm thinking; which keeps me in check.

But the filter's stopped working. Everything's piling out in a big, random stream, and I can't stop it.

'Sometimes I think I believe in God, because how else did we all get here? But then I think, yes but what about war and stuff . . .'

'. . . wear G-strings because they don't give you VPL. But they're *so* uncomfortable . . .'

'. . . size eight, and I didn't know what to do, so I just said "Wow those are absolutely fantastic . . ."'

'. . . roasted peppers, my complete favourite food . . .'

'. . . joined a book group, but I just couldn't get through *Great Expectations*. So I just skimmed the back and pretended I'd read it . . .'

'. . . I gave him all his goldfish food, I honestly don't know what happened . . .'

'. . . just have to *hear* that Carpenters song "Close to You" and I start crying . . .'

'. . . *really* wish I had bigger boobs. I mean, not Page 3 size, not completely enormous and stupid, but you know, bigger. Just to know what it's like . . .'

'. . . perfect date would start off with champagne just *appearing* at the table, as if by magic . . .'

'. . . I just cracked, I secretly bought this huge tub of Häagen-Dazs and scoffed the lot, and I never told Lissy . . .'

I'm unaware of anything around us. The world has narrowed to me and this stranger, and my mouth, spewing out all my innermost thoughts and secrets.

I barely know what I'm saying any more. All I know is, it feels good.

Is this what therapy is like?

'. . . name was Danny Nussbaum. Mum and Dad were downstairs watching *Ben Hur*, and I remember thinking, if this is what the world gets so excited about, then the world's mad . . .'

'. . . lie on my side, because that way your cleavage looks bigger . . .'

'. . . works in market research. I remember thinking the very first time I saw him, wow, he's good-looking. He's very tall and blond, because he's half-Swedish, and he has these amazing blue eyes. So he asked me out . . .'

'. . . always have a glass of sweet sherry before a date, just to calm my nerves . . .'

'He's wonderful. Connor's completely wonderful. I'm just so lucky. Everyone's always telling me how great he is. He's sweet, and he's good, and he's successful and everyone calls us the perfect couple . . .'

'. . . I'd never tell anyone this in a million years. But sometimes I think he's almost *too* good-looking. A bit like one of those dolls? Like Ken. Like a blond Ken.'

And now I'm on the subject of Connor, I'm saying things I've never said to anyone. Things I never even realized were in my head.

'. . . gave him this lovely leather watch for Christmas, but he wears this orange digital thing because it can tell him the temperature in Poland or something stupid . . .'

'. . . took me to all these jazz concerts and I pretended to enjoy them to be polite, so now he thinks I love jazz . . .'

'. . . every single Woody Allen film off by heart and says each line before it comes and it drives me crackers . . .'

'. . . just looks at me as though I'm speaking some foreign language . . .'

'. . . determined to find my G spot, so we spent the whole weekend doing it in different positions, and by the end I was just knackered, all I wanted was a pizza and *Friends* . . .'

'. . . he kept saying, what was it like, what was it like? So in the end I just made some stuff up, I said it was absolutely amazing, and it felt as though my whole body was opening up like a flower, and he said, what sort of flower, so I said a begonia . . .'

'. . . can't expect the initial passion to last. But how do you tell if the passion's faded in a good, long-term-commitment way or in a crap, we-don't-fancy-each-other-any-more way . . .'

'. . . knight in shining armour is not a realistic option. But there's a part of me that wants a huge, amazing romance. I want passion. I want to be swept off my feet. I want an earthquake, or a . . . I don't know, a huge whirlwind . . . something *exciting*. Sometimes I feel as if there's this whole new, thrilling life waiting for me out there, and if I can just—'

'Excuse me, miss?'

'What?' I look up dazedly. 'What is it?' The air hostess with the French plait is smiling down at me.

'We've landed.' I stare at her.

'We've *landed*?'

This doesn't make sense. How can we have landed? I look around – and sure enough, the plane's still. We're on the ground.

I feel like Dorothy. A second ago I was swirling around in Oz, clicking my heels together, and now I've woken up all flat and quiet and normal again.

'We aren't bumping any more,' I say stupidly.

'We stopped bumping quite a while ago,' says the American man.

'We're . . . we're not going to die.'

'We're not going to die,' he agrees.

I look at him as though for the first time – and it hits me. I've been blabbering non-stop for an hour to this complete stranger. God alone knows what I've been saying.

I think I want to get off this plane right now.

'I'm sorry,' I say awkwardly. 'You should have stopped me.'

'That would have been a little difficult.' There's a tiny smile at his lips. 'You were on a bit of a roll.'

'I'm so embarrassed!' I try to smile, but I can't even look this guy in the eye. I mean, I told him about my knickers. I told him about my *G spot*.

'Don't worry about it. We were all stressed out. That was some flight.' He picks up his knapsack and gets up from his seat – then looks back at me. 'Will you be OK getting back home?'

'Yes. I'll be fine. Thanks. Enjoy your visit!' I call after him, but I don't think he hears.

Slowly I gather my things together and make my way off the plane. I feel sweaty, my hair's all over the place, and my head is starting to throb.

The airport seems so bright and still and calm after the intense atmosphere of the plane. The ground seems so firm. I sit quietly on a plastic chair for a while, trying to get myself together, but as I stand up at last, I still feel dazed. I walk along in a slight blur, hardly able to believe I'm here. I'm alive. I honestly never thought I'd make it back on the ground.

'Emma!' I hear someone calling as I come out of Arrivals, but I don't look up. There are loads of Emmas in this world.

'Emma! Over here!'

I raise my head in disbelief. Is that . . .

No. It can't be, it can't—

It's Connor.

He looks heart-breakingly handsome. His skin has that Scandinavian tan, and his eyes are bluer than ever, and he's running towards me. This makes no sense. What's he doing here? As we reach each other he grabs me and pulls me tight to his chest.

'Thank God,' he says huskily. 'Thank God. Are you OK?'

'Connor, what— what are you doing here?'

'I phoned the airline to ask what time you'd be landing, and they told me the plane had hit terrible turbulence. I just had to come to the airport.' He gazes down at me. 'Emma, I watched your plane land. They sent an ambulance straight out to it. Then you didn't appear. I thought . . .' He swallows hard. 'I don't know exactly what I thought.'

'I'm fine. I was just . . . trying to get myself together. Oh God, Connor, it was terrifying.' My voice is suddenly all shaky, which is ridiculous, because I'm perfectly safe now. 'At one point I honestly thought I was going to die.'

'When you didn't come through the barrier . . .' Connor breaks off and stares at me silently for a few seconds. 'I think I realized for the first time quite how deeply I feel about you.'

'Really?' I falter.

My heart's thumping. I think I might fall over at any moment.

'Emma, I think we should . . .'

Get married? My heart jumps in fear. Oh my God.

36

He's going to ask me to marry him, right here in the airport. What am I going to say? I'm not ready to get married. But if I say no he'll stalk off in a huff. Shit. OK. What I'll say is, Gosh, Connor, I need a little time to . . .

'. . . move in together,' he finishes.

I am such a deluded moron. Obviously he wasn't going to ask me to *marry* him.

'What do you think?' he strokes my hair gently.

'Erm . . .' I rub my dry face, playing for time, unable to think straight. Move in with Connor. It kind of makes sense. Is there a reason why not? I feel all confused. Something's tugging at my brain; trying to send me a message . . .

And into my head slide some of the things I said on the plane. Something about never having been properly in love. Something about Connor not really understanding me.

But then . . . that was just drivel, wasn't it? I mean, I thought I was about to die, for God's sake. I wasn't exactly at my most lucid.

'Connor, what about your big meeting?' I say, suddenly recalling.

'I cancelled it.'

'You cancelled it?' I stare at him. 'For me?'

I feel really wobbly now. My legs are barely holding me up. I don't know if it's the aftermath of the plane journey or love.

Oh God, just look at him. He's tall and he's handsome, and he cancelled a big meeting, and he came to rescue me.

It's love. It has to be love.

'I'd love to move in with you, Connor,' I whisper, and to my utter astonishment, burst into tears.

THREE

I wake up the next morning with sunlight dazzling my eyelids and a delicious smell of coffee in the air.

'Morning!' comes Connor's voice from far above.

'Morning,' I mumble, without opening my eyes.

'D'you want some coffee?'

'Yes please.'

I turn over and bury my throbbing head in the pillow, trying to sink into sleep again for a couple of minutes. Which normally I would find very easy. But today, something's niggling at me. Have I forgotten something?

As I half listen to Connor clattering around in the kitchen, and the tinny background sound of the telly, my mind gropes blearily around for clues. It's Saturday morning. I'm in Connor's bed. We went out for supper – oh God, that awful plane ride . . . he came to the airport, and he said . . .

We're moving in together!

I sit up, just as Connor comes in with two mugs and a cafetière. He's dressed in a white waffle robe and looks completely gorgeous. I feel a prickle of pride, and reach over to give him a kiss.

'Hi,' he says, laughing. 'Careful.' He hands me my coffee. 'How are you feeling?'

'All right.' I push my hair back off my face. 'A bit groggy.'

'I'm not surprised.' Connor raises his eyebrows. 'Quite a day yesterday.'

'Absolutely.' I nod, and take a sip of coffee. 'So. We're . . . going to live together!'

'If you're still on for it?'

'Of course! Of course I am!' I smile brightly.

And it's true. I am.

I feel as though overnight, I've turned into a grown-up. I'm moving in with my boyfriend. Finally my life is going the way it should!

'I'll have to give Andrew notice . . .' Connor gestures towards the wall, on the other side of which is his flat-mate's room.

'And I'll have to tell Lissy and Jemima.'

'And we'll have to find the right place. And you'll have to promise to keep it tidy.' He gives me a teasing grin.

'I like that!' I feign outrage. 'You're the one with fifty million CDs.'

'That's different!'

'How is it different, may I ask?' I plant my hand on my hip, like someone in a sitcom, and Connor laughs.

There's a pause, as though we've both run out of steam, and we take a sip of coffee.

'So anyway,' says Connor after a while, 'I should get going.' Connor is attending a course on computers this weekend. 'I'm sorry I'll miss your parents,' he adds.

And he really is. I mean, as if he wasn't already the perfect boyfriend, he actually *enjoys* visiting my parents.

'That's OK,' I say benevolently. 'It doesn't matter.'

'Oh, and I forgot to tell you.' Connor gives me a mysterious grin. 'Guess what I've got tickets for?'

'Ooh!' I say excitedly. 'Um . . .'

I'm about to say 'Paris!'

'The jazz festival!' Connor beams. 'The Dennisson Quartet! It's their last concert of the year. Remember we heard them at Ronnie Scott's?'

For a moment I can't quite speak.

'Wow!' I manage at last. 'The . . . Dennisson Quartet! I do remember.'

They played clarinets. On and on and on, for about two hours, without even taking a breath.

'I knew you'd be pleased.' Connor touches my arm affectionately, and I give him a feeble smile.

'Oh, I am!'

The thing is, I probably will get to like jazz one day. In fact, I'm positive I will.

I watch fondly as he gets dressed, flosses his teeth and picks up his briefcase.

'You wore my present,' he says with a pleased smile, glancing at my discarded underwear on the floor.

'I . . . often wear them,' I say, crossing my fingers behind my back. 'They're so gorgeous!'

'Have a lovely day with your family.' Connor comes over to the bed to kiss me, and then hesitates. 'Emma?'

'Yes?'

He sits down on the bed and gazes seriously at me. Gosh, his eyes are so blue.

'There's something I wanted to say.' He bites his lip. 'You know we always speak frankly to each other about our relationship.'

'Er . . . yes,' I say, feeling a little apprehensive.

'This is just an idea. You may not like it. I mean . . . it's completely up to you.'

I gaze at Connor in puzzlement. His face is growing pink, and he looks really embarrassed.

Oh my God. Is he going to start getting kinky? Does he want me to dress up in outfits and stuff?

I wouldn't mind being a nurse, actually. Or

40

Catwoman from *Batman.* That would be cool. I could get some shiny boots . . .

'I was thinking that . . . perhaps . . . we could . . .' He stops awkwardly.

'Yes?' I put a supportive hand on his arm.

'We could . . .' He stops again.

'Yes?'

There's another silence. I almost can't breathe. What does he want us to do? What?

'We could start calling each other "darling",' he says in an embarrassed rush.

'What?' I say blankly.

'It's just that . . .' Connor flushes pinker. 'We're going to be living together. It's quite a commitment. And I noticed recently, we never seem to use any . . . terms of endearment.'

I stare at him, feeling caught out.

'Don't we?'

'No.'

'Oh.' I take a sip of coffee. Now I think about it, he's right. We don't. Why don't we?

'So what do you think? Only if you want to.'

'Absolutely!' I say quickly. 'I mean, you're right. Of course we should.' I clear my throat. 'Darling!'

'Thanks, darling,' he says, with a loving smile, and I smile back, trying to ignore the tiny protests inside my head.

This doesn't feel right.

I don't feel like a darling.

Darling is a married person with pearls and a four-wheel-drive.

'Emma?' Connor's staring at me. 'Is something wrong?'

'I'm not sure!' I give a self-conscious laugh. 'I just don't know if I feel like a "darling". But . . . you know. It may grow on me.'

41

'Really? Well, we can use something else. What about "dear"?'

Dear? Is he serious?

'No,' I say quickly. 'I think "darling" is better.'

'Or "sweetheart" . . . "honey" . . . "angel" . . .'

'Maybe. Look, can we just leave it?'

Connor's face falls, and I feel bad. Come on. I can call my boyfriend 'darling', for God's sake. This is what growing up's all about. I'm just going to have to get used to it.

'Connor, I'm sorry,' I say. 'I don't know what's wrong with me. Maybe I'm still a bit tense after that flight.' I take his hand. 'Darling.'

'That's all right, darling.' He smiles back at me, his sunny expression restored, and gives me a kiss. 'See you later.'

You see. Easy.

Oh God.

Anyway. It doesn't matter. I expect all couples have this kind of awkward-ish moment. It's probably perfectly normal.

It takes me about half an hour to get from Connor's place in Maida Vale to Islington, which is where I live, and as I open the door I find Lissy on the sofa. She's surrounded by papers and has a frown of concentration on her face. She works so hard, Lissy. She really overdoes it sometimes.

'What are you working on?' I say sympathetically. 'Is it that fraud case?'

'No, it's this article,' says Lissy abstractly, and lifts up a glossy magazine. 'It says since the days of Cleopatra, the proportions of beauty have been the same, and there's a way to work out how beautiful you are, scientifically. You do all these measurements . . .'

'Oh right!' I say interestedly. 'So what are you?'

'I'm just working it out.' She frowns at the page again. 'That makes 53 . . . subtract 20 . . . makes . . . Oh my God!' She stares at the page in dismay. 'I only got 33!'

'Out of what?'

'A hundred! 33 out of a hundred!'

'Oh Lissy. That's crap.'

'I know,' says Lissy seriously. 'I'm ugly. I knew it. You know, all my life I've kind of secretly *known*, but—'

'No!' I say, trying not to laugh. 'I meant the magazine's crap! You can't measure beauty with some stupid index. Just *look* at you!' I gesture at Lissy, who has the biggest grey eyes in the world, and gorgeous clear pale skin and is frankly stunning, even if her last haircut was a bit severe. 'I mean, who are you going to believe? The mirror or a stupid mindless magazine article?'

'A stupid mindless magazine article,' says Lissy, as though it's perfectly obvious.

I know she's half joking. But ever since her boyfriend Simon chucked her, Lissy's had really low self-esteem. I'm actually a bit worried about her.

'Is that the golden proportion of beauty?' says our other flatmate Jemima, tapping into the room in her kitten heels. She's wearing pale pink jeans and a tight white top and as usual, she looks perfectly tanned and groomed. In theory, Jemima has a job, working in a sculpture gallery. But all she ever seems to do is have bits of her waxed and plucked and massaged, and go on dates with city bankers, whose salary she always checks out before she says yes.

I do get on with Jemima. Kind of. It's just that she tends to begin all her sentences '*If* you want a rock on your finger,' and '*If* you want an SW3 address,' and '*If* you want to be known as a seriously good dinner-party hostess.'

I mean, I wouldn't *mind* being known as a seriously good dinner-party hostess. You know. It's just not exactly highest on my list of priorities right now.

Plus, Jemima's idea of being a seriously good dinner-party hostess is inviting lots of rich friends over, decorating the whole flat with twiggy things, getting caterers to cook loads of yummy food and telling everyone she made it herself, then sending her flatmates (me and Lissy) out to the cinema for the night and looking affronted when they dare creep back in at midnight and make themselves a hot chocolate.

'I did that quiz,' she says now, picking up her pink Louis Vuitton bag. Her dad bought it for her as a present when she broke up with a guy after three dates. Like she was heartbroken.

Mind you, he had a yacht, so she probably was heart-broken.

'What did you get?' says Lissy.

'Eighty-nine.' She spritzes herself with perfume, tosses her long blond hair back and smiles at herself in the mirror. 'So Emma, is it true you're moving in with Connor?' I gape at her.

'How did you know that?'

'Word on the street. Andrew called Rupes this morning about cricket, and he told him.'

'Are you moving in with Connor?' says Lissy incredulously. 'Why didn't you tell me?'

'I was about to, honestly. Isn't it great?'

'Bad move, Emma.' Jemima shakes her head. 'Very bad tactics.'

'Tactics?' says Lissy, rolling her eyes. '*Tactics?* Jemima, they're having a relationship, not playing chess!'

'A relationship *is* a game of chess,' retorts Jemima, brushing mascara onto her lashes. 'Mummy says you

44

always have to look ahead. You have to plan strategically. If you make the wrong move, you've had it.'

'That's rubbish!' says Lissy defiantly. 'A relationship is about like minds. It's about soulmates finding each other.'

'Soulmates!' says Jemima dismissively, and looks at me. 'Just remember, Emma, *if* you want a rock on your finger, don't move in with Connor.'

Her eyes give a swift, Pavlovian glance to the photograph on the mantelpiece of her meeting Prince William at a charity polo match.

'Still holding out for Royalty?' says Lissy. 'How much younger is he than you, again, Jemima?'

'Don't be stupid!' she snaps, colour tinging her cheeks. 'You're so immature sometimes, Lissy.'

'Anyway, I don't *want* a rock on my finger,' I retort.

Jemima raises her perfectly arched eyebrows as though to say, 'you poor, ignorant fool', and picks up her bag.

'Oh,' she suddenly adds, her eyes narrowing. 'Has either of you borrowed my Joseph jumper?'

There's a tiny beat of silence.

'No,' I say innocently.

'I don't even know which one it is,' says Lissy, with a shrug.

I can't look at Lissy. I'm sure I saw her wearing it the other night.

Jemima's blue eyes are running over me and Lissy like some kind of radar scanners.

'Because I have very slender arms,' she says warningly, 'and I really don't want the sleeves stretched. And don't think I won't notice, because I will. Ciao.'

The minute she's gone Lissy and I look at each other.

'Shit,' says Lissy. 'I think I left it at work. Oh well, I'll pick it up on Monday.' She shrugs and goes back to reading the magazine.

OK. So the truth is, we do both occasionally borrow Jemima's clothes. Without asking. But in our defence, she has so many, she hardly ever notices. Plus according to Lissy, it's a basic human right that flatmates should be able to borrow each others' clothes. She says it's practically part of the unwritten British constitution.

'And anyway,' adds Lissy, 'she owes it to me for writing her that letter to the council about all her parking tickets. You know, she never even said thank you.' She looks up from an article on Nicole Kidman. 'So what are you doing later on? D'you want to see a film?'

'I can't,' I say reluctantly. 'I've got my mum's birthday lunch.'

'Oh yes, of course.' She pulls a sympathetic face. 'Good luck. I hope it's OK.'

Lissy is the only person in the world who has any idea how I feel about visiting home. And even she doesn't know it all.

FOUR

But as I sit on the train down, I'm resolved that this time will be better. I was watching a Cindy Blaine show the other day, all about reuniting long-lost daughters with their mothers, and it was so moving I soon had tears running down my face. At the end, Cindy gave this little homily about how it's far too easy to take our families for granted and that they gave us life and we should cherish them. And suddenly I felt really chastened.

So these are my resolutions for today:

I will not:

Let my family stress me out.

Feel jealous of Kerry, or let Nev wind me up.

Look at my watch, wondering how soon I can leave.

I will:

Stay serene and loving and remember that we are all sacred links in the eternal circle of life.

(I got that from Cindy Blaine, too.)

Mum and Dad used to live in Twickenham, which is where I grew up. But now they've moved out of London to a village in Hampshire. I arrive at their house just after twelve, to find Mum in the kitchen with my cousin Kerry. She and her husband Nev have moved out too, to a village about five minutes' drive from Mum and Dad, so they see each other all the time.

I feel a familiar pang as I see them, standing side by

side by the stove. They look more like mother and daughter than aunt and niece. They've both got the same feather-cut hair – although Kerry's is highlighted more strongly than Mum's – they're both wearing brightly coloured tops which show a lot of tanned cleavage, and they're both laughing. On the counter, I notice a bottle of white wine already half gone.

'Happy birthday!' I say, hugging Mum. As I glimpse a wrapped parcel on the kitchen table, I feel a little thrill of anticipation. I have got Mum the *best* birthday present. I can't wait to give it to her!

'Hi*ya*!' says Kerry, turning round in her apron. Her blue eyes are heavily made-up, and round her neck she's wearing a diamond cross which I haven't seen before. Every time I see Kerry she has a new piece of jewellery. 'Great to see you, Emma! We don't see enough of you. Do we, Aunty Rachel?'

'We certainly don't,' says Mum, giving me a hug.

'Shall I take your coat?' says Kerry, as I put the bottle of champagne I've brought into the fridge. 'And what about a drink?'

This is how Kerry always talks to me. As though I'm a visitor.

But never mind. I'm not going to stress about it. Sacred links in the eternal circle of life.

'It's OK,' I say, trying to sound pleasant. 'I'll get it.' I open the cupboard where glasses are always kept, to find myself looking at tins of tomatoes.

'They're over here,' says Kerry, on the other side of the kitchen. 'We moved everything around! It makes much more sense now.'

'Oh right. Thanks.' I take the glass she gives me and take a sip of wine. 'Can I do anything to help?'

'I don't *think* so . . .' says Kerry, looking critically around the kitchen. 'Everything's pretty much done. So I said to Elaine,' she adds to Mum, '"Where did you get

48

those shoes?" And she said M&S! I couldn't believe it!'

'Who's Elaine?' I say, trying to join in.

'At the golf club,' says Kerry.

Mum never used to play golf. But when she moved to Hampshire, she and Kerry took it up together. And now all I hear about is golf matches, golf club dinners, and endless parties with chums from the golf club.

I did once go along, to see what it was all about. But first of all they have all these stupid rules about what you can wear, which I didn't know, and some old guy nearly had a heart attack because I was in jeans. So they had to find me a skirt, and a spare pair of those clumpy shoes with spikes. And then when we got on to the course I couldn't hit the ball. Not I couldn't hit the ball *well*: I literally could not make contact with the ball. So in the end they all exchanged glances and said I'd better wait in the clubhouse.

'Sorry, Emma, can I just get past you . . .' Kerry reaches over my shoulder for a serving dish.

'Sorry,' I say, and move aside. 'So, is there really nothing I can do, Mum?'

'You could feed Sammy,' she says, giving me a pot of goldfish food. She frowns anxiously. 'You know, I'm a bit worried about Sammy.'

'Oh,' I say, feeling a spasm of alarm. 'Er . . . why?'

'He just doesn't seem *himself*.' She peers at him in his bowl. 'What do you think? Does he look right to you?'

I follow her gaze and pull a thoughtful face, as though I'm studying Sammy's features.

Oh God. I never thought she would notice. I tried as hard as I could to get a fish that looked just like Sammy. I mean he's orange, he's got two fins, he swims around . . . What's the difference?

'He's probably just a bit depressed,' I say at last. 'He'll get over it.'

49

Please don't let her take him to the vet or anything, I silently pray. I didn't even check if I got the right sex. Do goldfishes even *have* sexes?

'Anything else I can do?' I say, sprinkling fish food lavishly over the water in an attempt to block her view of him.

'We've pretty much got it covered,' says Kerry kindly.

'Why don't you go and say hello to Dad?' says Mum, sieving some peas. 'Lunch won't be for another ten minutes or so.'

I find Dad and Nev in the sitting room, in front of the cricket. Dad's greying beard is as neatly trimmed as ever, and he's drinking beer from a silver tankard. The room has recently been redecorated, but on the wall there's still a display of all Kerry's swimming cups. Mum polishes them regularly, every week.

Plus my couple of riding rosettes. I think she kind of flicks those with a duster.

'Hi, Dad,' I say, giving him a kiss.

'Emma!' He puts a hand to his head in mock-surprise. 'You made it! No detours! No visits to historic cities!'

'Not today!' I give a little laugh. 'Safe and sound.'

There was this time, just after Mum and Dad had moved to this house, when I took the wrong train on the way down and ended up in Salisbury, and Dad always teases me about it.

'Hi, Nev.' I peck him on the cheek, trying not to choke on the amount of aftershave he's wearing. He's in chinos and a white roll-neck, and has a heavy gold bracelet round his wrist, plus a wedding ring with a diamond set in it. Nev runs his family's company, which supplies office equipment all round the country, and he met Kerry at some

50

convention for young entrepreneurs. Apparently they struck up conversation admiring each other's Rolex watches.

'Hi, Emma,' he says. 'D'you see the new motor?'

'What?' I peer at him blankly – then recall a glossy new car on the drive when I arrived. 'Oh yes! Very smart.'

'Mercedes 5 Series.' He takes a slug of beer. 'Forty-two grand list price.'

'Gosh.'

'Didn't pay that, though.' He taps the side of his nose. 'Have a guess.'

'Erm . . . forty?'

'Guess again.'

'Thirty-nine?'

'Thirty-seven-two-fifty,' says Nev triumphantly. 'And free CD changer. Tax deductible,' he adds.

'Right. Wow.'

I don't really know what else to say, so I perch on the side of the sofa and eat a peanut.

'That's what you're aiming for, Emma!' says Dad. 'Think you'll ever make it?'

'I . . . don't know. Er . . . Dad, that reminds me. I've got a cheque for you.' Awkwardly I reach in my bag and get out a cheque for £300.

'Well done,' says Dad. 'That can go on the tally.' His green eyes twinkle as he puts it in his pocket. 'It's called learning the value of money. It's called learning to stand on your own two feet!'

'Valuable lesson,' says Nev, nodding. He takes a slug of beer and grins at Dad. 'Just remind me, Emma – what career is it this week?'

When I first met Nev it was just after I'd left the estate agency to become a photographer. Two and a half years ago. And he makes this same joke every time I see him. Every single bloody—

51

OK, calm down. Happy thoughts. Cherish your family. Cherish Nev.

'It's still marketing!' I say brightly. 'Has been for over a year now.'

'Ah. Marketing. Good, good!'

There's silence for a few minutes, apart from the cricket commentary. Suddenly Dad and Nev simultaneously groan as something or other happens on the cricket pitch. A moment later they groan again.

'Right,' I say. 'Well, I'll just . . .'

As I get up from the sofa, they don't even turn their heads.

I go out to the hall and pick up the cardboard box which I brought down with me. Then I go through the side gate, knock on the annexe door and push it cautiously.

'Grandpa?'

Grandpa is Mum's dad, and he's lived with us ever since he had his heart operation, ten years ago. At the old house in Twickenham he just had a bedroom, but this house is bigger, so he has his own annexe of two rooms, and a tiny little kitchen, tacked onto the side of the house. He's sitting in his favourite leather armchair, with the radio playing classical music, and on the floor in front of him are about six cardboard packing cases full of stuff.

'Hi, Grandpa,' I say.

'Emma!' He looks up, and his face lights up. 'Darling girl. Come here!' I bend over to give him a kiss, and he squeezes my hand tight. His skin is dry and cool, and his hair is even whiter than it was last time I saw him.

'I've got some more Panther Bars for you,' I say, nodding to my box. Grandpa is completely addicted to Panther energy bars, and so are all his friends at the bowling club, so I use my allowance to buy him a boxful for every time I come home.

'Thank you, my love,' Grandpa beams. 'You're a good girl, Emma.'

'Where should I put them?'

We both look helplessly around the cluttered room.

'What about over there, behind the television?' says Grandpa at last. I pick my way across the room, dump the box on the floor, then retrace my steps, trying not to tread on anything.

'Now, Emma, I read a very worrying newspaper article the other day,' says Grandpa as I sit down on one of the packing cases. 'About safety in London.' He gives me a beady look. 'You don't travel on public transport in the evenings, do you?'

'Erm . . . hardly ever,' I say, crossing my fingers behind my back. 'Just now and then, when I absolutely have to . . .'

'Darling girl, you mustn't!' says Grandpa, looking agitated. 'Teenagers in hoods with flick-knives roam the underground, it said. Drunken louts, breaking bottles, gouging one another's eyes out . . .'

'It's not *that* bad—'

'Emma, it's not worth the risk! For the sake of a taxi fare or two.'

I'm pretty sure that if I asked Grandpa what he thought the average taxi fare was in London, he'd say five shillings.

'Honestly, Grandpa, I'm really careful,' I say reassuringly. 'And I do take taxis.'

Sometimes. About once a year.

'Anyway. What's all this stuff?' I ask, to change the subject, and Grandpa gives a gusty sigh.

'Your mother cleared out the attic last week. I'm just sorting out what to throw away and what to keep.'

'That seems like a good idea.' I look at the pile of rubbish on the floor. 'Is this stuff you're throwing away?'

'No! I'm keeping all that.' He puts a protective hand over it.

'So where's the pile of stuff to throw out?'

There's silence. Grandpa avoids my gaze.

'Grandpa! You have to throw *some* of this away!' I exclaim, trying not to laugh. 'You don't need all these old newspaper cuttings. And what's this?' I reach past the newspaper cuttings and fish out an old yo-yo. 'This is rubbish, surely.'

'Jim's yo-yo.' Grandpa reaches for the yo-yo, his eyes softening. 'Good old Jim.'

'Who was Jim?' I say, puzzled. I've never even heard of a Jim before. 'Was he a good friend of yours?'

'We met at the fairground. Spent the afternoon together. I was nine.' Grandpa is turning the yo-yo over and over in his fingers.

'Did you become friends?'

'Never saw him again.' He shakes his head mistily. 'I've never forgotten it.'

The trouble with Grandpa is, he never forgets anything.

'Well, what about some of these cards?' I pull out a bundle of old Christmas cards.

'I never throw away cards.' Grandpa gives me a long look. 'When you get to my age; when the people you've known and loved all your life start to pass away . . . you want to hang onto any memento. However small.'

'I can understand that,' I say, feeling touched. I reach for the nearest card, open it and my expression changes. 'Grandpa! This is from Smith's Electrical Maintenance, 1965.'

'Frank Smith was a very good man—' starts Grandpa.

'No!' I put the card firmly on the floor. 'That's going. And nor do you need one from . . .' I open the next card. 'Southwestern Gas Supplies. And you don't need twenty old copies of *Punch*.' I deposit them on the pile. 'And what are these?' I reach into the box again and pull out an envelope of photos. 'Are these actually of anything you really want to—'

Something shoots through my heart and I stop, mid-stream.

I'm looking at a photograph of me and Dad and Mum, sitting on a bench in a park. Mum's wearing a flowery dress, and Dad's wearing a stupid sunhat, and I'm on his knee, aged about nine, eating an ice-cream. We all look so happy together.

Wordlessly, I turn to another photo. I've got Dad's hat on and we're all laughing helplessly at something. Just us three.

Just us. Before Kerry came into our lives.

I still remember the day she arrived. A red suitcase in the hall, and a new voice in the kitchen, and an unfamiliar smell of perfume in the air. I walked in and there she was, a stranger, drinking a cup of tea. She was wearing school uniform, but she still looked like a grown-up to me. She already had an enormous bust, and gold studs in her ears, and streaks in her hair. And at suppertime, Mum and Dad let her have a glass of wine. Mum kept telling me I had to be very kind to her, because her mother had died. We all had to be very kind to Kerry. That was why she got my room.

I leaf through the rest of the pictures, trying to swallow the lump in my throat. I remember this place now. The park we used to go to, with swings and slides. But it was too boring for Kerry, and I desperately wanted to be like her, so I said it was boring too, and we never went again.

'Knock knock!' I look up with a start, and Kerry's standing at the door, holding her glass of wine. 'Lunch is ready!'

'Thanks,' I say. 'We're just coming.'

'Now, Gramps!' Kerry wags her finger reprovingly at Grandpa, and gestures at the packing cases. 'Haven't you got anywhere with this lot yet?'

'It's difficult,' I hear myself saying defensively. 'There are a lot of memories in here. You can't just throw them out.'

'If you say so.' Kerry rolls her eyes. 'If it were me, the whole lot'd go in the bin.'

I cannot cherish her. I cannot do it. I want to throw my treacle tart at her.

We've been sitting round the table now for forty minutes and the only voice we've heard is Kerry's.

'It's all about image,' she's saying now. 'It's all about the right clothes, the right look, the right walk. When I walk along the street, the message I give the world is "I am a successful woman".'

'Show us!' says Mum admiringly.

'Well.' Kerry gives a false-modest smile. 'Like this.' She pushes her chair back and wipes her mouth with her napkin.

'You should watch this, Emma,' says Mum. 'Pick up a few tips!'

As we all watch, Kerry starts striding round the room. Her chin is raised, her boobs are sticking out, her eyes are fixed on the middle distance, and her bottom is jerking from side to side.

She looks like a cross between an ostrich and one of the androids in *Attack of the Clones*.

'I should be in heels, of course,' she says, without stopping.

'When Kerry goes into a conference hall, I tell you, heads turn,' says Nev proudly, and takes a sip of wine. 'People stop what they're doing and stare at her!'

I bet they do.

Oh God. I want to giggle. I mustn't. I mustn't.

'Do you want to have a go, Emma?' says Kerry. 'Copy me?'

'Er . . . I don't think so,' I say. 'I think I probably . . . picked up the basics.'

Suddenly I give a tiny snort and turn it into a cough.

'Kerry's trying to help you, Emma!' says Mum. 'You should be grateful! You are good to Emma, Kerry.'

She beams fondly at Kerry, who simpers back. And I take a swig of wine.

Yeah, right. Kerry really wants to help me.

That's why when I was completely desperate for a job and asked her for work experience at her company, she said no. I wrote her this long, careful letter, saying I realized it put her in an awkward situation, but I'd really appreciate any chance, even a couple of days running errands.

And she sent back a standard rejection letter.

I was so totally mortified, I never told anyone. Especially not Mum and Dad.

'You should listen to some of Kerry's business tips, Emma,' Dad is saying sharply. 'Maybe if you paid more attention you'd do a bit better in life.'

'It's only a walk,' quips Nev with a chortle. 'It's not a miracle cure!'

'Nev!' says Mum half reprovingly.

'Emma knows I'm joking, don't you, Emma?' says Nev easily and fills up his glass with more wine.

'Of course!' I say, forcing myself to smile gaily.

Just wait till I get promoted.

Just wait. Just wait.

'Emma! Earth to Emma!' Kerry is waving a comical hand in front of my face. 'Wake up, Dopey! We're doing presents.'

'Oh right,' I say, coming to. 'OK. I'll just go and get mine.'

As Mum opens a camera from Dad and a purse from

Grandpa, I start to feel excited. I *so* hope Mum likes my present.

'It doesn't look much,' I say as I hand her the pink envelope. 'But you'll see when you open it . . .'

'What can it be?' Mum says, looking intrigued. She rips open the envelope, opens the flowered card, and stares at it. 'Oh, Emma!'

'What is it?' says Dad.

'It's a day at a spa!' says Mum in delight. 'A whole day of pampering.'

'What a good idea,' says Grandpa, and pats my hand. 'You always have good ideas for presents, Emma.'

'Thank you, love. How thoughtful!' Mum leans over to kiss me, and I feel a warm glow inside. I had the idea a few months ago. It's a really nice day-long package, with free treatments and everything.

'You get champagne lunch,' I say eagerly. 'And you can keep the slippers!'

'Wonderful!' says Mum. 'I'll look forward to it. Emma, that's a lovely present!'

'Oh dear,' says Kerry, giving a little laugh. She looks at the large creamy envelope in her own hands. 'My present's slightly upstaged, I'm afraid. Never mind. I'll change it.'

I look up, alert. There's something about Kerry's voice. I know something's up. I just know it.

'What do you mean?' says Mum.

'It doesn't matter,' says Kerry. 'I'll just . . . find something else. Not to worry.' She starts to put the envelope away in her bag.

'Kerry, love!' says Mum. 'Stop that! Don't be silly. What is it?'

'Well,' says Kerry. 'It's just that Emma and I seem to have had the same idea.' She hands Mum the envelope with another little laugh. 'Can you believe it?'

My whole body stiffens in apprehension.

No.

No. She can't have done what I think she's done.

There's complete silence as Mum opens the envelope.

'Oh my goodness!' she says, taking out a gold embossed brochure. 'What's this? Le Spa Meridien?' Something falls out, into her hands, and she stares at it. 'Tickets to *Paris*? Kerry!'

She has. She's ruined my present.

'For both of you,' adds Kerry, a little smugly. 'Uncle Brian, too.'

'Kerry!' says Dad in delight. 'You marvel!'

'It is supposed to be rather good,' says Kerry with a complacent smile. 'Five-star accommodation . . . the chef has three Michelin stars . . .'

'I don't believe this,' says Mum. She's leafing excitedly through the brochure. 'Look at the swimming pool! Look at the gardens!'

My flowery card is lying, forgotten, amid the wrapping paper.

All at once I feel close to tears. She knew. She *knew*.

'Kerry, you knew,' I suddenly blurt out, unable to stop myself. 'I told you I was giving Mum a spa treat. I *told* you! We had that conversation about it, months ago. In the garden!'

'Did we?' says Kerry casually. 'I don't remember.'

'You do! Of course you remember.'

'Emma!' says Mum sharply. 'It was a simple mistake. Wasn't it, Kerry?'

'Of course it was!' says Kerry, opening her eyes in wide innocence. 'Emma, if I've spoiled things for you, I can only apologize—'

'There's no need to apologize, Kerry love,' says Mum. 'These things happen. And they're *both* lovely presents. *Both* of them.' She looks at my card again. 'Now, you two girls are best friends! I don't like to see you quarrelling. Especially on my birthday.'

Mum smiles at me, and I try to smile back. But inside, I feel about ten years old again. Kerry always manages to wrong-foot me. She always has done, ever since she arrived. Whatever she did, everyone took her side. She was the one whose mother had died. We all had to be nice to her. I could never, ever win.

Trying to pull myself together, I reach for my wine glass and take a huge swig. Then I find myself surreptitiously glancing at my watch. I can leave at four if I make an excuse about trains running late. That's only another hour and a half to get through. And maybe we'll watch telly or something . . .

'A penny for your thoughts, Emma,' says Grandpa, patting my hand with a little smile, and I look up guiltily.

'Er . . . nothing,' I say, and force a smile. 'I wasn't really thinking about anything.'

FIVE

Anyway. It doesn't matter, because I'm going to get a promotion. Then Nev will stop making cracks about my career, and I'll be able to pay back Dad. Everyone will be really impressed – and it'll be fantastic!

I wake up on Monday morning feeling totally bouncy and positive, and get dressed in my usual work outfit of jeans and a nice top, this one from French Connection.

Well, not exactly French Connection. To be honest, I bought it at Oxfam. But the *label* says French Connection. And while I'm still paying off Dad I don't have much choice about where I shop. I mean, a new top from French Connection costs about fifty quid, whereas this one cost £7.50. And it's practically new!

As I skip up the tube steps, the sun's shining and I'm full of optimism. Imagine if I do get promoted. Imagine telling everybody. Mum will say, 'How was your week?' and I'll say, 'Well, actually . . .'

No, what I'll do is wait until I go home, and then just nonchalantly hand over my new business card.

Or maybe I'll just drive up in my company car I think in excitement! I mean, I'm not sure any of the other marketing executives have cars – but you never know, do you? They might introduce it as a new thing. Or they might say, 'Emma, we've chosen you specially—'

'Emma!'

I look round to see Katie, my friend from Personnel,

climbing the tube steps behind me, panting slightly. Her curly red hair is all tousled, and she's holding one shoe in her hand.

'What on earth happened?' I say as she reaches the top.

'My stupid shoe,' says Katie disconsolately. 'I only had it mended the other day, and the heel's just come off.' She flaps it at me. 'I paid six quid for that heel! God, this day is such a disaster. The milkman forgot to bring me any milk, and I had a *terrible* weekend . . .'

'I thought you were spending it with Charlie,' I say in surprise. 'What happened?'

Charlie is Katie's latest man. They've been seeing each other for a few weeks and she was supposed to be visiting his country cottage, which he's doing up at the weekends.

'It was awful! As soon as we arrived, he said he was going off to play golf.'

'Oh right.' I try to find a positive angle. 'Well, at least he's comfortable with you. He can just act normally.'

'Maybe.' She looks at me doubtfully. 'So then he said, how did I feel about helping out a bit while he was gone? So I said of course – and then he gave me this paintbrush, and three pots of paint and said I should get the sitting room done if I worked fast.'

'*What?*'

'And then he came back at six o'clock – and said my brushwork was careless!' Her voice rises woefully. 'It wasn't careless! I only smudged one bit, and that's because the stupid ladder wasn't long enough.'

I stare at her.

'Katie, you're not telling me you actually painted the room.'

'Well . . . yes.' She looks at me with huge blue eyes. 'You know, to help out. But now I'm starting to think . . . is he just using me?'

I'm almost speechless with disbelief.

'Katie, of course he's using you,' I manage at last. 'He wants a free painter-decorator! You have to chuck him. Immediately. Now!'

Katie is silent for a few seconds, and I eye her a bit nervously. Her face is blank, but I can tell lots of things are going on beneath the surface. It's a bit like when Jaws disappears underneath the rippling water, and you just know that any minute—

'Oh God, you're right!' she suddenly bursts out. 'You're right. He's been using me! It's my own fault. I should have realized when he asked me if I had any experience in plumbing or roofing.'

'When did he ask you that?' I say incredulously.

'On our first date! I thought he was just, you know, making conversation.'

'Katie, it's not your fault.' I squeeze her arm. 'You weren't to know.'

'But what is it about me?' Katie stops still in the street. 'Why do I only attract complete shits?'

'You don't!'

'I do! Look at the men I've been out with.' She starts counting off on her fingers. 'Daniel borrowed all that money off me and disappeared to Mexico. Gary chucked me as soon as I found him a job. David was two-timing me. Do you see a pattern emerging?'

'I . . . um . . .' I say helplessly. 'Possibly . . .'

'I just think I should give up.' Her face falls. 'I'm never going to find anyone nice.'

'No,' I say at once. 'Don't give up! Katie, I just know your life is going to turn around. You're going to find some lovely, kind, wonderful man—'

'But where?' she says hopelessly.

'I . . . don't know.' I cross my fingers behind my back. 'But I know it'll happen. I've got a really strong feeling about it.'

'Really?' She stares at me. 'You do?'

'Absolutely!' I think quickly for a moment. 'Look, here's an idea. Why don't you try . . . going to have lunch at a different place today. Somewhere completely different. And maybe you'll meet someone there.'

'You think?' She gazes at me. 'OK. I'll try it.'

She gives a gusty sigh, and we start walking along the pavement again. 'The *only* good thing about the weekend,' she adds as we reach the corner, 'is I finished making my new top. What do you think?'

She proudly takes off her jacket and does a twirl, and I stare at her for a few seconds, not quite sure what to say.

It's not that I don't *like* crochet . . .

OK. It is that I don't like crochet.

Especially pink scoop-neck open-weave crochet tops. You can actually see glimpses of her bra through it.

'It's . . . amazing,' I manage at last. 'Absolutely fantastic!'

'Isn't it great?' She gives me a pleased smile. 'And it was so quick to do! I'm going to make the matching skirt next.'

'That's great,' I say faintly. 'You're so clever.'

'Oh, it's nothing! I just enjoy it.'

She smiles modestly, and puts her jacket back on. 'So anyway, how about you?' she adds as we start to cross the road. 'Did you have a nice weekend? I bet you did. I bet Connor was completely wonderful and romantic. I bet he took you out for dinner or something.'

'Actually, he asked me to move in with him,' I say awkwardly.

'Really?' Katie gazes wistfully at me. 'God, Emma, you two make the perfect couple. You give me faith that it can happen. It all seems so easy for you.'

I can't help feeling a little flicker of pleasure inside. Me and Connor. The perfect couple. Role models for other people.

'It's not *that* easy,' I say with a modest little laugh. 'I mean, we argue, like anyone else.'

'Do you?' Katie looks surprised. 'I've never seen you argue.'

'Of course we do!'

I rack my brain for a moment, trying to remember the last time Connor and I had a fight. I mean, obviously we do *have* arguments. Loads of them. All couples do. It's only healthy.

Come on, this is silly. We must have—

Yes. There was that time by the river when I thought those big white birds were geese and Connor thought they were swans. Exactly. We're normal. I knew it.

We're nearing the Panther building now, and as we walk up the pale stone steps, each with a granite panther jumping across it, I start feeling a bit nervous. Paul will want a full report on how the meeting went with Glen Oil.

What shall I say?

Well, obviously I'll be completely frank and honest. Without actually telling him the truth—

'Hey, look.' Katie's voice interrupts me and I follow her gaze. Through the glass front of the building I can see a commotion in the foyer. This isn't normal. What's going on?

God, has there been a fire, or something?

As Katie and I push our way through the heavy revolving glass doors, we look at each other in bewilderment. The whole place is in turmoil. People are scurrying about, someone's polishing the brass banister, someone else is polishing the fake plants, and

Cyril, the senior office manager, is shooing people into lifts.

'Could you please go to your offices! We don't want you hanging around the reception area. You should all be at your desks by now.' He sounds completely stressed out. 'There's nothing to see down here! Please go to your desks.'

'What's happening?' I say to Dave the security guard, who's lounging against the wall with a cup of tea as usual. He takes a sip, swills it around his mouth and gives us a grin.

'Jack Harper's visiting.

'*What?*' We both gawp at him.

'Today?'

'Are you *serious*?'

In the world of the Panther Corporation, this is like saying the Pope's visiting. Or Father Christmas. Jack Harper is the joint founder of the Panther Corporation. He *invented* Panther Cola. I know this because I've typed out blurbs about him approximately a million times. 'It was 1987 when young, dynamic business partners Jack Harper and Pete Laidler bought up the ailing Zoot soft-drinks company, repackaged Zootacola as Panther Cola, invented the slogan "Don't Pause", and thus made marketing history.'

No wonder Cyril's in a tizz.

'In about five minutes.' Dave consults his watch. 'Give or take.'

'But . . . but how come?' says Katie. 'I mean, just out of the blue like this.'

Dave's eyes twinkle. He's obviously been telling people the news all morning and is thoroughly enjoying himself.

'He wants to have a look round the UK operation, apparently.'

'I thought he wasn't active in the business any more,'

says Jane from Accounts, who's come up behind us in her coat and is listening, agog. 'I thought ever since Pete Laidler died he was all grief-stricken and reclusive. On his ranch, or whatever it is.'

'That was three years ago,' points out Katie. 'Maybe he's feeling better.'

'Maybe he wants to sell us off, more like,' says Jane darkly.

'Why would he do that?'

'You never know.'

'My theory,' says Dave, and we all bend our heads to listen, 'is he wants to see if the plants are shiny enough.' He nods his head towards Cyril, and we all giggle.

'Be careful,' Cyril is snapping. 'Don't damage the stems.' He glances up. 'What are you all still doing there?'

'Just going!' says Katie, and we head towards the stairs, which I always use because it means I don't have to bother with the gym. Plus luckily Marketing is on the first floor. We've just reached the landing when Jane squeaks 'Look! Oh my God! It's him!'

A limousine has purred up the street and stopped right in front of the glass doors.

What is it about some cars? They look so gleaming and burnished, as if they're made out of a completely different metal from normal cars.

As if by clockwork, the lift doors at the other end of the foyer open, and out strides Graham Hillingdon, the chief executive, plus the managing director and about six others, all looking immaculate in dark suits.

'That's enough!' Cyril is hissing at the poor cleaners in the foyer. 'Go! Leave it!'

The three of us stand, goggling like children, as the passenger door of the limousine opens. A moment later, out gets a man with blond hair in a navy blue overcoat. He's wearing dark glasses and is holding a very expensive-looking briefcase.

Wow. He looks like a million dollars.

Graham Hillingdon and the others are all outside by now, lined up on the steps. They shake his hand in turn, then usher him inside, where Cyril is waiting.

'Welcome to the Panther Corporation UK,' Cyril says fulsomely. 'I hope your journey was pleasant?'

'Not too bad, thanks,' says the man, in an American accent.

'As you can see, this is very much a *normal* working day . . .'

'Hey look,' murmurs Katie. 'Kenny's stuck outside the doors.'

Kenny Davey, one of the designers, is hovering uncertainly on the steps outside in his jeans and baseball boots, not knowing whether to come in or not. He puts a hand to the door, then retreats a little, then comes up to the door again and peers uncertainly inside.

'Come in, Kenny!' says Cyril, opening the door with a rather savage smile. 'One of our designers, Kenny Davey. You should have been here ten minutes ago, Kenny. Still, never mind!' He pushes a bewildered Kenny towards the lifts, then glances up and shoos us away in irritation.

'Come on,' says Katie, 'we'd better go.' And, trying not to giggle, the three of us hurry up the stairs.

The atmosphere in the marketing department is a bit like my bedroom used to be before we had parties in the sixth form. People are brushing their hair, spraying perfume, shuffling papers around and gossiping excitedly. As I walk past the office of Neil Gregg, who is in charge of media strategy, I see him carefully lining up his Marketing Effectiveness awards on his desk, while

Fiona his assistant is polishing the framed photographs of him shaking hands with famous people.

I'm just hanging up my coat on the rack when the head of our department, Paul, pulls me aside.

'What the fuck happened at Glen Oil? I had a very strange email from Doug Hamilton this morning. You poured a drink over him?'

I stare at him in shock. Doug Hamilton *told* Paul? But he promised he wouldn't!

'It wasn't like that,' I say quickly. 'I was just trying to demonstrate the many fine qualities of Panther Prime and I . . . I kind of spilled it.' Paul raises his eyebrows, not in a friendly way.

'All right. It was a lot to ask of you.'

'It wasn't,' I say quickly. 'I mean, it would have been fine, if . . . what I mean is, if you give me another chance, I'll do better. I promise.'

'We'll see.' He looks at his watch. 'You'd better get on. Your desk is a fucking mess.'

'OK. Um, what time will my appraisal be?'

'Emma, in case you hadn't heard, Jack Harper's visiting us today,' says Paul, in his most sarcastic voice. 'But of course, if you think your appraisal's more important than the guy who *founded* the company—'

'I didn't mean . . . I just . . .'

'Go and tidy your desk,' says Paul in a bored voice. 'And if you spill fucking Panther Prime over Harper, you're fired.'

As I scuttle to my desk, Cyril comes into the room, looking hassled.

'Attention!' he says, clapping his hands. 'Attention everyone! This is an informal visit, nothing more. Mr Harper will come in, perhaps talk to one or two of you, observe what you do. So I want you all just to act normally, but obviously, at your highest standards . . . What are these papers?' he suddenly snaps, looking at a neat pile of proofs in the corner next to Fergus Grady's desk.

'That's the . . . um . . . artwork for the new Panther Gum campaign,' says Fergus, who is very shy and creative. 'I haven't quite got room on my desk.'

'Well, they can't stay here!' Cyril picks them up and shoves them at him. 'Get rid of them. Now, if he asks any of you a question, just be pleasant and natural. When he arrives, I want you all at work. Just doing typical tasks which you would naturally be doing in the course of a normal day.' He looks around distractedly. 'Some of you could be on the phone, some could be typing at your computers . . . a couple of you could be creatively brainstorming . . . Remember, this department is the hub of the company. The Panther Corporation is renowned for its marketing brilliance!'

He stops and we all stare dumbly at him.

'Get on!' He claps his hands again. 'Don't just stand there. You!' He points to me. 'Come on. Move!'

Oh, God. My desk is completely covered with stuff. I open a drawer and sweep a whole load of papers inside, then in slight panic, begin to tidy the pens in my stationery pot. At the next desk, Artemis Harrison is redoing her lipstick.

'It'll be really inspirational to meet him,' she says, admiring herself in her hand mirror. 'You know, a lot of people think he single-handedly changed the face of marketing practice.' Her eyes fall on me. 'Is that a new top, Emma? Where's it from?'

'Er, French Connection,' I say after a pause.

'I was in French Connection at the weekend.' Her eyes are narrowing. 'I didn't see that design.'

'Well, they'd probably sold out.' I turn away and pretend to be reorganizing my top drawer.

'What do we call him?' Caroline is saying. 'Mr Harper or Jack?'

'Five minutes alone with him,' Nick, one of the marketing executives, is saying feverishly into his phone. 'That's all I need. Five minutes to pitch him the website idea. I mean, Jesus, if he went for it—'

God, the air of excitement is infectious. With a spurt of adrenalin, I find myself reaching for my comb and checking my lip-gloss. I mean, you never know. Maybe he'll somehow spot my potential. Maybe he'll pull me out of the crowd!

'OK, folks,' says Paul, striding into the department. 'He's on this floor. He's going into Admin first . . .'

'On with your everyday tasks!' exclaims Cyril. 'Now!'

Fuck. What's my everyday task?

I pick up my phone and press my voice-mail code. I can be listening to my messages.

I look around the department – and see that everyone else has done the same thing.

We can't *all* be on the phone. This is so stupid! OK, I'll just switch on my computer and wait for it to warm up.

As I watch the screen changing colour, Artemis starts talking in a loud voice.

'I think the whole essence of the concept is *vitality*,' she says, her eye constantly flicking towards the door. 'D'you see what I mean?'

'Er, yes,' says Nick. 'I mean, in a modern marketing environment, I think we need to be looking at a . . . um . . . fusion of strategy and forward-thinking vision . . .'

God, my computer's slow today. Jack Harper will arrive and I'll still be staring at it like a moron.

I know what I'll do. I'll be the person getting a coffee. I mean, what could be more natural than that?

'I think I'll get a coffee,' I say self-consciously, and get up from my seat.

'Could you get me one?' says Artemis, looking up briefly. 'So anyway, on my MBA course . . .'

The coffee machine is near the entrance to the department, in its own little alcove. As I'm waiting for the noxious liquid to fill my cup, I glance up, and see Graham Hillingdon walking out of the admin department, followed by a couple of others. Shit! He's coming!

OK. Keep cool. Just wait for the second cup to fill, nice and natural . . .

And there he is! With his blond hair and his expensive-looking suit, and his dark glasses. But to my slight surprise, he steps back, out of the way.

In fact, no-one's even looking at him. Everyone's attention is focused on some other guy. A guy in jeans and a black turtleneck who's walking out now.

As I stare in fascination, he turns. And as I see his face I feel an almighty thud, as though a bowling ball's landed hard in my chest.

Oh my God.

It's him.

The same dark eyes. The same lines etched around them. The stubble's gone, but it's definitely him.

It's the man from the plane.

What's he doing here?

And why is everyone's attention on him? He's speaking now, and they're lapping up every word he says.

He turns again, and I instinctively duck back out of sight, trying to keep calm. What's he doing here? He can't—

That can't be—

That can't possibly be—

With wobbly legs, I walk back to my desk, trying not to drop the coffee on the floor.

'Hey,' I say to Artemis, my voice pitched slightly too

high. 'Erm . . . do you know what Jack Harper looks like?'

'No,' she says, and takes her coffee. 'Thanks.'

'Dark hair,' says someone.

'Dark?' I swallow. 'Not blond?'

'He's coming this way!' hisses someone. 'He's coming!'

With weak legs I sink into my chair and sip my coffee, not tasting it.

'. . . our head of marketing and promotion, Paul Fletcher,' I can hear Graham saying.

'Good to meet you, Paul,' comes the same dry, American voice.

It's him. It's definitely him.

OK, keep calm. Maybe he won't remember me. It was one short flight. He probably takes a lot of flights.

'Everyone.' Paul is leading him into the centre of the office. 'I'm delighted to introduce our founding father, the man who has influenced and inspired a generation of marketeers – Jack Harper!'

A round of applause breaks out, and Jack Harper shakes his head, smiling. 'Please,' he says. 'No fuss. Just do what you would normally do.'

He starts to walk around the office, pausing now and then to talk to people. Paul is leading the way, making all the introductions, and following them silently everywhere is the blond man.

'Here he comes!' Artemis hisses, and everyone at our end of the office stiffens.

My heart starts to thump, and I shrink into my chair, trying to hide behind my computer. Maybe he won't recognize me. Maybe he won't remember. Maybe he won't—

Fuck. He's looking at me. I see the flash of surprise in his eyes, and he raises his eyebrows.

He recognizes me.

Please don't come over, I silently pray. Please don't come over.

'And who's this?' he says to Paul.

'This is Emma Corrigan, one of our junior marketing assistants.'

He's walking towards me. Artemis has stopped talking. Everyone's staring. I'm hot with embarrassment.

'Hello,' he says pleasantly.

'Hello,' I manage. 'Mr Harper.'

OK, so he recognizes me. But that doesn't necessarily mean he remembers anything I said. A few random comments thrown out by a person in the next-door seat. Who's going to remember that? Maybe he wasn't even *listening*.

'And what do you do?'

'I, um, assist the marketing department and I help with setting up promotional initiatives,' I mumble.

'Emma was in Glasgow only last week on business,' puts in Paul, giving me a completely phoney smile. 'We believe in giving our junior staff responsibility as early as possible.'

'Very wise,' says Jack Harper, nodding. His gaze runs over my desk and alights with sudden interest on my polystyrene cup. He looks up and meets my eye. 'How's the coffee?' he asks pleasantly. 'Tasty?'

Like a tape recording in my head, I suddenly hear my own stupid voice, prattling on.

The coffee at work is the most disgusting stuff you've ever drunk, absolute poison . . .'

'It's great!' I say. 'Really . . . delicious!'

'I'm very glad to hear it.' There's a spark of amusement in his eyes, and I feel myself redden.

He remembers. Fuck. He remembers.

'And this is Artemis Harrison,' says Paul. 'One of our brightest young marketing executives.'

'Artemis,' says Jack Harper thoughtfully. He takes a few steps towards her work station. 'That's a nice big desk you've got there, Artemis.' He smiles at her. 'Is it new?'

'. . . *this new desk arrived the other day, and she just took it . . .*'

He remembers everything, doesn't he? Everything.

Oh God. What the fuck else did I say?

I'm sitting perfectly still, while Artemis makes some showy-off reply, with my pleasant, good-employee expression. But my mind is frantically spooling back, trying to remember, trying to piece together what I said. I mean, God, I told this man everything about myself. *Everything.* I told him what sort of knickers I wear, and what flavour ice-cream I like, and how I lost my virginity, and—

My blood runs cold.

I'm remembering something I should not have told him.

Something I should not have told anyone.

'. . . *I know I shouldn't have done it, but I so wanted to get the job . . .*'

I told him about faking the A grade on my CV.

Well, that's it. I'm dead.

He'll fire me. I'll get a record for being dishonest and no-one will ever employ me again, and I'll end up on a 'Britain's Worst Jobs' documentary, clearing up cow poo, saying brightly 'It's not too bad, really.'

OK. Don't panic. There must be something I can do. I'll apologize. Yes. I'll say it was an error of judgement which I now deeply regret, and I never meant to mislead the company, and—

No. I'll say, 'Actually, I *did* get an A grade, haha, silly me I forgot!' And then I'll forge a GCSE certificate with one of those calligraphy kits. I mean, he's American. He'll never know.

No. He's bound to find out. Oh God. Oh God.

OK, maybe I'm over-reacting here. Let's just get things in proportion. Jack Harper is a huge important guy. Look at him! He's got limos and flunkies, and a huge great company which makes millions every year. He doesn't care if one of his employees got a poxy A grade or not. I mean, honestly!

I laugh out loud in my nerves, and Artemis gives me an odd look.

'I'd just like to say that I'm very glad to meet you all,' says Jack Harper, looking around the silent office. 'And also introduce my assistant Sven Petersen.' He gestures to the guy with blond hair. 'I'll be staying here for a few days so I hope I'll get to know a few of you better. As you're aware, Pete Laidler, who founded the Panther Corporation with me, was British. For that reason, among many others, this country has always been immensely important to me.'

A sympathetic murmur goes around the office. He lifts a hand, nods, and walks away, followed by Sven and all the executives. There's silence until he's gone, then an excited babble breaks out.

I feel my whole body sag in relief. Thank God. Thank *God*.

Honestly, I'm such a moron. Fancy thinking even for a moment that Jack Harper would remember what I said. Let alone care about it! Fancy thinking he would take time out of his busy, important schedule, for something as tiny and insignificant as whether I faked my CV or not! As I reach for my mouse and click on a new document, I'm actually smiling.

'Emma.' I look up to see Paul standing over my desk. 'Jack Harper would like to see you,' he says curtly.

'What?' My smile fades away. 'Me?'

'The meeting room in five minutes.'

'Did he say why?'

'No.'

Paul strides off, and I gaze unseeingly at my computer screen, feeling sick.

I was right first time.

I'm going to lose my job.

I'm going to lose my job because of one stupid comment on one stupid plane ride.

Why did I have to get upgraded? *Why* did I have to open my stupid mouth? I'm just a stupid, *stupid* blabbermouth.

'Why does Jack Harper want to see you?' says Artemis, sounding put out.

'I don't know,' I say.

'Is he seeing anyone else?'

'I don't know!' I say distractedly.

To stop her asking any more questions, I start typing drivel into my computer, my mind whirring round and round.

I can't lose this job. I can't ruin yet another career.

He can't fire me. He just can't. It's not fair. I didn't know who he was. I mean, obviously, if he'd *told* me he was my employer, I would never have mentioned my CV. Or . . . any of it.

And anyway, it's not as if I faked my *degree*, is it? It's not as if I've got a criminal record or something. I'm a good employee. I try really hard and I don't skive off that often, *and* I put in all that overtime with the sportswear promotion, *and* I organized the Christmas raffle . . .

I'm typing harder and harder, and my face is growing red with agitation.

'Emma.' Paul is looking meaningfully at his watch.

'Right.' I take a deep breath and stand up.

I'm not going to let him fire me. I'm just not going to let it happen.

I stride across the office and down the corridor to the

77

meeting room, knock on the door and push it open.

Jack Harper is sitting on a chair at the conference table, scribbling something in a notebook. As I come in, he looks up, and the grave expression on his face makes my stomach turn over.

But I have to defend myself. I *have* to keep this job.

'Hi,' he says. 'Can you close the door?' He waits until I've done so, then looks up. 'Emma, we need to talk about something.'

'I'm aware that we do,' I say, trying to keep my voice steady. 'But I'd like to say my part first, if I may.'

For a moment Jack Harper looks taken aback – then he raises his eyebrows.

'Sure. Go ahead.'

I walk into the room, take a deep breath and look him straight in the eye.

'Mr Harper, I know what you want to see me about. I know it was wrong. It was an error of judgement which I deeply regret. I'm extremely sorry, and it will never happen again. But in my defence . . .' I can hear my voice rising in emotion. 'In my defence, I had no idea who you were on that plane ride. And I don't believe I should be penalized for what was an honest genuine mistake.'

There's a pause.

'You think I'm penalizing you?' says Jack Harper at last, with a frown.

How can he be so callous?

'Yes! You must realize I would never have mentioned my CV if I'd known who you were! It was like a . . . a honeytrap! You know, if this was a court the judge would throw it out. They wouldn't even let you—'

'Your CV?' Jack Harper's brow clears. 'Ah! The A grade on your résumé.' He gives me a penetrating look. 'The falsified A grade, I should say.'

Hearing it out loud like that silences me. I can feel my face growing hotter and hotter.

'You know, a lot of people would call that fraud,' says Jack Harper, leaning back in his chair.

'I know they would. I know it was wrong. I shouldn't have . . . But it doesn't affect the way I do my job. It doesn't *mean* anything.'

'You think?' He shakes his head thoughtfully. 'I don't know. Going from a C grade to an A grade . . . that's quite a jump. What if we need you to do some math?'

'I can do maths,' I say desperately. 'Ask me a maths question. Go on, ask me anything.'

'OK.' His mouth is twitching. 'Eight nines.'

I stare at him, my heart racing, my mind blank. Eight nines. I've got no idea. Fuck. OK, once nine is nine. Two nines are—

No. I've got it. Eight tens are 80. So eight *nines* must be—

'Seventy-two!' I cry, and flinch as he gives a tiny half-smile. 'It's seventy-two,' I add more calmly.

'Very good.' He gestures politely to a chair. 'Now. Have you finished what you wanted to say or is there more?'

I rub my face confusedly. 'You're . . . not going to fire me?'

'No,' says Jack Harper patiently. 'I'm not going to fire you. Now can we talk?'

As I sit down, a horrible suspicion starts growing in my mind.

'Was . . .' I clear my throat. 'Was my CV what you wanted to see me about?'

'No,' he says mildly. 'That wasn't what I wanted to see you about.'

I want to die.

I want to die right here, right now.

'Right.' I smooth back my hair, trying to compose myself; trying to look businesslike. 'Right. Well. So er, what did you . . . what . . .'

'I have a small favour to ask you.'

'Right!' I feel a thud of anticipation. 'Anything! I mean . . . what is it?'

'For various reasons,' says Jack Harper slowly, 'I would prefer it that nobody knows I was in Scotland last week.' He meets my eyes. 'So I would like it very much if we could keep our little meeting between ourselves.'

'Right!' I say after a pause. 'Of course! Absolutely. I can do that.'

'You haven't told anyone?'

'No. No-one. Not even my . . . I mean, no-one. I haven't told anyone.'

'Good. Thank you very much, I appreciate it.' He smiles, and gets up from his chair. 'Nice to meet you again, Emma. I'm sure I'll see you again.'

'That's it?' I say, taken aback.

'That's it. Unless you had anything else you wanted to discuss.'

'No!' I get to my feet hurriedly, banging my ankle on the table leg.

I mean, what did I think? That he was going to ask me to head up his exciting new international project?

Jack Harper opens the door, and holds it politely for me. And I'm halfway out when I stop. 'Wait.'

'What is it?'

'What shall I say you wanted to talk to me about?' I say awkwardly. 'Everyone's going to ask me.'

'Why not say we were discussing logistics?' He raises his eyebrows and closes the door.

SIX

For the rest of the day there's a kind of festive atmosphere at work. But I just sit there, unable to believe what just happened. And as I travel home that evening, my heart is still pounding at the unlikeliness of it all. At the *injustice* of it all.

He was a stranger. He was supposed to be a *stranger*. The whole point about strangers is, they disappear into the ether, never to be seen again. Not turn up at the office. Not ask you what eight nines are. Not turn out to be your mega-boss employer.

Well, all I can say is, that's taught me. My parents always said never talk to strangers, and they were right. I'm never telling a stranger anything again. *Ever*.

I've arranged to go to Connor's flat in the evening, and when I arrive I feel my body expand in relief. Away from the office. Away from all the endless Jack Harper talk. And Connor's already cooking. I mean, how perfect is that? The kitchen is full of a wonderful garlicky-herby smell, and there's a glass of wine already waiting for me on the table.

'Hi!' I say, and give him a kiss.

'Hi, darling!' he says, looking up from the stove.

Shit. I totally forgot to say Darling. OK, how am I going to remember this?

I know. I'll write it on my hand.

'Have a look at those. I downloaded them from the Internet.' Connor gestures to a folder on the table with a wide smile. I open it, and find myself looking at a grainy black and white picture of a room with a sofa and a pot plant.

'Flat details!' I say, taken aback. 'Wow. That's quick. I haven't even given notice yet.'

'Well, we need to start looking,' says Connor. 'Look, that one's got a balcony. And there's one with a working fireplace!'

'Gosh!'

I sit down on a nearby chair and peer at the blurry photograph, trying to imagine me and Connor living in it together. Sitting on that sofa. Just the two of us, every single evening.

I wonder what we'll talk about.

Well! We'll talk about . . . whatever we always talk about.

Maybe we'll play Monopoly. Just if we get bored or anything.

I turn to another sheet and feel a pang of excitement.

This flat has wooden floors and shutters! I've *always* wanted wooden floors and shutters. And look at that cool kitchen, with all granite worktops . . .

Oh, this is going to be so great. I can't wait!

I take a happy slug of wine, and am just sinking comfortably back when Connor says, 'So! Isn't it exciting about Jack Harper coming over.'

Oh God. Please. Not *more* talk about bloody Jack Harper.

'Did you get to meet him?' he adds, coming over with a bowl of peanuts. 'I heard he went into Marketing.'

'Um, yes, I met him.'

'He came into Research this afternoon, but I was at a meeting.' Connor looks at me, agog. 'So what's he like?'

'He's . . . I don't know. Dark hair . . . American . . . So how did the meeting go?'

Connor totally ignores my attempt to change the subject.

'Isn't it exciting, though?' His face is glowing. 'Jack Harper!'

'I suppose so.' I shrug. 'Anyway—'

'Emma! Aren't you excited?' Connor looks astonished. 'We're talking about the founder of the company! We're talking about the man who came up with the concept of Panther Cola. Who took an unknown brand, repackaged it and sold it to the world! He turned a failing company into a huge, successful corporation. And now we're all getting to meet him. Don't you find that thrilling?'

'Yes,' I say at last. 'It's . . . thrilling.'

'This could be the opportunity of a lifetime for all of us. To learn from the genius himself! You know, he's never written a book, he's never shared his thoughts with anyone except Pete Laidler . . .' He reaches into the fridge for a can of Panther Cola and cracks it open. Connor has to be the most loyal employee in the world. I once bought a Pepsi when we were out on a picnic, and he nearly had a hernia.

'You know what I would love above anything?' he says, taking a gulp. 'A one-to-one with him.' He looks at me, his eyes shining. 'A one-to-one with Jack Harper! Wouldn't that be the most fantastic career boost?'

A one-to-one with Jack Harper.

Yup, that boosted my career great.

'I suppose,' I say reluctantly.

'Of course it would be! Just having the chance to listen to him. To hear what he has to say! I mean, the guy's been shut away for three years. What ideas must he have been generating all this time? He must have so many insights and theories, not just about marketing, but about business . . . about the way people work . . . about life itself.'

Connor's enthusiastic voice is like salt rubbing into my sore skin. So, let's just see quite how spectacularly I have played this wrong, shall we? I'm sitting on a plane next to the great Jack Harper, creative genius and source of all wisdom on business and marketing, not to mention the great mysteries of life itself.

And what do I do? Do I ask him insightful questions? Do I engage him in intelligent conversation? Do I learn anything from him at all?

No. I blabber on about what kind of underwear I prefer.

Great career move, Emma. One of the best.

The next day, Connor is off to a meeting first thing, but before he goes he digs out an old magazine article about Jack Harper.

'Read this,' he says, through a mouthful of toast. 'It's good background information.'

I don't *want* any background information! I feel like retorting, but Connor's already out of the door.

I'm tempted to leave it behind and not even bother looking at it, but it's quite a long journey from Connor's place to work, and I haven't got any magazines with me. So I take the article with me, and grudgingly start reading it on the tube, and I suppose it is quite an interesting story. How Harper and Péte Laidler were friends, and they decided to go into business, and Jack was the creative one and Pete was the extrovert playboy one, and they became multimillionaires together, and they were so close they were practically like brothers. And then Pete was killed in a car crash. And Jack was so devastated he shut himself away from the world and said he was giving it all up.

And of course now I read all this I'm starting to feel a bit stupid. I should have recognized Jack Harper. I mean, I certainly recognize Pete Laidler. For one thing he looks – looked – just like Robert Redford. And for another, he was all over the papers when he died. I can remember it vividly now, even though I had nothing to do with the Panther Corporation then. He crashed his Mercedes, and everyone said it was just like Princess Diana.

I'm so busy reading, I nearly miss my stop and have to make one of those stupid dashes for the doors, where everyone looks at you like: You complete moron, did you not know that your stop was coming up? And then, as the doors close, I realize I've left the article behind on the tube.

Oh well. I'd kind of got the gist of it.

It's a bright sunshiny morning, and I head towards the juice bar where I usually pop in before work. I've got into the habit of picking up a mango smoothie every morning, because it's healthy.

And also because there is a very cute New Zealand guy who works behind the counter, called Aidan. (In fact, I had a miniature crush on him, before I started going out with Connor.) When he isn't working in the smoothie bar he's doing a course on sports science, and he's always telling me stuff about essential minerals, and what your carb-ratio should be.

'Hiya,' he says as I come in. 'How's the kick-boxing going?'

'Oh!' I say, colouring slightly. 'It's great, thanks.'

'Did you try that new manoeuvre I told you about?'

'Yes! It really helped!'

'I thought it would,' he says, looking pleased, and goes off to make my mango smoothie.

OK. So the truth is, I don't really do kick-boxing. I did try it once, at our local leisure centre, and to be honest, I was shocked! I had no idea it would be so *violent*. But Aidan was so enthused about it, and kept saying how it would transform my life, I couldn't bring

85

myself to admit I'd given up after only one session. It just seemed so lame. So I kind of . . . fibbed. And I mean, it's not like it matters. He'll never know. It's not as if I ever see him outside the smoothie bar.

'That's one mango smoothie,' says Aidan.

'And a chocolate brownie,' I say. 'For . . . my colleague.' Aidan picks up the brownie and pops it in a bag.

'You know, that colleague of yours needs to think about her refined sugar levels,' he says with a concerned frown. 'That must be – four brownies this week?'

'I know,' I say earnestly. 'I'll tell her. Thanks, Aidan.'

'No problem!' says Aidan. 'And remember: one-two-swivel!'

'One-two-swivel,' I repeat brightly. 'I'll remember!'

As I arrive at the office, Paul appears out of his room, snaps his fingers at me and says, 'Appraisal.'

My stomach gives an almighty lurch, and I nearly choke on my last bite of chocolate brownie. Oh God. This is it. I'm not ready.

Yes I am. Come on. Exude confidence. I am a woman on her way somewhere.

Suddenly I remember Kerry and her 'I am a successful woman' walk. I know Kerry's an obnoxious cow, but she does have her own travel agency and make zillions of pounds a year. She must be doing something right. Maybe I should give it a go. Cautiously I stick out my bust, lift my head and start striding across the office with a fixed, alert expression on my face.

'Have you got period pain or something?' says Paul crudely as I reach his door.

'No!' I say in shock.

'Well you look very odd. Now sit down.' He shuts

86

the door, sits down at his desk and opens a form marked Staff Appraisal Review. 'I'm sorry I couldn't see you yesterday. But what with Jack Harper's arrival, everything got buggered up.'

'That's OK.'

I try to smile but my mouth is suddenly dry. I can't believe how nervous I feel. This is worse than a school report.

'OK. So . . . Emma Corrigan.' He looks at the form and starts ticking boxes. 'Generally, you're doing fine. You're not generally late . . . you understand the tasks given to you . . . you're fairly efficient . . . you work OK with your colleagues . . . blah blah . . . blah . . . Any problems?' he says, looking up.

'Er . . . no.'

'Do you feel racially harassed?'

'Er . . . no.'

'Good.' He ticks another box. 'Well I think that's it. Well done. Can you send Nick in to see me?'

What? Has he forgotten?

'Um, what about my promotion?' I say, trying not to sound too anxious.

'Promotion?' He stares at me. 'What promotion?'

'To Marketing Executive.'

'What the fuck are you talking about?'

'It said. It said in the ad for my job . . .' I pull the crumpled ad out of my jeans pocket, where it's been since yesterday. '"Possible promotion after a year."' It says it right there.' I push it across the desk, and he looks at it with a frown.

'Emma, that was only for exceptional candidates. You're not ready for a promotion. You'll have to prove yourself first.'

'But I'm doing everything as well as I can! If you just give me a chance—'

'You had the chance at Glen Oil.' Paul raises his

eyebrows at me and I feel a twinge of humiliation. 'Emma, bottom line is, you're not ready for a higher position. In a year we'll see.'

'A *year*?'

'OK? Now hop it.'

My mind is whirling. I have to accept this in a calm, dignified way. I have to say something like 'I respect your decision, Paul', shake his hand and leave the room. This is what I have to do.

The only trouble is, I can't seem to get up out of my chair.

After a few moments Paul looks puzzledly at me. 'That's it, Emma.'

I can't move. Once I leave this room, it's over.

'Emma?'

'Please promote me,' I say desperately. 'Please. I have to get a promotion to impress my family. It's the only thing I want in the whole world, and I'll work so hard, I promise, I'll come in at weekends, and I'll . . . I'll wear smart suits . . .'

'*What?*' Paul is staring at me as though I've turned into a goldfish.

'You don't have to pay me any more salary! I'll do all the same jobs as before. I'll even pay to have my new business cards printed! I mean, it won't make any difference to you. You won't even *know* I've been promoted!'

I break off, breathing hard.

'I think you'll find that's not quite the point of promotion, Emma,' says Paul sarcastically. 'I'm afraid the answer's no. Even more so.'

'But—'

'Emma, a word of advice. If you want to get ahead, you have to create your own chances. You have to carve out your own opportunities. Now seriously.

88

Could you please fuck off out of my office and get Nick for me?'

As I leave I can see him raising his eyes to heaven and scribbling something else on my form.

Great. He's probably writing 'Deranged lunatic, seek medical help'.

As I walk dejectedly back to my desk, Artemis looks up with a beady expression. 'Oh, Emma,' she says, 'your cousin Kerry just called for you.'

'Really?' I say in surprise. Kerry never phones me at work. In fact she never phones me at all. 'Did she leave a message?'

'Yes, she did. She wanted to know, have you heard about your promotion yet?'

OK. This is now official. I hate Kerry.

'Oh right,' I say, trying to sound as though this is some boring, everyday enquiry. 'Thanks.'

'Are you being promoted, Emma? I didn't know that!' Her voice is high and piercing, and I see a couple of people raise their heads in interest. 'So, are you going to become a marketing executive?'

'No,' I mutter, my face hot with humiliation. 'I'm not.'

'Oh!' Artemis pulls a mock-confused face. 'So why did she—'

'Shut up, Artemis,' says Caroline. I give her a grateful look and slump into my chair.

Another whole year. Another whole year of being the crappy marketing assistant, and everyone thinking I'm useless. Another year of being in debt to Dad, and Kerry and Nev laughing at me, and feeling like a complete failure. I switch on my computer and dispiritedly type a couple of words. But suddenly all my energy's gone.

'I think I'll get a coffee,' I say. 'Does anyone want one?'

'You can't get a coffee,' says Artemis, giving me an odd look. 'Haven't you seen?'

'What?'

'They've taken the coffee machine away,' says Nick. 'While you were in with Paul.'

'Taken it away?' I look at him, puzzled. 'But why?'

'Dunno,' he says, walking off towards Paul's office. 'They just came and carted it away.'

'We're getting a new machine!' says Caroline, walking past with a bundle of proofs. 'That's what they were saying downstairs. A really nice one, with proper coffee. Ordered by Jack Harper, apparently.'

She moves off, and I stare after her.

Jack Harper ordered a new coffee machine?

'Emma!' Artemis is saying impatiently. 'Did you hear that? I want you to find the leaflet we did for the Tesco promotion two years ago. Sorry, Mummy,' she says into the phone. 'Just telling my assistant something.'

Her assistant. God, it pisses me off when she says that.

But to be honest, I'm feeling a bit too dazed to get annoyed.

It's nothing to do with me, I tell myself firmly as I root around at the bottom of the filing cabinet. It's ridiculous to think I had anything to do with it. He was probably planning to order new coffee anyway. He was probably—

I stand up with a pile of files in my arms and nearly drop them all on the floor.

There he is.

Standing right in front of me.

'Hello again.' His eyes crinkle in a smile. 'How are you doing?'

90

'Er . . . good, thanks.' I swallow hard. 'I just heard about the coffee machine. Um . . . thanks.'

'No problem.'

'Now everyone!' Paul comes striding up behind him. 'Mr Harper is going to be sitting in on the department this morning.'

'Please.' Jack Harper smiles. 'Call me Jack.'

'Right you are. *Jack* is going to be sitting in this morning. He's going to observe what you do, find out how we operate as a team. Just behave normally, don't do anything special.' Paul's eyes alight on me and he gives me an ingratiating smile. 'Hi there, Emma! How are you doing? Everything OK?'

'Er, yes thanks, Paul,' I mutter. 'Everything's great.'

'Good! A happy staff, that's what we like. And, while I've got your attention,' he coughs a little self-consciously, 'let me just remind you that our Corporate Family Day is coming up, a week on Saturday. A chance for us all to let our hair down, enjoy meeting each other's families, and have some fun!'

We all stare at him a bit blankly. Until this moment, Paul has always referred to this as the Corporate Fuckwit Day and said he'd rather have his balls torn off than bring any member of his family to it.

'Anyway, back to work, everyone! Jack, let me get you a chair.'

'Just ignore me,' says Jack Harper pleasantly, as he sits down in the corner. 'Behave normally.'

Behave normally. Right. Of course.

So that would be sit down, take my shoes off, check my emails, put some hand cream on, eat a few Smarties, read my horoscope on iVillage, read Connor's horoscope, write 'Emma Corrigan, Managing Director' several times in swirly letters on my notepad, add a border of flowers, send an email to Connor, wait a few minutes to see if he replies, take a swig of mineral water and then finally get round to finding the Tesco leaflet for Artemis.

I don't think so.

As I sit back down at my desk, my mind is working quickly. Create your own chances. Carve out your own opportunities. That's what Paul said.

And what is this if not an opportunity?

Jack Harper himself is sitting here, watching me work. The great Jack Harper. Boss of the entire corporation. Surely I can impress him *somehow*?

OK, perhaps I haven't got off to the most brilliant start with him. But maybe this is my chance to redeem myself! If I can just somehow show that I'm really bright and motivated . . .

As I sit, leafing through the file of promotional literature, I'm aware that I'm holding my head slightly higher than usual, as though I'm in a posture class. And as I glance around the office, everyone else seems to be in a posture class, too. Before Jack Harper arrived, Artemis was on the phone to her mum, but now she's put on her horn-rimmed glasses and is typing briskly, occasionally pausing to smile at what she's written in a 'what a genius I am' way. Nick was reading the sports section of the *Telegraph*, but now I can see him studying some documents with graphs in them, with a deep frown.

'Emma?' says Artemis in a falsely sweet voice. 'Have you found that leaflet I was asking you for? Not that there's *any* hurry—'

'Yes, I have!' I say. I push back my chair, stand up, and walk over to her desk. I'm trying to look as natural as possible. But God, this is like being on telly or something. My legs aren't working properly and my smile is pasted onto my face and I have a horrible conviction I might suddenly shout 'Pants!' or something.

'Here you are, Artemis,' I say, and carefully lay the leaflet on her desk.

'Bless you!' says Artemis. Her eyes meet mine brightly and I realize she's acting, too. She puts her hand on mine, and gives me a twinkly smile. 'I don't know what we'd do without you, Emma!'

'That's quite all right!' I say, matching her tone. 'Any time!'

Shit, I think as I walk back to my desk. I should have said something cleverer. I should have said, 'Teamwork is what keeps this operation together.'

OK, never mind. I can still impress him.

Trying to act as normally as possible I open a document and start to type as quickly and efficiently as I can, my back ramrod straight. I've never known the office this quiet. Everyone's tapping away, no-one's chatting. It's like being in an exam. My foot's itching, but I don't dare scratch it.

How on earth do people do those fly-on-the-wall documentaries? I feel completely exhausted, and it's only been about five minutes.

'It's very quiet in here,' says Jack Harper, sounding puzzled. 'Is it normally this quiet?'

'Er . . .' We all look around uncertainly at each other.

'Please, don't mind me. Talk away like you normally would. You must have office discussions.' He gives a friendly smile. 'When I worked in an office, we talked about everything under the sun. Politics, books . . . For instance, what have you all been reading recently?'

'Actually, I've been reading the new biography of Mao Tse Tung,' says Artemis at once. 'Fascinating stuff.'

'I'm in the middle of a history of fourteenth-century Europe,' says Nick.

'I'm just re-reading Proust,' says Caroline, with a modest shrug. 'In the original French.'

'Ah.' Jack Harper nods, his face unreadable. 'And . . . Emma, is it? What are you reading?'

'Um, actually . . .' I swallow, playing for time.

I cannot say *Celebrity Doodles – What Do They Mean?* Even though it is actually very good. Quick. What's a serious book?

'You were reading *Great Expectations*, weren't you, Emma?' says Artemis. 'For your book club.'

'Yes!' I say in relief. 'Yes, that's right—'

And then I stop abruptly as I meet Jack Harper's gaze. Fuck.

Inside my head, my own voice from the plane is babbling away innocently.

'. . . *just skimmed the back cover and pretended I'd read it . . .*'

'*Great Expectations*,' says Jack Harper thoughtfully. 'What did you think of it, Emma?'

I don't *believe* he asked me that.

For a few moments I can't speak.

'Well!' I clear my throat at last. 'I thought it . . . it was really . . . extremely . . .'

'It's a wonderful book,' says Artemis earnestly. 'Once you fully understand the symbolism.'

Shut *up*, you stupid show-off. Oh God. What am I going to say?

'I thought it really . . . resonated,' I say at last.

'What resonated?' says Nick.

'The . . . um . . .' I clear my throat. 'The resonances.'

There's a puzzled silence.

'The resonances . . . resonated?' says Artemis.

'Yes,' I say defiantly. 'They did. Anyway, I've got to get on with my work.' I turn away with a roll of my eyes and start typing feverishly.

OK. So the book discussion didn't go that well. But that was just sheer bad luck. Think positive. I can still do this. I can still impress him—

'I just don't know what's wrong with it!' Artemis is saying in a girly voice. 'I water it every day.'

She pokes her spider plant and gazes at Jack Harper winsomely. 'Do you know anything about plants, Jack?'

'I don't, I'm afraid,' says Jack, and looks over at me, his face deadpan. 'What do you think could be wrong with it, Emma?'

'. . . *sometimes, when I'm pissed off with Artemis . . .*'

'I . . . I have no idea,' I say at last, and carry on typing, my face flaming.

OK. Never mind. It doesn't matter. So I watered one little plant with orange juice. So what?

'Has anyone seen my World Cup mug?' says Paul, walking into the office with a frown. 'I can't seem to find it anywhere.'

'. . . *I broke my boss's mug last week and hid the pieces in my handbag. . .*'

Shit.

OK. Never mind. So I broke one tiny mug, too. It doesn't matter. Just keep typing.

'Hey Jack,' says Nick, in a matey, lads-together voice. 'Just in case you don't think we have any fun, look up there!' He nods towards the picture of a photo-copied, G-stringed bottom which has been up on the noticeboard since Christmas. 'We still don't know who it is . . .'

'. . . *I had a few too many drinks at the last Christmas party . . .*'

OK, now I want to die. Someone please kill me.

'Hi, Emma!' comes Katie's voice, and I look up to see her hurrying into the office, her face pink with excitement. When she sees Jack Harper, she stops dead. 'Oh!'

'It's all right. I'm simply a fly on the wall.' He waves a friendly hand at her. 'Go ahead. Say whatever you were going to say.'

'Hi Katie!' I manage. 'What is it?'

As soon as I say her name, Jack Harper looks up again, a riveted expression on his face.

I do not like the look of that riveted expression.

What did I tell him about Katie? What? My mind spools furiously back. What did I say? What did I—

I feel an internal lurch. Oh God.

'. . . *we have this secret code where she comes in and says, "Can I go through some numbers with you, Emma?" and it really means "Shall we nip out to Starbucks . . ."*'

I told him our skiving code.

I stare desperately at Katie's eager face, trying somehow to convey the message to her.

Do not say it. Do *not* say you want to go over some numbers with me.

But she's completely oblivious.

'I just . . . erm . . .' She clears her throat in a businesslike way and glances self-consciously at Jack Harper. 'Could I possibly go over some numbers with you, Emma?'

Fuck.

My face floods with colour. My whole body is prickling.

'You know,' I say, in a bright, artificial voice, 'I'm not sure that'll be possible today.'

Katie stares at me in surprise.

'But I have to . . . I really *need* you to go over some numbers with me.' She nods in excitement.

'I'm quite tied up here with my work, Katie!' I force a smile, simultaneously trying to telegraph 'Shut *up*!'

'It won't take long! Just quickly.'

'I really don't think so.'

Katie is practically hopping from foot to foot.

'But Emma, they're very . . . *important* numbers. I really need to . . . to tell you about them . . .'

'Emma.' At Jack Harper's voice I jump as though I've been stung. He leans towards me confidentially. 'Maybe you should go over the numbers.'

I stare back at him for a few moments, unable to speak, blood pounding in my ears.

'Right,' I manage after a long pause. 'OK. I'll do that.'

SEVEN

As I walk along the street with Katie, half of me is numb with horror, and half almost wants to burst into hysterical laughter. Everyone else is in the office, trying as hard as they can to impress Jack Harper. And here I am, strolling off nonchalantly under his nose for a cappuccino.

'I'm sorry I interrupted you,' says Katie brightly, as we push our way through the doors of Starbucks. 'With Jack Harper there and everything. I had no idea he'd be just *sitting* there! But you know, I was really subtle,' she adds reassuringly. 'He'll never know what we're up to.'

'I'm sure you're right,' I manage. 'He'll never guess in a million years.'

'Are you OK, Emma?' Katie looks at me curiously.

'I'm fine!' I say with a kind of shrill hilarity. 'I'm absolutely fine! So . . . why the emergency summit?'

'I *had* to tell you. Two cappuccinos, please.' Katie beams at me excitedly. 'You won't believe it!'

'What is it?'

'I've got a date. I met a new guy!'

'No!' I say, staring at her. 'Really? That was quick.'

'Yes, it happened yesterday, just like you said! I deliberately walked further than usual in my lunch hour, and I found this really nice place where they were serving lunch. And there was this nice man in the line next to me – and he struck up a conversation with me. Then we shared a table and chatted some more . . .

and I was just leaving, when he said did I fancy having a drink some time?' She takes the cappuccinos with a beam. 'So we're going out this evening.'

'That's fantastic!' I say in delight. 'So come on, what's he like?'

'He's lovely. He's called Phillip! He's got these lovely twinkly eyes, and he's really charming and polite, and he's got a great sense of humour . . .'

'He sounds amazing!'

'I know. I have a really good feeling about him.' Katie's face glows as we sit down. 'I really do. He just seems different. And I know this sounds really stupid, Emma . . .' she hesitates. 'But I feel you somehow *brought* him to me.'

'Me?' I gape at her.

'You gave me the confidence to speak to him.'

'But all I said was—'

'You said you knew I'd meet someone. You had faith in me. And I did!' Her eyes begin to shine. 'I'm sorry,' she whispers, and dabs her eyes with a napkin. 'I'm just a bit overcome.'

'Oh Katie.'

'I just really think my life is going to turn around. I think everything's going to get better. And it's all down to you, Emma!'

'Really, Katie,' I say awkwardly. 'It was nothing.'

'It wasn't nothing!' she gulps. 'And I wanted to do something for you in return.' She rummages in her bag and pulls out a large piece of orange crochet. 'So I made you this last night.' She looks at me expectantly. 'It's a headscarf.'

For a few moments, I can't move. A crochet headscarf.

'Katie,' I manage at last, turning it over in my fingers. 'Really, you . . . you shouldn't have!'

'I wanted to! To say thank you.' She looks at me

earnestly. 'Especially after you lost that crochet belt I made for you for Christmas.'

'Oh!' I say, feeling a pang of guilt. 'Er, yes. That was ... such a shame.' I swallow. 'It was a lovely belt. I was really upset to lose it.'

'Oh what the hell!' Her eyes well up again. 'I'll make you a new belt, too.'

'No!' I say in alarm. 'No, Katie, don't do that.'

'But I want to!' She leans forward and gives me a hug. 'That's what friends are for!'

It's another twenty minutes before we finish our second cappuccinos and head back for the office. As we approach the Panther building I glance at my watch and see with a lurch that we've been gone thirty-five minutes in all.

'Isn't it amazing we're getting new coffee machines?' says Katie as we hurry up the steps.

'Oh . . . yes. It's great.'

My stomach has started to churn at the thought of facing Jack Harper again. I haven't felt so nervous since I took my grade one clarinet exam and when the examiner asked me what my name was I burst into tears.

'Well, see you later,' says Katie as we reach the first floor. 'And thanks, Emma.'

'No problem,' I say. 'See you later.'

As I start to walk along the corridor towards the marketing department, I'm aware that my legs aren't moving quite as quickly as usual. In fact, as the door is nearing, they're getting slower, and slower . . . and slower . . .

One of the secretaries from Accounts overtakes me, with a brisk high-heeled pace, and gives me an odd look.

Oh God. I can't go in there.

Yes I can. It'll be fine. I'll just sit down very quietly

and get on with my work. Maybe he won't even notice me.

Come on. The longer I leave it, the worse it'll be. I take a deep breath, close my eyes, take a few steps into the marketing department, and open them.

There's a hubbub around Artemis's desk, and no sign of Jack Harper.

'I mean, maybe he's going to rethink the whole company,' someone's saying.

'I've heard this rumour he's got a secret project . . .'

'He can't completely centralize the marketing function,' Artemis is saying, trying to raise her voice above everyone else's.

'Where's Jack Harper?' I say, trying to sound casual.

'He's gone,' says Nick, and I feel a whoosh of relief. Gone! He's gone!

'Is he coming back?'

'Don't think so. Emma, have you done those letters for me yet? Because I gave them to you three days ago—'

'I'll do them now,' I say, and beam at Nick. As I sit down at my desk, I feel as light as a helium balloon. Cheerfully I kick off my shoes, reach for my Evian bottle – and stop.

There's a folded piece of paper resting on my keyboard, with 'Emma' written on it in a handwriting I don't recognize.

Puzzled, I look around the office. No-one's looking at me, waiting for me to find it. In fact no-one seems to have noticed. They're all too busy talking about Jack Harper.

Slowly I unfold it and stare at the message inside.

Hope your meeting was productive. I always find numbers give me a real buzz.

Jack Harper

It could have been worse. It could have read 'Clear your desk'.

Even so, for the rest of the day, I'm completely on edge. Every time anyone walks into the department I feel a little spasm of panic. And when someone starts talking loudly outside our door about how 'Jack says he may pop back into Marketing', I seriously consider hiding in the loos until he's gone.

On the dot of 5.30 I stop typing mid-sentence, close my computer down and grab my coat. I'm not waiting around for him to reappear. I all but run down the stairs, and only begin to relax when I'm safely on the other side of the big glass doors.

The tubes are miraculously quick for once, and I arrive home within twenty minutes. As I push open the front door of the flat I can hear a strange noise coming from Lissy's room. A kind of thumping, bumping sound. Maybe she's moving her furniture around.

'Lissy,' I call as I go into the kitchen. 'You will not believe what happened today.' I open the fridge, take out a bottle of Evian and hold it against my hot fore-head. After a while I open the bottle and take a few swigs, then wander out into the hall again to see Lissy's door opening.

'Lissy!' I begin. 'What on earth were you—'

And then I halt, as out of the door comes not Lissy, but a man.

A man! A tall thin guy in trendy black trousers and steel spectacles.

'Oh,' I say, taken aback. 'Er . . . hi.'

'Emma!' says Lissy, following him out. She's wearing a T-shirt over some grey leggings I've never seen before, is drinking a glass of water and looks startled to see me. 'You're home early.'

'I know. I was in a hurry.'

'This is Jean-Paul,' says Lissy. 'Jean-Paul, my flat-mate Emma.'

'Hello, Jean-Paul,' I say with a friendly smile.

'Good to meet you, Emma,' says Jean-Paul, in a French accent.

God, French accents are sexy. I mean, they just are.

'Jean-Paul and I were just . . . um . . . going over some case notes,' says Lissy.

'Oh right,' I say brightly. 'Lovely!'

Case notes. Yeah, right. Because that would really make a whole load of thumping noises.

Lissy is such a dark horse!

'I must be going,' says Jean-Paul, looking at Lissy.

'I'll just see you out,' she says, flustered.

She disappears out of the front door, and I can hear the two of them murmuring on the landing.

I take a few more swigs of Evian, then walk into the sitting room and slump down heavily on the sofa. My whole body's aching from sitting rigid with tension all day. This is seriously bad for my health. How on earth am I going to survive a whole week of Jack Harper?

'So!' I say as Lissy walks back into the room. 'What's going on?'

'What do you mean?' she says shiftily.

'You and Jean-Paul! How long have you two been . . .'

'We're not,' starts Lissy, turning red. 'It's not . . . We were going over case notes. That's all.'

'Sure you were.'

'We were! That's all it was!'

'OK,' I say, raising my eyebrows. 'If you say so.'

Lissy sometimes gets like this, all shy and abashed. I'll just have to get her pissed one night, and she'll admit it.

'So how was your day?' she says, sinking onto the floor and reaching for a magazine.

How was my day?

I don't even know where to start.

'My day,' I say at last. 'My day was a bit of a nightmare.'

'Really?' says Lissy, looking up in surprise.

'No, take that back. It was a *complete* nightmare.'

'What happened?' Lissy's attention is fully grabbed. 'Tell me!'

'OK.' I take a deep breath and smooth my hair back, wondering where on earth to start. 'OK, remember I had that awful flight back from Scotland last week?'

'Yes!' Lissy's face lights up. 'And Connor came to meet you and it was all really romantic . . .'

'Yes. Well.' I clear my throat. 'Before that. On the flight. There was this . . . this man sitting next to me. And the plane got really turbulent.' I bite my lip. 'And the thing is, I honestly thought we were all going to die and this was the last person I would ever see, and . . . I . . .'

'Oh my God!' Lissy claps her hand over her mouth. 'You didn't have sex with him.'

'Worse! I told him all my secrets.'

I'm expecting Lissy to gasp, or say something sympathetic like 'Oh no!' but she's staring at me blankly.

'What secrets?'

'My secrets. You know.'

Lissy looks as if I've told her I've got an artificial leg. 'You have *secrets*?'

'Of course I have secrets!' I say. 'Everyone has a few secrets.'

'I don't!' she says at once, looking offended. 'I don't have any secrets.'

'Yes you do!'

'Like what?'

'Like . . . like . . . OK.' I start counting off on my fingers. 'You never told your dad it was you who lost the garage key that time.'

'That was ages ago!' says Lissy scornfully.

'You never told Simon you were hoping he might propose to you . . .'

'I wasn't!' says Lissy, colouring. 'Well, OK, maybe I was . . .'

'You think that sad guy next door fancies you . . .'

'That's not a *secret*!' she says, rolling her eyes.

'Oh right. Shall I tell him, then?' I lean back towards the open window. 'Hey Mike,' I call. 'Guess what? Lissy thinks you—'

'Stop!' says Lissy frantically.

'You see? You have got secrets. Everyone has secrets. The *Pope* probably has a few secrets.'

'OK,' says Lissy. 'OK. You've made your point. But I don't understand what the problem is. So you told some guy on a plane your secrets—'

'And now he's turned up at work.'

'What?' Lissy stares at me. 'Are you serious? Who is he?'

'He's . . .' I'm about to say Jack Harper's name when I remember the promise I made. 'He's just this . . . this guy who's come in to observe,' I say vaguely.

'Is he senior?'

'He's . . . yes. You could say he's pretty senior.'

'Blimey.' Lissy frowns, thinking for a few moments. 'Well, does it really matter? If he knows a few things about you.'

'Lissy, it wasn't just a few things.' I feel myself flush slightly. 'It was *everything*. I told him I faked a grade on my CV.'

'You faked a grade on your *CV*?' echoes Lissy in shock. 'Are you serious?'

'I told him about feeding Artemis's spider plant orange juice, I told him I find G-strings uncomfortable . . .'

I tail off to see Lissy staring at me, aghast.

'Emma,' she says at last. 'Have you ever *heard* the phrase "too much information?"'

'I didn't *mean* to say any of it!' I retort defensively. 'It just kind of came out! I'd had three vodkas, and I thought we were about to die. Honestly, Lissy, you would have been the same. Everyone was screaming, people were praying, the plane was lurching around . . .'

'So you blab all your secrets to your boss.'

'But he *wasn't* my boss on the plane!' I cry in frustration. 'He was just some stranger. I was never supposed to see him again!'

There's silence as Lissy takes this all in.

'You know, this is like what happened to my cousin,' she says at last. 'She went to a party, and there, right in front of her, was the doctor who'd delivered her baby two months before.'

'Ooh.' I pull a face.

'Exactly! She said she was so embarrassed, she had to leave. I mean, he'd seen everything! She said somehow it didn't matter when she was in a hospital room, but when she saw him standing there, holding a glass of wine and chatting about house prices, it was a different matter.'

'Well, this is the same,' I say hopelessly. 'He knows all my most intimate, personal details. But the difference is, I can't just leave! I have to sit there and pretend to be a good employee. And he *knows* I'm not.'

'So what are you going to do?'

'I don't know! I suppose all I can do is try to avoid him.'

'How long is he over for?'

'The rest of the week,' I say despairingly. 'The whole week.'

I pick up the zapper and turn on the television and for a few moments we stare silently at a load of dancing models in Gap jeans.

The ad finishes, and I look up again, to see Lissy looking at me curiously.

'What?' I say. 'What is it?'

'Emma . . .' She clears her throat awkwardly. 'You don't have any secrets from *me*, do you?'

'From *you*?' I say, slightly thrown.

A series of images flashes rapidly through my mind. That weird dream I once had about Lissy and me being lesbians. Those couple of times I've bought supermarket carrots and sworn to her they were organic. The time when we were fifteen and she went to France and I got off with Mike Appleton whom she had a complete crush on, and never told her.

'No! Of course not!' I say, and quickly take a sip of water. 'Why? Have you got any from me?'

Two dots of pink appear on Lissy's cheeks.

'No, of course I haven't!' she says in an unnatural voice. 'I was just . . . wondering.' She reaches for the TV guide and starts to flip through it, avoiding my gaze. 'You know. Just out of interest.'

'Yes, well.' I give a shrug. 'So was I.'

Wow. Lissy's got a secret. I wonder what it—

Of course. Like she was really going over case notes with that guy. Does she think I'm a complete moron?

EIGHT

I arrive at work the next morning with exactly one aim. Avoid Jack Harper.

It should be easy enough. The Panther Corporation is a huge company in a huge building. He'll be busy in other departments today. He'll probably be tied up in loads of meetings. He'll probably spend all day on the eleventh floor or something.

Even so, as I approach the big glass doors, my pace slows down and I find myself peering inside to see if he's about.

'All right, Emma?' says Dave the security guard, coming to open the door for me. 'You look lost.'

'No! I'm fine, thanks!' I give a relaxed little laugh, my eyes darting about the foyer.

I can't see him anywhere. OK. This is going to be fine. He probably isn't in yet. He probably isn't even coming in today. I throw my hair back confidently, walk briskly across the marble floor, and start to walk up the stairs.

'Jack!' I suddenly hear as I'm nearing the first floor. 'Have you got a minute?'

'Sure.'

It's his voice. Where on earth—

I turn around, bewildered, and spot him on the landing above, talking to Graham Hillingdon. My heart gives a huge jump, and I clutch the brass banister. Shit. If he looked down now he'd see me.

Why does he have to stand right *there*? Doesn't he have some big important office he can go to?

Anyway. It doesn't matter. I'll just . . . take a different route. Very slowly I take a few steps back down the stairs, trying not to click my heels on the marble or move suddenly in case I attract his attention. Moira from Accounts walks past as I'm carefully stepping backwards and gives me an odd look, but I don't care. I have to get away.

As soon as I'm out of his view I feel myself relax, and walk more quickly back down to the foyer. I'll go by lift, instead. No problem. I step confidently across the floor, and I'm right in the middle of the huge expanse of marble when I freeze.

'That's right.' It's his voice again. And it seems to be getting nearer. Or am I just paranoid?

'. . . think I'll take a good look at . . .'

My head swivels around. Where is he now? Which direction is he going in?

'. . . really think that . . .'

Shit. He's coming down the stairs. There's nowhere to hide!

Without thinking twice I almost run to the glass doors, push them open, and hurry out of the building. I scuttle down the steps, run about a hundred yards down the road and stop, panting.

This is not going well.

I stand on the pavement for a few minutes in the morning sunshine, trying to estimate how long he will stay in the foyer, then cautiously approach the glass doors again. New tactic. I will walk to my office so incredibly quickly, I can't catch anyone's eye. So it won't matter if I pass Jack Harper or not. I will simply stride along without looking right or left and oh my God there he is, talking to Dave.

Without quite meaning to, I find myself running

back down the steps and along the street again.

This is getting ridiculous. I can't stay out here on the street all day. I have to get to my desk. Come on, think. There must be a way round this. There must be—

Yes! I have a totally brilliant idea. This will definitely work.

Three minutes later I approach the doors of the Panther building once more, totally engrossed in an article in *The Times*. I can't see anything around me. And no-one can see my face. This is the perfect disguise!

I push the door open with my shoulder, walk across the foyer and up the stairs, all without looking up. As I stride along the corridor towards the marketing department, I feel all cocooned and safe, buried in my *Times*. I should do this more often. No-one can get me in here. It's a really reassuring feeling, almost as though I'm invisible, or—

'Ow! Sorry!'

I've crashed into someone. Shit. I lower my paper, to see Paul staring at me, rubbing his head.

'Emma, what the fuck are you doing?'

'I was just reading *The Times*,' I say feebly. 'I'm really sorry.'

'All right. Anyway, where the hell have you been? I want you to do teas and coffees at the departmental meeting. Ten o'clock.'

'What teas and coffees?' I say, puzzled. They don't usually have any refreshments at the departmental meeting. In fact, usually only about six people turn up.

'We're having teas and coffees today,' he says. 'And biscuits. All right? Oh, and Jack Harper's coming along.'

'What?' I stare at him in consternation.

'Jack Harper's coming along,' repeats Paul impatiently. 'So hurry up.'

'Do I have to go?' I say before I can stop myself.

'What?' Paul stares at me with a blank frown.

'I was just wondering if I . . . have to go, or whether . . .' I tail off feebly.

'Emma, if you can serve tea and coffee by telepathy,' says Paul sarcastically, 'then you're more than welcome to stay at your desk. If not, would you most kindly get your arse in gear and up to the conference room. You know, for someone who wants to advance their career . . .' He shakes his head and stalks off.

How can this day have gone so wrong already and I haven't even sat down yet?

I dump my bag and jacket at my desk, hurry back down the corridors to the lifts, and press the Up button. A moment later, one pings in front of me, and the doors open.

No. No.

This is a bad dream.

Jack Harper is standing alone in the lift, in old jeans and a brown cashmere sweater.

Before I can stop myself I take a startled step backwards. Jack Harper puts his mobile phone away, tilts his head to one side and gives me a quizzical look.

'Are you getting into the elevator?' he says mildly.

I'm stuffed. What can I say? I can't say 'No, I just pressed the button for fun, haha!'

'Yes,' I say at last and walk into the lift with stiff legs. 'Yes I am.'

The doors close, and we begin to travel upwards in silence. I've got a knot of tension in my stomach.

'Erm, Mr Harper,' I say awkwardly, and he looks up. 'I just wanted to apologize for my . . . for the, um, shirking episode the other day. It won't happen again.'

'You have drinkable coffee now,' says Jack Harper, raising his eyebrows. 'So you shouldn't need to go to Starbucks, at any rate.'

'I know. I'm really sorry,' I say, my face hot. 'And may I assure you, that was the very last time I will ever do such a thing.' I clear my throat. 'I am fully committed to the Panther Corporation, and I look forward to serving this company as best as I can, giving one hundred per cent, every day, now and in the future.'

I almost want to add 'Amen'.

'Really.' Jack looks at me, his mouth twitching. 'That's . . . great.' He thinks for a moment. 'Emma, can you keep a secret?'

'Yes,' I say apprehensively. 'What is it?'

Jack leans close and whispers, 'I used to play hookey too.'

'What?' I stare at him.

'In my first job,' he continues in his normal voice. 'I had a friend I used to hang out with. We had a code, too.' His eyes twinkle. 'One of us would ask the other to bring him the Leopold file.'

'What was the Leopold file?'

'It didn't exist.' He grins. 'It was just an excuse to get away from our desks.'

'Oh. Oh right!'

Suddenly I feel a bit better.

Jack Harper used to *skive*? I would have thought he was too busy being a brilliant creative dynamic genius, or whatever he is.

The lift stops at floor 3 and the doors open, but no-one gets in.

'So, your colleagues seemed a very pleasant lot,' says Jack as we start travelling up again. 'A very friendly, industrious team. Are they like that all the time?'

'Absolutely!' I say at once. 'We enjoy cooperating with one another, in an integrated, team-based . . . um

112

. . . operational . . .' I'm trying to think of another long word when I make the mistake of catching his eye.

He *knows* this is bullshit, doesn't he?

Oh God. What is the point?

'OK.' I lean against the lift wall. 'In real life, we don't behave anything like that. Paul usually shouts at me six times a day, and Nick and Artemis hate each other, and we don't usually sit around discussing literature. We were all faking it.'

'You amaze me.' His mouth twitches. 'The atmosphere in the admin department also seemed very false. My suspicions were aroused when two employees spontaneously started singing the Panther Corporation song. I didn't even know there *was* a Panther Corporation song.'

'Neither did I,' I say in surprise. 'Is it any good?'

'What do you think?' He raises his eyebrows comically and I give a little giggle.

It's bizarre, but the atmosphere between us isn't remotely awkward any more. In fact, it almost feels like we're old friends or something.

'How about this Corporate Family Day?' he says. 'Looking forward to it?'

'Like having teeth pulled out,' I say bluntly.

'I got that vibe.' He nods, looking amused. 'And what . . .' He hesitates. 'What do people think about me?' He casually rumples his hair. 'You don't have to answer if you don't want to.'

'No, everyone likes you!' I think for a few moments. 'Although . . . some people think your friend is creepy.'

'Who, Sven?' Jack stares at me for a minute, then throws back his head and laughs. 'I can assure you, Sven is one of my oldest, closest friends, and he's not in the least bit creepy. In fact—'

He breaks off as the lift doors ping. We both snap back into impassive expressions and move slightly away from each other. The doors open, and my stomach gives a lurch.

Connor is standing on the other side.

As he sees Jack Harper his face lights up as though he can't believe his luck.

'Hi there!' I say, trying to sound natural.

'Hi,' he says, his eyes shining with excitement, and walks into the lift.

'Hello,' says Jack pleasantly. 'Which floor would you like?'

'Nine, please.' Connor swallows. 'Mr Harper, may I quickly introduce myself?' He eagerly holds out his hand. 'Connor Martin from Research. You're coming to visit our department later on today.'

'It's a pleasure to meet you, Connor,' says Jack kindly. 'Research is vital for a company like ours.'

'You're so right!' says Connor, looking thrilled. 'In fact, I'm looking forward to discussing with you the latest research findings on Panther Sportswear. We've come up with some very fascinating results involving customer preferences on fabric thickness. You'll be amazed!'

'I'm . . . sure I will,' says Jack. 'I look forward to it.'

Connor gives me an excited grin.

'You've already met Emma Corrigan from our marketing department?' he says.

'Yes, we've met.' Jack's eyes gleam at me.

We travel for a few seconds in an awkward silence.

This is weird.

No. It's not weird. It's fine.

'How are we doing for time?' says Connor. He glances at his watch and in slight horror, I see Jack's eyes falling on it.

Oh God.

'. . . I gave him a really nice watch, but he insists on wearing this orange digital thing . . .'

114

'Wait a minute!' says Jack, dawn breaking over his face. He stares at Connor as through seeing him for the first time. 'Wait a minute. You're Ken.'

Oh no.

Oh no, oh no, oh no, oh no, oh no, oh—

'It's Connor,' says Connor puzzledly. 'Connor Martin.'

'I'm sorry!' Jack hits his head with his fist. 'Connor. Of course. And you two –' he gestures to me '– are an item?'

Connor looks uncomfortable.

'I can assure you, sir, that at work our relationship is strictly professional. However, in a private context, Emma and I arc . . . yes, having a personal relationship.'

'That's wonderful!' says Jack encouragingly, and Connor beams, like a flower blossoming in the sun.

'In fact,' he adds proudly, 'Emma and I have just decided to move in together.'

'Is that so?' Jack shoots me a look of genuine surprise. 'That's . . . great news. When did you make that decision?'

'Just a couple of days ago,' says Connor. 'At the airport.'

'At the airport,' echoes Jack Harper after a short silence. 'Very interesting.'

I can't look at Jack Harper. I'm staring desperately at the floor. Why can't this bloody lift go quicker?

'Well, I'm sure you'll be very happy together,' Jack Harper says to Connor. 'You seem very compatible.'

'Oh we are!' says Connor at once. 'We both love jazz, for a start.'

'Is that so?' says Jack thoughtfully. 'You know, I can't think of anything nicer in the world than a shared love of jazz.'

He's taking the piss. This is unbearable.

'Really?' says Connor eagerly.

'Absolutely.' Jack nods. 'I'd say jazz, and . . . Woody Allen films.'

'We love Woody Allen films!' says Connor in amazed delight. 'Don't we, Emma!'

'Yes,' I say a little hoarsely. 'Yes, we do.'

'Now Connor, tell me,' says Jack in confidential tones. 'Did you ever find Emma's . . .'

If he says 'G spot' I will die. I will die. I will *die*.

'. . . presence here distracting? Because I can imagine I would!' Jack gives Connor a friendly smile, but Connor doesn't smile back.

'As I said, sir,' he says, a little stiffly, 'Emma and I operate on a strictly professional basis whilst at work. We would never dream of abusing the company's time for our own . . . ends.' He flushes. 'I mean, by ends, I don't mean . . . I meant . . .'

'I'm glad to hear it,' says Jack, looking amused.

God, why does Connor have to be such a *goody-goody*?

The lift pings, and I feel relief drain over me. Thank God, at last I can escape—

'Looks like we're all going to the same place,' says Jack Harper with a grin. 'Connor, why don't you lead the way?'

I can't cope with this. I just can't cope. As I pour out cups of tea and coffee for members of the marketing department, I'm outwardly calm, smiling at everyone and even chatting pleasantly. But inside I'm all unsettled and confused. I don't want to admit it to myself, but seeing Connor through Jack Harper's eyes has thrown me.

I love Connor, I tell myself over and over. I didn't mean any of what I said on the plane. I love him. I run my eyes over his face, trying to reassure myself. There's no doubt about it. Connor is good-looking by any standards. He glows with good health. His hair is shiny and his eyes are blue and he's got a gorgeous dimple when he smiles.

Jack Harper, on the other hand, looks kind of weary and dishevelled. He's got shadows under his eyes and his hair is all over the place. *And* there's a hole in his jeans.

But even so. It's as if he's some kind of magnet. I'm sitting here, my attention firmly on the tea trolley, and yet somehow I can't keep my eyes off him.

It's because of the plane, I keep telling myself. It's just because we were in a traumatic situation together; that's why. No other reason.

'We need more lateral thinking, people,' Paul is saying. 'The Panther Bar is simply not performing as it should. Connor, you have the latest research statistics?'

Connor stands up, and I feel a flip of apprehension on his behalf. I can tell he's really nervous from the way he keeps fiddling with his cuffs.

'That's right, Paul.' He picks up a clipboard and clears his throat. 'In our latest survey, 1,000 teenagers were questioned on aspects of the Panther Bar. Unfortunately, the results were inconclusive.'

He presses his remote control. A graph appears on the screen behind him, and we all stare at it obediently.

'Seventy-four per cent of 10–14-year-olds felt the texture could be more chewy,' says Connor earnestly. 'However, 67 per cent of 15–18-year-olds felt the texture could be more crunchy, while 22 per cent felt it could be *less* crunchy . . .'

I glance over Artemis's shoulder and see she's written 'Chewy/crunchy??' on her notepad.

Connor presses the remote control again, and another graph appears.

'Now, 46 per cent of 10–14-year-olds felt the flavour was too tangy. However, 33 per cent of 15–18-year-olds felt it was not tangy enough, while . . .'

Oh God. I know it's Connor. And I love him and everything. But can't he make this sound a bit more *interesting*?

I glance over to see how Jack Harper is taking it and he raises his eyebrows at me. Immediately I flush, feeling disloyal.

He'll think I was laughing at Connor. Which I wasn't. I wasn't.

'And 90 per cent of female teenagers would prefer the calorie content to be reduced,' Connor concludes. 'But the same proportion would also like to see a thicker chocolate coating.' He gives a helpless shrug.

'They don't know what the hell they want,' says someone.

'We polled a broad cross-section of teenagers,' says Connor, 'including Caucasians, Afro-Caribbeans, Asians, and . . . er . . .' he peers at the paper. 'Jedi knights.'

'Teenagers!' says Artemis, rolling her eyes.

'Briefly remind us of our target market, Connor,' says Paul with a frown.

'Our target market . . .' Connor consults another clipboard, 'is aged 10–18, in full or part time education. He/she drinks Panther Cola four times a week, eats burgers three times a week, visits the cinema twice a week, reads magazines and comics but not books, is most likely to agree with the lifestyle statement "It's more important to be cool than rich". . .' he looks up. 'Shall I go on?'

'Does he/she eat toast for breakfast?' says somebody thoughtfully. 'Or cereal?'

118

'I . . . I'm not sure,' says Connor, riffling quickly through his pages. 'We could do some more research . . .'

'I think we get the picture,' says Paul. 'Does anyone have any thoughts on this?'

All this time, I've been plucking up courage to speak, and now I take a deep breath.

'You know, my grandpa really likes Panther Bars!' I say. Everyone swivels in their chairs to look at me, and I feel my face grow hot.

'What relevance does that have?' says Paul with a frown.

'I just thought I could . . .' I swallow. 'I could maybe ask him what he thinks . . .'

'With all due respect, Emma,' says Connor, with a smile which verges on patronizing, 'your grandfather is hardly in our target demographic!'

'Unless he started very young,' quips Artemis.

I flush, feeling stupid, and pretend to be re-organizing the teabags.

To be honest, I feel a bit hurt. Why did Connor have to say that? I know he wants to be all professional and proper when we're at work. But that's not the same as being mean, is it? I'd always stick up for him.

'My own view,' Artemis is saying, 'is that if the Panther Bar isn't performing, we should axe it. It's quite obviously a problem child.'

I look up in slight dismay. They can't axe the Panther Bar! What will Grandpa take to his bowling tournaments?

'Surely a fully cost-based, customer-oriented re-branding—' begins somebody.

'I disagree.' Artemis leans forward. 'If we're going to maximise our concept innovation in a functional and logistical way, then surely we need to focus on our strategic competencies—'

'Excuse me,' says Jack Harper, lifting a hand. It's the first time he's spoken, and everyone turns to look. There's a prickle of anticipation in the air, and Artemis glows smugly. 'Yes, Mr Harper?' she says.

'I have no idea what you're talking about,' he says.

The whole room reverberates in shock, and I give a snort of laughter without quite meaning to.

'As you know, I've been out of the business arena for a while.' He smiles. 'Could you please translate what you just said into standard English?'

'Oh,' says Artemis, looking discomfited. 'Well, I was simply saying, that from a strategic point of view, notwithstanding our corporate vision . . .' she tails off at his expression.

'Try again,' he says kindly. 'Without using the word strategic.'

'Oh,' says Artemis again, and rubs her nose. 'Well, I was just saying that . . . we should . . . concentrate on . . . on what we do well.'

'Ah!' Jack Harper's eyes gleam. 'Now I understand. Please, carry on.'

He glances at me, rolls his eyes and grins, and I can't help giving a tiny grin back.

After the meeting, people trickle out of the room, still talking, and I go round the table, picking up coffee cups.

'It was very good to meet you, Mr Harper,' I can hear Connor saying eagerly. 'If you'd like a transcript of my presentation . . .'

'You know, I don't think that will be necessary,' Jack says in that dry, quizzical voice. 'I think I more or less got the gist.'

Oh God. Doesn't Connor *realize* he's trying too hard?

I balance all the cups in precarious piles on the trolley, then start collecting up the biscuit wrappers.

'Now, I'm due in the design studio right about now,' Jack Harper's saying, 'but I don't quite remember where it is . . .'

'Emma!' says Paul sharply. 'Can you please show Jack to the design studio? You can clear up the rest of the coffee later.'

I freeze, clutching an orange cream wrapper.

Please, no more.

'Of course,' I manage at last. 'It would be a . . . pleasure. This way.'

Awkwardly, I usher Jack Harper out of the meeting room and we begin to walk down the corridor, side by side. My face is tingling slightly as people try not to stare at us, and I'm aware of everyone else in the corridor turning into self-conscious robots as soon as they see him. People in adjacent offices are nudging each other excitedly, and I hear at least one person hissing 'He's coming!'

Is it like this everywhere Jack Harper goes?

'So,' he says conversationally after a while. 'You're moving in with Ken.'

'It's *Connor*,' I say. 'And yes.'

'Looking forward to it?'

'Yes. Yes, I am.'

We've reached the lifts and I press the button. I can feel his quizzical eyes on me. I can *feel* them.

'What?' I say defensively, turning to look at him.

'Did I say anything?' He raises his eyebrows. As I see the expression on his face I feel stung. What does he know about it?

'I know what you're thinking,' I say, lifting my chin defiantly. 'But you're quite wrong.'

'I'm wrong?'

'Yes! You're . . . misapprehended.'

'*Misapprehended?*'

He looks as if he wants to laugh, and a small voice

121

inside my head is telling me to stop. But I can't. I have to explain to him how it is.

'Look. I know I might have made certain . . . comments to you on the plane,' I begin, clenching my fists tightly at my side. 'But what you have to know is that that conversation took place under duress, in extreme circumstances, and I said a lot of things I didn't really mean. A lot of things, actually!'

There! That tells him.

'I see,' says Jack thoughtfully. 'So . . . you *don't* like double chocolate chip Häagen-Dazs ice-cream.'

I gaze at him, discomfited.

'I . . .' I clear my throat several times. 'Some things, obviously, I *did* mean—'

The lift doors ping, and both our heads jerk up.

'Jack!' says Cyril, standing on the other side of the doors. 'I wondered where you were.'

'I've been having a nice chat with Emma here,' says Jack. 'She kindly offered to show me the way.'

'Ah.' Cyril's eyes run dismissively over me. 'Well, they're waiting for you in the studio.'

'So, um . . . I'll just go, then,' I say awkwardly.

'See you later,' says Jack with a grin. 'Good talking to you, Emma.'

NINE

As I leave the office that evening I feel all agitated, like one of those snow globes. I was perfectly happy being an ordinary, dull little Swiss village. But now Jack Harper's come and shaken me up, and there are snowflakes all over the place, whirling around, not knowing what they think any more.

And bits of glitter, too. Tiny bits of shiny, secret excitement.

Every time I catch his eye or hear his voice, it's like a dart to my chest.

Which is ridiculous. Ridiculous.

Connor is my boyfriend. Connor is my future. He loves me and I love him and I'm moving in with him. And we're going to have wooden floors and shutters and granite worktops. So there.

So there.

I arrive home to find Lissy on her knees in the sitting room, helping Jemima into the tightest black suede dress I've ever seen.

'Wow!' I say, as I put down my bag. 'That's amazing!'

'There!' pants Lissy, and sits back on her heels. 'That's the zip done. Can you breathe?'

Jemima doesn't move a muscle. Lissy and I glance at each other.

'Jemima!' says Lissy in alarm. 'Can you breathe?'

'Kind of,' says Jemima at last. 'I'll be fine.' Very slowly, with a totally rigid body, she totters over to where her Louis Vuitton bag is resting on a chair.

'What happens if you need to go to the loo?' I say, staring at her.

'Or go back to his place?' says Lissy with a giggle.

'It's only our second date! I'm not going to go back to his place!' Jemima says in horror. 'That's not the way to –' she struggles for breath '– to get a rock on your finger.'

'But what if you get carried away with desire for each other?'

'What if he gropes you in the taxi?'

'He's not *like* that,' says Jemima, with a roll of her eyes. 'He happens to be the First Assistant Under-Secretary to the Secretary of the Treasury, *actually*.'

I meet Lissy's eyes and I can't help it, I give a snort of laughter.

'Emma, don't laugh,' says Lissy, deadpan. 'There's nothing wrong with being a secretary. He can always move up, get himself a few qualifications . . .'

'Oh ha ha, very funny,' says Jemima crossly. 'You know, he'll be knighted one day. I don't think you'll be laughing then.'

'Oh, I expect I will,' says Lissy. 'Even more so.' She suddenly focuses on Jemima, who is still standing by the chair, trying to reach her bag. 'Oh my God! You can't even pick up your bag, can you?'

'I can!' says Jemima, making one last desperate effort to bend her body. 'Of course I can. There!' She manages to scoop up the strap on the end of one of her acrylic fingernails, and triumphantly swings it onto her shoulder. 'You see?'

'What if he suggests dancing?' says Lissy slyly. 'What will you do then?'

A look of total panic briefly crosses Jemima's face, then disappears.

'He won't,' she says scornfully. 'Englishmen never suggest dancing.'

'Fair point.' Lissy grins. 'Have a good time.'

As Jemima disappears out of the door, I sink down heavily onto the sofa and reach for a magazine. I glance up at Lissy, but she's staring ahead with a preoccupied look on her face.

'Conditional!' she says suddenly. 'Of course! How could I have been so *stupid*?'

She scrabbles around under the sofa, pulls out several old newspaper crosswords and starts searching through them.

Honestly. As if being a top lawyer didn't use up enough brain power, Lissy spends her whole time doing crosswords and games of chess by correspondence, and special brainy puzzles which she gets from her geeky society of extra-clever people. (It's not *called* that, of course. It's called something like 'Mindset – for people who like to think'. Then at the bottom it casually mentions that you need an IQ of 600 in order to join.)

And if she can't solve a clue, she doesn't just throw it out, saying 'stupid puzzle' like I would. She saves it. Then about three months later, when we're watching *EastEnders* or something, she'll suddenly come up with the answer. And she's ecstatic! Just because she gets the last word in the box, or whatever.

Lissy's my oldest friend, and I really love her. But sometimes I really do *not* understand her.

'What's that?' I say, as she writes in the answer. 'Some crossword from 1993?'

'Ha ha,' she says absently. 'So what are you doing this evening?'

'I thought I'd have a quiet evening in,' I say, flicking through the magazine. 'In fact, I might go through my clothes,' I add, as my eyes fall on an article entitled 'Essential Wardrobe Upkeep'.

'Do what?'

'I thought I'd check them all for missing buttons and drooping hems,' I say, reading the article. 'And brush all my jackets with a clothes brush.'

'Have you got a clothes brush?'

'With a hairbrush then.'

'Oh right.' She shrugs. 'Oh well. Because I was just wondering, do you want to go out?'

'Ooh!' My magazine slithers to the floor. 'Where?'

'Guess what I've got?' She raises her eyebrows tantalizingly, then fishes in her bag. Very slowly she pulls out a large, rusty keyring, to which a brand new Yale is attached.

'What's that?' I begin, puzzledly – then suddenly realize. 'No!'

'Yes! I'm in!'

'Oh my God! Lissy!'

'I know!' Lissy beams at me. 'Isn't it fab?'

The key which Lissy is holding is the coolest key in the world. It opens the door to a private members' club in Clerkenwell, which is completely happening and impossible to get into.

And Lissy got in!

'Lissy, you're the coolest!'

'No I'm not,' she says, looking pleased. 'It was Jasper at my chambers. He knows everyone on the committee.'

'Well I don't care who it was. I'm so impressed!'

I take the key from her and look at it in fascination, but there's nothing on it. No name, no address, no logo, no nothing. It looks a bit like the key to my dad's garden shed, I find myself thinking. But obviously way, way cooler, I add hastily.

'So who do you think'll be there?' I look up. 'You

know, apparently Madonna's a member. And Jude and Sadie! And that gorgeous new actor from *EastEnders*. Except everyone says he's gay really . . .'

'Emma,' interrupts Lissy. 'You do know celebrities aren't guaranteed.'

'I know!' I say, a little offended.

Honestly. Who does Lissy think I am? I'm a cool and sophisticated Londoner. I don't get excited by stupid celebrities. I was just *mentioning* it, that's all.

'In fact,' I add after a pause, 'it probably spoils the atmosphere if the place is stuffed full of famous people. I mean, can you think of anything worse than sitting at a table, trying to have a nice normal conversation, while all around you are movie stars and supermodels and . . . and pop stars . . .'

There's a pause while we both think about this.

'So,' says Lissy casually. 'We might as well go and get ready.'

'Why not?' I say, equally casually.

Not that it will take long. I mean, I'm only going to throw on a pair of jeans. And maybe quickly wash my hair, which I was going to do anyway.

And maybe do a quick face-mask.

An hour later Lissy appears at the door of my room, dressed in jeans, a tight black corset top and her Bertie heels which I happen to know always give her a blister.

'What do you think?' she says, in the same casual voice. 'I mean, I haven't really made much effort—'

'Neither have I,' I say, blowing on my second coat of nail polish. 'I mean, it's just a relaxed evening out. I'm hardly even bothering with makeup.' I look up and stare at Lissy. 'Are those false eyelashes?'

'No! I mean . . . yes. But you weren't supposed to notice. They're called natural look.' She goes over to the mirror and bats her eyelids at herself worriedly. 'Are they really obvious?'

'No!' I say reassuringly, and reach for my blusher brush. When I look up again, Lissy is staring at my shoulder.

'What's that?'

'What?' I say innocently, and touch the little diamanté heart on my shoulder blade. 'Oh *this*. Yes, it just sticks on. I thought I'd just put it on for fun.' I reach for my halterneck top, tie it on, and slide my feet into my pointy suede boots. I got them in a Sue Ryder shop a year ago, and they're a bit scuffed up, but in the dark you can hardly tell.

'Do you think we look too much?' says Lissy as I go and stand next to her in front of the mirror. 'What if they're all in jeans?'

'We're in jeans!'

'But what if they're in big thick jumpers and we look really stupid?'

Lissy is always completely paranoid about what everyone else will be wearing. When it was her first chambers Christmas party and she didn't know whether 'black tie' meant long dresses or just sparkly tops, she made me come and stand outside the door with about six different outfits in carrier bags, so she could quickly change. (Of course the original dress she'd put on was fine. I *told* her it would be.)

'They won't be wearing big thick jumpers,' I say. 'Come on, let's go.'

'We can't!' Lissy looks at her watch. 'It's too early.'

'Yes we can. We can be just having a quick drink on our way to *another* celebrity party.'

'Oh yes.' Lissy brightens. 'Cool. Let's go!'

It takes us about fifteen minutes by bus to get from Islington to Clerkenwell. Lissy leads me down an

empty road near to Smithfield Market, full of ware-
houses and empty office buildings. Then we turn a
corner, and then another corner, until we're standing
in a small alley.

'Right,' says Lissy, standing under a street lamp and
consulting a tiny scrap of paper. 'It's all hidden away
somewhere.'

'Isn't there a sign?'

'No. The whole point is, no-one except members
knows where it is. You have to knock on the right door
and ask for Alexander.'

'Who's Alexander?'

'Dunno.' Lissy shrugs. 'It's their secret code.'

Secret code! This gets cooler and cooler. As Lissy
squints at an intercom set in the wall, I look idly
around. This street is completely nondescript. In fact,
it's pretty shabby. Just rows of identical doors and
blanked-out windows and barely any sign of life. But
just think. Hidden behind this grim façade is the whole
of London celebrity society!

'Hi, is Alexander there?' says Lissy nervously.
There's a moment's silence, then as if by magic, the
door clicks open.

Oh my God. This is like Aladdin or something.
Looking apprehensively at each other, we make our
way down a lit corridor pulsing with music. We come
to a flat, stainless steel door, and Lissy reaches for her
key. As it opens, I quickly tug at my top and casually
rearrange my hair.

'OK,' Lissy mutters. 'Don't look. Don't stare. Just be
cool.'

'All right,' I mutter back, and follow Lissy into the
club. As she shows her membership card to a girl at a
desk, I stare studiously at her back, and as we walk
through into a large, dim room, I keep my eyes fixed
on the beige carpet. I'm not going to gawp at the

celebrities. I'm not going to stare. I'm not going to—

'Look out!'

Oops. I was so busy gazing at the floor, I blundered right into Lissy.

'Sorry,' I whisper. 'Where shall we sit down?'

I don't dare look around the room for a free seat, in case I see Madonna and she thinks I'm staring at her. 'Here,' says Lissy, gesturing to a wooden table with an odd little jerk of her head.

Somehow we manage to sit down, stow our bags and pick up the lists of cocktails, all the time rigidly staring at each other.

'Have you seen anyone?' I murmur.

'No. Have you?'

'No.' I open the cocktail menu and run my eyes down it. God this is a strain. My eyes are starting to ache. I want to look around. I want to *see* the place.

'Lissy,' I hiss. 'I'm going to have a look round.'

'Really?' Lissy stares at me anxiously, as though I'm Steve McQueen announcing he's going over the wire. 'Well . . . OK. But be careful. Be *discreet*.'

'I will. I'll be fine!'

OK. Here we go. A quick, non-gawping sweep. I lean back in my chair, take a deep breath, then allow my eyes to skim swiftly round the room, taking in as much detail as quickly as I can. Low lighting . . . lots of purple sofas and chairs . . . a couple of guys in T-shirts . . . three girls in jeans and jumpers, God, Lissy's going to freak . . . a couple whispering to each other . . . a guy with a beard reading *Private Eye* . . . and that's it.

That can't be it.

This can't be right. Where's Robbie Williams? Where's Jude and Sadie? Where are all the super-models?

'Who did you see?' hisses Lissy, still staring at the cocktail menu.

'I'm not sure,' I whisper uncertainly. 'Maybe that guy with the beard is some famous actor?'

Casually, Lissy turns in her seat and gives him a look.

'I don't think so,' she says at last, turning back.

'Well, how about the guy in the grey T-shirt?' I say, gesturing hopefully. 'Is he in a boy band or something?'

'Mmm . . . no. I don't think so.'

There's silence as we look at each other.

'Is *anyone* famous here?' I say at last.

'Celebrities aren't guaranteed!' says Lissy defensively.

'I know! But you'd think—'

'Hi!' A voice interrupts us and we both look round, to see two of the girls in jeans approaching our table. One of them is smiling at me nervously. 'I hope you don't mind, but my friends and I were just wondering – aren't you that new one in *Hollyoaks*?'

Oh, for God's sake.

Anyway. I don't care. We didn't come here to see tacky celebrities taking coke and showing off. We just came to have a nice quiet drink together.

We order strawberry daiquiris and some luxury mixed nuts (£4.50, for a small bowl. Don't even *ask* how much the drinks cost). And I have to admit, I feel a bit more relaxed now I know there's no-one famous to impress.

'How's your work going?' I ask, as I sip my drink.

'Oh, it's fine,' says Lissy with a vague shrug. 'I saw the Jersey Fraudster today.'

The Jersey Fraudster is this client of Lissy's who keeps being charged with fraud and appealing and – because Lissy's so brilliant – getting let out. One minute he's wearing handcuffs, the next he's dressed in hand-made suits and taking her to lunch at the Ritz.

'He tried to buy me a diamond brooch,' says Lissy, rolling her eyes. 'He had this Asprey's catalogue and he kept saying "That one's rather jolly." And I was like, "Humphrey, you're in prison! Concentrate!"' She shakes her head, takes a sip of her drink, and looks up. 'So . . . what about your man?'

I know at once she means Jack, but I don't want to admit that's where my mind has leapt to, so I attempt a blank look and say, 'Who, Connor?'

'No, you dope! Your stranger on the plane. The one who knows everything about you.'

'Oh *him.*' I feel a flush coming to my cheeks, and look down at my embossed paper coaster.

'Yes, him! Have you managed to avoid him?'

'No,' I admit. 'He won't bloody leave me alone.'

I break off as a waiter puts two fresh strawberry daiquiris on the table. When he's gone, Lissy gives me a close look.

'Emma, do you fancy this guy?'

'No, of course I don't *fancy* him,' I say hotly. 'He just . . . disconcerts me, that's all. It's a completely natural reaction. You'd be the same. Anyway, it's fine. I only have to get through until Friday. Then he'll be gone.'

'And then you'll be moving in with Connor.' Lissy takes a sip of her daiquiri and leans forward. 'You know, I reckon he's going to ask you to marry him!'

I feel a tiny lurch in my stomach, which is probably just my drink going down or something.

'You're so lucky,' says Lissy wistfully. 'You know, he put up those shelves in my room the other day without even asking! How many men would do that?'

'I know. He's just . . . great.' There's a pause, and I start to shred my paper coaster into little bits. 'I suppose the only *tiny* little thing would be that it's not that romantic any more.'

'You can't expect it to be romantic for ever,' says Lissy. 'Things change. It's natural to become a bit more steady.'

'Oh, I know that!' I say. 'We're two mature, sensible people, and we're having a loving, steady relationship. Which, you know, is just what I want out of life. Except . . .' I clear my throat awkwardly. 'We don't have sex *that* often any more . . .'

'That's a common problem in long-term relationships,' says Lissy knowledgeably. 'You need to spice it up.'

'With what?'

'Have you tried handcuffs?'

'No! Have you?' I stare at Lissy, riveted.

'A long time ago,' she says with a dismissive shrug. 'They weren't all that . . . Um . . . why not try doing it somewhere different. Try doing it at work!'

At work! Now, that's a good idea. Lissy is so clever.

'OK!' I say. 'I'll try that!'

I reach for my bag, get out a pen and write 'shag@work' on my hand, next to where I've written 'nb: darling'.

Suddenly I'm filled with fresh enthusiasm. This is a brilliant plan. I'll shag Connor at work tomorrow, and it will be the best sex we've ever had, and the sparkle will come back, and we'll be madly in love again. Easy. And that will show Jack Harper.

No. This is nothing to do with Jack Harper. I don't know why that slipped out.

There's only one tiny hitch to my scheme. Which is that it's not quite as easy to shag your boyfriend at work as you'd think. I hadn't quite appreciated before how *open* everything is in our office. And how many glass partitions there are. And how many people there are, walking around all the time.

By eleven o'clock the next morning I still haven't managed to put a game plan together. I think I'd kind of pictured doing it behind a pot plant somewhere. But now I actually look at them, pot plants are tiny! And all frondy. There's no way Connor and I would be able to hide behind one, let alone risk any . . . movement.

We can't do it in the loos. The girls' loos always have people in there, gossiping and putting on their makeup, and the men's loos . . . yuck. No way.

We can't do it in Connor's office because the walls are completely made of glass and there aren't any blinds or anything. Plus people are always coming in and out of it to get stuff out of his filing cabinet.

Oh, this is ridiculous. People having affairs must have sex at the office all the time. Is there some special secret shagging room I don't know about?

I can't email Connor and ask for suggestions, because it's crucial that I surprise him. The shock element will be a huge turn-on and make it really sizzling hot and romantic. Plus there's a tiny risk that if I warn him he'll go all corporate on me and insist we take an hour's unpaid leave for it, or something.

I'm just wondering whether we could creep out onto the fire escape, when Nick comes out of Paul's office saying something about margins.

My head jerks up, and I feel a twinge of apprehension. There's something I've been trying to pluck up courage to say to him since that big meeting yesterday.

'Hey Nick,' I say as he walks by my desk. 'Panther Bars are your product, aren't they?'

'If you can call them a product,' he says, rolling his eyes.

'Are they going to axe them?'

'More than likely.'

'Well, listen,' I say quickly. 'Can I have a tiny bit of the marketing budget to put a coupon ad in a magazine?' Nick puts his hands on his hips and stares at me.

'Do what?'

'Put in an ad. It won't be very expensive, I promise. No-one will even notice.'

'Where?'

'*Bowling Monthly*,' I say, flushing slightly. 'My grandpa gets it.'

'Bowling *what*?'

'Please! Look, you don't have to do anything. I'll sort it all out. It'll be a drop in the ocean compared to all the other ads you've run.' I stare at him entreatingly. 'Please . . . please . . .'

'Oh all right!' he says impatiently. 'It's a dead duck, anyway.'

'Thanks!' I beam at him, then as he walks off, reach for the phone and dial Grandpa's number.

'Hi Grandpa!' I say as his answermachine beeps. 'I'm putting a money-off coupon ad for Panther Bars in *Bowling Monthly*. So tell all your friends! You can stock up cheaply. I'll see you soon, OK?'

'Emma?' Grandpa's voice suddenly booms into my ear. 'I'm here! Just screening.'

'Screening?' I echo, trying not to sound too surprised. Grandpa screens?

'It's my new hobby. Have you not heard of it? You listen to your friends leaving messages and laugh at them. Most amusing. Now Emma, I was meaning to ring you. I saw a very alarming piece on the news yesterday, about muggings in central London.'

Not this again.

'Grandpa—'

'Promise me you don't take London transport, Emma.'

'I er . . . promise,' I say, crossing my fingers. 'Grandpa, I have to go, really. But I'll call again soon. Love you.'

'Love you too, darling girl.'

As I put the phone down I feel a tiny glow of satisfaction. That's one thing done.

But what about Connor?

'I'll just have to go and fish it out of the archives,' Caroline is saying across the office, and my head pops up.

The archive room. Of course. Of course! No-one goes to the archive room unless they absolutely have to. It's way down in the basement, and it's all dark with no windows and loads of old books and magazines, and you end up grovelling on the floor to get what you want.

It's perfect.

'I'll go,' I say, trying to sound nonchalant. 'If you like. What do you have to find?'

'Would you?' says Caroline gratefully. 'Thanks, Emma. It's an old ad in some defunct magazine. This is the reference . . .' She hands me a piece of paper and I take it, feeling a thrill of excitement. As she walks away, I demurely pick up my phone and dial Connor's number.

'Hey Connor,' I say in a low, husky voice. 'Meet me in the archive room. I've got something I want to show you.'

'What?'

'Just . . . be there,' I say, feeling like Sharon Stone.

Ha! Office shag here I come!

I hurry down the corridor as quickly as I can, but as I pass Admin I'm accosted by Wendy Smith, who wants to know if I'd like to play in the netball team. So I don't actually get to the basement for a few minutes, and when I open the door, Connor is standing there, looking at his watch.

That's rather annoying. I'd planned to be waiting for him. I was going to be sitting on a pile of books which I would have quickly constructed, one leg crossed over the other and my skirt hitched up seductively.

Oh well.

'Hi,' I say, in the same husky voice.

'Hi,' says Connor, with a frown. 'Emma, what is this? I'm really busy this morning.'

'I just wanted to see you. A lot of you.' I push the door shut with an abandoned gesture and trail my finger down his chest, like an aftershave commercial. 'We never make love spontaneously any more.'

'What?' Connor stares at me.

'Come on.' I start unbuttoning his shirt with a sultry expression. 'Let's do it. Right here, right now.'

'Are you *crazy*?' says Connor, pushing my fingers out of the way and hastily rebuttoning his shirt. 'Emma, we're in the office!'

'So what? We're young, we're supposed to be in love . . .' I trail a hand even further down, and Connor's eyes widen.

'Stop!' he hisses. 'Stop right now! Emma, are you drunk or something?'

'I just want to have sex! Is that too much to ask?'

'Is it too much to ask that we do it in bed like normal people?'

'But we don't *do* it in bed! I mean, hardly ever!'

There's a sharp silence.

'Emma,' says Connor at last. 'This isn't the time or the place—'

'It is! It could be! This is how we get the spark back! Lissy said—'

'You discussed our sex life with Lissy?' Connor looks aghast.

'Obviously I didn't mention *us*,' I say, hastily backtracking. 'We were just talking about . . . about couples in general, and she said doing it at work can be . . . sexy! Come on, Connor!' I shimmy close to him and pull one of his hands inside my bra. 'Don't you find this exciting? Just the thought that someone could be walking down the corridor right now . . .' I come to a halt as I hear a sound.

I think someone *is* walking down the corridor right now.

Oh shit.

'I can hear footsteps!' Connor hisses, and pulls sharply away from me, but his hand stays exactly where it is, inside my bra. He stares at it in horror. 'I'm stuck! My bloody watch. It's snagged on your jumper!' He yanks at it. 'Fuck! I can't move my arm!'

'Pull it!'

'I *am* pulling it!' He looks frantically around. 'Where are some scissors?'

'You're not cutting my jumper,' I say in horror.

'Do you have any other suggestions?' He yanks sharply again, and I give a muffled shriek. 'Ow! Stop it! You'll ruin it!'

'Oh I'll ruin it. And that's our major concern, is it?'

'I've always hated that stupid watch! If you'd just worn the one I gave you—'

I break off. There are definitely footsteps approaching. They're nearly outside the door.

'Fuck!' Connor's looking around distractedly. 'Fucking . . . fucking . . .'

'Calm down! We'll just shuffle into the corner,' I hiss. 'Anyway, they might not even come in.'

'This was a great idea, Emma,' he mutters furiously, as we do a hasty, awkward shuffle across the room together. 'Really great.'

'Don't blame me!' I retort. 'I just wanted to get a bit of passion back into our—' I freeze as the door opens.

No. God, no.

I feel lightheaded with shock.

Jack Harper is standing in the doorway, holding a big bundle of old magazines.

Slowly, his eyes run over us, taking in Connor's angry expression, his hand inside my bra, my agonized face.

'Mr Harper,' Connor begins to stutter. 'I'm so very, very sorry. We're . . . we didn't . . .' He clears his throat. 'Can I just say how mortified I am . . . we both are . . .'

'I'm sure you are,' says Jack. His face is blank and unreadable; his voice as dry as ever. 'Perhaps the pair of you could adjust your dress before returning to your desks?'

The door closes behind him, and we stand motionless, like waxworks.

'Look, can you just get your bloody hand out of my top?' I say at last, suddenly feeling irritated beyond belief with Connor. All my desire for sex has vanished. I feel completely livid with myself. And Connor. And everybody.

TEN

Jack Harper leaves today.

Thank God. Thank God. Because I really couldn't cope with any more of . . . of *him*. If I can just keep my head down and avoid him until five o'clock and then run out of the door, then everything will be fine. Life will be back to normal and I will stop feeling as if my radar's been skewed by some invisible magnetic force.

I don't know why I'm in such a jumpy, irritable mood. Because although I nearly died of embarrassment yesterday, things are pretty good. First of all, it doesn't look like Connor and I are going to get the sack for having sex at work, which was my immediate fear. And secondly, my brilliant plan worked. As soon as we got back to our desks, Connor started sending me apologetic emails. And then last night we had sex. Twice. With scented candles.

I think Connor must have read somewhere that girls like scented candles during sex. Maybe in *Cosmo*. Because every time he brings them out, he gives me this 'aren't I considerate?' look, and I have to say 'Oh! Scented candles! How lovely!'

I mean, don't get me wrong. I don't *mind* scented candles. But it's not as if they actually do anything, is it? They just stand there and burn. And then at crucial moments I find myself thinking 'I hope the scented candle doesn't fall over', which is a bit distracting.

Anyway. So we had sex.

140

And tonight we're going to look at a flat together. It doesn't have a wooden floor or shutters – but it has a Jacuzzi in the bathroom, which is pretty cool. So my life is coming together nicely. I don't know why I'm feeling so pissed off. I don't know what's—

I don't want to move in with Connor, says a tiny voice in my brain before I can stop it.

No. That can't be right. That cannot possibly be right. Connor is perfect. Everyone knows that.

But I don't want to—

Shut up. We're the Perfect Couple. We have sex with scented candles. And we go for walks by the river. And we read the papers on Sundays with cups of coffee in pyjamas. That's what perfect couples do.

But—

Stop it!

I swallow hard. Connor is the one good thing in my life. If I didn't have Connor, what would I have?

The phone rings on my desk, interrupting my thoughts, and I pick it up.

'Hello, Emma?' comes a familiar dry voice. 'This is Jack Harper.'

My heart gives an almighty leap of fright and I nearly spill my coffee. I haven't seen him since the hand-in-bra incident. And I really don't want to.

I should never have answered my phone.

In fact, I should never have come into work today.

'Oh,' I say. 'Er . . . hi!'

'Would you mind coming up to my office for a moment?'

'What . . . me?' I say nervously.

'Yes, you.'

I clear my throat.

'Should I . . . bring anything?'

'No, just yourself.'

He rings off, and I stare at my phone for a few

moments, feeling a coldness in my spine. I should have known it was too good to be true. He's going to fire me after all. Gross . . . negligence . . . negligent grossness.

I mean, it is pretty gross, getting caught with your boyfriend's hand in your top at work.

OK. Well, there's nothing I can do.

I take a deep breath, stand up and make my way up to the eleventh floor. There's a desk outside his door, but no secretary is sitting there, so I go straight up to the door and knock.

'Come in.'

Cautiously I push the door open. The room is huge and bright and panelled, and Jack is sitting at a circular table with six people gathered round on chairs. Six people I've never seen before, I suddenly realize. They're all holding pieces of paper and sipping water, and the atmosphere is a bit tense.

Have they gathered to watch me being fired? Is this some kind of how-to-fire-people training?

'Hello,' I say, trying to keep as composed as possible. But my face is hot and I know I look flustered.

'Hi.' Jack's face crinkles in a smile. 'Emma . . . relax. There's nothing to worry about. I just wanted to ask you something.'

'Oh, right,' I say, taken aback.

OK, now I'm totally confused. What on earth could he have to ask me?

Jack reaches for a piece of paper and holds it up so I can see it clearly. 'What do you think this is a picture of?' he says.

Oh fucketty fuck.

This is your worst nightmare. This is like when I went for that interview at Laines Bank and they showed me a squiggle and I said I thought it looked like a squiggle.

Everyone is staring at me. I so want to get it right. If only I knew what right was.

I stare at the picture, my heart beating quickly. It's a graphic of two round objects. Kind of irregular in shape. I have absolutely no idea what they're supposed to be. None at all. They look like . . . they look like . . .

Suddenly I see it.

'It's nuts! Two walnuts!'

Jack explodes with laughter, and a couple of people give muffled giggles which they hastily stifle.

'Well, I think that proves my point,' says Jack.

'Aren't they walnuts?' I look helplessly around the table.

'They're supposed to be ovaries,' says a man with rimless spectacles tightly.

'*Ovaries?*' I stare at the page. 'Oh, right! Well, yes. Now you say it, I can definitely see a . . . an ovary-like . . .'

'Walnuts.' Jack wipes his eyes.

'I've explained, the ovaries are simply *part* of a range of symbolic representations of womanhood,' says a thin guy defensively. 'Ovaries to represent fertility, an eye for wisdom, this tree to signify the earth mother . . .'

'The point is, the images can be used across the entire range of products,' says a woman with black hair, leaning forward. 'The health drink, clothing, a fragrance . . .'

'The target market responds well to abstract images,' adds Rimless Spectacle Guy. 'The research has shown—'

'Emma.' Jack looks at me again. 'Would *you* buy a drink with ovaries on it?'

'Er . . .' I clear my throat, aware of a couple of hostile faces pointing my way. 'Well . . . probably not.'

A few people exchange glances.

'This is so irrelevant,' someone is muttering.

'Jack, three creative teams have been at work at this,' the black-haired woman says earnestly. 'We can't start from scratch. We simply cannot.'

Jack takes a swig of water from an Evian bottle, wipes his mouth and looks at her.

'You know I came up with the slogan "Don't Pause" in two minutes on a bar napkin?'

'Yes, we know,' mutters the guy in rimless spectacles.

'We are not selling a drink with ovaries on it.' He exhales sharply, and runs a hand through his dishevelled hair. Then he pushes his chair back. 'OK, let's take a break. Emma, would you be kind enough to assist me in carrying some of these folders down to Sven's office?'

God, I wonder what all that was about. But I don't quite dare ask. Jack marches me down the corridor, and into a lift and presses the ninth-floor button, without saying anything. After we've descended for about two seconds he presses the emergency button, and we grind to a halt. Then, finally, he looks at me.

'Are you and I the only sane people in this building?'

'Um . . .'

'What happened to instincts?' His face is incredulous. 'No-one knows a good idea from a terrible one any more. Ovaries.' He shakes his head. 'Fucking *ovaries*!'

I can't help it. He looks so outraged, and the way he says 'ovaries!' suddenly seems the funniest thing in the world, and before I know it, I've started laughing. For an instant Jack looks astounded, and then his face kind of crumples, and suddenly he's laughing too. His nose screws right up when he laughs, just like a baby's and somehow this makes it seem about a million times funnier.

Oh God. I really am laughing now. I'm giving tiny little snorts, and my ribs hurt, and every time I look at him I give another gurgle. My nose is running, and I haven't got a tissue . . . I'll have to blow my nose on the picture of the ovaries . . .

'Emma, why are you with that guy?'

'What?' I look up, still laughing, until I realize that Jack's stopped. He's looking at me, with an unreadable expression on his face.

'Why are you with that guy?' he repeats.

My gurgles peter out, and I push my hair back off my face.

'What do you mean?' I say, playing for time.

'Connor Martin. He's not going to make you happy. He's not going to fulfil you.'

I stare at him, feeling wrong-footed.

'Who says?'

'I've got to know Connor. I've sat in meetings with him. I've seen how his mind works. He's a nice guy – but you need more than a nice guy.' Jack gives me a long, shrewd look. 'My guess is, you don't really want to move in with him. But you're afraid of ducking out.'

I feel a swell of indignation. How dare he read my mind and get it so . . . so *wrong*. Of course I want to move in with Connor.

'Actually, you're quite mistaken,' I say cuttingly. 'I'm looking forward to moving in with him. In fact . . . in fact, I was just sitting at my desk, thinking how I can't wait!'

So there.

Jack's shaking his head.

'You need someone with a spark. Who excites you.'

'I told you, I didn't *mean* what I said on the plane.

Connor *does* excite me!' I give him a defiant look. 'I mean . . . when you saw us last, we were pretty passionate, weren't we?'

'Oh, that.' Jack shrugs. 'I assumed that was a desperate attempt to spice up your love life.'

I stare at him in fury.

'That was not a desperate attempt to spice up my love life!' I almost spit at him. 'That was simply a . . . a spontaneous act of passion.'

'Sorry,' says Jack mildly. 'My mistake.'

'Anyway, why do you care?' I fold my arms. 'What does it matter to you whether I'm happy or not?'

There's a sharp silence, and I find I'm breathing rather quickly. I meet his dark eyes, and quickly look away again.

'I've asked myself that same question,' says Jack. He shrugs. 'Maybe it's because we experienced that extraordinary plane ride together. Maybe it's because you're the only person in this whole company who hasn't put on some kind of phoney act for me.'

I would have put on an act! I feel like retorting. If I'd had a choice!

'I guess what I'm saying is . . . I feel as if you're a friend,' he says. 'And I care what happens to my friends.'

'Oh,' I say, and rub my nose.

I'm about to say politely that he feels like a friend, too, when he adds, 'Plus anyone who recites Woody Allen films line for line *has* to be a loser.'

I feel a surge of outrage on Connor's behalf.

'You don't know anything about it!' I exclaim. 'You know, I wish I'd never sat next to you on that stupid plane! You go around, saying all these things to wind me up, behaving as though you know me better than anyone else—'

'Maybe I do,' he says, his eyes glinting.

146

'What?'

'Maybe I do know you better than anyone else.'

I stare back at him, feeling a breathless mixture of anger and exhilaration. I suddenly feel like we're playing tennis. Or dancing.

'You do not know me better than anyone else!' I retort, in the most scathing tones I can muster.

'I know you won't end up with Connor Martin.'

'You don't know that.'

'Yes I do.'

'No you don't.'

'I do.'

He's starting to laugh.

'No you don't! If you want to know, I'll probably end up marrying Connor.'

'Marry Connor?' says Jack, as though this is the funniest joke he's ever heard.

'Yes! Why not? He's tall, and he's handsome, and he's kind and he's very . . . he's . . .' I'm floundering slightly. 'And anyway, this is my personal life. You're my boss, and you only met me last week, and frankly, this is none of your business!'

Jack's laughter vanishes, and he looks as though I've slapped him. For a few moments he stares at me, saying nothing. Then he takes a step back and releases the lift button.

'You're right,' he says in a completely different voice. 'Your personal life is none of my business. I overstepped the mark, and I apologize.'

I feel a spasm of dismay.

'I . . . I didn't mean—'

'No. You're right.' He stares at the floor for a few moments, then looks up. 'So, I leave for the States tomorrow. It's been a very pleasant stay, and I'd like to thank you for all your help. Will I see you at the drinks party tonight?'

147

'I . . . I don't know,' I say.

The atmosphere has disintegrated.

This is awful. It's horrible. I want to say something, I want to put it back to the way it was before, all easy and joking. But I can't find the words.

We reach the ninth floor, and the doors open.

'I think I can manage these from here,' Jack says. 'I really only asked you along for the company.'

Awkwardly, I transfer the folders to his arms.

'Well, Emma,' he says in the same formal voice. 'In case I don't see you later on . . . it was nice knowing you.' He meets my eyes and a glimmer of his old, warm expression returns. 'I really mean that.'

'You too,' I say, my throat tight.

I don't want him to go. I don't want this to be the end. I feel like suggesting a quick drink. I feel like clinging to his hand and saying: Don't leave.

God, what's *wrong* with me?

'Have a good journey,' I manage as he shakes my hand. Then he turns on his heel and walks off down the corridor.

I open my mouth a couple of times to call after him – but what would I say? There's nothing to say. By tomorrow morning he'll be on a plane back to his life. And I'll be left here in mine.

I feel leaden for the rest of the day. Everyone else is talking about Jack Harper's leaving party, but I leave work half an hour early. I go straight home and make myself some hot chocolate, and I'm sitting on the sofa, staring into space when Connor lets himself into the flat.

I look up as he walks into the room, and immediately I know something's different. Not with him. He hasn't changed a bit.

But I have. I've changed.

'Hi,' he says, and kisses me lightly on the head. 'Shall we go?'

'Go?'

'To look at the flat on Edith Road. We'll have to hurry if we're going to make it to the party. Oh, and my mother's given us a house-warming present. It was delivered to work.'

He hands me a cardboard box. I pull out a glass teapot and look at it blankly.

'You can keep the tea-leaves separate from the water. Mum says it really does make a better cup of tea—'

'Connor,' I hear myself saying. 'I can't do this.'

'It's quite easy. You just have to lift the—'

'No.' I shut my eyes, trying to gather some courage, then open them again. 'I can't do *this*. I can't move in with you.'

'What?' Connor stares at me. 'Has something happened?'

'Yes. No.' I swallow. 'I've been having doubts for a while. About us. And recently they've . . . they've been confirmed. If we carry on, I'll be a hypocrite. It's not fair to either of us.'

'*What?*' Connor rubs his face. 'Emma, are you saying you want to . . . to . . .'

'I want to break up,' I say, staring at the carpet.

'You're joking.'

'I'm not joking!' I say in sudden anguish. 'I'm not joking, OK?'

'But . . . this is ridiculous! It's ridiculous!' Connor's pacing around the room like a rattled lion. Suddenly he looks at me.

'It's that plane journey.'

'What?' I jump as though I've been scalded. 'What do you mean?'

'You've been different ever since that plane ride down from Scotland.'

'No I haven't!'

'You have! You've been edgy, you've been tense . . .'
Connor squats down in front of me and takes my
hands. 'Emma, I think maybe you're still suffering
some kind of trauma. You could have counselling.'

'Connor, I don't need counselling!' I jerk my hands
away. 'But maybe you're right. Maybe that plane ride
did . . .' I swallow. 'Affect me. Maybe it brought my life
into perspective and make me realize a few things.
And one of the things I've realized is, we aren't right
for each other.'

Slowly Connor sinks down onto the carpet, his face
bewildered.

'But things have been great! We've been having lots
of sex—'

'I know.'

'Is there someone else?'

'No!' I say sharply. 'Of course there's no-one else!' I
rub my finger roughly up and down the cover of the
sofa.

'This isn't you talking,' says Connor suddenly. 'It's
just the mood you're in. I'll run you a nice hot bath,
light some scented candles . . .'

'Connor, please!' I cry. 'No more scented candles!
You have to listen to me. And you have to believe me.'
I look straight into his eyes. 'I want to break up.'

'I *don't* believe you!' he says, shaking his head. 'I
know you, Emma! You're not that kind of person.
You wouldn't just throw away something like
that. You wouldn't—'

He stops in shock as, with no warning, I hurl the
glass teapot to the floor.

We both stare at it, stunned.

'It was supposed to break,' I explain after a pause.
'And that was going to signify that yes, I would throw
something away. If I knew it wasn't right for me.'

150

'I think it has broken,' says Connor, picking it up and examining it. 'At least, there's a hairline crack.'

'There you go.'

'We could still use it—'

'No. We couldn't.'

'We could get some Sellotape.'

'But it would never work properly.' I clench my fists by my sides. 'It just . . . wouldn't work.'

'I see,' says Connor after a pause.

And I think, finally, he does.

'Well . . . I'll be off then,' he says at last. 'I'll phone the flat people and tell them that we're . . .' He stops, and roughly wipes his nose.

'OK,' I say, in a voice which doesn't sound like mine. 'Can we keep it quiet from everyone at work?' I add. 'Just for the moment.'

'Of course,' he says gruffly. 'I won't say anything.'

He's halfway out of the door when abruptly he turns back, reaching in his pocket. 'Emma, here are the tickets for the jazz festival,' he says, his voice cracking a little. 'You have them.'

'What?' I stare at them in horror. 'No! Connor, you have them! They're yours!'

'*You* have them. I know how much you've been looking forward to hearing the Dennisson Quartet.' He pushes the brightly coloured tickets roughly into my hand and closes my fingers over them.

'I . . . I . . .' I swallow. 'Connor . . . I just . . . I don't know what to say.'

'We'll always have jazz,' says Connor in a choked-up voice, and closes the door behind him.

ELEVEN

So now I have no promotion *and* no boyfriend. And puffy eyes from crying. And everyone thinks I'm mad.

'You're mad,' Jemima says, approximately every ten minutes. It's Saturday morning, and we're in our usual routine of dressing gowns, coffee, and nursing hangovers. Or in my case, break-ups. 'You do realize you had him?' She frowns at her toenail, which she's painting baby pink. 'I would have predicted a rock on your finger within six months.'

'I thought you said I'd ruined all my chances by agreeing to move in with him,' I retort sulkily.

'Well, in Connor's case I think you would have been safe and dry.' She shakes her head. 'You're crazy.'

'Do you think I'm crazy?' I say, turning to Lissy, who's sitting in the rocking chair with her arm round her knees, eating a piece of raisin toast. 'Be honest.'

'Er . . . no,' says Lissy unconvincingly. 'Of course not!'

'You do!'

'It's just . . . you seemed like such a great couple.'

'I know we did. I know we looked great on the outside.' I pause, trying to explain. 'But the truth is, I never felt I was being myself. It was always a bit like we were acting. You know. It didn't seem *real*, somehow.'

'That's *it*?' interrupts Jemima, staring at me as though I'm talking gibberish. 'That's the reason you broke up?'

'It's a pretty good reason, don't you think?' says Lissy loyally.

Jemima stares at us both blankly.

'Of course not! Emma, if you'd just stuck it out and acted being the perfect couple for long enough, you would have *become* the perfect couple.'

'But . . . but we wouldn't have been happy!'

'You would have been the perfect couple,' says Jemima, as though explaining something to a very stupid child. '*Obviously* you would have been happy.' She cautiously stands up, her toes splayed by bits of pink foam, and starts making her way towards the door. 'And anyway. Everyone pretends in a relationship.'

'No they don't! Or at least, they shouldn't.'

'Of course they should! All this being honest with each other is totally overrated.' She gives us a knowing look. 'My mother's been married to my father for thirty years, and he still has no idea she isn't a natural blonde.'

She disappears out of the room and I exchange glances with Lissy.

'Do you think she's right?' I say.

'No,' says Lissy uncertainly. 'Of course not! Relationships should be built on . . . on trust . . . and truth . . .' She pauses, and looks at me anxiously. 'Emma, you never told me you felt that way about Connor.'

'I . . . didn't tell anyone.'

This isn't quite true, I immediately realize. But I'm hardly going to tell my best friend that I told more to a complete stranger than to her, am I?

'Well, I really wish you'd confided in me more,' says Lissy earnestly. 'Emma, let's make a new resolution. We'll tell each other *everything* from now on. We shouldn't have secrets from one another, anyway. We're best friends!'

'It's a deal!' I say, with a sudden warm burst of emotion. Impulsively I lean forward and give her a hug.

Lissy's so right. We should confide in each other. We shouldn't keep things from each other. I mean, we've known each other for over twenty years, for God's sake.

'So, if we're telling each other everything . . .' Lissy takes a bite of raisin toast and gives me a sidelong look. 'Did your chucking Connor have anything to do with that man? The man from the plane?'

I feel a tiny pang inside which I ignore by taking a sip of coffee.

Did it have anything to do with him? No. No, it didn't.

'No,' I say without looking up. 'Nothing.'

We both watch the television screen for a few moments, where Kylie Minogue is being interviewed.

'Oh, OK!' I say, suddenly remembering. 'So if we're asking each other questions . . . what were you *really* doing with that guy Jean-Paul in your room?'

Lissy takes a breath.

'And don't tell me you were looking at case notes,' I add. 'Because that wouldn't make all that thumping bumping noise.'

'Oh!' says Lissy, looking cornered. 'OK. Well . . . we were . . .' She takes a gulp of coffee and avoids my gaze. 'We were . . . um . . . having sex.'

'What?' I stare at her, disconcerted.

'Yes. We were having sex. That's why I didn't want to tell you. I was embarrassed.'

'You and Jean-Paul were having sex?'

'Yes!' She clears her throat. 'We were having passionate . . . raunchy . . . animalistic sex.'

There's something wrong here.

'I don't believe you,' I say, giving her a long look. 'You weren't having sex.'

The pink dots on Lissy's cheeks deepen in colour.

'Yes we were!'

'No you weren't! Lissy, what were you *really* doing?'

'We were having sex, OK?' says Lissy agitatedly.
'He's my new boyfriend and . . . that's what we were
doing! Now just leave me alone.' She gets up flusteredly, scattering raisin toast crumbs, and heads out
of the room, tripping slightly on the rug.

I stare after her, completely agog.

Why is she lying? What on earth was she doing in
there? What's more embarrassing than sex, for God's
sake? I'm so intrigued I almost feel cheered up.

To be honest, it's not the greatest weekend of my life.
It's made even less great when the post arrives and I
get a postcard from Mum and Dad from Le Spa
Meridien, telling me what a fantastic time they're
having. And even *less* great when I read my horoscope
in the *Mail*, and it tells me I may just have made a big
mistake.

But by Monday morning, I'm feeling better. I *haven't*
made a mistake. My new life starts today. I'm going to
forget all about love and romance and concentrate on
my career. Maybe I'll even look for a new job.

As I come out of the tube station, I start to like this
idea a lot. I'll apply for a job as Marketing Executive at
Coca-Cola or somewhere. And I'll get it. And Paul will
suddenly realize what a terrible mistake he made, not
promoting me. And he'll ask me to stay, but I'll say,
'It's too late. You had your chance.' And then he'll beg,
'Emma, is there anything I can do to change your
mind?' And then *I'll* say—

By the time I reach the office, Paul is grovelling on
the floor as I sit nonchalantly on his desk, holding one
knee (I also seem to be wearing a new trouser suit and

Prada shoes) saying, 'You know, Paul, all you had to do was treat me with a little respect—'

Shit. My eyes focus and I stop in my tracks, hand on the glass doors. There's a blond head in the foyer.

Connor. A wave of panic overcomes me. I can't go in there. I can't do it. I can't—

Then the head moves, and it's not Connor at all, it's Andrea from Accounts. I push the door open, feeling like a complete moron. God, I'm a mess. I have to get a grip of myself, because I will run into Connor before too long, and I'm just going to have to handle it.

At least no-one at work knows yet, I think as I walk up the stairs. That would make things a million times harder. To have people coming up to me and saying—

'Emma, I'm so sorry to hear about you and Connor!'

'What?' My head jerks up in shock and I see a girl called Nancy coming towards me.

'It was such a bolt from the blue! Of all the couples to split up, I would never have said you two. But it just shows, you never can tell . . .'

I stare at her dazedly.

'How . . . how do you know?'

'Oh, everyone knows!' says Nancy. 'You know there was a little drinks do on Friday night? Well, Connor came to it, and he got quite drunk. And he told everyone. In fact, he made a little speech!'

'He . . . he did what?'

'It was quite touching, really. It was all about how the Panther Corporation felt like his family, and how he knew we would all support him through this difficult time. And you, of course,' she adds as an after-thought. 'Although since you were the one who broke it off, Connor's really the wounded party.' She leans forward confidentially. 'I have to say, a lot of the girls were saying you must have a screw loose!'

I cannot believe this. Connor gave a speech about

our break-up. After promising to keep it quiet. And now everyone's on *his* side.

'Right,' I say at last. 'Well, I'd better get on—'

'It just seems such a shame.' Nancy eyes me inquisitively. 'You two seemed so perfect!'

'I know we did.' I force a smile. 'Anyway. See you later.'

I head for the new coffee machine and am staring into space, trying to get my head round this, when a tremulous voice interrupts me.

'Emma?' I look up and my heart sinks. It's Katie, staring at me as though I've grown three heads.

'Oh hi!' I say, trying to sound breezy.

'Is it true?' she whispers. 'Is it true? Because I won't believe it's true until I hear you say it with your own lips.'

'Yes,' I say reluctantly. 'It's true. Connor and I have broken up.'

'Oh God.' Katie's breathing becomes quicker and quicker. 'Oh my God. It's true. Oh my God, oh my God, I really can't cope with this . . .'

Shit. She's hyperventilating. I grab an empty sugar bag and shove it over her mouth.

'Katie, calm down!' I say helplessly. 'Breathe in . . . and out . . .'

'I've been having panic attacks all weekend,' she manages, between breaths. 'I woke up last night in a cold sweat and I just thought to myself, if this is true, the world doesn't make sense any more. It simply makes no sense.'

'Katie, we broke up! That's all. People break up all the time.'

'But you and Connor weren't just people! You were *the* couple. I mean, if you can't make it, why should any of the rest of us bother even trying?'

'Katie, we weren't *the* couple!' I say, trying to keep my temper. 'We were *a* couple. And it went wrong, and . . . and these things happen.'

'But—'

'And to be honest, I'd rather not talk about it.'

'Oh,' she says, and stares at me over the bag. 'Oh God, of course. Sorry, Emma. I didn't . . . I just . . . you know, it was such a shock!'

'Come on, you haven't told me how your date with Phillip went yet,' I say firmly. 'Cheer me up with some good news.'

Katie's breathing has gradually calmed, and she removes the bag from her face.

'Actually, it went really well,' she says. 'We're going to see each other again!'

'Well there you go,' I say encouragingly.

'He's so charming. And gentle. And we have the same sense of humour, and we like the same things.' A bashful smile spreads across Katie's face. 'In fact, he's lovely!'

'He sounds wonderful! You see?' I squeeze her arm. 'You and Phillip will probably be a far better couple than Connor and I ever were. Do you want a coffee?'

'No thanks, I've got to go. We've got a meeting with Jack Harper about personnel. See you.'

'OK, see you,' I say absently.

About five seconds later, my brain clicks into gear.

'Wait a second.' I hurry down the corridor and grab her shoulder. 'Did you just say Jack Harper?'

'Yes.'

'But . . . but he's gone. He left on Friday.'

'No he didn't. He changed his mind.'

I stare at her in disbelief.

'He changed his mind?'

'Yes.'

'So . . .' I swallow. 'So he's here?'

'Of course he's here!' says Katie with a laugh. 'He's upstairs.'

Suddenly my legs won't work properly.

'Why . . .' I clear my throat, which has gone a little husky. 'Why did he change his mind?'

'Who knows?' Katie shrugs. 'He's the boss. He can do what he likes, can't he? Mind you, he seems very down to earth.' She reaches into her pocket for a packet of gum, and offers it to me. 'He was really nice to Connor after he gave his little speech . . .'

I feel a fresh jolt.

'Jack Harper heard Connor's speech? About us breaking up?'

'Yes! He was standing right next to him.' Katie unwraps her gum. 'And afterwards he said something really nice like he could just imagine how Connor was feeling. Wasn't that sweet?'

I need to sit down. I need to think. I need to . . .

'Emma, are you OK?' says Katie in dismay. 'God, I'm so insensitive—'

'No. It's fine,' I say dazedly. 'I'm fine. I'll see you later.'

My mind is whirling as I walk into the marketing department.

This is not the way it was supposed to happen. Jack Harper was supposed to be back in America. He was supposed to have no idea that I went straight home from our conversation and chucked Connor.

I feel a smart of humiliation. He'll think I chucked Connor because of what he said to me in the lift, won't he? He'll think it was all because of him. Which it wasn't. It so *wasn't*.

At least, not completely . . .

Maybe that's why . . .

No. It's ridiculous to think that his staying has anything to do with me. Ridiculous. I don't know why I'm so jumpy.

As I near my desk, Artemis looks up from a copy of *Marketing Week.*

'Oh Emma. I was sorry to hear about you and Connor.'

'Thanks,' I say. 'But I don't really want to talk about it if that's OK.'

'Fine,' says Artemis. 'Whatever. I was just being polite.' She looks at a Post-It on her desk. 'There's a message for you from Jack Harper, by the way.'

'What?' I start.

Shit. I didn't mean to sound so rattled. 'I mean, what is it?' I add more calmly.

'Could you please take the –' She squints at the paper. '– the Leopold file to his office. He said you'd know what it was. But if you can't find it, it doesn't matter.'

I stare at her, my heart hammering in my chest.

The Leopold file.

It was just an excuse to get away from our desks . . .

It's a secret code. He wants to see me.

Oh my God. Oh my God.

I have never been more excited and thrilled and petrified. All at once.

I sit down and stare at my blank screen for a minute. Then with trembling fingers I take out a blank file. I wait until Artemis has turned away, then write 'Leopold' on the side of it, trying to disguise my handwriting.

Now what do I do?

Well, it's obvious. I take it upstairs to his office.

Unless . . . Oh fuck. Am I being really, really stupid here? Is there a real Leopold file?

Hastily I go into the company database and do a

quick search for 'Leopold'. But nothing comes up.

OK. I was right first time.

I'm about to push my chair back when I suddenly have a paranoid thought. What if someone stops me and asks what the Leopold file is? Or what if I drop it on the floor and everyone sees it's empty?

Quickly, I open a new document, invent a fancy letterhead and type a letter from a Mr Ernest P. Leopold to the Panther Corporation. I send it over to print, stroll over to the printer and whisk it out before anyone else can see what it is. Not that anyone else is remotely interested.

'Right,' I say casually, tucking it into the cardboard folder. 'Well, I'll just take that file up, then . . .'

Artemis doesn't even raise her head.

As I walk along the corridors my stomach is churning, and I feel all prickly and self-conscious, as though everyone in the building must know what I'm doing. There's a lift waiting to go up, but I head for the stairs, firstly so I won't have to talk to anyone and secondly because my heart's beating so fast, I feel like I need to use up a bit of nervous energy.

Why does Jack Harper want to see me? Because if it's to tell me he was right all along about Connor, then he can just . . . he can just bloody well . . . Suddenly I have a flashback to that awful atmosphere in the lift, and my stomach turns over. What if it's really awkward? What if he's angry with me?

I don't have to go, I remind myself. He did give me an out. I could easily phone his secretary and say, 'Sorry, I couldn't find the Leopold file,' and that would be the end.

For an instant I hesitate on the marble stairs, my fingers tightly clutching the cardboard. And then I carry on walking.

*　　*　　*

As I near the door of Jack's office I see that it's being guarded not by one of the secretaries, but by Sven.

Oh God. I know Jack has said he's his oldest friend, but I can't help it. I do find this guy creepy.

'Hi,' I say. 'Er . . . Mr Harper asked me to bring up the Leopold file.'

Sven looks at me, and for an instant it's as if a little silent communication is passing between us. He knows, doesn't he? He probably uses the Leopold file code himself. He picks up his phone and after a moment says, 'Jack, Emma Corrigan here with the Leopold file.' Then he puts down the phone, and without smiling, says, 'Go straight in.'

I walk in, feeling prickly with self-consciousness. The room is huge and panelled, and Jack's sitting behind a big wooden desk. When he looks up, his eyes are warm and friendly, and I feel myself relax just the teeniest bit.

'Hello,' he says.

'Hello,' I reply, and there's a short silence.

'So, um, here's the Leopold file,' I say, and hand him the cardboard folder.

'The Leopold file.' He laughs. 'Very good.' Then he opens it and looks at the sheet of paper in surprise. 'What's this?'

'It's a . . . it's a letter from Mr Leopold of Leopold and Company.'

'You composed a letter from Mr Leopold?' He sounds astonished, and suddenly I feel really stupid.

'Just in case I dropped the file on the floor and someone saw,' I mumble. 'I thought I'd just quickly make something up. It's not important.' I try to take it back, but Jack moves it out of my reach.

'"From the office of Ernest P. Leopold",' he reads aloud, and his face crinkles in delight. 'I see he wishes to order 6,000 cases of Panther Cola. Quite a customer, this Leopold.'

'It's for a corporate event,' I explain. 'They normally use Pepsi, but recently one of their employees tasted Panther Cola, and it was so good . . .'

'They simply had to switch,' finishes Jack. '"May I add that I am delighted with all aspects of your company, and have taken to wearing a Panther jogging suit, which is quite the most comfortable sportswear I have ever known."' He stares at the letter, then looks up with a smile. To my surprise, his eyes are shining slightly. 'You know, Pete would have adored this.'

'Pete Laidler?' I say hesitantly.

'Yup. It was Pete who came up with the whole Leopold file manoeuvre. This was the kind of stuff he did all the time.' He taps the letter. 'Can I keep it?'

'Of course,' I say, a little taken aback.

He folds it up and puts it in his pocket, and for a few moments there's silence.

'So,' says Jack at last. He raises his head and looks at me with an unreadable expression. 'You broke up with Connor.'

My stomach gives a flip. I don't know what to say.

'So.' I lift my chin defiantly. 'You decided to stay.'

'Yes, well . . .' He stretches out his fingers and studies them briefly. 'I thought I might take a closer look at some of the European subsidiaries.' He looks up. 'How about you?'

He wants me to say I chucked Connor because of him, doesn't he? Well, I'm not going to. No way.

'Same reason.' I nod. 'European subsidiaries.'

Jack's mouth twitches reluctantly into a smile.

'I see. And are you . . . OK?'

'I'm fine. Actually, I'm enjoying the freedom of being single again.' I gesture widely with my arms. 'You know, the liberation, the flexibility . . .'

'That's great. Well then, maybe this isn't a good time to . . .' He stops.

'To what?' I say, a little too quickly.

'I know you must be hurting right now,' he says carefully. 'But I was wondering.' He pauses for what seems like for ever, and I can feel my heart thumping hard against my ribs. 'Would you like to have dinner some time?'

He's asked me out. He's asked me out.

I almost can't move my mouth.

'Yes,' I say at last. 'Yes, that would be lovely.'

'Great!' He pauses. 'The only thing is, my life is kind of complicated right now. And what with our office situation . . .' He spreads his hands. 'It might be an idea to keep this to ourselves.'

'Oh, I completely agree,' I say quickly. 'We should be discreet.'

'So shall we say . . . how about tomorrow night? Would that suit you?'

'Tomorrow night would be perfect.'

'I'll come and pick you up. If you email me your address. Eight o'clock?'

'Eight it is!'

As I leave Jack's office, Sven glances up and raises his eyebrows, but I don't say anything. I head back to the marketing department, trying as hard as I can to keep my face dispassionate and calm. But excitement is bubbling away in my stomach, and a huge smile keeps licking over my face.

Oh my God. Oh my God. I'm going out to dinner with Jack Harper. I just . . . I can't believe—

Oh, who am I kidding? I knew this was going to happen. As soon as I heard he hadn't gone to America. I knew.

TWELVE

I have never seen Jemima look quite so appalled.

'He knows all your *secrets*?' She's looking at me as though I've just proudly informed her I'm going out with a mass-murderer. 'What on earth do you mean?'

'I sat next to him on a plane, and I told him everything about myself.'

I frown at my reflection in the mirror and tweak out another eyebrow hair. It's seven o'clock, I've had my bath, I've blow-dried my hair and now I'm on my makeup.

'And now he's asked her out,' says Lissy, hugging her knees. 'Isn't it romantic?'

'You are joking, aren't you?' says Jemima, looking aghast. 'Tell me this is a joke.'

'Of course I'm not joking! What's the problem?'

'You're going out with a man who knows everything about you.'

'Yes.'

'And you're asking me what's the *problem*?' Her voice rises incredulously. 'Are you *crazy*?'

'Of course I'm not crazy!'

'I *knew* you fancied him,' says Lissy for about the millionth time. 'I knew it. Right from the moment you started talking about him.' She looks at my reflection. 'I'd leave that right eyebrow alone now.'

'Really?' I peer at my face.

'Emma, you don't tell men all about yourself! You

have to keep something back! Mummy always told me, you should never let a man see your feelings or the contents of your handbag.'

'Well, too late,' I say, slightly defiantly. 'He's seen it all.'

'Then it's never going to work,' says Jemima. 'He'll never respect you.'

'Yes he will.'

'Emma,' says Jemima, almost pityingly. 'Don't you understand? You've already lost.'

'I haven't *lost*!'

Sometimes I think Jemima sees men not as people, but as alien robots, who must be conquered by any means possible.

'You're not being very helpful, Jemima,' puts in Lissy. 'Come on. You've been on loads of dates with rich businessmen. You must have some good advice!'

'All right.' Jemima sighs, and puts her bag down. 'It's a hopeless cause, but I'll do my best.' She starts ticking off on her fingers. 'The first thing is to look as well groomed as possible.'

'Why do you think I'm plucking my eyebrows?' I say with a grimace.

'Fine. OK, the next thing is, you can show an interest in his hobbies. What does he like?'

'Dunno. Cars, I think. He has all these vintage cars on his ranch, apparently.'

'Well then!' Jemima brightens. 'That's good. Pretend you like cars, suggest visiting a car show. You could flick through a car magazine on the way there.'

'I can't,' I say, taking a glug from my pre-date relaxer glass of Harvey's Bristol Cream. 'I told him on the plane that I hate vintage cars.'

'You did *what*?' Jemima looks as if she wants to hit me. 'You told the man you're dating that you hate his favourite hobby?'

'I didn't know I would be going on a date with him then, did I?' I say defensively, reaching for my foundation. 'And anyway, it's the truth. I hate vintage cars. The people in them always look so smug and pleased with themselves.'

'What's the *truth* got to do with anything?' Jemima's voice rises in agitation. 'Emma, I'm sorry, I can't help you. This is a disaster. You're completely vulnerable. It's like going into battle in a nightie.'

'Jemima, this is not a battle,' I retort, rolling my eyes. 'And it's not a chess game. It's dinner with a nice man!'

'You're so cynical, Jemima,' chimes in Lissy. '*I* think it's really romantic! They're going to have the perfect date, because there won't be any of that awkwardness. He knows what Emma likes. He knows what she's interested in. They're obviously already completely compatible.'

'Well, I wash my hands of it,' says Jemima, still shaking her head. 'What are you going to wear?' Her eyes narrow. 'Where's your outfit?'

'My black dress,' I say innocently. 'And my strappy sandals.' I gesture to the back of the door, where my black dress is hanging up.

Jemima's eyes narrow even further. She would have made a really good SS officer, I often think.

'You're not going to borrow anything of mine.'

'No!' I say indignantly. 'Honestly Jemima, I do have my own clothes, you know.'

'Fine. Well. Have a good time.'

Lissy and I wait until her footsteps have tapped down the corridor and the front door has slammed.

'Right!' I say excitedly, but Lissy lifts a hand.

'Wait.'

We both sit completely still for a couple of minutes. Then we hear the sound of the front door being opened very quietly.

'She's trying to catch us out,' hisses Lissy. 'Hi!' she says, raising her voice. 'Is anyone there?'

'Oh hi,' says Jemima, appearing at the door of the room. 'I forgot my lip-gloss.' Her eyes do a quick sweep of the room.

'I don't think you'll find it in here,' says Lissy innocently.

'No. Well.' Her eyes travel suspiciously round the room again. 'OK. Have a nice evening.'

Again her footsteps tap down the corridor, and again the front door slams.

'Right!' says Lissy. 'Let's go.'

We unpeel the Sellotape from Jemima's door, and Lissy makes a little mark where it was. 'Wait!' she says, as I'm about to push the door open. 'There's another one at the bottom.'

'You should have been a spy,' I say, watching her carefully peel it off.

'OK,' she says, her brow furrowed in concentration. 'There have to be some more booby traps.'

'There's Sellotape on the wardrobe, too,' I say. 'And . . . Oh my God!' I point up. A glass of water is balanced on top of the wardrobe, ready to drench us if we open the door.

'That cow!' says Lissy as I reach up for it. 'You know, I had to spend all evening fielding calls for her the other night, and she wasn't even grateful.'

She waits until I've put the water down safely, then reaches for the door. 'Ready?'

'Ready.'

Lissy takes a deep breath, then opens the wardrobe door. Immediately, a loud, piercing siren begins to wail. 'Wee-oo wee-oo wee-oo . . .'

'Shit!' she says, banging the door shut. 'Shit! How did she do that?'

'It's still going!' I say agitatedly. 'Make it stop. Make it stop!'

'I don't know how to! You probably need a special code!'

We're both jabbing frantically at the wardrobe, patting it, searching for an off-switch.

'I can't see a button, or a switch or anything . . .'

Abruptly the noise stops, and we stare at each other, panting slightly.

'Actually,' says Lissy after a long pause. 'Actually, I think that might have been a car alarm outside.'

'Oh,' I say. 'Oh right. Yes, maybe it was.'

Looking a bit sheepish, Lissy reaches for the door again, and this time it's silent. 'OK,' she says. 'Here goes.'

'Wow,' we breathe as one as she swings the door open.

Jemima's wardrobe is like a treasure chest. It's like a Christmas stocking. It's new, shiny, gorgeous clothes, one after another, all neatly folded and hung on scented hangers, like in a shop. All the shoes in shoe-boxes with Polaroids on the front. All the belts hanging neatly from hooks. All the bags are neatly lined up on a shelf. It's a while since I borrowed anything from Jemima, and every single item seems to have changed since then.

'She must spend about an hour a day keeping this tidy,' I say with a slight sigh, thinking of the jumble of my own wardrobe.

'She does,' says Lissy. 'I've seen her.'

Mind you, Lissy's wardrobe is even worse. It consists of a chair in her room, on which everything is heaped in a great big pile. She says putting stuff away makes her brain ache, and as long as it's clean, what does it matter?

'So!' says Lissy with a grin, and reaches for a white

sparkly dress. 'What look would Madam like this evening?'

I don't wear the white sparkly dress. But I do try it on. In fact, we both try on quite a lot of stuff, and then have to put it all back, very carefully. At one point another car alarm goes off outside, and we both jump in terror, then immediately pretend we weren't fazed.

In the end, I go for this amazing new red top of Jemima's with slashed shoulders, over my own black DKNY chiffon trousers (£25 from the Notting Hill Housing Trust shop) and Jemima's silver high heels from Prada. And then, although I wasn't intending to, at the last minute I grab a little black Gucci bag.

'You look amazing!' says Lissy as I do a twirl. 'Completely fab!'

'Do I look too smart?'

'Of course not! Come on, you're going out to dinner with a multimillionaire.'

'Don't *say* that!' I exclaim, feeling nerves clutch my stomach. I look at my watch. It's almost eight o'clock.

Oh God. Now I really am starting to feel nervous. In the fun of getting ready, I'd almost forgotten what it was all for.

Keep calm, I tell myself. It's just dinner. That's all it is. Nothing special. Nothing out of the—'

'Fuck!' Lissy's looking out of the window in the sitting room. 'Fuck! There's a great big car outside!'

'What? Where?' I hurry to join her, my heart galloping. As I follow her gaze, I almost can't breathe.

An enormous posh car is waiting outside our house. I mean, *enormous*. It's silver and shiny, and looks incredibly conspicuous in our tiny little street. In fact I can see some people looking curiously out of the house opposite.

And all at once I'm really scared. What am I doing?

This is a world I know nothing about. When we were sitting on those plane seats, Jack and I were just two people on an equal level. But look at us now. Look at the world he lives in – and look at the world I live in.

'Lissy,' I say in a tiny voice. 'I don't want to go.'

'Yes you do!' says Lissy – but I can see, she's just as freaked out as me.

The buzzer goes, and we jump.

I feel like I might throw up.

OK. OK. Here I go.

'Hi,' I say into the intercom. 'I'll . . . I'll be right down.' I put the phone down and look at Lissy.

'Well,' I say in a trembling voice. 'This is it!'

'Emma.' Lissy grabs my hands. 'Before you go. Don't take any notice of what Jemima said. Just have a lovely time.' She hugs me tightly. 'Call me if you get a chance.'

'I will.'

I take one last look at myself in the mirror, then open the door and make my way down the stairs.

I open the door, and Jack's standing there, wearing a jacket and tie. He smiles at me, and all my fears fly away like butterflies. Jemima's wrong. This isn't me against him. This is me *with* him.

'Hi,' he says, smiling warmly. 'You look very nice.'

'Thanks.'

I reach for the door handle, but a man in a peaked cap rushes forward to open it for me.

'Silly me!' I say nervously.

I can't quite believe I'm getting into this car. Me. Emma Corrigan. I feel like a princess. I feel like a movie star.

I sit down on the plushy seat, trying not to think how different this is from any car I've ever been in, ever.

'Are you OK?' says Jack.

'Yes! I'm fine!' My voice is a nervous squeak.

'Emma,' says Jack. 'We're going to have fun. I promise. Did you have your pre-date sweet sherry?'

How did he know—

Oh yes. I told him on the plane.

'Yes, I did actually,' I admit.

'Would you like some more?' He opens the bar and I see a bottle of Harvey's Bristol Cream sitting on a silver platter.

'Did you get that especially for me?' I say in disbelief.

'No, it's my favourite tipple.' His expression is so deadpan, I can't help laughing. 'I'll join you,' he says, as he hands me a glass. 'I've never tasted this before.' He pours himself a deep measure, takes a sip, and splutters. 'Are you serious?'

'It's yummy! It tastes like Christmas!'

'It tastes like . . .' He shakes his head. 'I don't even want to tell you what it tastes like. I'll stick to whisky if you don't mind.'

'OK,' I say with a shrug. 'But you're missing out.' I take another sip and grin happily at him. I'm completely relaxed already.

This is going to be the perfect date.

THIRTEEN

We arrive at a restaurant in Mayfair which I've never been to before. In fact I'm not even sure I've been to Mayfair before. It's so completely posh, why ever would I?

'It's a kind of private place,' Jack murmurs as we walk through a pillared courtyard. 'Not many people know about it.'

'Mr Harper. Miss Corrigan,' says a man in a Nehru suit, appearing out of nowhere. 'Please come this way.'

Wow! They know my name!

We glide past more pillars into an ornate room in which about three other couples are seated. There's a couple to our right, and as we walk past, a middle-aged woman with platinum hair and a gold jacket catches my eye.

'Well, hello!' she says. 'Rachel!'

'What?' I look around, bewildered. Is she looking at me?

She gets up from her seat and, lurching slightly, comes and gives me a kiss. 'How are you, darling? We haven't seen you for ages!'

OK, you can smell the alcohol from five yards away. And as I glance over at her dinner partner, he looks just as bad.

'I think you've made a mistake,' I say politely. 'I'm not Rachel.'

'Oh!' The woman stares at me for a moment. Then

she glances at Jack and her face snaps in under-standing. 'Oh! Oh, I see. Of course you're not.' She gives me a little wink.

'No!' I say in horror. 'You don't understand. I'm *really* not Rachel. I'm Emma.'

'Emma. Of course!' She nods conspiratorially. 'Well, have a wonderful dinner! And call me some time.'

As she stumbles back to her chair, Jack gives me a quizzical look.

'Is there something you want to tell me?'

'Yes,' I say. 'That woman is extremely drunk.' As I meet his gaze, I can't help giving a tiny giggle, and his mouth twitches.

'So, shall we sit down? Or do you have any more long-lost friends you'd like to greet?'

I look around the room consideringly.

'No, I think that's probably it.'

'If you're sure. Take your time. You're sure that elderly gentleman over there isn't your grandfather?'

'I don't *think* so . . .'

'Also, you should know that pseudonyms are fine by me,' Jack adds. 'I myself often go by the name of Egbert.'

I give a snort of laughter and hastily stifle it. This is a posh restaurant. People are already looking at us.

We're shown to a table in the corner, by the fire. A waiter helps me into my chair and fluffs a napkin over my knee, while another pours out some water, and yet another offers me a bread roll. Exactly the same is happening on Jack's side of the table. We have six people dancing attendance on us! I want to catch Jack's eye and laugh, but he looks unconcerned, as if this is perfectly normal.

Perhaps it *is* normal for him, it strikes me. Oh God. Perhaps he has a butler who makes him tea and irons his newspaper every day.

But what if he does? I mustn't let any of this faze me.

'So,' I say, as all the waiting staff melt away. 'What shall we have to drink?' I've already eyed up the drink which that woman in gold has got. It's pink and has slices of watermelon decorating the glass, and looks absolutely delicious.

'Already taken care of,' says Jack with a smile, as one of the waiters brings over a bottle of champagne, pops it open and starts pouring. 'I remember you telling me on the plane, your perfect date would start off with a bottle of champagne appearing at your table as if by magic.'

'Oh,' I say, quelling a tiny feeling of disappointment. 'Er . . . yes! So I did.'

'Cheers,' says Jack, and lightly clinks my glass.

'Cheers.' I take a sip, and it's delicious champagne. It really is. All dry and delicious.

I wonder what the watermelon drink tastes like.

Stop it. Champagne is perfect. Jack's right, this is the perfect start to a date.

'The first time I ever had champagne was when I was six years old—' I begin.

'At your Aunt Sue's,' says Jack with a smile. 'You took all your clothes off and threw them in the pond.'

'Oh right,' I say, halted mid-track. 'Yes, I've told you, haven't I?'

So I won't bore him with that anecdote again. I sip my champagne and quickly try to think of something else to say. Something that he doesn't already know.

Is there anything?

'I've chosen a very special meal, which I think you'll like,' says Jack, with a smile. 'All pre-ordered, just for you.'

'Gosh!' I say, taken aback. 'How . . . wonderful.'

A meal specially pre-ordered for me! Wow. That's incredible.

Except . . . choosing your food is half the fun of eating out, isn't it? It's almost my favourite bit.

Anyway. It doesn't matter. It'll be perfect. It *is* perfect.

OK. Let's start a conversation.

'So what do you like doing in your spare time?' I ask, and Jack gives a shrug.

'I hang out. I watch baseball. I fix my cars . . .'

'You have a collection of vintage cars! That's right. Wow. I really . . . um . . .'

'You hate vintage cars.' He smiles. 'I remember.'

Damn. I was hoping he might have forgotten.

'I don't hate the cars themselves,' I say quickly. 'I hate the people who . . . who . . .'

Shit. That didn't quite come out right. I take a quick gulp of champagne, but it goes down the wrong way and I start coughing. Oh God, I'm really spluttering. My eyes are weeping.

And now the other six people in the room have all turned to stare.

'Are you OK?' says Jack in alarm. 'Have some water. You like Evian, right?'

'Er . . . yes. Thanks.'

Oh, bloody hell. I hate to admit that Jemima could be right about anything. But it would have been a lot easier if I could just have said brightly, 'Oh, I adore vintage cars!'

Anyway. Never mind.

As I'm gulping my water, a plate of roasted peppers somehow materializes in front of me.

'Wow!' I say in delight. 'I love roasted peppers.'

'I remembered.' Jack looks rather proud of himself. 'You said on the plane that your favourite food was roasted peppers.'

'Did I?' I stare at him, a bit surprised.

Gosh. I don't remember that. I mean, I *like* roasted peppers, but I wouldn't have said—

'So I called the restaurant and had them make it specially for you. I can't eat peppers,' Jack adds, as a plate of scallops appears in front of him, 'otherwise I would join you.'

I gape at his plate. Oh my God. Those scallops look amazing. I *adore* scallops.

'Bon appetit!' says Jack cheerfully.

'Er . . . yes! Bon appetit.'

I take a bite of roasted pepper. It's delicious. And it was very thoughtful of him to remember.

But I can't help eyeing up his scallops. They're making my mouth water. And look at that green sauce! God, I bet they're succulent and perfectly cooked . . .

'Would you like a bite?' says Jack, following my gaze.

'No!' I say, jumping. 'No thanks. These peppers are absolutely – perfect!' I beam at him and take another huge bite.

Suddenly Jack claps a hand on his pocket.

'My mobile,' he says. 'Emma, would you mind if I took this? It could be something important.'

'Of course not,' I say. 'Go ahead.'

When he's gone, I just can't help it. I reach over, and spear one of his scallops. I close my eyes as I chew it, letting the flavour flood through my taste buds. That is just divine. That is the best food I've ever tasted in my life. I'm just wondering whether I could get away with eating a second one if I shifted the others around his plate a bit, when I smell a whiff of gin. The woman in the golden jacket is right by my ear.

'Tell me quickly!' she says. 'What's going on?'

'We're . . . having dinner.'

'I can see that!' she says impatiently. 'But what about Jeremy? Does he have any idea?'

Oh God.

'Look,' I say helplessly. 'I'm not who you think I am—'

'I can see that! I would never have thought you had this in you.' The woman squeezes my arm. 'Well, good for you. Have some fun, that's what I say! You took your wedding band off,' she adds, glancing at my left hand. 'Smart girl . . . oops! He's coming! I'd better go!'

She lurches away again, as Jack sits back down in his place, and I lean forward, already half giggling. Jack is going to love this.

'Guess what!' I say. 'I have a husband called Jeremy! My friend over there just came over and told me. So what do you reckon? Has Jeremy been having a dalliance too?'

There's silence, and Jack looks up, a strained expression on his face.

'I'm sorry?' he says.

He wasn't listening to a word I was saying.

I can't say the whole thing again. I'll just feel stupid. In fact, I already feel stupid. 'It doesn't matter,' I say, and force a smile.

There's another silence and I cast around for something to say. 'So, um, I have a confession to make,' I say, gesturing to his plate. 'I pinched one of your scallops.'

I wait for him to pretend to be shocked, or angry. Or *anything*.

'That's OK,' he says abstractedly, and begins to fork the rest of them into his mouth.

I don't understand. What's happened? Where's the banter gone? He's completely changed.

*   *   *

By the time we've finished our tarragon chicken with rocket salad and chips, my entire body is tensed up with misery. This date is a disaster. A complete disaster. I've made every effort possible to chat, and joke and be funny. But Jack's taken two more calls, and the rest of the time he's been broody and distracted, and to be honest I might as well not be there.

I feel like crying with disappointment. I just don't understand it. It was going so well. We were getting on so fantastically. What went wrong?

'I'll just go and freshen up,' I say, as our main-course plates are removed, and Jack simply nods.

The Ladies is more like a palace than a loo, with gold mirrors, plushy chairs and a woman in uniform to give you a towel. For a moment I feel a bit shy about phoning Lissy in front of her, but she must have seen it all before, mustn't she?

'Hi,' I say, as Lissy picks up. 'It's me.'

'Emma! How's it going?'

'It's awful,' I say dolefully.

'What do you mean?' she says in horror. 'How can it be awful? What's happened?'

'That's the worst thing.' I slump into a chair. 'It all started off brilliantly. We were laughing and joking, and the restaurant's amazing, and he'd ordered this special menu just for me, all full of my favourite things . . .'

I swallow hard. Now I put it like that, it does all sound pretty perfect.

'It sounds wonderful,' says Lissy in astonishment. 'So how come—'

'So then he had this call on his mobile.' I blow my nose. 'And ever since, he's barely said a word to me. He keeps disappearing off to take calls, and I'm left on my own, and when he comes back the conversation's

179

all strained and stilted, and he's obviously only half paying attention.'

'Maybe he's worried about something, but he doesn't want to burden you with it,' says Lissy after a pause.

'That's true,' I say slowly. 'He does look pretty hassled.'

'Maybe something awful has happened but he doesn't want to ruin the mood. Just try talking to him. Share his worries!'

'OK,' I say, feeling more cheerful. 'OK, I'll try that. Thanks, Lissy.'

I walk back to the table feeling slightly more positive. A waiter materializes to help me with my chair, and as I sit down, I give Jack the warmest, most sympathetic look I can muster. 'Jack, is everything OK?'

He frowns.

'Why do you say that?'

'Well, you keep disappearing off. I just wondered if there was anything . . . you wanted to talk about.'

'It's fine,' he says curtly. 'Thanks.' His tone is very much 'subject closed' but I'm not going to give up that easily.

'Have you had some bad news?'

'No.'

'Is it . . . a business thing?' I persist. 'Or . . . or is it some kind of personal . . .'

Jack looks up, a sudden flash of anger in his face.

'I said, it's nothing. Quit it.'

Great. That puts me in my place, doesn't it?

'Would you both care for dessert?' A waiter's voice interrupts me, and I give him a strained smile.

'Actually, I don't think so.'

I've had enough of this evening. I just want to get it over and go home.

'Very well.' The waiter smiles at me. 'Any coffee?'

'She does want dessert,' says Jack, over my head.

What? *What* did he just say? The waiter looks at me hesitantly.

'No I don't!' I say firmly.

'Come on, Emma,' says Jack, and now his warm, teasing tone is back. 'You don't have to pretend with me. You told me on the plane, this is what you always say. You say you don't want a dessert, when really, you do.'

'Well, this time, I really don't.'

'It's specially created for you.' Jack leans forward. 'Häagen-Dazs, meringue, Bailey's sauce on the side . . .'

Suddenly I feel completely patronized. How does he know what I want? Maybe I just want fruit. Maybe I want nothing. He has no idea about me. None at all.

'I'm not hungry.' I push my chair back.

'Emma, I know you. You want it, really—'

'You *don't* know me!' I cry angrily, before I can stop myself. 'Jack, you may know a few random facts about me. But that doesn't mean you know me!'

'What?' Jack stares at me.

'If you knew me,' I say in a trembling voice, 'you would have realized that when I go out to dinner with someone, I like them to listen to what I'm saying. I like them to treat me with a bit of respect, and not tell me to "quit it" when all I'm doing is trying to make conversation . . .'

Jack is staring at me in astonishment.

'Emma, are you OK?'

'No. I'm not OK! You've practically ignored me all evening.'

'That's not fair.'

'You have! You've been on autopilot. Ever since your mobile phone started going . . .'

'Look.' Jack rubs his face. 'A few things are going on

181

in my life at the moment, they're very important—'

'Fine. Well, let them go on without me.'

Tears are stinging my eyes as I stand up and reach for my bag. I so wanted this to be a perfect evening. I had such high hopes. I can't believe it's gone so wrong.

'That's right! You tell him!' the woman in gold supportively calls from across the room. 'You know, this girl's got a lovely husband of her own,' she exclaims to Jack. 'She doesn't need you!'

'Thank you for dinner,' I say, staring fixedly at the tablecloth, as one of the waiters magically appears at my side with my coat.

'Emma,' says Jack, getting to his feet in disbelief. 'You're not seriously going.'

'I am.'

'Give it another chance. Please. Stay and have some coffee. I promise I'll talk—'

'I don't want any coffee,' I say, as the waiter helps me on with my coat.

'Mint tea, then. Chocolates! I ordered you a box of Godiva truffles . . .' His tone is entreating, and just for an instant I waver. I love Godiva truffles.

But no, I've made up my mind.

'I don't care,' I gulp. 'I'm going. Thank you very much,' I add to the waiter. 'How did you know I wanted my coat?'

'We make it our business to know,' says the waiter discreetly.

'You see?' I say to Jack. '*They* know me.'

There's an instant in which we stare at each other.

'Fine,' says Jack at last, and gives a resigned shrug. 'Fine. Daniel will take you home. He should be waiting outside in the car.'

'I'm not going home in your car!' I say in horror. 'I'll make my own way, thanks.'

'Emma. Don't be stupid.'

'Goodbye. And thanks very much,' I add to the waiter. 'You were all very attentive and nice to me.'

I hurry out of the restaurant to discover it's started to rain. And I don't have an umbrella.

Well, I don't care. I'm going anyway. I stride along the streets, skidding slightly on the wet pavement, feeling raindrops mingling with tears on my face. I have no idea where I am. I don't even know where the nearest tube is, or where . . .

Hang on. There's a bus stop. I look down the numbers and see one that goes to Islington.

Well, fine. I'll take the bus home. And then I'll have a nice cup of hot chocolate. And maybe some ice-cream in front of the telly.

It's one of those bus shelters with a roof and little seats, and I sit down, thanking God my hair won't get any wetter. I'm just staring blankly at a car advertisement, wondering what that Häagen-Dazs pudding tasted like and whether the meringue was the stiff white kind or that gorgeous chewy, caramel kind, when a big silver car purrs up at the pavement.

I don't believe it.

'Please,' says Jack, getting out. 'Let me take you home.'

'No,' I say, without turning my head.

'You can't stay here in the rain.'

'Yes I can. Some of us live in the real world, you know.'

I turn away and pretend to be studying a poster about AIDS. The next moment Jack has arrived in the bus shelter. He sits down in the little seat next to mine and for a while we're both silent.

'I know I was terrible company this evening,' he says eventually. 'And I'm sorry. I'm also sorry I can't tell you anything about it. But my life is . . . complicated.

183

And some bits of it are very delicate. Do you understand?'

No, I want to say. No, I don't understand, when I've
told you every single little thing about me.

'I suppose,' I say, with a tiny shrug.

The rain is beating down even harder, thundering on
the roof of the shelter and creeping into my – Jemima's
– silver sandals. God, I hope it won't stain them.

'I'm sorry the evening was a disappointment to you,'
says Jack, lifting his voice above the noise.

'It wasn't,' I say, suddenly feeling bad. 'I just . . . I
had such high hopes! I wanted to get to know you a
bit, and I wanted to have fun . . . and for us to laugh . . .
and I wanted one of those pink cocktails, not
champagne . . .'

Shit. *Shit.* That slipped out before I could stop it.

'But . . . you like champagne!' says Jack, looking
stunned. 'You told me. Your perfect date would start
off with champagne.'

I can't quite meet his eye.

'Yes, well. I didn't know about the pink cocktails
then, did I?'

Jack throws back his head and laughs.

'Fair point. Very fair point. And I didn't even give
you a choice, did I?' He shakes his head ruefully. 'You
were probably sitting there thinking, damn this guy,
can't he tell I want a pink cocktail?'

'No!' I say at once, but my cheeks are turning
crimson, and Jack is looking at me with such a comical
expression that I want to hug him.

'Oh Emma. I'm sorry.' He shakes his head. 'I wanted
to get to know you too. And I wanted to have fun, too.
It sounds like we both wanted the same things. And
it's my fault we didn't get them.'

'It's not *your* fault,' I mumble awkwardly.

'This is not the way I planned for things to go.' He

looks at me seriously. 'Will you give me another chance?'

A big red double-decker bus rumbles up to the bus stop, and we both look up.

'I've got to go,' I say, standing up. 'This is my bus.'

'Emma, don't be silly. Come in the car.'

'No. I'm going on the bus!'

The automatic doors open, and I step onto the bus. I show my travelcard to the driver and he nods.

'You're seriously considering riding on this thing?' says Jack, stepping on behind me. He peers dubiously at the usual motley collection of night bus riders. 'Is this *safe*?'

'You sound like my grandpa! Of course it's safe. It goes to the end of my road.'

'Hurry up!' says the driver impatiently to Jack. 'If you haven't got the money, get off.'

'I have American Express,' says Jack, feeling in his pocket.

'You can't pay a bus fare with American Express!' I say, rolling my eyes. 'Don't you know anything? And anyway.' I stare at my travelcard for a few seconds. 'I think I'd rather be on my own, if you don't mind.'

'I see,' says Jack in a different voice. 'I guess I'd better get off,' he says to the driver. Then he looks at me. 'You haven't answered me. Can we try again? Tomorrow night. And this time we'll do whatever you want. You call the shots.'

'OK.' I'm trying to give a noncommittal shrug, but as I meet his eye I find myself smiling, too.

'Eight o'clock again?'

'Eight o'clock. And leave the car behind,' I add firmly. 'We'll do things my way.'

'Great! I look forward to it. Goodnight, Emma.'

'Goodnight.'

As he turns to get off, I climb up the stairs to the top

deck of the bus. I head for the front seat, the place I always used to sit when I was a child, and stare out at the dark, rainy, London night. If I stare for long enough, the street lights become blurred like a kaleidoscope. Like fairyland.

Swooshing round my mind are images of the woman in gold, the pink cocktail, Jack's face as I said I was leaving, the waiter bringing me my coat, Jack's car arriving at the bus stop . . . I can't quite work out what I think. All I can do is sit there, staring out, aware of familiar, comforting sounds around me. The old-fashioned grind and roar of the bus engine. The noise of the doors swishing open and shut. The sharp ring of the request bell. People thumping up the stairs and thumping back down again.

I can feel the bus lurch as we turn corners, but I'm barely aware of where we're going. Until after a while, familiar sights outside start to impinge on my consciousness, and I realize we're nearly at my street. I gather myself, reach for my bag, and totter along to the top of the stairs.

Suddenly the bus makes a sharp swing left, and I grab for a seat handle, trying to steady myself. Why are we turning left? I look out of the window, thinking I'll be really pissed off if I end up having to walk, and blink in astonishment.

Surely we're not—

Surely this can't be—

But we are. I peer down through the window, dumbfounded. We're in my tiny little road.

And now we've stopped outside my house.

I hurry down the stairs, nearly breaking my ankle, and stare at the driver.

'Number 41 Ellerwood Road,' he says with a flourish.

No. This can't be happening.

Bewildered, I look around the bus, and a couple of drunk teenagers stare blankly back.

'What's going on?' I look at the driver. 'Did he *pay* you?'

'Five hundred quid,' says the driver, and winks at me. 'Whoever he is, love, I'd hold onto him.'

Five hundred quid? Oh my God.

'Thanks,' I say dazedly. 'I mean, thanks for the ride.'

Feeling as though I'm in a dream, I get off the bus and head for the front door. But Lissy has already got there and is opening it.

'Is that a *bus*?' she says, staring. 'What's it doing here?'

'It's my bus,' I say. 'It took me home.'

I wave to the driver, who waves back, and the bus rumbles off into the night.

'I don't believe it!' says Lissy slowly, gazing as it disappears round the corner. She turns to look at me. 'So . . . it was OK in the end?'

'Yes,' I say. 'Yes. It was . . . OK.'

FOURTEEN

OK. Don't tell anyone. Do *not* tell anyone.

Do not tell anyone that you were on a date with Jack Harper last night.

I mean, not that I'm exactly planning to tell anyone. But as I arrive at work the next day I feel almost convinced I'm going to blurt it out by mistake.

Or someone's going to guess. I mean, surely it must be obvious from my face. From my clothes. From the way I'm walking. I feel as though everything I do screams 'Hey, guess what I did last night?'

'Hiya,' says Caroline as I make myself a cup of coffee. 'How are you?'

'I'm fine, thanks!' I say, giving a guilty jump. 'I just had a quiet evening in last night. Just . . . really quiet! With my flatmate. We watched three videos, *Pretty Woman*, *Notting Hill* and *Four Weddings*. Just the two of us. No-one else.'

'Right,' says Caroline, looking a bit bemused. 'Lovely!'

Oh God. I'm losing it. Everyone knows this is how criminals get caught. They add too many details and trip themselves up.

Right, no more babbling. Stick to one-word answers.

'Hi,' says Artemis as I sit down at my desk.

'Hi,' I say, forcing myself not to add anything else. Not even about which kind of pizza Lissy and I ordered, even though I've got a whole story ready

188

about how the pizza company thought we said green pepper instead of pepperoni, ha ha, what a mix-up.

I'm supposed to be doing some filing this morning, but instead I find myself taking out a piece of paper and starting a list of possible date venues where I can take Jack tonight.

1. Pub. No. Far too boring.
2. Movie. No. Too much sitting, not talking to each other.
3. Ice skating. I have no idea why I put that, since I can't even skate. Except it was in *Splash*.
4.

God, I've run out of ideas already. How crap is this? I stare at the sheet blankly, half-tuning into the idle conversation which is going on around me.

'. . . really working on some secret project, or is that just a rumour?'

'. . . company in a new direction, apparently, but no-one knows exactly what he's . . .'

'. . . *is* this Sven guy anyway? I mean, what function does he have?'

'He's with Jack, isn't he?' says Amy, who works in Finance but fancies Nick, so is always finding excuses to come into our office. 'He's Jack's lover.'

'*What?*' I say, suddenly sitting up, and snapping the end of my pencil. Luckily everyone's too busy gossiping to notice.

Jack gay? Jack gay?

That's why he didn't kiss me goodnight. He only wants me to be a friend. He'll introduce me to Sven and I'll have to pretend to be all cool with it, like I knew all along—

'Is Jack Harper gay?' Caroline is saying in astonishment.

189

'I just assumed he was,' says Amy with a shrug. 'He looks gay, don't you think?'

'Not really,' says Caroline, screwing up her face. 'Not groomed enough.'

'I don't think he looks gay!' I say, trying to sound light-hearted and just kind of vaguely interested.

'He's not gay,' chimes in Artemis authoritatively. 'I read a old profile of him in *Newsweek*, and he was dating the female president of Origin Software. And it said before that he went out with some supermodel.'

A huge surge of relief floods through me.

I knew he wasn't gay. Obviously I knew he wasn't gay.

Honestly, do these people have nothing better to do than engage in stupid mindless speculation about people they don't know?

'So is Jack seeing anyone at the moment?'

'Who knows?'

'He's pretty sexy, don't you think?' says Caroline with a wicked grin. 'I wouldn't mind.'

'Yeah right,' says Nick. 'You probably wouldn't mind his private jet, either.'

'Apparently, he hasn't had a relationship since Pete Laidler died,' says Artemis crisply. 'So I doubt you've got much of a chance.'

'Bad luck, Caroline,' says Nick, with a laugh.

I feel really uncomfortable, listening to this. Maybe I should leave the room until they've stopped. But then, maybe that would draw attention to myself.

Just for an instant, I find myself imagining what would happen if I stood up and said, 'Actually I had dinner with Jack Harper last night.' They'd all stare at me, dumbfounded, and maybe somebody would gasp, and . . .

Oh, who am I kidding? They wouldn't even believe

190

me, would they? They'd say I was suffering from delusions.

'Hi, Connor,' comes Caroline's voice, interrupting my thoughts.

Connor? My head jerks up in slight dismay. And there he is, with no warning. approaching my desk with a wounded look on his face.

What's he doing here?

Has he found out about me and Jack?

My heart starts to thump hard and I nervously push my hair back. I've spotted him a couple of times around the building, but this is our first moment face to face, since we broke up.

'Hi,' he says.

'Hi,' I reply awkwardly, and there's silence.

Suddenly I notice my unfinished list of date ideas lying prominently on my desk. Shit. As casually as possible I reach for it, screw it up and nonchalantly drop it in the bin.

All the gossip about Sven and Jack has petered out. I know everyone in the office is listening to us, even if they're pretending to be doing something else. It's like we're the in-house soap opera or something.

And I know which character I am. I'm the heartless bitch who chucked her lovely, decent man for no good reason.

Oh God. The thing is, I do feel guilty, I really do. Every time I see Connor, or even think about him, I get a horrible tight feeling in my chest. But does he *have* to have such an expression of injured dignity on his face? A kind of you've-mortally-wounded-me-but-I'm-such-a-good-person-I-forgive-you look.

I can feel my guilt ebbing away and annoyance starting to ebb in.

'I only came up,' says Connor at last, 'because I'd put us down to do a stint on the Pimm's stall together at the Corporate Family Day. Obviously when I did so, I thought we'd be—', He breaks off, looking more wounded than ever. 'Anyway. But I don't mind going through with it. If you don't.'

I'm not going to be the one to say I can't bear to stand next to him for half an hour.

'I don't mind!' I say.

'Fine.'

'Fine.'

There's another awkward pause.

'I found your blue shirt, by the way,' I say, with a tiny shrug. 'I'll bring it in.'

'Thanks. I think I've got some stuff of yours, too . . .'

'Hey,' says Nick, coming over towards us with a wicked, eyes gleaming, let's-shit-stir expression. 'I saw you with someone last night.'

My heart gives a huge, terrified bound. Fuck! Fuck fuck OK . . . OK . . . It's OK. He's not looking at me. He's looking at Connor.

Who the hell was Connor with?

'That was just a friend,' says Connor stiffly.

'Are you sure?' says Nick. 'You looked pretty friendly to me.'

'Shut up, Nick,' says Connor, looking pained. 'It's far too early to be thinking of . . . moving on. Isn't it, Emma?'

'Er . . . yes.' I swallow several times. 'Absolutely. Definitely.'

Oh God.

Anyway. Never mind. I'm not going to worry about Connor. I have an important date to think about. And thank goodness, by the end of the day I have at last come up with the perfect venue. In fact I'm amazed I didn't think of it before! There is one tiny little hitch – but I'll easily overcome it.

Sure enough, it only takes me about half an hour to

persuade Lissy that when they said 'The key shall in no circumstances be transferred to any non-member' in the rules, they didn't really mean it. At last she reaches into her bag and hands it to me, an anxious expression on her face.

'Don't lose it!'

'I won't! Thanks, Liss.' I give her a hug. 'Honestly, I'll do the same for you when I'm a member of an exclusive club.'

'You remember the password, don't you?'

'Yes. Alexander.'

'Where are you going?' says Jemima, coming into my room all dressed up to go out. She gives me a critical look. 'Nice top. Where's it from?'

'Oxfam. I mean, Whistles.'

I've decided tonight I'm not even going to *try* to borrow anything from Jemima. I'm going to wear all my own clothes, and if Jack doesn't like it, he can lump it.

'I was meaning to ask,' Jemima says, narrowing her eyes. 'You two didn't go into my room last night, did you?'

'No,' says Lissy innocently. 'Why, did it look like we had?'

Jemima was out until three, and by the time she got back, everything was back in place. Sellotape and everything. We couldn't have been more careful.

'No,' admits Jemima reluctantly. 'Nothing was out of place. But I just got a *feeling*. As though someone had been in there.'

'Did you leave the window open?' says Lissy. 'Because I read this article recently, about how monkeys are being sent into houses to steal things.'

'*Monkeys?*' Jemima stares at her.

'Apparently. The thieves train them.'

Jemima looks perplexedly from Lissy to me, and I force myself to keep a straight face.

193

'Anyway,' I say quickly, to change the subject. 'You might like to know that you were wrong about Jack. I'm going out with him again tonight. It wasn't a disastrous date at all!'

There's no need to add the small detail that we had a big row and I stormed out and he had to follow me to the bus stop. Because the point is, we're having a second date.

'I wasn't wrong,' says Jemima. 'You just wait. I predict doom.'

I pull a face at her behind her back as she leaves, and start putting on my mascara 'What's the time?' I say, frowning as I blob a bit on my eyelid.

'Ten to eight,' says Lissy. 'How are you going to get there?'

'Cab.'

Suddenly the buzzer goes, and we both look up.

'He's early,' says Lissy. 'That's a bit weird.'

'He can't be early!' We hurry into the sitting room, and Lissy gets to the window first.

'Oh my God,' she says, looking down to the street below. 'It's Connor.'

'*Connor?*' I stare at her in horror. 'Connor's here?'

'He's holding a box of stuff. Shall I buzz him up?'

'No! Pretend we're not in!'

'Too late,' says Lissy, and pulls a face. 'Sorry. He's seen me.'

The buzzer sounds again, and we look at each other helplessly.

'OK,' I say at last. 'I'm going down.'

Shit shit shit . . .

I pelt downstairs and breathlessly open the door. And there, standing on the doorstep, is Connor, wearing the same martyred expression he had at the office.

'Hi,' he says. 'Here are the things I was telling you about. I thought you might need them.'

'Er, thanks,' I say, grabbing the box, which seems to contain one bottle of L'Oréal shampoo and some jumper I've never seen in my life. 'I haven't quite sorted out your stuff yet, so I'll bring it to the office, shall I?'

I dump the box on the stairs, and quickly turn back before Connor thinks I'm inviting him in.

'So, um, thanks,' I say. 'It was really good of you to stop by.'

'No problem,' says Connor. He gives a heavy sigh. 'Emma . . . I was thinking perhaps we could use this as an opportunity to talk. Maybe we could have a drink, or supper even.'

'Gosh,' I say brightly. 'I'd love that. I really would. But to be honest, now isn't a completely brilliant time.'

'Are you going out?' His face falls.

'Um, yes. With Lissy.' I glance surreptitiously at my watch. It's six minutes to eight. 'So anyway, I'll see you soon. You know, around the office . . .'

'Why are you so flustered?' Connor is staring at me.

'I'm not flustered!' I say, and lean casually against the doorframe.

'What's wrong?' His eyes narrow suspiciously, and he looks past me into the hall. 'Is something going on?'

'Connor,' I put a reassuring hand on his arm. 'Nothing's going on. You're imagining things.'

At that moment, Lissy appears behind me at the door.

'Um, Emma, there's a very urgent phone call for you,' she says in a really stilted voice. 'You'd better come straight away . . . oh, hello Connor!'

Unfortunately Lissy is the worst liar in the world.

'You're trying to get rid of me!' says Connor, looking from Lissy to me in bewilderment.

'No we're not!' says Lissy, flushing bright red.

'Hang on,' says Connor suddenly, staring at my

outfit. 'Hang on a minute. I don't . . . are you going on a . . . date?'

My mind works quickly. If I deny it, we'll probably get into some huge argument. But if I admit the truth, maybe he'll stalk off in a huff.

'You're right,' I say. 'I've got a date.'

There's a shocked silence.

'I don't believe this,' says Connor, shaking his head, and to my dismay, sinks heavily down onto the garden wall. I glance at my watch. Three minutes to eight. Shit!

'Connor . . .'

'You told me there wasn't anyone else! You promised, Emma!'

'There wasn't! But . . . there is now. And he'll be here soon . . . Connor, you really don't want to get into this.' I grab his arm and try to lift him up, but he weighs about twelve stone. 'Connor, please. Don't make this more painful for everyone.'

'I suppose you're right.' At last Connor gets to his feet. 'I'll go.'

He walks to the gate, his back hunched in defeat, and I feel a pang of guilt, mixed with an urgent desire for him to hurry. Then, to my horror, he turns back.

'So, who is it?'

'It's . . . it's someone you don't know,' I say, crossing my fingers behind my back. 'Look, we'll have lunch soon and have a good talk. Or something, I promise.'

'OK,' says Connor, looking more wounded than ever. 'Fine. I get the message.'

I watch, unable to breathe, as he shuts the gate behind him and walks slowly along the street. Keep walking, keep walking . . . don't stop . . .

As he finally rounds the corner, Jack's silver car appears at the other end of the street.

'Oh my God,' says Lissy, staring at it.

196

'Don't!' I sink onto the stone wall. 'Lissy, I can't cope with this.'

I feel shaky. I think I need a drink. And I've only got mascara on one set of eyelashes, I abruptly realize.

The silver car pulls up in front of the house, and out gets the same uniformed driver as before. He opens the passenger door, and Jack steps out.

'Hi!' he says, looking taken aback to see me. 'Am I late?'

'No! I was just . . . um . . . sitting here. You know. Taking in the view.' I gesture across the road, where I notice for the first time that a man with a huge belly is changing the wheel on his caravan. 'Anyway!' I say, hastily standing up, 'Actually, I'm not quite ready. Do you want to come up for a minute?'

'Sure,' says Jack with a smile. 'That would be nice.'

'And send your car away,' I add. 'You weren't supposed to have it!'

'You weren't supposed to be sitting outside your house and catch me out,' retorts Jack with a grin. 'OK, Daniel, that's it for the night.' He nods to the driver. 'I'm in this lady's hands from now on.'

'This is Lissy, my flatmate,' I say as the driver gets back into the car. 'Lissy, Jack.'

'Hi,' says Lissy with a self-conscious grin, as they shake hands.

As we make our way up the stairs to our flat, I'm suddenly aware of how narrow they are, and how the cream paint on the walls is all scuffed, and the carpet smells of cabbage. Jack probably lives in some enormous grand mansion. He probably has a marble staircase or something.

But so what? We can't all have marble.

Anyway, it's probably awful. All cold and clattery. You probably trip on it all the time, and it probably chips really easily—

'Emma, if you want to get ready, I'll fix Jack a drink,' says Lissy, with a smile that says: He's nice!

'Thanks,' I say, shooting back an 'isn't he?' look. I hurry into my room and hurriedly start applying mascara to my other eye.

A few moments later there's a little knock at my door.

'Hi!' I say, expecting Lissy. But in comes Jack, holding out a glass of sweet sherry.

'Oh, thanks!' I say gratefully. 'I could do with a drink.'

'I won't come in,' he says politely.

'No, it's fine. Sit down!'

I gesture to the bed, but it's covered with clothes. And my dressing table stool is piled high with magazines. Damn, I should have tidied up a bit.

'I'll stand,' says Jack with a little smile. He takes a sip of what looks like whisky, and looks around my room in fascination. 'So this is your room. Your world.'

'Yes.' I flush slightly, unscrewing my lip-gloss. 'It's a bit messy—'

'It's very nice. Very homey.' I can see him taking in the shoes piled in the corner, the fish mobile hanging from my light, the mirror with necklaces strung over the side, and a new skirt hanging on the wardrobe door.

'Cancer Research?' he says puzzledly, looking at the label. 'What does that—'

'It's a shop,' I say, a little defiantly. 'A second-hand shop.'

'Ah.' He nods in tactful comprehension. 'Nice bedcover,' he adds, smiling.

'It's ironic,' I say hastily. 'It's an ironic statement.'

God, how embarrassing. I should have changed it.

Now Jack's staring incredulously at my open

dressing-table drawer, crammed with makeup. 'How many lipsticks do you have?'

'Er, a few . . .' I say, hastily closing it.

Maybe it wasn't such a great idea to let Jack come in here. He's picking up my Perfectil vitamins, and examining them. I mean, what's so interesting about *vitamins*? Now he's looking at Katie's crochet belt.

'What's this? A snake?'

'It's a belt,' I say, screwing up my face as I put in an earring. 'I know. It's hideous. I can't stand crochet.'

Where's my other earring? Where?

Oh, OK, here it is. Now what's Jack doing?

I turn to see him looking in fascination at my exercise chart, which I put up in January after I'd spent the entire Christmas eating Quality Street.

'"Monday, 7 a.m.",' he reads aloud. '"Brisk jog round block. Forty sit-ups. Lunch time: yoga class. Evening: Pilates tape. Sixty sit-ups."' He takes a sip of whisky. 'Very impressive. You do all this?'

'Well,' I say after a pause. 'I don't exactly manage every *single* . . . I mean, it was quite an ambitious . . . you know . . . er . . . Anyway!' I quickly spritz myself with perfume. 'Let's go!'

I have to get him out of here quickly before he does something like spot a Tampax and ask me what it is. I mean, honestly! Why on earth is he so *interested* in everything?

FIFTEEN

As we head out into the balmy evening, I feel light and happy with anticipation. Already there's a completely different atmosphere from yesterday night. No scary cars; no posh restaurants. It feels more casual. More fun.

'So,' says Jack, as we walk up to the main road. 'An evening out, Emma-style.'

'Absolutely!' I stick out my hand and hail a taxi, and give the name of the road in Clerkenwell off which the little alley runs.

'We're allowed to go by taxi, are we?' says Jack mildly as we get in. 'We don't have to wait for a bus?'

'As a very special treat,' I say with mock severity.

'So, are we eating? Drinking? Dancing?' says Jack, as we move off down the street.

'Wait and see!' I beam at him. 'I just thought we could have a really laid-back, spontaneous evening.'

'I guess I over-planned last night,' says Jack after a pause.

'No, it was lovely!' I say kindly. 'But sometimes you can put *too* much thought into things. You know, sometimes it's better just to go with the flow and see what happens.'

'You're right.' Jack smiles. 'Well, I look forward to going with the flow.'

As we whiz along Upper Street, I feel quite proud of

myself. It just shows I'm a true Londoner. I can take my guests to little places off the beaten track. I can find spots which aren't just the obvious venues to go. I mean, not that Jack's restaurant wasn't amazing. But how much cooler will this be? A secret club! And I mean, who knows, Madonna might be there this evening!

After about twenty minutes we get to Clerkenwell. I insist on paying the taxi fare, and lead Jack down the alley.

'Very interesting,' says Jack, looking around. 'So where are we heading?'

'Just wait,' I say enigmatically. I head for the door, press the buzzer and take Lissy's key out of my pocket with a little *frisson* of excitement.

He is going to be so impressed. He is going to be *so* impressed!

'Hello?' comes a voice.

'Hello,' I say casually. 'I'd like to speak to Alexander, please.'

'Who?' says the voice.

'Alexander,' I repeat, and give a knowing smile. Obviously they have to double-check.

'Ees no Alexander here.'

'You don't understand. Al-ex-and-er,' I enunciate clearly.

'Ees no Alexander.'

Maybe I got the wrong door, it suddenly occurs to me. I mean, I remember it as being this one – but maybe it was this other one with the frosted glass. Yes. That one looks quite familiar, actually.

'Tiny hitch,' I smile at Jack, and press the new bell.

There's silence. I wait a few minutes, then try again, and again. There's no reply. OK. So . . . it's not this one either.

Fuck.

I am a moron. Why didn't I check the address? I was just so sure I'd remember where it was.

'Is there a problem?' says Jack.

'No!' I say at once, and smile brightly. 'I'm just trying to recall exactly . . .'

I look up and down the street, trying not to panic. Which one was it? Am I going to have to ring every single doorbell in the street? I take a few steps along the pavement, trying to trigger my memory. And then, through an arch, I spy another alley, almost identical to this one.

I feel a huge thud of horror. Am I in the right *alley*, even? I dart forward and peer into the other alley. It looks exactly the same. Rows of nondescript doors and blanked-out windows.

My heart starts to beat more quickly. What am I going to do? I can't try every single doorbell in every bloody alley in the vicinity. It never once occurred to me that this might happen. Not once. I never even thought to—

OK, I'm being stupid. I'll call Lissy! She'll tell me. I pull out my mobile and dial home, but immediately it clicks onto answerphone.

'Hi, Lissy, it's me,' I say, trying to sound light and casual. 'A tiny little hitch has happened, which is that I can't remember exactly which door the club is behind. Or actually . . . which alley it's in either. So if you get this, could you give me a call? Thanks!'

I look up to see Jack watching me.

'Everything OK?'

'Just a slight glitch,' I say, and give a relaxed little laugh. 'There's this secret club along here somewhere, but I can't quite remember where.'

'Never mind,' says Jack nicely. 'These things happen.'

I jab the number for home again, but it's engaged.

Quickly I dial Lissy's mobile number, but it's switched off.

Oh fuck. Fuck. We can't stand here in the street all night.

'Emma,' says Jack cautiously. 'Would you like me to make a reservation at—'

'No!' I jump as though stung. Jack's not going to reserve anything. I've said I'll organize this evening, and I will. 'No thanks. It's OK.' I make a snap decision. 'Change of plan. We'll go to Antonio's instead.'

'I could call the car . . .' begins Jack.

'We don't need the car!' I stride purposefully towards the main road and thank God, a taxi's coming along with its light on. I flag it down, open the door for Jack and say to the driver,

'Hi, Antonio's on Sanderstead Road in Clapham, please.'

Hurrah. I have been grown-up and decisive and saved the situation.

'Where's Antonio's?' says Jack, as the taxi begins to speed away.

'It's a bit out of the way, in south London. But it's really nice. Lissy and I used to go there when we lived in Wandsworth. It's got huge pine tables, and gorgeous food, and sofas and stuff. And they never chivvy you.'

'It sounds perfect.' Jack smiles, and I smile proudly back.

OK, it should *not* take this long to get from Clerkenwell to Clapham. We should have got there ages ago. I mean, it's only down the road!

After about half an hour, I lean forward and say to the driver yet again, 'Is there a problem?'

'Traffic, love.' He gives an easy shrug. 'What can you do?'

You can find a clever traffic-avoiding back route like taxi drivers are supposed to! I want to yell furiously. But instead I say politely, 'So . . . how long do you think it'll be before we get there?'

'Who knows?'

I sink back on my seat, feeling my stomach churning with frustration.

We should have gone somewhere in Clerkenwell. Or Covent Garden. I am such a moron . . .

'Emma, don't worry,' says Jack. 'I'm sure it'll be great when we get there.'

'I hope so,' I say with a weak smile.

I can't make small talk. I'm using every ounce of concentration in willing the taxi to go faster. I stare out of the window, giving an inward cheer every time the postcodes on the street signs get closer to where we want to be. SW3 . . . SW11 . . . SW4!

At last! We're in Clapham. Nearly there . . .

Shit. Another bloody red traffic light. I almost can't keep still on my seat And the driver's just sitting there, like it doesn't matter.

OK, it's green! Go! Go now!

But he's pulling off in this leisurely way, as though we've got all day . . . he's chuntering down the street . . . now he's giving way to another driver! *What is he doing?*

OK. Calm down, Emma. Here's the street. We're finally here.

'So this is it!' I say, trying to sound relaxed as we get out of the taxi. 'Sorry it took a while.'

'No problem,' says Jack. 'This place looks great!'

As I hand the fare to the taxi driver, I have to admit I'm pretty pleased we came. Antonio's looks absolutely amazing! There are fairy lights decorating the familiar green façade, and helium balloons tied to the canopy, and music and laughter spilling out of the open door. I can even hear people singing inside.

'It's not normally quite *this* buzzing!' I say with a laugh, and head for the door. I can already see Antonio standing just inside.

'Hi!' I say as I push the door open. 'Antonio!'

'Emma!' says Antonio, who's standing by the door holding a glass of wine. His cheeks are flushed and he's beaming even more widely than usual. *'Bellissima!'* He kisses me on each cheek, and I feel a flood of warm relief. I was right to come here. I know the management. They'll make sure we have a wonderful time.

'This is Jack,' I say, grinning at him.

'Jack! Wonderful to meet you!' Antonio kisses Jack on each cheek too, and I giggle.

'So, could we have a table for two?'

'Ah . . .' He pulls a face of regret. 'Sweetheart, we're closed!'

'What?' I stare back at him, baffled. 'But . . . but you're not closed. People are here!' I look around at all the merry faces.

'It's a private party!' He raises his glass to someone across the room and shouts something in Italian. 'My nephew's wedding. You ever meet him? Guido. He served here a few summers ago.'

'I . . . I'm not sure.'

'He met a lovely girl at the law school. You know, he's qualified now. You ever need legal advice . . .'

'Thanks. Well . . . congratulations.'

'I hope the party goes well,' says Jack, and squeezes my arm briefly. 'Never mind, Emma, you couldn't have known.'

'Darling, I'm sorry!' says Antonio, seeing my face. 'Another night, I'll give you the best table we have. You call in advance, you let me know . . .'

'I'll do that,' I manage a smile. 'Thanks, Antonio.'

I can't even look at Jack. I dragged him all the way down to bloody Clapham for this.

I have to redeem this situation. Quickly.

'We'll go to the pub,' I say as soon as we're outside on the pavement. 'I mean, what's wrong with just sitting down with a nice drink?'

'Sounds good,' says Jack mildly, and follows me as I hurry down the street to a sign reading The Nag's Head, and push the door open. I've never been in this pub before, but surely it's bound to be fairly—

OK. Maybe not.

This has to be the grimmest pub I've ever seen in my life. Threadbare carpet, no music, and with no signs of life except a single man with a paunch.

I cannot have a date with Jack in here. I just can't.

'Right!' I say, swinging the door shut again, 'Let's think again.' I quickly look up and down the street, but apart from Antonio's everything is shut except for a couple of grotty takeaway places and a minicab firm. 'Well . . . let's just grab a taxi and head back to town!' I say, with a kind of shrill brightness. 'It won't take too long.'

I stride to the edge of the pavement and stick out my hand.

During the next three minutes not a single car passes by. Not just no taxis. No vehicles at all.

'Kind of quiet,' observes Jack at last.

'Well, this is really a residential area. Antonio's is a bit of a one-off.'

Outwardly, I'm still quite calm. But inside I'm starting to panic. What are we going to do? Should we try to walk to Clapham High Street? But it's bloody miles away.

I glance at my watch and see with a dart of shock that it's 9.15. We've spent over an hour faffing about and we haven't even had a drink. And it's all my fault. I

206

can't even organize one simple evening without it going catastrophically wrong.

Suddenly I want to burst into tears. I want to sink down on the pavement and bury my head in my hands and sob.

'How about pizza?' says Jack, and my head jerks up in sudden hope.

'Why? Do you know a pizza place round—'

'I see pizza for sale.' He nods at one of the grotty take-away places. 'And I see a bench.' He gestures to the other side of the road, where there's a tiny railed garden with paving and trees and a wooden bench. 'You get the pizza.' He smiles at me. 'I'll save the bench.'

I have never felt so mortified in my entire life. Ever.

Jack Harper takes me to the grandest, poshest restaurant in the world. And I take him to a park bench in Clapham.

'Here's your pizza,' I say, carrying the hot boxes over to where he's sitting. 'I got margarita, ham and mushroom and pepperoni.'

I can't quite believe this is going to be our supper. I mean, they aren't even *nice* pizzas. They aren't even gourmet, roasted-artichoke type of pizzas. They're just cheap slabs of dough pastry with melted, congealed cheese, and a few dodgy toppings.

'Perfect,' says Jack with a smile. He takes a large bite, then reaches into his inside pocket. 'Now, this was supposed to be your going home present, but since we're here . . .'

I gape as he produces a small, stainless steel cocktail shaker and two matching cups. He unscrews the top of the shaker and to my astonishment, pours a pink, transparent liquid into each cup.

Is that . . .

'I don't believe it!' I gaze at him, wide-eyed.

'Well, come on. I couldn't let you wonder all your life what it tasted like, could I?' He hands me a cup and raises his towards me. 'Your good health.'

'Cheers.' I take a sip of the cocktail . . . and oh my God it's yummy. Sharp and sweet, with a kick of vodka.

'Good?'

'Delicious!' I say, and take another sip.

He's being so nice to me. He's pretending he's having a good time. But what does he think inside? He must despise me. He must think I'm a complete and utter dizzy cow.

'Emma, are you OK?'

'Not really,' I say in a thick voice. 'Jack, I'm so sorry. I really am. I honestly had it all planned. We were going to go to this really cool club where celebrities go, and it was going to be really good fun . . .'

'Emma.' Jack puts his drink down and looks at me. 'I wanted to spend this evening with you. And that's what we're doing.'

'Yes. But—'

'That's what we're doing,' he repeats firmly.

Slowly he leans towards me and my heart starts to pound. Oh my God. Oh my God. He's going to kiss me. He's going to—

'Arrgh! Arrgh! Arrrgh!'

I leap up off the bench in total panic. A spider is running up my leg. A big black spider. 'Get it off!' I say, frantically. 'Get it off!'

With one brisk swipe, Jack brushes the spider off onto the grass, and I subside back on the bench, my heart racing.

And of course, the mood's completely ruined. Great. Just marvellous. Jack tries to kiss me and I shriek in horror. I'm really doing splendidly tonight.

Why was I so pathetic? I think furiously. Why did I

scream? I should have just gritted my teeth!

Not *literally* gritted my teeth, obviously. But I should have been cool. In fact, I should have been so swept away that I didn't even *notice* the spider.

'I don't suppose you're afraid of spiders,' I say to Jack, giving an awkward laugh. 'I don't suppose you're afraid of anything.'

Jack gives a noncommittal little smile in return.

'*Are* you afraid of anything?' I persist.

'Real men don't get afraid,' he says jokily.

In spite of myself, I feel a tiny prickle of discontent. Jack's not the best person in the world at talking about himself.

'So, where did you get this scar?' I ask, gesturing to his wrist.

'It's a long, boring story.' He smiles. 'You don't want to hear it.'

I do! my mind immediately says. I do want to hear it. But I just smile, and take another sip of my drink.

Now he's just staring ahead into the distance, as if I'm not even there.

Did he forget about kissing me?

Should I kiss him? No. No.

'Pete loved spiders,' he says suddenly. 'Kept them as pets. Huge, furry ones. And snakes.'

'Really?' I pull a face.

'Crazy. He was a crazy fucking guy.' He exhales sharply.

'You . . . still miss him,' I say hesitantly.

'Yes. I still miss him.'

There's another silence. In the distance I can hear a group of people leaving Antonio's, shouting to each other in Italian.

'Did he leave any family?' I say cautiously, and immediately Jack's face closes up.

'Some,' he says.

'Do you see them still?'

'Occasionally.' He exhales sharply, then turns and smiles. 'You have tomato sauce on your chin.' As he reaches up to wipe it away, he meets my eyes. Slowly, he's bending towards me. Oh my God. This is it, this is really it. This is—'

'Jack.'

We both leap in shock, and I drop my cocktail on the ground. I turn round, and stare in utter disbelief. Sven is standing at the gate of the tiny garden.

What the bloody fuck is Sven doing here?

'Great timing,' murmurs Jack. 'Hi, Sven.'

'But . . . but what's he doing here?' I stare at Jack. 'How did he know where we were?'

'He called while you were getting the pizza.' Jack sighs and rubs his face. 'I didn't know he'd get here this quickly. Emma . . . something's come up. I need to have a quick word with him. I promise it won't take long. OK?'

'OK,' I say with a little shrug. After all, what else can I say? But inside, my whole body is pulsing in frustration, bordering on anger. Trying to keep calm, I reach for the cocktail shaker, pour the remains of the pink cocktail into my cup and take a deep swig.

Jack and Sven are standing by the gate having an animated conversation in low voices. I take a sip of cocktail and casually shift along the bench so I can hear better.

'. . . what to do from here . . .'

'. . . plan B . . . back up to Glasgow . . .'

'. . . urgent . . .'

I look up and find myself meeting Sven's eye. Quickly I look away again, pretending to be studying the ground. Their voices descend even lower, and I can't hear a word. Then Jack breaks off and comes towards me.

'Emma . . . I'm really sorry about this. But I'm going to have to go.'

'*Go?*' I stare at him in dismay. 'What, now?'

'I'm going to have to go away for a few days. I'm sorry.' He sits down beside me on the bench. 'But . . . it's pretty important.'

'Oh. Oh, right.'

'Sven's ordered a car for you to take you home.'

Great, I think savagely. Thanks a lot, Sven.

'That was really . . . thoughtful of him,' I say, and trace a pattern in the dirt with my shoe.

'Emma, I really have to go,' says Jack, seeing my face. 'But I'll see you when I get back, OK? At the Corporate Family Day. And we'll . . . take it from there.'

'OK.' I try to smile. 'That would be great.'

'I had a good time tonight.'

'So did I,' I say, staring down at the bench. 'I had a really good time.'

'We'll have a good time again.' Gently he lifts my chin until I'm looking straight at him. 'I promise, Emma.'

He leans forward and this time there's no hesitation. His mouth lands on mine, sweet and firm. He's kissing me. Jack Harper is kissing me on a park bench.

His mouth is opening mine, his stubble is rough against my face. His arm creeps around me and pulls me towards him, and my breath catches in my throat. I find myself reaching under his jacket, feeling the ridges of muscle beneath his shirt, wanting to rip it off. Oh God, I want this. I want more.

Suddenly he pulls away, and I feel as if I've been wrenched out of a dream.

'Emma, I have to go.'

My mouth is prickly wet. I can still feel his skin on mine. My entire body is throbbing. This can't be the end. It can't.

211

'Don't go,' I hear myself saying thickly. 'Half an hour.'

What am I suggesting? That we do it under a *bush*?

Frankly, yes. Anywhere would do. I have never in my life been so desperate for a man.

'I don't want to go.' His dark eyes are almost opaque. 'But I have to.' He takes my hand, and I cling onto his, trying to prolong contact for as long as possible.

'So . . . I'll . . . I'll see you.' I can barely talk properly.

'I can't wait.'

'Neither can I.'

'Jack.' We both look up to see Sven at the gate.

'OK,' calls Jack. We stand up and I discreetly look away from Jack's slightly strange posture.

I could ride along in the car and—

No. *No*. Rewind. I did not think that.

When we reach the road, I see two silver cars waiting by the pavement. Sven is standing by one, and the other is obviously for me. Bloody hell. I feel like I've suddenly become part of the royal family or something.

As the driver opens the door for me, Jack touches my hand briefly. I want to grab him for a final snog, but somehow I manage to control myself.

'Bye,' he murmurs.

'Bye,' I murmur back.

Then I get into the car, the door closes with an expensive clunk, and we purr away.

SIXTEEN

We'll take it from there. That could mean . . .

Or it could mean . . .

Oh God. Every time I think about it, my stomach gives an excited little fizz. I can't concentrate at work. I can't think about anything else.

The Corporate Family Day is a company event, I keep reminding myself. *Not* a date. It'll be a strictly work occasion, and there probably won't be any opportunity at all for Jack and me to do more than say hello in a formal, boss–employee manner. Possibly shake hands. Nothing more.

But . . . you never know what might happen next.

We'll take it from there.

Oh God. Oh God.

On Saturday morning I get up extra early, exfoliate all over, Immac under my arms, rub in my most expensive body cream and paint my toenails.

Just because it's always a good thing to be well groomed. No other reason.

I choose my Gossard lacy bra and matching knickers, and my most flattering bias cut summer dress.

Then, with a slight blush, I pop some condoms into my bag. Simply because it's always good to be prepared. This is a lesson I learned when I was eleven years old at Brownies, and it's always stayed with me. OK, maybe Brown Owl was talking about spare hankies and sewing kits rather than condoms, but the principle is the same, surely?

I look in the mirror, give my lips a final coat of gloss and spray Allure all over me. OK. Ready for sex.

I mean, for Jack.

I mean . . . Oh God. Whatever.

The family day is happening at Panther House, which is the Panther Corporation's country house in Hertfordshire. They use it for training and conferences and creative brainstorming days, none of which I ever get invited to. So I've never been here before, and as I get out of the taxi, I have to admit I'm pretty impressed. It's a really nice big old mansion, with lots of windows and pillars at the front. Probably dating from the . . . older period.

'Fabulous Georgian architecture,' says someone as they crunch past on the gravel drive.

Georgian. That's what I meant.

I follow the sounds of music and walk round the house to find the event in full swing on the vast lawn. Brightly coloured bunting is festooning the back of the house, tents are dotting the grass, a band is playing on a little bandstand and children are shrieking on a bouncy castle.

'Emma!' I look up to see Cyril advancing towards me, dressed as a joker with a red and yellow pointy hat. 'Where's your costume?'

'Costume!' I try to look surprised. 'Gosh! Um . . . I didn't realize we had to have one.'

This is not entirely true. Yesterday evening at about five o'clock, Cyril sent round an urgent email to everyone in the company, reading: A REMINDER: AT THE CFD, COSTUMES ARE COMPULSORY FOR ALL PANTHER EMPLOYEES.

But honestly. How are you supposed to produce a costume with five minutes' warning? And no way was

I going to come here today in some hideous nylon outfit from the party shop.

Plus let's face it, what can they do about it now?

'Sorry,' I say vaguely, looking around for Jack. 'Still, never mind . . .'

'You people! It was on the memo, it was in the newsletter . . .' He takes hold of my shoulder as I try to walk away. 'Well, you'll have to take one of the spare ones.'

'What?' I look at him blankly. 'What spare ones?'

'I had a feeling this might happen,' says Cyril with a slight note of triumph, 'so I made advance provisions.'

A cold feeling starts to creep over me. He can't mean—

He can't possibly mean—

'We've got plenty to choose from,' he's saying.

No. No way. I have to escape. Now.

I give a desperate wriggle, but his hand is like a clamp on my shoulder. He chivvies me into a tent, where two middle-aged ladies are standing beside a rack of . . . oh my God. The most revolting, lurid man-made-fibre costumes I've ever seen. Worse than the party shop. Where did he *get* these from?

'No,' I say in panic. 'Really. I'd rather stay as I am.'

'Everybody has to wear a costume,' says Cyril firmly. 'It was in the memo!'

'But . . . but this *is* a costume!' I quickly gesture to my dress. 'I forgot to say. It's um . . . a twenties summer garden-party costume, very authentic . . .'

'Emma, this is a fun day,' snaps Cyril. 'And part of that fun derives from seeing our fellow employees and family in amusing outfits. Which reminds me, where is your family?'

'Oh.' I pull the regretful face I've been practising all week. 'They . . . actually, they couldn't make it.'

215

Which could be because I didn't tell them anything about it.

'You did tell them about it?' He eyes me suspiciously. 'You sent them the leaflet?'

'Yes!' I cross my fingers behind my back. 'Of course I told them. They would have loved to be here!'

'Well. You'll have to mingle with other families and colleagues. Here we are. Snow White.' He shoves a horrendous nylon dress with puffy sleeves towards me.

'I don't want to be Snow White—' I begin, then break off as I see Moira from Accounts miserably being pushed into a big shaggy gorilla costume. 'OK.' I grab the dress. 'I'll be Snow White.'

I almost want to cry. My beautiful flattering dress is lying in a calico bag, ready for collection at the end of the day. And I am wearing an outfit which makes me look like a six-year-old. A six-year-old with zero taste and colour-blindness.

As I emerge disconsolately from the tent, the band is briskly playing the 'Oom-pa-pa' song from *Oliver*, and someone is making an incomprehensible, crackly announcement over the loudspeaker. I look around, squinting against the sun, trying to work out who everyone is behind their disguises. I spot Paul walking along on the grass, dressed as a pirate, with three small children hanging off his legs.

'Uncle Paul! Uncle Paul!' one is shrieking. 'Do your scary face again!'

'I want a lolly!' yells another. 'Uncle Paul, I want a lolleeee!'

'Hi, Paul,' I say miserably. 'Are you having a good time?'

'Whoever invented Corporate Family Days should be shot,' he says without a flicker of humour. 'Get the hell off my foot!' he snaps at one of the children, and they all shriek with delighted laughter.

'Mummy, I don't *need* to spend a penny,' mutters Artemis, as she walks by dressed as a mermaid, in the company of a commanding woman in a huge hat.

'Artemis, there's no need to be so touchy!' booms the woman.

This is so weird. People with their families are completely different. Thank God mine aren't here.

I wonder where Jack is. Maybe he's in the house. Maybe I should—

'Emma!' I look up, and see Katie heading towards me. She's dressed in a totally bizarre carrot costume, holding the arm of an elderly man with grey hair. Who must be her father, I suppose.

Which is a bit weird, because I thought she said she was coming with—

'Emma, this is Phillip!' she says radiantly. 'Phillip, meet my friend Emma. She's the one who brought us together!'

Wh- what?

No. I don't believe it.

This is her new man? *This* is Phillip? But he has to be at least seventy!

In a total blur, I shake his hand, which is dry and papery, just like Grandpa's, and manage to make a bit of small talk about the weather. But all the time, I'm in total shock.

Don't get me wrong. I am not ageist. I am not anything-ist. I think people are all the same, whether they're black or white, male or female, young or—

But he's an old man! He's *old*!

'Isn't he lovely?' says Katie fondly, as he goes off to get some drinks. 'He's so thoughtful. Nothing's too much trouble. I've never been out with a man like him before!'

'I can believe that,' I say, my voice a little strangled. 'What exactly is the age gap between you two?'

'I'm not sure,' says Katie in surprise. 'I've never asked. Why?'

Her face is shiny and happy and totally oblivious. Has she not *noticed* how old he is?

'No reason!' I clear my throat. 'So . . . er . . . remind me. Where exactly did you meet Phillip again?'

'You know, silly!' says Katie, mock-chidingly. 'You suggested I should try somewhere different for lunch, remember? Well, I found this really unusual place, tucked away in a little street. In fact, I really recommend it.'

'Is it . . . a restaurant? A café?'

'Not exactly,' she says thoughtfully. 'I've never been anywhere like it before. You go in and someone gives you a tray, and you collect your lunch and then eat it, sitting at all these tables. And it only costs two pounds! And afterwards they have free entertainment! Like sometimes it's bingo or whist . . . sometimes it's a singsong round the piano. One time they had this brilliant tea dance! I've made loads of new friends.'

I stare at her for a few silent seconds.

'Katie,' I say at last. 'This place. It couldn't possibly be – a day care centre for the elderly?'

'Oh!' she says, looking taken aback. 'Erm . . .'

'Try and think. Is everyone who goes there on the . . . old side?'

'Gosh,' she says slowly, and screws up her brow. 'Now you mention it, I suppose everyone is kind of quite . . . mature. But honestly Emma, you should come along.' Her face brightens. 'We have a real laugh!'

'You're still *going* there?' I stare at her.

'I go every day,' she says in surprise. 'I'm on the social committee.'

'Hello again!' says Phillip cheerily, reappearing

218

with three glasses. He beams at Katie and gives her a kiss on the cheek, and she beams back. And suddenly I feel quite heart-warmed. OK, it's weird. But they do seem to make a really sweet couple.

'The man behind the stall seemed rather stressed out, poor chap,' says Phillip, as I take my first delicious sip of Pimm's, closing my eyes to savour it.

Mmm. There is absolutely nothing nicer on a summer's day than a nice cold glass of—

Hang on a minute. My eyes open. Pimm's.

Shit. I promised to do the Pimm's stall with Connor, didn't I? I glance at my watch and realize I'm already ten minutes late. Oh, bloody hell. No wonder he's stressed out.

I hastily apologize to Phillip and Katie, then hurry as fast as I can to the stall, which is in the corner of the garden. There I find Connor manfully coping with a huge queue all on his own. He's dressed as Henry VIII, with puffy sleeves and breeches, and has a huge red beard stuck to his face. He must be absolutely boiling.

'Sorry,' I mutter, sliding in beside him. 'I had to get into my costume. What do I have to do?'

'Pour out glasses of Pimm's,' says Connor curtly. 'One pound fifty each. Do you think you can manage?'

'Yes!' I say, a bit nettled. 'Of course I can manage!'

For the next few minutes we're too busy serving Pimm's to talk. Then the queue melts away, and we're left on our own again.

Connor isn't even looking at me, and he's clanking glasses around so ferociously I'm afraid he might break one. Why is he in such a bad mood?

'Connor, look, I'm sorry I'm late.'

'That's all right,' he says stiffly, and starts chopping a bundle of mint as though he wants to kill it. 'So, did you have a nice time the other evening?'

219

That's what this is all about.

'Yes, I did, thanks,' I say after a pause.

'With your new mystery man.'

'Yes,' I say, and surreptitiously scan the crowded lawn, searching for Jack.

'It's someone at work, isn't it?' Connor suddenly says, and my stomach gives a small plunge.

'Why do you say that?' I say lightly.

'That's why you won't tell me who it is.'

'It's not that! It's just . . . look, Connor, can't you just respect my privacy?'

'I think I have a right to know who I've been dumped for.' He shoots me a reproachful look.

'No you don't!' I retort, then realize that sounds a bit mean. 'I just don't think it's very helpful to discuss it.'

'Well, I'll work it out.' His jaw sets grimly. 'It won't take me long.'

'Connor, please. I really don't think—'

'Emma, I'm not stupid.' He gives me an appraising look. 'I know you a lot better than you think I do.'

I feel a flicker of uncertainty. Maybe I've underestimated Connor all this time. Maybe he does know me. Oh God. What if he guesses?

I start to slice up a lemon, constantly scanning the crowd. Where is Jack, anyway?

'I've got it,' says Connor suddenly, and I look up to see him staring at me triumphantly. 'It's Paul, isn't it?'

'What?' I gape back at him, wanting to laugh. 'No, it's not Paul! Why on earth should you think it was Paul?'

'You keep looking at him.' He gestures to where Paul is standing nearby, moodily swigging a bottle of beer. 'Every two minutes!'

'I'm not looking at him,' I say hurriedly. 'I'm just looking at . . . I'm just taking in the atmosphere.'

'So why is he hanging around here?'

'He's not! Honestly, Connor, take it from me, I'm not going out with Paul.'

'You think I'm a fool, don't you?' says Connor with a flash of anger.

'I don't think you're a fool! I just . . . I think this is a pointless exercise. You're never going to—'

'Is it Nick?' His eyes narrow. 'You and he have always had a bit of a spark going.'

'No!' I say impatiently. 'It's not Nick.'

Honestly. Clandestine affairs are hard enough as it is, without your ex-boyfriend subjecting you to the third degree. I should never have agreed to do this stupid Pimm's stall.

'Oh my God,' Connor says in a lowered voice. 'Look.'

I look up, and my stomach gives an enormous lurch. Jack is walking over the grass towards us, dressed as a cowboy, with leather chaps and a checked shirt and a proper cowboy hat.

He looks so completely and utterly sexy, I feel quite faint.

'He's coming this way!' hisses Connor. 'Quick! Tidy up that lemon peel. Hello, sir,' he says in a louder voice. 'Would you like a glass of Pimm's?'

'Thank you very much, Connor,' says Jack with a smile. Then he looks at me. 'Hello, Emma. Enjoying the day?'

'Hello,' I say, my voice about six notches higher than usual. 'Yes, it's . . . lovely!' With trembling hands I pour out a glass of Pimm's and give it to him.

'Emma! You forgot the mint!' says Connor.

'It doesn't matter about the mint,' says Jack, his eyes fixed on mine.

'You can have some mint if you want it,' I say, gazing back.

'It looks fine just the way it is.' His eyes give a tiny flash, and he takes a deep gulp of Pimm's.

This is so unreal. We can't keep our eyes off each other. Surely it's completely obvious to everyone else what's going on? Surely Connor must realize? Quickly I look away and pretend to be busying myself with the ice.

'So, Emma,' says Jack casually. 'Just to talk work briefly. That extra typing assignment I asked you about. The Leopold file.'

'Er yes?' I say, flusteredly dropping an ice-cube onto the counter.

'Perhaps we could have a quick word about it before I go?' He meets my eyes. 'I have a suite of rooms up at the house.'

'Right,' I say, my heart pounding. 'OK.'

'Say . . . one o'clock?'

'One o'clock it is.'

He saunters off, holding his glass of Pimm's, and I stand staring after him, dripping an ice-cube onto the grass.

A suite of rooms. That can only mean one thing.

Jack and I are going to have sex.

And suddenly, with no warning, I feel really, really nervous.

'I've been so stupid!' exclaims Connor, abruptly putting down his knife. 'I've been so *blind*.' He turns to face me, his eyes burning blue. 'Emma, I know who your new man is.'

I feel a huge spasm of fear.

'No you don't,' I say quickly. 'Connor, you don't know who it is. Actually, it's not anyone from work. I just made that up. It's this guy who lives over in west London, you've never met him, his name is . . . um . . . Gary, he works as a postman.'

'Don't lie to me! I know exactly who it is.' He folds his arms and gives me a long, penetrating look. 'It's Tristan from Design, isn't it?'

* * *

As soon as our stint on the stall is up, I escape from Connor and go and sit under a tree with a glass of Pimm's, glancing at my watch every two minutes. I can't quite believe how nervous I am about this. Maybe Jack knows loads of tricks. Maybe he'll expect me to be really sophisticated. Maybe he'll expect all kinds of amazing manoeuvres that I've never even heard of.

I mean . . . I don't think I'm *bad* at sex.

You know. Generally speaking. All things considered.

But what sort of standard are we talking about here? I feel like I've been competing in tiny little local shows and suddenly I'm taking on the Olympics. Jack Harper is an international multimillionaire. He must have dated models and . . . and gymnasts . . . women with enormous perky breasts . . . kinky stuff involving muscles I don't even think I *possess*.

How am I ever going to match up? How? I'm starting to feel sick. This was a bad, bad idea. I'm never going to be as good as the president of Origin Software, am I? I can just imagine her, with her long legs and $400 underwear and honed, tanned body . . . maybe a whip in her hand . . . maybe her bisexual glamour model friend at the ready to spice things up . . .

OK, just stop. This is getting ridiculous. I'll be fine. I'm *sure* I'll be fine. It'll be like doing a ballet exam – once you get into it, you forget to be nervous. My old ballet teacher always used to say to us, 'As long as you keep your legs nicely turned out and a smile on your face, you'll do splendidly.'

Which I guess kind of applies here, too.

I glance at my watch and feel a fresh spasm of fright. It's one o'clock. On the dot.

Time to go and have sex. I stand up, and do a few

surreptitious limbering-up exercises, just in case. Then I take a deep breath and, with a thumping heart, begin to walk towards the house. I've just reached the edge of the lawn when a shrill voice hits my ears.

'There she is! Emma! Cooee!'

That sounded just like my mum. Weird. I stop briefly, and turn round, but I can't see anyone. It must be a hallucination. It must be subconscious guilt trying to throw me, or something.

'Emma, turn round! Over here!'

Hang on. That sounded like Kerry.

I peer bewilderedly at the crowded scene, my eyes squinting in the sunshine. I can't see anything. I'm looking all around, but I can't see—

And then suddenly, like a Magic Eye, they spring into view. Kerry, Nev, and my mum and dad. Walking towards me. All in costume. Mum is wearing a Japanese kimono and holding a picnic basket. Dad is dressed as Robin Hood and holding two fold-up chairs. Nev is in a Superman costume and holding a bottle of wine. And Kerry is wearing an entire Marilyn Monroe outfit, including platinum blond wig and high-heeled shoes, and complacently soaking up the stares.

What's going on?

What are they *doing* here?

I didn't tell them about the Corporate Family Day. I know I didn't. I'm *positive* I didn't.

'Hi, Emma!' says Kerry as she gets near. 'Like the outfit?' She gives a little shimmy and pats her blond wig.

'Who are you supposed to be, darling?' says Mum, looking in puzzlement at my nylon dress. 'Is it Heidi?'

'I . . .' I rub my face. 'Mum . . . What are you doing here? I never – I mean, I forgot to tell you.'

'I know you did,' says Kerry. 'But your friend Artemis told me all about it the other day, when I phoned.'

I stare at her, unable to speak.

I will kill Artemis. I will murder her.

'So what time's the fancy dress contest?' says Kerry, winking at two teenage boys who are gawping at her. 'We haven't missed it, have we?'

'There . . . there isn't a contest,' I say, finding my voice.

'Really?' Kerry looks put out.

I don't believe her. This is why she's come here, isn't it? To win a stupid competition.

'You came all this way just for a fancy dress contest?' I can't resist saying.

'Of course not!' Kerry quickly regains her usual scornful expression. 'Nev and I are taking your mum and dad to Hanwood Manor. It's near here. So we thought we'd drop in.'

I feel a sparkle of relief. Thank God. We can have a little chat, then they can be on their way.

'We've brought a picnic,' says Mum. 'Now, let's find a nice spot.'

'Do you think you've got time for a picnic?' I say, trying to sound casual. 'You might get caught in traffic. In fact, maybe you should head off now, just to be on the safe side . . .'

'The table's not booked until seven!' says Kerry, giving me an odd look. 'How about under that tree?'

I watch dumbly as Mum shakes out a plaid picnic rug, and Dad sets up the two chairs. I cannot sit down and have a family picnic when Jack is waiting to have sex with me. I have to do something, quick. *Think.*

'Um, the thing is,' I say in sudden inspiration, 'the

thing is, actually, I won't be able to stay. We've all got duties to do.'

'Don't tell me they can't give you half an hour off,' says Dad.

'Emma's the linchpin of the whole organization!' says Kerry with a sarky giggle. 'Can't you tell?'

'Emma!' Cyril is approaching the picnic rug. 'Your family came after all! And in costume. Jolly good!' He beams around, his joker's hat tinkling in the breeze. 'Now make sure you all buy a raffle ticket . . .'

'Oh, we will,' says Mum. 'And we were wondering . . .' She smiles at him. 'Could Emma possibly have some time off her duties to have a picnic with us?'

'Absolutely!' says Cyril. 'You've done your stint on the Pimm's stall, haven't you, Emma? You can relax now.'

'Lovely!' says Mum. 'Isn't that good news, Emma?'

'That's great!' I manage at last with a fixed smile.

I have no choice. I have no way out of this. With stiff knees I sink down onto the rug and accept a glass of wine.

'So, is Connor here?' asks Mum, decanting chicken drumsticks onto a plate.

'Ssh! Don't Mention Connor!' says Dad in his Basil Fawlty voice.

'I thought you were supposed to be moving in with him,' says Kerry, taking a swig of champagne. 'What happened there?'

'She made him breakfast,' quips Nev, and Kerry giggles.

I try to smile, but my face won't quite do it. It's ten past one. Jack will be waiting. What can I do?

As Dad passes me a plate, I see Sven passing by.

'Sven,' I say quickly. 'Um, Mr Harper was kindly asking earlier on about my family. And whether they were here or not. Could you possibly tell him that they've . . . they've unexpectedly turned up?' I look up at him desperately and his face flickers in comprehension.

'I'll pass on the message,' he says.

And that's the end of that.

SEVENTEEN

I once read an article called 'Make Things Go Your Way' which said if a day doesn't turn out as you intended, you should go back, charting the differences between your Goals and your Results, and this will help you learn from your mistakes.

OK. Let's just chart exactly how much this day has diverged from the original plan I had this morning.

Goal: Look like sexy and sophisticated woman in beautiful, flattering dress.

Result: Look like Heidi/Munchkin extra in lurid puffy nylon sleeves.

Goal: Make secret assignation with Jack.

Result: Make secret assignation with Jack then fail to turn up.

Goal: Have fantastic sex with Jack in romantic location.

Result: Have peanut-barbecued chicken drumstick on picnic rug.

Overall Goal: Euphoria.

Overall Result: Complete misery.

All I can do is stare dumbly down at my plate, telling myself this can't last for ever. Dad and Nev have made about a million jokes about Don't Mention Connor. Kerry has shown me her new Swiss watch which cost £4,000 and boasted about how her company is expanding yet again. And now she's telling us how she played golf with the chief executive of British Airways last week and he tried to head-hunt her.

'They all try it on,' she says, taking a huge bite of chicken drumstick. 'But I say to them, if I *needed* a job . . .' She tails off. 'Did you want something?'

'Hi there,' comes a dry, familiar voice from above my head.

Very slowly I raise my head, blinking in the light.

It's Jack. Standing there against the blue sky in his cowboy outfit. He gives me a tiny, almost imperceptible smile, and I feel my heart lift. He's come to get me. I should have known he would.

'Hi!' I say, half-dazedly. 'Everyone, this is—'

'My name's Jack,' he cuts across me pleasantly. 'I'm a friend of Emma's. Emma . . .' He looks at me, his face deliberately blank. 'I'm afraid you're needed.'

'Oh dear!' I say with a whoosh of relief. 'Oh well, never mind, these things happen.'

'That's a shame!' says Mum. 'Can't you at least stay for a quick drink? Jack, you're welcome to join us, have a chicken drumstick or some quiche.'

'We have to go,' I say hurriedly. 'Don't we, Jack?'

'I'm afraid we do,' he says, and holds out a hand to pull me up.

'Sorry, everyone,' I say.

'We don't mind!' says Kerry with the same sarky laugh. 'I'm sure you've some vital job to do, Emma. In fact, I expect the whole event would collapse without you!'

Jack stops. Very slowly, he turns round.

'Let me guess,' he says pleasantly. 'You must be Kerry.'

'Yes!' she says in surprise. 'That's right.'

'And Mum . . . Dad . . .' He surveys the faces. 'And you have to be . . . Nev?'

'Spot on!' says Nev with a chortle.

'Very good!' says Mum with a laugh. 'Emma must have told you a bit about us.'

'Oh . . . she has,' agrees Jack, looking around the picnic rug again with a kind of odd fascination on his face. 'You know, there might be time for that drink after all.'

What? *What* did he say?

'Good,' says Mum. 'It's always nice to meet friends of Emma's!'

I watch in total disbelief as Jack settles comfortably down on the rug. He was supposed to be *rescuing* me from all this. Not joining in. Slowly I sink down beside him.

'So, you work for this company, Jack?' says Dad, pouring him a glass of wine.

'In a way,' says Jack after a pause. 'You could say . . . I used to.'

'Are you between jobs?' says Mum tactfully.

'You could put it like that, I guess.' His face crinkles in a little smile.

'Oh dear!' says Mum sympathetically. 'What a shame. Still, I'm sure something will come up.'

Oh God. She has absolutely no idea who he is. None of my family has any idea who Jack is.

I'm really not at all sure I like this.

'I saw Danny Nussbaum the other day in the post office, Emma,' adds Mum, briskly slicing some tomatoes. 'He asked after you.'

Out of the corner of my eye I can see Jack's eyes brightening.

'Gosh!' I say, my cheeks growing hot. 'Danny Nussbaum! I haven't thought about him for ages.'

'Danny and Emma used to step out together,' Mum explains to Jack with a fond smile. 'Such a nice boy. Very *bookish*. He and Emma used to study together in her bedroom, all afternoon.'

230

I cannot look at Jack. I cannot.

'You know . . . *Ben Hur*'s a fine film,' Jack suddenly says in thoughtful tones. 'A very fine film.' He smiles at Mum. 'Don't you think?'

I am going to kill him.

'Er . . . yes!' says Mum, a bit confused. 'Yes, I've always liked *Ben Hur*.' She cuts Jack a huge chunk of quiche and adds a slice of tomato. 'So, Jack,' she says sympathetically as she hands him a paper plate. 'Are you getting by financially?'

'I'm doing OK,' Jack replies gravely.

Mum looks at him for a moment. Then she rummages in the picnic basket and produces another Sainsbury's quiche, still in its box.

'Take this,' she says, pressing it on him. 'And some tomatoes. They'll tide you over.'

'Oh no,' says Jack at once. 'Really, I couldn't—'

'I won't take no for an answer. I insist!'

'Well, that's truly kind.' Jack gives her a warm smile.

'You want some free career advice, Jack?' says Kerry, munching a piece of chicken.

My heart gives a nervous flip. Please, *please* don't try to get Jack to do the successful woman walk.

'Now, you want to listen to Kerry,' puts in Dad proudly. 'She's our star! She has her own company.'

'Is that so?' says Jack politely.

'My own travel agency,' says Kerry with a complacent smile. 'Started from scratch. Now we have forty staff and a turnover of just over two million. And you know what my secret is?'

'I . . . have no idea,' says Jack.

Kerry leans forward and fixes him with her blue eyes.

'Golf.'

'Golf!' echoes Jack.

'Business is all about networking,' says Kerry. 'It's

all about contacts. I'm telling you, Jack, I've met most of the top businesspeople in the country on the golf course. Take any company. Take *this* company.' She spreads her arm around the scene. 'I know the top guy here. I could call him up tomorrow if I wanted to.'

I stare at her, frozen in horror.

'Really?' says Jack, sounding riveted. 'Is that so?'

'Oh yes.' She leans forward confidentially. 'And I mean, the *top* guy.'

'The top guy,' echoes Jack. 'I'm impressed.'

'Perhaps Kerry could put in a good word for you, Jack!' exclaims Mum in sudden inspiration. 'You'd do that, wouldn't you, Kerry love?'

I would burst into hysterical laughter. If it wasn't so completely and utterly hideous.

'I guess I'll have to take up golf without delay,' says Jack. 'Meet the right people.' He raises his eyebrows at me. 'What do you think, Emma?'

I can barely talk. I am beyond embarrassment. I just want to disappear into the rug and never be seen again.

'Mr Harper?' A voice interrupts and I breathe in relief. We all look up to see Cyril bending awkwardly down to Jack.

'I'm extremely sorry to interrupt, sir,' he says, glancing puzzledly around at my family as though trying to discern any reason at all why Jack Harper might be having a picnic with us. 'But Malcolm St John is here and would like a very brief word.'

'Of course,' says Jack, and smiles politely at Mum. 'If you could just excuse me a moment.'

As he carefully balances his glass on his plate and gets to his feet, the whole family exchanges confused glances.

'Giving him a second chance, then!' calls out Dad jocularly to Cyril.

'I'm sorry?' says Cyril, taking a couple of steps towards us.

'That chap Jack,' says Dad, gesturing to Jack, who's talking to a guy dressed in a navy blazer. 'You're thinking of taking him on again, are you?'

Cyril looks stiffly from Dad to me and back again.

'It's OK, Cyril!' I call lightly. 'Dad, shut up, OK?' I mutter. 'He owns the company.'

'What?' Everyone stares at me.

'He owns the company,' I say, my face hot. 'So just . . . don't make any jokes about him.'

'The man in the jester's suit owns the company?' says Mum, looking in surprise at Cyril.

'No! *Jack* does! Or at least, some great big chunk of it.' They're all still looking completely blank. 'Jack's one of the founders of the Panther Corporation!' I hiss in frustration. 'He was just trying to be modest.'

'Are you saying that guy is Jack Harper?' says Nev in disbelief.

'Yes!'

There's a flabbergasted silence. As I look around, I see that a piece of chicken drumstick has fallen out of Kerry's mouth.

'Jack Harper – the multimillionaire,' says Dad, just to make sure.

'*Multimillionaire?*' Mum looks totally confused. 'So . . . does he still want the quiche?'

'Of course he doesn't want the quiche!' says Dad testily. 'What would he want a quiche for? He can buy a million bloody quiches!'

Mum's eye starts flicking around the picnic rug in slight agitation.

'Quick!' she says suddenly. 'Put the crisps into a bowl. There's one in the hamper—'

'They're fine as they are . . .' I begin helplessly.

'Millionaires don't eat crisps from the packet!' she

233

hisses. She plops the crisps in a plastic bowl and hastily starts straightening the rug. 'Brian! Crumbs on your beard!'

'So how the hell do *you* know Jack Harper?' says Nev.

'I . . . I just know him,' I colour slightly. 'We've worked together and stuff, and he's kind of become a . . . a friend. But listen, don't act any differently,' I say quickly, as Jack shakes the hand of the blazer guy, and starts coming back towards the picnic rug. 'Just act the way you were before . . .'

Oh God. Why am I even bothering? As Jack approaches, my entire family is sitting bolt upright, staring at him in awe-struck silence.

'Hi!' I say, as naturally as possible, then quickly glare around at them.

'So . . . Jack!' says Dad self-consciously. 'Have another drink! Is this wine all right for you? Because we can easily nip to the wine shop, get something with a proper vintage.'

'It's great, thanks,' says Jack, looking a little baffled.

'Jack, what else can I get you to eat?' says Mum, flustered. 'I've got some gourmet salmon rolls some-where. Emma, give Jack your plate!' she snaps. 'He can't eat off paper.'

'So . . . Jack,' says Nev in a matey voice. 'What does a guy like you drive, then? No, don't tell me.' He lifts his hand. 'A Porsche. Am I right?'

Jack meets my eye with a quizzical expression, and I stare back him beseechingly, trying to convey to him that I had no choice, that I'm really sorry, that basically I want to die . . .

'I take it my cover's been blown,' he says with a grin.

'Jack!' exclaims Kerry, who has regained her compo-sure. She gives him an ingratiating smile and thrusts out her hand. 'Good to meet you properly.'

'Absolutely!' says Jack. 'Although . . . didn't we just meet?'

'As *professionals*,' says Kerry smoothly. 'One business-owner to another. Here's my card, and if you ever need any help with travel arrangements of any sort, please give me a call. Or if you wanted to meet up socially . . . perhaps the four of us could go out some time! Play a round? Couldn't we, Emma?'

I stare at her blankly. Since when have Kerry and I ever socialized together?

'Emma and I are practically sisters, of course,' she adds sweetly, putting her arm round me. 'I'm sure she's told you.'

'Oh, she told me a few things,' says Jack, his expression unreadable. He takes a bite of roast chicken and starts to chew it.

'We grew up together, we shared everything.' Kerry gives me a squeeze and I try to smile, but her perfume is nearly choking me.

'Isn't that nice!' says Mum in pleasure. 'I wish I had a camera.'

Jack doesn't reply. He's just giving Kerry this long, appraising look.

'We couldn't be closer!' Kerry's smile grows even more ingratiating. She's squeezing me so hard, her talons are digging into my flesh. 'Could we, Ems?'

'Er, no,' I say at last. 'No, we couldn't.'

Jack's still chewing his chicken. He swallows it, then looks up.

'So, I guess that must have been a pretty tough decision for you when you had to turn Emma down,' he says conversationally to Kerry. 'You two being so close, and all.'

'Turn her down?' Kerry gives a tinkling laugh. 'I don't know what on earth you—'

'That time she applied for work experience in your

235

firm and you turned her down,' says Jack pleasantly, and takes another bite of chicken.

I can't quite move.

That was a secret. That was supposed to be a secret.

'What?' says Dad, half laughing. 'Emma applied to Kerry?'

'I . . . I don't know what you're talking about!' says Kerry, going a little pink.

'I *think* I have this right,' says Jack, chewing. 'She offered to work for no money . . . but you still said no.' He looks perplexed for a moment. 'Interesting decision.'

Very slowly, Mum and Dad's expressions are changing.

'But of course, fortunate for us here at the Panther Corporation,' Jack adds cheerfully. 'We're *very* glad Emma didn't make a career in the travel industry. So I guess I have to thank you, Kerry! As one business-owner to another.' He smiles at her. 'You did us a big favour.'

Kerry is completely puce.

'Kerry, is this true?' says Mum sharply. 'You wouldn't help Emma when she asked?'

'You never told us about this, Emma.' Dad looks completely taken aback.

'I was embarrassed, OK?' I say, my voice jumping a bit.

'Bit cheeky of Emma to ask,' says Nev, taking a huge bite of pork pie. 'Using family connections. That's what you said, wasn't it, Kerry?'

'Cheeky?' echoes Mum in disbelief. 'Kerry, if you remember, we lent you the money to start that company. You wouldn't *have* a company without this family.'

'It wasn't like *that*,' says Kerry, darting an annoyed look at Nev. 'There's been a . . . a crossed wire. Some confusion!' She pats her hair, and gives me another smile. 'Obviously I'd be *delighted* to help you with your career, Ems. You should have said before! Just call me at the office, I'll do anything I can . . .'

I gaze back at her, full of loathing. I cannot *believe* she is trying to wriggle out of this. She is the most two-faced cow in the entire world.

'There's no crossed wire, Kerry,' I say, as calmly as I can. 'We both know exactly what happened. I asked you for help and you wouldn't give it to me. And fine, it's your company and it was your decision and you had every right to make it. But don't try and say it didn't happen, because it did.'

'Emma!' says Kerry, with a little laugh, and tries to reach for my hand. 'Silly girl! I had no idea! If I'd known it was important . . .'

If she'd known it was important? How could she not know it was important?

I jerk my hand away and stare back at Kerry. I can feel all the old hurt and humiliation building up inside me, rising up like hot water inside a pipe, until suddenly the pressure is unbearable.

'Yes you did!' I hear myself crying. 'You knew exactly what you were doing! You *knew* how desperate I was! Ever since you've arrived in this family you've tried to squash me down. You tease me about my crap career. You boast about yourself. I spend my entire life feeling small and stupid. Well, fine. You win, Kerry! You're the star and I'm not. You're the success and I'm the failure. But just don't pretend to be my best friend, OK? Because you're not, and you never will be!'

I finish, and look around the gobsmacked picnic rug, breathing hard. I have a horrible feeling I might burst into tears, any moment.

I meet Jack's eye and he gives me a tiny, way-to-go

smile. Then I risk a brief glance at Mum and Dad. They're both looking paralysed, as if they don't know what on earth to do.

The thing is, our family just doesn't *do* loud, emotional outbursts.

In fact, I'm not entirely sure what to do next myself.

'So, um . . . I'll be going, then,' I say, my voice shaking. 'I'll be off. Come on, Jack. We've got work to do.'

With wobbly legs, I turn on my heel and head off, stumbling slightly on the grass. Adrenalin is pumping round my body. I'm so wound up, I barely know what I'm doing.

'That was fantastic, Emma,' comes Jack's voice in my ear. 'You were great! Absolutely . . . logistical assessment,' he adds more loudly as we pass Cyril.

'I've never spoken like that in my life,' I say. 'I've never . . . operational management,' I quickly add, as we pass a couple of people from Accounts.

'I guessed as much,' he says, shaking his head. 'Jesus, that cousin of yours . . . valid assessment of the market.'

'She's a total – spreadsheet,' I say quickly as we pass Connor. 'So . . . I'll get that typed up for you, Mr Harper.'

Somehow we make it into the house and up the stairs. Jack leads me along a corridor, produces a key and opens a door. And we're in a room. A large, light, cream-coloured room. With a big double bed in it. The door closes, and suddenly all my nerves flood back. This is it. Finally this is it. Jack and me. Alone in a room. With a bed.

Then I catch sight of myself in a gilded mirror, and gasp in dismay. I'd forgotten I was in the stupid Snow White costume. My face is red and blotchy, my eyes are welling up, hair is all over the place, and my bra strap is showing.

This is *so* not how I thought I was looking.

'Emma, I'm really sorry I waded in there.' Jack's looking at me ruefully. 'I was way out of line. I had no right to butt in like that. I just . . . that cousin of yours got under my skin—'

'No!' I interrupt, turning to face him. 'It was *good*! I've never told Kerry what I thought of her before. Ever! It was . . . it was . . .' I tail off, breathing hard.

For a still moment there's silence. Jack's gazing at my flushed face. I'm staring back, my ribcage rising and falling, blood beating in my ears. Then suddenly he bends forward and kisses me.

His mouth is opening mine, and he's already tugging the elastic sleeves of my Snow White costume down off my shoulders, unhooking my bra. I'm fumbling for his shirt buttons. His mouth reaches my nipple and I'm starting to gasp with excitement when he pulls me down onto the sun-warmed carpet.

Oh my God, this is quick. He's ripping off my knickers. His hands are . . . his fingers are . . . I'm panting helplessly . . . We're going so fast I can barely register what's happening. This is nothing like Connor. This is nothing like I've ever – A minute ago I was standing at the door, fully clothed, and now I'm already – he's already –

'Wait,' I manage to say. 'Wait, Jack. I just need to tell you something.'

'What?' Jack looks at me with urgent, aroused eyes. 'What is it?'

'I don't know any tricks,' I whisper, a little gruffly.

'You don't what?' He pulls away slightly and stares at me.

'Tricks! I don't know any tricks,' I say defensively. 'You know, you've probably had sex with zillions of supermodels and gymnasts and they know all sorts of amazing . . .' I tail off at his expression. 'Never mind,' I say quickly. 'It doesn't matter. Forget it.'

'I'm intrigued,' says Jack. 'Which particular tricks did you have in mind?'

Why did I ever open my stupid mouth? Why?

'I didn't!' I say, growing hot. 'That's the whole point, I don't *know* any tricks.'

'Neither do I,' says Jack, totally deadpan. 'I don't know one trick.'

I feel a sudden giggle rise inside me.

'Yeah, right.'

'It's true. Not one.' He pauses thoughtfully, running a finger around my shoulder. 'Oh, OK. Maybe one.'

'What?' I say at once.

'Well . . .' He looks at me for a long moment, then shakes his head. 'No.'

'Tell me!' And now I can't help giggling out loud.

'Show, not tell,' he murmurs against my ear, and pulls me towards him. 'Did nobody ever teach you that?'

EIGHTEEN

I'm in love.

I, Emma Corrigan, am in love.

For the first time ever in my entire life, I'm totally, one hundred per cent in love! I spent all night with Jack at the Panther mansion. I woke up in his arms. We had sex about ninety-five times and it was just . . . perfect. (And somehow tricks didn't even seem to come into it. Which was a bit of a relief.)

But it's not just the sex. It's everything. It's the way he had a cup of tea waiting for me when I woke up. It's the way he turned on his laptop especially for me to look up all my Internet horoscopes and helped me choose the best one. He knows all the crappy, embarrassing bits about me which I normally try and hide from any man for as long as possible . . . and he loves me anyway.

So he didn't exactly *say* he loved me. But he said something even better. I still keep rolling it blissfully round my head. We were lying there this morning, both just kind of staring up at the ceiling, when all at once I said, without quite intending to, 'Jack, how come you remembered about Kerry turning me down for work experience?'

'What?'

'How come you remembered about Kerry turning me down?' I swivelled my head slowly to look at him.

241

'And not just that. Every single thing I told you on that plane. Every little detail. About work, about my family, about Connor . . . everything. You remember it all. And I just don't get it.'

'What don't you get?' said Jack with a frown.

'I don't get why someone like you would be interested in my stupid, boring little life,' I said, my cheeks prickling with embarrassment.

Jack looked at me silently for a moment.

'Emma, your life is not stupid and boring.'

'It is!'

'It's not.'

'Of course it is! I never do anything exciting, I never do anything clever, I haven't got my own company, or invented anything—'

'You want to know why I remember all your secrets?' interrupted Jack. 'Emma, the minute you started talking on that plane – I was gripped.'

I stared at him in disbelief.

'You were gripped?' I said, to make sure. 'By me?'

'I was gripped,' he repeated gently, and he leant over and kissed me.

Gripped!

Jack Harper was gripped by my life! By me!

And the point is, if I'd never spoken to him on that plane – and if I'd never blurted out all that stuff – then this would never have happened. We would never have found each other. It was fate. I was *meant* to get on that plane. I was *meant* to get upgraded. I was *meant* to spill my secrets.

As I arrive home, I'm glowing all over. A lightbulb has switched on inside me. Suddenly I know what the meaning of life is. Jemima is wrong. Men and women aren't enemies. Men and women are *soulmates*. And if they were just honest, right from the word go, then they'd all realize it. All this being mysterious and aloof is complete rubbish. Everyone should share their secrets straight away!

I'm so inspired, I think I'm going to write a book on relationships. It will be called 'Don't Be Scared To Share', and it will show that men and women should be honest with each other and they'll communicate better, and understand each other, and never have to pretend about anything, ever again. And it could apply to families, too. And politics! Maybe if world leaders all told each other a few personal secrets, then there wouldn't be any more wars! I think I'm really on to something.

I float up the stairs and unlock the door of our flat.

'Lissy!' I call. 'Lissy, I'm in love!'

There isn't any reply, and I feel a twinge of disappointment. I wanted someone to talk to. I wanted someone to tell all about my brilliant new theory of life and—

I hear a thumping sound from her room, and stand completely still in the hallway, transfixed. Oh my God. The mysterious thumping sounds. There's another one. Then two more. What on earth—

And then I see it, through the door of the sitting room. On the floor, next to the sofa. A briefcase. A black leather briefcase. It's him. It's Jean-Paul. He's in there. Right this minute! I take a few steps forward and stare at her door, intrigued.

What are they *doing*?

I just don't believe her story that they're having sex. But what else could it be? What else could it possibly—

OK . . . Just stop. It's none of my business. If Lissy doesn't want to tell me what she's up to, she doesn't want to tell me. Feeling very mature, I walk into the kitchen and pick up the kettle to make myself a cup of coffee.

Then I put it down again. *Why* doesn't she want to tell me? *Why* does she have a secret from me? We're best friends! I mean it was *she* who said we shouldn't have any secrets.

I can't stand this. Curiosity is niggling at me like a burr. It's unbearable. And this could be my only chance to find out the truth. But how? I can't just walk in there. Can I?

All of a sudden, a little thought occurs to me. Suppose I *hadn't* seen the briefcase? Suppose I'd just walked into the flat perfectly innocently, like I normally do, and happened to go straight to Lissy's door and happened to open it? Nobody could blame me then, could they? It would just be an honest mistake.

I come out of the kitchen, listen intently for a moment, then quickly tiptoe back towards the front door.

Start again. I'm walking into the flat for the first time.

'Hi, Lissy!' I call self-consciously, as though a camera's trained on me. 'Gosh! I wonder where she is. Maybe I'll . . . um . . . try her bedroom!'

I walk down the corridor, attempting a natural stride, arrive at her door and give the tiniest of knocks.

There's no response from inside. The thumping noises have died down. I stare at the blank wood, feeling a sudden apprehension.

Am I really going to do this?

Yes, I am. I just *have* to know.

I grasp the handle, open the door – and give a scream of terror.

The image is so startling, I can't make sense of it. Lissy's naked. They're both naked. She and the guy are tangled together in the strangest position I've ever, ever . . . her legs are up in the air, and his are twisted round her, and they're both scarlet in the face and panting.

'I'm sorry!' I stutter. 'God, I'm sorry!'

'Emma, wait!' I hear Lissy shout as I scuttle away to my room, slam the door and sink onto my bed.

My heart is pounding. I almost feel sick. I've never been so shocked in my entire life. I should never have opened that door. I should *never* have opened that door.

She was telling the truth! They were having sex! But I mean, what kind of weird, contorted sex was that? Bloody hell. I never realized. I never—

I feel a hand on my shoulder, and give a fresh scream.

'Emma, calm down!' says Lissy. 'It's me! Jean-Paul's gone.'

I can't look up. I can't meet her eye.

'Lissy, I'm sorry,' I gabble, staring at the floor. 'I'm sorry! I didn't mean to do that. I should never have . . . your sex life is your own affair.'

'Emma, we weren't having sex, you dope!'

'You were! I saw you! You didn't have any clothes on.'

'We did have clothes on. Emma, look at me!'

'No!' I say in panic. 'I don't want to look at you!'

'*Look* at me!'

Apprehensively, I raise my head, and gradually my eyes focus on Lissy, standing in front of me.

Oh. Oh . . . right. She's wearing a flesh-coloured leotard.

'Well what were you doing if you weren't having sex?' I say, almost accusingly. 'And why are you wearing that?'

'We were dancing,' says Lissy, looking embarrassed.

'What?' I stare at her in utter bewilderment.

'We were dancing, OK? That's what we were doing!'

'*Dancing?* But . . . why were you dancing?'

This makes no sense at all. Lissy and a French guy

called Jean-Paul dancing in her bedroom? I feel like I've landed in the middle of some weird dream.

'I've joined this group,' says Lissy after a pause.

'Oh my God. Not a cult—'

'No, not a cult. It's just . . .' She bites her lip. 'It's some lawyers who've got together and formed a . . . a dance group.'

A dance group?

For a few moments I can't quite speak. Now that my shock's died down, I have this horrible feeling that I might possibly be about to laugh.

'You've joined a group of . . . dancing lawyers.'

'Yes.' Lissy nods.

An image pops into my head of a bunch of portly barristers dancing around in their wigs and I can't help it, I give a snort of laughter.

'You see!' cries Lissy. 'That's why I didn't tell you. I *knew* you'd laugh!'

'I'm sorry!' I say. 'I'm sorry! I'm not laughing. I think it's really great!' Another hysterical giggle bursts from me. 'It's just . . . I don't know. Somehow the idea of dancing lawyers . . .'

'We're not all lawyers,' she says defensively. 'There are a couple of merchant bankers, too, and a judge . . . Emma, stop laughing!'

'I'm sorry,' I say helplessly. 'Lissy, I'm not laughing at you, honestly.' I take a deep breath and try desperately to clamp my lips together. But all I can see is merchant bankers dressed in tutus, clutching their briefcases, dancing to *Swan Lake*. A judge leaping across the stage, robes flying.

'It's not funny!' Lissy's saying. 'It's just a few like-minded professionals who want to express themselves through dance. What's wrong with that?'

'I'm sorry,' I say again, wiping my eyes and trying to regain control of myself. 'Nothing's wrong with it. I think it's brilliant. So . . . are you having a show, or anything?'

'It's in three weeks. That's why we've been doing extra practices.'

'Three weeks?' I stare at her, my laughter melting away. 'Weren't you going to *tell* me?'

'I . . . I hadn't decided,' she says, scuffing her dancing shoe on the floor. 'I was embarrassed.'

'Don't be embarrassed!' I say in dismay. 'Lissy, I'm sorry I laughed. I think it's brilliant. And I'm going to come and watch. I'll sit right in the front row . . .'

'Not the front row. You'll put me off.'

'I'll sit in the middle, then. Or at the back. Wherever you want me.' I give her a curious look. 'Lissy, I never knew you could dance.'

'Oh, I can't,' she says at once. 'I'm crap. It's just a bit of fun. D'you want a coffee?'

As I follow Lissy into the kitchen, she gives me a raised-eyebrow look. 'So, you've got a bit of a nerve, accusing *me* of having sex. Where were you last night?'

'With Jack,' I admit with a dreamy smile. 'Having sex. All night.'

'I knew it!'

'Oh God, Lissy. I'm completely in love with him.'

'In *love*?' She flicks on the kettle. 'Emma, are you sure? You've only known him about five minutes.'

'That doesn't matter! We're already complete soulmates. There's no need to pretend with him . . . or try to be something I'm not . . . and the sex is amazing . . . He's everything I never had with Connor. Everything. And he's *interested* in me. You know, he asks me questions all the time, and he seems really genuinely fascinated by the answers.'

I spread my arms with a blissful smile and sink down onto a chair. 'You know, Lissy, all my life I had this feeling that something wonderful was about to happen to me. I always just . . . *knew* it, deep down inside. And now it has.'

'So where is he now?' says Lissy, shaking coffee into the cafetière.

'He's going away for a bit. He's going to brainstorm some new concept with a creative team.'

'What?'

'I dunno. He didn't say. It'll be really intense and he probably won't be able to phone me. But he's going to email every day,' I add happily.

'Biscuit?' says Lissy, opening the tin.

'Oh, er . . . yes. Thanks.' I take a digestive and give it a thoughtful nibble. 'You know, I've got this whole new theory about relationships. It's so simple. Everyone in the world should be more honest with each other. Everyone should share! Men and women should share, families should share, world leaders should share!'

'Hmm.' Lissy looks at me silently for a few moments. 'Emma, did Jack ever tell you why he had to go rushing off in the middle of the night that time?'

'No,' I say in surprise. 'But it's his business.'

'Did he ever tell you what all those phone calls were about on your first date?'

'Well . . . no.'

'Has he told you anything about himself other than the bare minimum?'

'He's told me plenty!' I say defensively. 'Lissy, what's your problem?'

'I don't have a problem,' she says mildly. 'I'm just wondering . . . is it you who's doing all the sharing?'

'What?'

'Is he sharing himself with you?' She pours hot water onto the coffee. 'Or are you just sharing yourself with him?'

'We're sharing with each other,' I say, looking away and fiddling with a fridge magnet.

Which is true, I tell myself firmly. Jack's shared loads with me! I mean, he's told me . . .

He's told me all about . . .

Well, anyway. He probably just hasn't been in the mood for talking very much. Is that a crime?

'Have some coffee,' says Lissy, handing me a mug.

'Thanks,' I say, a touch grudgingly, and Lissy sighs.

'Emma, I'm not trying to spoil things. He does seem really lovely—'

'He is! Honestly, Lissy, you don't know what he's like. He's so romantic. Do you know what he said this morning? He said the minute I started talking on that plane, he was gripped.'

'Really?' Lissy gazes at me. 'He said that? That is pretty romantic.'

'I told you!' I can't help beaming at her. 'Lissy, he's perfect!'

NINETEEN

For the next couple of weeks, nothing can pierce my happy glow. Nothing. I waft into work on a cloud, sit all day smiling at my computer terminal, then waft home again. Paul's sarcastic comments bounce off me like bubbles. I don't even notice when Artemis introduces me to a visiting advertising team as her personal secretary. They can all say what they like. Because what they don't know is that when I'm smiling at my computer, it's because Jack has just sent me another funny little email. What they don't know is that the guy who employs them all is in love with me. *Me.* Emma Corrigan. The junior.

'Well, of course, I had several in-depth conversations with Jack Harper on the subject,' I can hear Artemis saying on the phone as I tidy up the proofs cupboard. 'Yup. And he felt – as I do – that the concept really needed to be refocused.'

Bullshit! She never had any in-depth conversations with Jack Harper. I'm almost tempted to email him straight away and tell him how she's using his name in vain.

Except that would be a bit mean.

And besides, she's not the only one. Everyone is dropping Jack Harper into their conversations, left, right and centre. It's as if now he's gone, everyone's suddenly pretending they were his best friend and he thought their idea was perfect.

Apart from me. I'm just keeping my head down and not mentioning his name at all.

Partly because I know that if I do, I'll blush bright red, or give some huge, goofy smile or something. Partly because I have a horrible feeling that if I once start talking about Jack, I won't be able to stop. But mainly because no-one ever brings the subject up with me. After all, what would I know about Jack Harper? I'm only the crappy assistant, after all.

'Hey!' says Nick, looking up from his phone. 'Jack Harper's going to be on television!'

'What?'

I feel a jolt of surprise. Jack's going to be on television?

How come he didn't tell me?

'Is a TV crew coming to the office, or anything?' says Artemis, smoothing down her hair.

'Dunno.'

'OK folks,' says Paul, coming out of his office. 'Jack Harper has done an interview on *Business Watch*, and it's being broadcast at twelve. A television is being set up in the large meeting room; anyone who would like to can go along and watch there. But we need one person to stay behind and man the phones.' His gaze falls on me. 'Emma. You can stay.'

'What?' I say blankly.

'You can stay and man the phones,' says Paul. 'OK?'

'No! I mean . . . I want to watch!' I say in dismay. 'Can't someone else stay behind? Artemis, can't you stay?'

'*I'm* not staying!' says Artemis at once. 'Honestly, Emma, don't be so selfish. It won't be at all interesting for you.'

'Yes it will!'

'No it won't.' She rolls her eyes.

'It will,' I say desperately. 'He's . . . he's my boss too!'

'Yes, well,' says Artemis sarcastically, 'I think there's a slight difference. You've barely even spoken to Jack Harper.'

'I have!' I say before I can stop myself. 'I have! I . . .' I break off, my cheeks turning pink. 'I . . . once went to a meeting he was at . . .'

'And served him a cup of tea?' Artemis meets Nick's eyes with a little smirk.

I stare at her furiously, blood pounding through my ears, wishing just once I could think of something really scathing and clever to put Artemis down.

'Enough, Artemis,' says Paul. 'Emma, you're staying here, and that's settled.'

By five to twelve the office is completely empty. Apart from me, a fly and a whirring fax machine. Disconsolately I reach into my desk drawer and take out an Aero. And a Flake for good measure. I'm just unwrapping the Aero and taking a big bite when the phone rings.

'OK,' comes Lissy's voice down the line. 'I've set the video.'

'Thanks, Liss,' I say through a mouthful of chocolate. 'You're a star.'

'I can't believe you're not allowed to watch.'

'I know. It's completely unfair.' I slump deeper in my chair and take another bite of Aero.

'Well, never mind, we'll watch it again tonight. Jemima's going to put the video on in her room too, so we should definitely catch it.'

'What's Jemima doing at home?' I say in surprise.

'She's taken a sickie so she can do a home spa day. Oh, and your dad rang,' she adds cautiously.

'Oh right.' I feel a flicker of apprehension. 'What did he say?'

I haven't talked to Mum or Dad since the débâcle at

the Corporate Family Day. I just can't bring myself to. It was all too painful and embarrassing, and for all I know, they've completely taken Kerry's side.

So when Dad rang here on the following Monday, I said I was really busy and I'd call him back – and, never did. And the same thing at home.

I know I'll have to talk to them some time. But not now. Not while I'm so happy.

'He'd seen the trailer for the interview,' says Lissy. 'He recognized Jack and just wondered if you knew about it. And he said . . .' She pauses. 'He really wanted to talk to you about a few things.'

'Oh.' I stare at my notepad, where I've doodled a huge spiral over a telephone number I was supposed to be keeping.

'Anyway, he and your mum are going to be watching it,' says Lissy. 'And your grandpa.'

Great. Just great. The entire world is watching Jack on television. The entire world except me.

When I've put the phone down, I go and get myself a coffee from the new machine, which actually does make a very nice *café au lait*. I come back and look around the quiet office, then go and pour orange juice into Artemis's spider plant. And some photocopier toner for good measure.

Then I feel a bit mean. It's not the plant's fault, after all.

'Sorry,' I say out loud, and touch one of its leaves. 'It's just your owner is a real cow. But then, you probably knew that.'

'Talking to your mystery man?' comes a sarcastic voice from behind me, and I turn round in shock, to see Connor standing in the doorway.

'Connor!' I say. 'What are you doing here?'

'I'm on my way to watch the TV interview. But I just wanted a quick word.' He takes a few steps into the office, and fixes me with an accusing stare. 'So. You lied to me.'

Oh shit. Has Connor guessed? Did he see something at the Corporate Family Day?

'What do you mean?' I say nervously.

'I've just had a little chat with Tristan from Design.' Connor's voice swells with indignation. 'He's gay! You're not going out with him at all, are you?'

He cannot be serious. Connor didn't *seriously* think I was going out with Tristan from Design, did he? I mean, Tristan could not look more gay if he wore leopardskin hotpants, carried a handbag, and walked around humming Barbra Streisand hits.

'No,' I say, managing to keep a straight face. 'I'm not going out with Tristan.'

'Well!' says Connor, nodding as though he's scored a hundred points and doesn't quite know what to do with them. 'Well. I just don't see why you feel it necessary to lie to me.' He lifts his chin in wounded dignity. 'That's all. I just would have thought we could be a little honest with each other.'

'Connor, it's just . . . it's complicated. OK?'

'Fine. Whatever. It's your boat, Emma.'

There's a slight pause.

'It's my what?' I say puzzledly. 'My *boat*?'

'Court,' he says with a flash of annoyance. 'I meant to say . . . the ball's in your court.'

'Oh right,' I say, none the wiser. 'Er . . . OK. I'll bear that in mind.'

'Good.' He gives me his most wounded-martyr look, and starts walking away.

'Wait!' I say suddenly. 'Hang on a minute! Connor, could you do me a real favour?' I wait until he turns, then pull a wheedling face. 'Could you possibly man the phones here while I quickly go and watch Jack Harper's interview?'

I know Connor isn't my number one fan at the moment. But I don't exactly have a lot of choice.

'Could I do *what*?' Connor stares at me in astonishment.

'Could you man the phones? Just for half an hour. I'd be so incredibly grateful . . .'

'I can't believe you're even *asking* me that!' says Connor incredulously. 'You *know* how important Jack Harper is to me! Emma, I really don't know what you've turned into.'

After he's stalked off, I sit there for twenty minutes. I take several messages for Paul, one for Nick and one for Caroline. I file a couple of letters. I address a couple of envelopes. And then suddenly, I've had it.

This is stupid. This is more than stupid. It's ridiculous. I love Jack. He loves me. I should be there, supporting him. I pick up my coffee and hurry along the corridor. The meeting room is crowded with people, but I edge in at the back, and squeeze between two guys who aren't even *watching* Jack, but are discussing some football match.

'What are *you* doing here?' says Artemis, as I arrive at her side. 'What about the phones?'

'No taxation without representation,' I hear myself responding coolly, which perhaps isn't exactly appropriate (I'm not even sure what it means), but has the desired effect of shutting her up.

I crane my neck so I can see over everyone's heads, and my eyes focus on the screen – and there he is. Sitting on a chair in a studio, in jeans and a white T-shirt. There's a bright blue backdrop and the words 'Business Inspirations' behind him, and two smart-looking interviewers sitting opposite him.

There he is. The man I love.

This is the first time I've seen him since we slept

together, it suddenly occurs to me. But his face is as warm as ever, and his eyes look all dark and glossy under the studio lights.

Oh God, I want to kiss him.

If no-one else was here I would go up to the television set and kiss it. I honestly would.

'What have they asked him so far?' I murmur to Artemis.

'They're talking to him about how he works. His inspirations, his partnership with Pete Laidler, stuff like that.'

'Sssh!' says someone else.

'Of course it was tough after Pete died,' Jack's saying. 'It was tough for all of us. But recently . . .' He pauses. 'Recently my life has turned around and I'm finding inspiration again. I'm enjoying it again.'

A small tingle runs over me.

He has to be referring to me. He has to be. I've turned his life around! Oh my God. That's even more romantic than 'I was gripped'.

'You've already expanded into the sports drinks market,' the male interviewer is saying. 'Now I believe you're looking to expand into the women's market.'

'What?'

There's a *frisson* around the room, and people start turning their heads.

'We're going into the women's market?'

'Since when?'

'I knew, actually,' Artemis is saying smugly. 'Quite a few people have known for a while—'

I stare at the screen, instantly recalling those people up in Jack's office. That's what the ovaries were for. Gosh, this is quite exciting. A new venture!

'Can you give us any further details about that?' the

male interviewer is saying. 'Will this be a soft drink marketed at women?'

'It's very early stages,' says Jack. 'But we're planning an entire line. A drink, clothing, a fragrance. We have a strong creative vision.' He smiles at the man. 'We're excited.'

'So, what's your target market this time?' asks the man, consulting his notes. 'Are you aiming at sports-women?'

'Not at all,' says Jack. 'We're aiming at . . . the girl on the street.'

'The "girl on the street"?' The female interviewer sits up, looking slightly affronted. 'What's that supposed to mean? Who is this girl on the street?'

'She's twenty-something,' says Jack after a pause. 'She works in an office, takes the tube to work, goes out in the evenings and comes home on the night bus . . . just an ordinary, nothing-special girl.'

'There are thousands of them,' puts in the man with a smile.

'But the Panther brand has always been associated with men,' chips in the woman, looking sceptical. 'With competition. With masculine values. Do you really think you can make the switch to the female market?'

'We've done research,' says Jack pleasantly. 'We feel we know our market.'

'Research!' she scoffs. 'Isn't this just another case of men telling women what they want?'

'I don't believe so,' says Jack, still pleasantly, but I can see a slight flicker of annoyance pass across his face.

'Plenty of companies have tried to switch markets without success. How do you know you won't just be another one of them?'

'I'm confident,' says Jack.

God, why is she being so aggressive? I think indignantly. Of course Jack knows what he's doing!

'You round up a load of women in some focus group and ask them a few questions! How does that tell you anything?'

'That's only a small part of the picture, I can assure you,' says Jack evenly.

'Oh, come on,' the woman says, leaning back and folding her arms. 'Can a company like Panther – can a man like you – *really* tap into the psyche of, as you put it, an ordinary, nothing-special girl?'

'Yes. I can!' Jack meets her gaze square-on. 'I know this girl.'

'You *know* her?' The woman raises her eyebrows.

'I know who this girl is,' says Jack. 'I know what her tastes are; what colours she likes. I know what she eats, I know what she drinks. I know what she wants out of life. She's size twelve but she'd like to be size ten. She . . .' he spreads his arms as though searching for inspiration. 'She eats Cheerios for breakfast and dips Flakes in her cappuccinos.'

I look in surprise at my hand, holding a Flake. I was about to dip it into my coffee. And . . . I had Cheerios this morning.

'We're surrounded these days by images of perfect, glossy people,' Jack is saying with animation. 'But this girl is real. She has bad hair days, and good hair days. She wears G-strings even though she finds them uncomfortable. She writes out exercise routines, then ignores them. She pretends to read business journals but hides celebrity magazines inside them.'

I stare blankly at the television screen.

Just . . . hang on a minute. This all sounds a bit familiar.

'That's *exactly* what you do, Emma,' says Artemis.

'I've seen your copy of *OK!* inside *Marketing Week*.'
She turns to me with a mocking laugh and her gaze
lands on my Flake.

'She loves clothes but she's not a fashion victim,'
Jack is saying on screen. 'She'll wear, maybe, a pair of
jeans . . .'

Artemis stares in disbelief at my Levis.

'. . . and a flower in her hair . . .'

Dazedly I lift a hand and touch the fabric rose in my
hair.

He can't—

He can't be talking about—

'Oh . . . my . . . God,' says Artemis slowly.

'What?' says Caroline, next to her. She follows
Artemis's gaze, and her expression changes.

'Oh my God! Emma! It's you!'

'It's not,' I say, but my voice won't quite work properly.

'It is!'

A few people start nudging each other and turning
to look at me.

'She reads fifteen horoscopes every day and chooses
the one she likes best . . .' Jack's voice is saying.

'It is you! It's exactly you!'

'. . . she scans the back of highbrow books and
pretends she's read them . . .'

'I *knew* you hadn't read *Great Expectations*!' says
Artemis triumphantly.

'. . . she adores sweet sherry . . .'

'Sweet *sherry*?' says Nick, turning in horror. 'You
cannot be serious.'

'It's Emma!' I can hear people saying on the other
side of the room. 'It's Emma Corrigan!'

'*Emma?*' says Katie, looking straight at me in disbelief. 'But . . . but . . .'

'It's not Emma!' says Connor all of a sudden, with a

laugh. He's standing over on the other side of the room, leaning against the wall. 'Don't be ridiculous! Emma's size eight, for a start. Not size twelve!'

'Size eight?' says Artemis with a snort of laughter.

'Size *eight*!' Caroline giggles. 'That's a good one!'

'Aren't you size eight?' Connor looks at me bewilderedly. 'But you said . . .'

'I . . . I know I did.' I swallow, my face like a furnace. 'But I was . . . I was . . .'

'Do you really buy all your clothes from thrift shops and pretend they're new?' says Caroline, looking up with interest from the screen.

'No!' I say defensively. 'I mean, yes, maybe . . . sometimes . . .'

'She weighs 135 pounds, but pretends she weighs 125,' Jack's voice is saying.

What? *What?*

My entire body contracts in shock.

'I do not!' I yell in outrage at the screen. 'I do not weigh anything like 135 pounds! I weigh . . . about . . . 128 . . . and a half . . .' I tail off as the entire room turns to stare at me.

'. . . hates crochet . . .'

There's an almighty gasp from across the room.

'You hate crochet?' comes Katie's disbelieving voice.

'No!' I say, swivelling in horror. 'That's wrong! I love crochet! You know I love crochet.'

But Katie is stalking furiously out of the room.

'She cries when she hears the Carpenters,' Jack's voice is saying on the screen. 'She loves Abba but she can't stand jazz . . .'

Oh no. Oh no oh no . . .

Connor is staring at me as though I have personally driven a stake through his heart.

'You can't stand . . . *jazz*?'

It's like one of those dreams where everyone can see your underwear and you want to run but you can't. I can't tear myself away. All I can do is stare ahead in agony as Jack's voice continues inexorably.

All my secrets. All my personal, private secrets. Revealed on television. I'm in such a state of shock, I'm not even taking them all in.

'She wears lucky underwear on first dates . . . she borrows designer shoes from her flatmate and passes them off as her own . . . pretends to kick-box . . . confused about religion . . . worries that her breasts are too small . . .'

I close my eyes, unable to bear it. My breasts. He mentioned my *breasts*. On *television*.

'When she goes out, she can play sophisticated, but on her bed . . .'

I'm suddenly faint with fear.

No. No. Please not this. Please, *please* . . .

'. . . she has a Barbie bedcover.'

A huge roar of laughter goes round the room, and I bury my face in my hands. I am beyond mortification. *No-one* was supposed to know about my Barbie bedcover. *No-one*.

'Is she sexy?' the interviewer is asking, and my heart gives a huge jump. I stare at the screen, unable to breathe for apprehension. What's he going to say?

'She's very sexual,' says Jack at once, and all eyes swivel towards me, agog. 'This is a modern girl who carries condoms in her purse.'

OK. Every time I think this can't get any worse, it does.

My *mother* is watching this. My *mother*.

'But maybe she hasn't reached her full potential . . . maybe there's a side of her which has been frustrated . . .'

I can't look at Connor. I can't look anywhere.

'Maybe she's willing to experiment . . . maybe she's had – I don't know – a lesbian fantasy about her best friend.'

No! No! My entire body clenches in horror. I have a sudden image of Lissy watching the screen at home, wide-eyed, clasping a hand over her mouth. She'll know it was her. I will never be able to look her in the eye again.

'It was a *dream*, OK?' I manage desperately, as everyone gawps at me. 'Not a fantasy. They're different!'

I feel like throwing myself at the television. Draping my arms over it. Stopping him.

But it wouldn't do any good, would it? A million TVs are on, in a million homes. People, everywhere, are watching.

'She believes in love and romance. She believes her life is one day going to be transformed into something wonderful and exciting. She has hopes and fears and worries, just like anyone. Sometimes she feels frightened.' He pauses, and adds in a softer voice, 'Sometimes she feels unloved. Sometimes she feels she will never gain approval from those people who are most important to her.'

As I stare at Jack's warm, serious face on the screen, I feel my eyes stinging slightly.

'But she's brave and goodhearted and faces her life head on . . .' He shakes his head dazedly and smiles at the interviewer. 'I'm . . . I'm so sorry. I don't know what happened there. I guess I got a little carried away. Could we—' His voice is abruptly cut off by the interviewer.

Carried away.

He got a little carried away.

This is like saying Hitler was a tad aggressive.

'Jack Harper, many thanks for talking to us,' the interviewer starts saying. 'Next week, we'll be chatting to the charismatic king of motivational videos, Ernie Powers. Meanwhile, many thanks again to . . .'

Everyone stares at the screen as she finishes her spiel and the programme's music starts. Then someone leans forward and switches the television off.

For a few seconds the entire room is silent. Everyone is gaping at me, as though they're expecting me to make a speech, or do a little dance or something. Some faces are sympathetic, some are curious, some are gleeful and some are just Jeez-am-I-glad-I'm-not-you.

Now I know exactly how zoo animals feel.

I am never visiting a zoo again.

'But . . . but I don't understand,' comes a voice from across the room, and all the heads swivel avidly towards Connor, like at a tennis match. He's staring at me, his face red with confusion. 'How does Jack Harper know so much about you?'

Oh God. I know Connor got a really good degree from Manchester University and everything. But sometimes he is so slow on the uptake.

The heads have swivelled back towards me again.

'I . . .' My whole body is prickling with embarrassment. 'Because we . . . we . . .'

I can't say it out loud. I just can't.

But I don't have to. Connor's face is slowly turning different colours.

'No,' he gulps, staring at me as though he's seen a ghost. And not just any old ghost. A really big ghost with clanky chains going 'Whoooarr!'

'No,' he says again. 'No. I don't believe it.'

'Connor—' says someone, putting a hand on his shoulder, but he shrugs it off.

'Connor, I'm really sorry,' I say helplessly.

'You're joking!' exclaims some guy in the corner,

who is obviously even slower than Connor, and has just had it spelled out to him, word for word. He looks up at me. 'So how long has this been going on?'

It's as if he opened the floodgates. Suddenly everyone in the entire room starts pitching questions at me. I can't hear myself think for the babble.

'Is that why he came to Britain? To see you?'

'Are you going to marry him?'

'You know, you don't *look* like you weigh 135 pounds . . .'

'Do you really have a Barbie bedspread?'

'So in the lesbian fantasy, was it just the two of you, or . . .'

'Have you had sex with Jack Harper at the office?'

'Is that why you dumped Connor?'

I can't cope with this. I have to get out of here. Now.

Without looking at anyone, I get to my feet and stumble out of the room. As I head down the corridor, I'm too dazed to think of anything other than I must get my bag and go. Now.

I enter the empty marketing department, where phones are shrilly ringing around. The habit's too ingrained, I can't ignore them.

'Hello?' I say, picking up one randomly.

'So!' comes Jemima's furious voice. '"She borrows designer shoes from her flatmate and passes them off as her own." Whose shoes might those be, then? Lissy's?'

'Look, Jemima, can I just . . . I'm sorry . . . I have to go,' I say feebly, and put the phone down.

No more phones. Get bag. Go.

As I zip up my bag with trembling hands, a couple of people who have followed me into the office are picking up some of the ringing phones.

'Emma, your grandad's on the line,' says Artemis, putting her hand over the receiver. 'Something about the night bus and he'll never trust you again?'

'You have a call from Harvey's Bristol Cream publicity department,' chimes in Caroline. 'They want to know where they can send you a free case of sweet sherry?'

'How did they get my name? How? Has the word spread already? Are the women on reception *telling* everybody?'

'Emma, I have your dad here,' says Nick. 'He says he needs to talk to you urgently . . .'

'I can't,' I say numbly. 'I can't talk to anybody. I have to . . . I have to . . .'

I grab my jacket and almost run out of the office and down the corridor to the stairs. Everywhere, people are making their way back to their offices after watching the interview, and they all stare at me as I hurry by.

'Emma!' As I'm nearing the stairs, a woman named Fiona, whom I barely know, grabs me by the arm. She weighs about 300 pounds and is always campaigning for bigger chairs and wider doorways. 'Never be ashamed of your body. Rejoice in it! The earth mother has given it to you! If you want to come to our workshop on Saturday . . .'

I tear my arm away in horror, and start clattering down the marble stairs. But as I reach the next floor, someone else grabs my arm.

'Hey, can you tell me which charity shops you go to?' It's a girl I don't even recognize. 'Because you always look really well dressed to me . . .'

'I adore Barbie dolls too!' Carol Finch from Accounts is suddenly in my path. 'Shall we start a club together, Emma?'

'I . . . I really have to go.'

I back away, then start running down the stairs. But people keep accosting me from all directions.

'I didn't realize I was a lesbian till I was thirty-three . . .'

'A lot of people are confused about religion. This is a leaflet about our Bible study group . . .'

'Leave me alone!' I yell in anguish. 'Everyone just leave me alone!'

I sprint for the entrance, the voices following me, echoing on the marble floor. As I'm frantically pushing against the heavy glass doors, Dave the security guard saunters up, and stares right at my breasts.

'They look all right to me, love,' he says encouragingly.

I finally get the door open, run outside and down the road, not looking right or left. At last I come to a halt, sink down on a bench and bury my head in my hands.

My body is still reverberating with shock.

I can barely form a coherent thought.

I have never been so completely and utterly embarrassed in all my life.

TWENTY

'Are you OK? Emma?'

I've been sitting on the bench for about five minutes, staring down at the pavement, my mind a whirl of confusion. Now there's a voice in my ear, above the everyday street sounds of people walking by and buses grinding and cars hooting. It's a man's voice. I open my eyes, blink in the sunlight and stare dazedly at a pair of green eyes that seem familiar.

Then suddenly I realize. It's Aidan from the smoothie bar.

'Is everything all right?' he's saying. 'Are you OK?'

For a few moments I can't quite reply. All my emotions have been scattered on the floor like a dropped tea tray, and I'm not sure which one to pick up first.

'I think that would have to be a no,' I say at last. 'I'm not OK. I'm not OK at all.'

'Oh.' He looks alarmed. 'Well . . . is there anything I can—'

'Would you be OK if all your secrets had been revealed on television by a man you trusted?' I say shakily. 'Would you be OK if you'd just been mortified in front of all your friends and colleagues and family?'

There's a bemused silence.

'*Would* you?'

'Er . . . probably not?' he hazards hurriedly.

'Exactly! I mean, how would you feel if someone

revealed in public that you . . . you wore women's underwear?'

He turns pale with shock.

'I don't wear women's underwear!'

'I know you don't wear women's underwear!' I expostulate. 'Or rather, I don't *know* that you don't, but just assuming for a moment that you did. How would you like it if someone just *told* everyone in a so-called business interview on television?'

Aidan stares at me, as though his mind is suddenly putting two and two together.

'Wait a moment. That interview with Jack Harper. Is that what you're talking about? We had it on in the smoothie bar.'

'Oh great!' I throw my hands in the air. 'Just great! Because you know, it would be a shame if anyone in the entire universe had missed it.'

'So, that's *you*? Who reads fifteen horoscopes a day and lies about her . . .' He breaks off at my expression. 'Sorry. Sorry. You must be feeling very hurt.'

'Yes. I am. I'm feeling hurt. And angry. And embarrassed.'

And I'm confused, I add silently. I'm so confused and shocked and bewildered I feel as though I can barely keep my balance on this bench. In the space of a few minutes, my entire world has turned upside down.

I thought Jack loved me. I thought he—

I thought he and I—

A searing pain suddenly hits me, and I bury my head in my hands.

'So, how did he know so much about you?' Aidan's saying tentatively. 'Are you and he . . . an item?'

'We met on a plane.' I look up, trying to keep control of myself. 'And . . . I spent the entire journey telling him everything about myself. And then we went on a few dates, and I thought . . .' My voice is starting to jump about. 'I honestly thought it might be . . . you know.' I feel my cheeks flame crimson. 'The real thing. But the truth is, he was never interested in me, was he? Not really. He just wanted to find out what an ordinary girl-on-the-street was like. For his stupid target market. For his stupid new women's line.'

As the realization hits me properly for the first time, a tear rolls down my cheek, swiftly followed by another one.

Jack used me.

That's why he asked me out to dinner. That's why he was so fascinated by me. That's why he found everything I said so interesting. That's why he was gripped.

It wasn't love. It was business.

Suddenly, without meaning to, I give a sob.

'I'm sorry,' I gulp. 'I'm sorry. I just . . . it's just been such a shock.'

'Don't worry,' says Aidan sympathetically. 'It's a completely natural reaction.' He shakes his head. 'I don't know much about big business, but it seems to me these guys don't get to the top without trampling over a few people on the way. They'd have to be pretty ruthless to be so successful.' He pauses, watching as I try, only half successfully, to stop my tears. 'Emma, can I offer a word of advice?'

'What?' I look up, wiping my eyes.

'Take it out in your kick-boxing. Use the aggression. *Use* the hurt.'

I stare at him in disbelief. Was he not *listening*?

'Aidan, I don't *do* kick-boxing!' I hear myself crying shrilly. 'I don't kick-box, OK? I never have!'

'You don't?' He looks confused. 'But you said—'

'I was lying!'

There's a short pause.

269

'Right,' says Aidan at last. 'Well . . . no worries! You could go for something with lower impact. T'ai Chi, maybe . . .' He gazes at me uncertainly. 'Listen, do you want a drink? Something to calm you down? I could make you a mango-banana blend with camomile flowers, throw in some soothing nutmeg.'

'No thanks.' I blow my nose, take a deep breath, then reach for my bag. 'I think I'll go home, actually.'

'Will you be OK?'

'I'll be fine.' I force a smile. 'I'm fine.'

But of course that's a lie too. I'm not fine at all. As I sit on the tube going home, tears pour down my face, one by one, landing in big wet drips on my skirt. People are staring at me, but I don't care. Why should I care? I've already suffered the worst embarrassment possible; a few extra people gawping is neither here nor there.

I feel so stupid. So *stupid*.

Of course we weren't soulmates. Of course he wasn't genuinely interested in me. Of course he never loved me.

A fresh pain rushes through me and I scrabble for a tissue.

'Don't worry, darling!' says a large lady sitting to my left, wearing a voluminous print dress covered with pineapples. 'He's not worth it! Now you just go home, wash your face, have a nice cup of tea . . .'

'How do you know she's crying over a man?' chimes in a woman in a dark suit aggressively. 'That is such a clichéd, counter-feminist perspective. She could be crying over anything! A piece of music, a line of poetry, world famine, the political situation in the Middle East.' She looks at me expectantly.

'Actually, I was crying over a man,' I admit.

The tube stops, and the woman in the dark suit rolls

her eyes at us and gets out. The pineapple lady rolls her eyes back.

'World famine!' she says scornfully, and I can't help giving a half-giggle. 'Now, don't you worry, love.' She gives me a comforting pat on the shoulder as I dab at my eyes. 'Have a nice cup of tea, and a few nice choco-late digestives, and have a nice chat with your mum. You've still got your mum, haven't you?'

'Actually, we're not really speaking at the moment,' I confess.

'Well then, your dad?'

Tacitly, I shake my head.

'Well . . . how about your best friend? You must have a best friend!' The pineapple lady gives me a comfort-ing smile.

'Yes, I have got a best friend,' I gulp. 'But she's just been informed on national television that I've been having secret lesbian fantasies about her.'

The pineapple lady stares at me silently for a few moments.

'Have a nice cup of tea,' she says at last, with less conviction. 'And . . . good luck, dear.'

I make my way slowly back from the tube station to our street. As I reach the corner I stop, blow my nose, and take a few deep breaths. The pain in my chest has receded slightly, and in its place I'm feeling thumping, jumping nerves.

How am I going to face Lissy after what Jack said on television? How?

I've known Lissy a long time. And I've had plenty of embarrassing moments in front of her. But none of them comes anywhere near this.

This is worse than the time when I threw up in her parents' bathroom. This is worse than the time she saw me kissing my reflection in the mirror and saying 'ooh, baby' in a sexy voice. This is even worse than the time she caught me writing a Valentine to our maths teacher, Mr Blake.

I am hoping against hope that she might have suddenly decided to go out for the day or something. But as I open the front door of the flat, there she is, coming out of the kitchen into the hall. And as she looks at me, I can already see it in her face. She's completely freaked out.

So that's it. Not only has Jack betrayed me. He's ruined my best friendship, too. Things will never be the same between me and Lissy again. It's just like *When Harry Met Sally*. Sex has got in the way of our relationship, and now we can't be friends any more because we want to sleep together.

No. Scratch that. We don't want to sleep together. We want to – No, the point is we *don't* want to—

Anyway. Whatever. It's not good.

'Oh!' she says, staring at the floor. 'Gosh! Um . . . hi, Emma!'

'Hi!' I reply in a strangled voice. 'I thought I'd come home. The office was just too . . . too awful . . .'

I tail off, and there's the most excruciating, prickling silence for a few moments.

'So . . . I guess you saw it,' I say at last.

'Yes, I saw it,' says Lissy, still staring at the floor, 'And I . . .' She clears her throat. 'I just wanted to say that . . . that if you want me to move out, then I will.'

A lump comes to my throat. I knew it. After twenty-one years, our friendship is over. One tiny secret comes out – and that's the end of everything.

'It's OK,' I say, trying not to burst into tears. 'I'll move out.'

'No!' says Lissy awkwardly. '*I'll* move out. This isn't your fault, Emma. It's been me who's been . . . leading you on.'

'What?' I stare at her. 'Lissy, you haven't been leading me on!'

'Yes I have.' She looks stricken. 'I feel terrible. I just never realized you had . . . those kind of feelings.'

'I don't!'

'But I can see it all now! I've been walking around half-dressed, no wonder you were frustrated!'

'I wasn't frustrated,' I say quickly. 'Lissy, I'm not a lesbian.'

'Bisexual, then. Or "multi-oriented". Whatever term you want to use.'

'I'm not bisexual, either! Or multi-whatever it was.'

'Emma, please!' Lissy grabs my hand. 'Don't be ashamed of your sexuality. And I promise, I'll support you a hundred per cent, whatever choice you decide to make—'

'Lissy, I'm not bisexual!' I cry. 'I don't need support! I just had one dream, OK? It wasn't a fantasy, it was just a weird dream, which I didn't intend to have, and it doesn't mean I'm a lesbian, and it doesn't mean I fancy you, and it doesn't mean anything.'

'Oh.' There's silence. Lissy looks taken aback. 'Oh, right. I thought it was a . . . a . . . you know.' She clears her throat. 'That you wanted to . . .'

'No! I just had a dream. Just one, stupid dream.'

'Oh. Right.'

There's a long pause, during which Lissy looks intently at her fingernails, and I study the buckle of my watch.

'So, did we actually . . .' says Lissy at last.

Oh God.

'Kind of,' I admit.

'And . . . was I any good?'

'What?' I gape at her.

'In the dream.' She looks straight at me, her cheeks bright pink. 'Was I any good?'

'Lissy . . .' I say, pulling an agonized face.

'I was crap, wasn't I? I was crap! I knew it.'

'No, of course you weren't crap!' I exclaim. 'You were . . . you were really . . .'

I cannot believe I'm seriously having a conversation about my best friend's sexual prowess as a dream lesbian.

'Look, can we just leave the subject? My day has been embarrassing enough already.'

'Oh. Oh God, yes,' says Lissy, suddenly full of remorse. 'Sorry. Emma. You must be feeling really . . .'

'Totally and utterly humiliated and betrayed?' I try to give a smile. 'Yup, that's pretty much how I feel.'

'Did anyone at the office see it, then?' says Lissy sympathetically.

'Did anyone at the office *see* it?' I wheel round. 'Lissy, they *all* saw it. They all knew it was me! And they were all laughing at me, and I just wanted to curl up and *die* . . .'

'Oh God,' says Lissy in distress. 'Really?'

'It was *awful*.' I close my eyes as fresh mortification washes over me. 'I have never been more embarrassed in my entire life. I have never felt more . . . exposed. The whole world knows I find G-strings uncomfortable and I don't really kick-box, and I've never read Dickens.' My voice is wobbling more and more, and then, with no warning, I give a huge sob. 'Oh God, Lissy. You were right. I feel such a complete . . . *fool*. He was just using me, right from the beginning. He was never really interested in me. I was just a . . . a market research project.'

'You don't know that!' she says in dismay.

'I do! Of course I do. That's why he was gripped. That's why he was so fascinated by everything I said. It wasn't because he loved me. It was because he real-ized he had his target customer, right next to him. The kind of normal, ordinary, girl-on-the-street he would never normally give the time of day to!' I give another huge sob. 'I mean, he said it on the television, didn't he? I'm just a nothing-special girl.'

'You are not,' says Lissy fiercely. 'You are *not* nothing-special!'

'I am! That's exactly what I am. I'm just an ordinary nothing. And I was so stupid, I believed it all. I honestly thought Jack loved me. I mean, maybe not exactly loved me.' I feel myself colour. 'But . . . you know. Felt about me like I felt about him.'

'I know.' Lissy looks like she wants to cry herself. 'I know you did.' She leans forward and gives me a huge hug.

Suddenly she draws awkwardly away. 'This isn't making you feel uncomfortable, is it? I mean, it's not . . . turning you on or anything—'

'Lissy, for the last time, I'm not a lesbian!' I cry in exasperation.

'OK!' she says hurriedly. 'OK. Sorry.' She gives me another tight hug, then stands up. 'Come on,' she says. 'You need a drink.'

We go onto the tiny, overgrown balcony which was described as 'spacious roof terrace' by the landlord when we first rented this flat, and sit in a patch of sun, drinking the schnapps which Lissy got duty-free last year. Each sip makes my mouth burn unbearably, but five seconds later sends a lovely soothing warmth all over my body.

'I should have known,' I say, staring into my glass. 'I should have known a big important millionaire like that would never really be interested in a girl like me.'

'I just can't believe it,' says Lissy, sighing for the thousandth time. 'I can't believe it was all made up. It was all so *romantic*. Changing his mind about going to

America . . . and the bus . . . and bringing you that pink cocktail . . .'

'But that's the point.' I can feel tears rising again, and fiercely blink them back. 'That's what makes it so humiliating. He knew exactly what I would like. I told him on the plane I was bored with Connor. He knew I wanted excitement, and intrigue, and a big romance. He just fed me everything he knew I'd like. And I believed it – because I wanted to believe it.'

'You honestly think the whole thing was one big plan?' Lissy bites her lip.

'Of course it was a plan,' I say tearfully. 'He deliberately followed me around, he watched everything I did, he wanted to get into my life! Look at the way he came and poked around my bedroom. No wonder he seemed so bloody interested. I expect he was taking notes all the time. I expect he had a Dictaphone in his pocket. And I just . . . invited him in.' I take a deep gulp of schnapps and give a little shudder. 'I am never going to trust a man again. Never.'

'But he seemed so nice!' says Lissy dolefully. 'I just can't believe he was being so cynical.'

'Lissy . . .' I look up. 'The truth is, a man like that doesn't get to the top without being ruthless and trampling over people. It just doesn't happen.'

'Doesn't it?' She stares back at me, her brow crumpled. 'Maybe you're right. God, how depressing.'

'Is that Emma?' comes a piercing voice, and Jemima appears on the balcony in a white robe and face mask, her eyes narrowed furiously. 'So! Miss I-never-borrow-your-clothes. What have you got to say about my Prada slingbacks?'

Oh God. There's no point lying about it, is there?

'They're really pointy and uncomfortable?' I say with a little shrug, and Jemima inhales sharply.

'I knew it! I knew it all along. You *do* borrow my

clothes. What about my Joseph jumper? What about my Gucci bag?'

'*Which* Gucci bag?' I shoot back defiantly.

For moment Jemima flounders for words.

'All of them!' she says at last. 'You know, I could sue you for this. I could take you to the cleaners!' She brandishes a piece of paper at me. 'I've got a list here of items of apparel which I fully suspect have been worn by someone other than me during the last three months—'

'Oh shut up about your stupid clothes,' says Lissy. 'Emma's really upset. She's been completely betrayed and humiliated by the man she thought loved her.'

'Well, surprise, surprise, let me just faint with shock,' says Jemima tartly. 'I could have told you that was going to happen. I *did* tell you! Never tell a man all about yourself, it's bound to lead to trouble. Did I not warn you?'

'You said she wouldn't get a rock on her finger!' exclaims Lissy. 'You didn't say, he will pitch up on television, telling the nation all her private secrets. You know, Jemima, you could be a bit more sympathetic.'

'No, Lissy, she's right,' I say miserably. 'She was completely right all along. If I'd just kept my stupid mouth shut, then none of this would have happened.' I reach for the schnapps bottle and morosely pour myself another glass. 'Relationships *are* a battle. They *are* a chess game. And what did I do? I just threw all my chess pieces down on the board at once, and said, "Here! Have them all!"' I take a gulp of my drink. 'The truth is, men and women should tell each other nothing. *Nothing.*'

'I couldn't agree more,' says Jemima. 'I'm planning to tell my future husband as little as possible—' She breaks off as the cordless phone in her hand gives a shrill ring.

'Hi!' she says, switching it on. 'Camilla? Oh. Er . . . OK. Just hang on a moment.'

She puts her hand over the receiver and looks at me, wide-eyed. 'It's Jack!' she mouths.

I stare back in utter shock.

Somehow I'd almost forgotten Jack existed in real life. All I can see is that face on the television screen, smiling and nodding and slowly leading me to my humiliation.

'Tell him Emma doesn't want to speak to him!' hisses Lissy.

'No! She *should* speak to him,' hisses back Jemima. 'Otherwise he'll think he's won.'

'But surely—'

'Give it to me!' I say, and grab the phone out of Jemima's hand, my heart thumping. 'Hi,' I say, in as curt a tone as I can muster.

'Emma, it's me,' comes Jack's familiar voice, and with no warning, I feel a rush of emotion which almost overwhelms me. I want to cry. I want to hit him, hurt him . . .

But somehow, I keep control of myself.

'I never want to speak to you again,' I say. I switch off the phone, breathing rather hard.

'Well done!' says Lissy.

An instant later the phone rings again.

'Please, Emma,' says Jack, 'just listen for a moment. I know you must be very upset. But if you just give me a second to explain—'

'Didn't you hear me?' I exclaim, my face flushing. 'You used me and you humiliated me and I never want to speak to you again, or see you, or hear you or . . . or . . .'

'Taste you,' hisses Jemima, nodding urgently.

'. . . or touch you again. Never ever. Ever.' I switch off the phone, march inside and yank the line out of the wall. Then, with trembling hands, I get my mobile out of my bag and, just as it begins to ring, switch it off.

As I emerge on the balcony again, I'm still half shaking with shock. I can't quite believe it's all ended like this. In one day, my entire perfect romance has crumbled into nothing.

'Are you OK?' says Lissy anxiously.

'I'm fine. I think.' I sink onto a chair. 'A bit shaky.'

'Now, Emma,' says Jemima, examining one of her cuticles. 'I don't want to rush you. But you know what you have to do, don't you?'

'What?'

'You have to get your revenge!' She looks up and fixes me with a determined gaze. 'You have to make him pay.'

'Oh no.' Lissy pulls a face. 'Isn't revenge really undignified? Isn't it better just to walk away?'

'What good is walking away?' retorts Jemima. 'Will walking away teach him a lesson? Will walking away make him wish he'd never crossed you?'

'Emma and I have always agreed we'd rather keep the moral high ground,' says Lissy determinedly. '"Living well is the best revenge." George Herbert.'

Jemima stares at her blankly for a few seconds.

'So anyway,' she says at last, turning back to me. 'I'd be delighted to help. Revenge is actually quite a speciality of mine, though I say it myself . . .'

I avoid Lissy's eyes.

'What did you have in mind?'

'Scrape his car, shred his suits, sew fish inside his curtains and wait for them to rot . . .' Jemima reels off instantly, as though reciting poetry.

'Did you learn that at finishing school?' says Lissy, rolling her eyes.

279

'I'm being a feminist, *actually*,' retorts Jemima. 'We women have to stand up for our rights. You know, before she married my father, Mummy went out with this scientist chap who practically jilted her. He changed his mind three weeks before the wedding, can you believe it? So one night she crept into his lab and pulled out all the plugs of his stupid machines. His whole research was ruined! She always says, that taught Emerson!'

'Emerson?' says Lissy, staring at her in disbelief. 'As in . . . Emerson Davies?'

'That's right! Davies.'

'Emerson Davies who nearly discovered a cure for smallpox?'

'Well, he shouldn't have messed Mummy about, should he?' says Jemima, lifting her chin mutinously. She turns to me. 'Another of Mummy's tips is chilli oil. You somehow arrange to have sex with the chap again, and then you say. "How about a little massage oil?" And you rub it into his . . . you know.' Her eyes sparkle. 'That'll hurt him where it counts!'

'Your *mother* told you this?' says Lissy.

'Yes,' says Jemima. 'It was rather sweet, actually. On my eighteenth birthday she sat me down and said we should have a little chat about men and women—'

Lissy is staring at her incredulously.

'In which she instructed you to rub chilli oil into men's genitals?'

'Only if they treat you badly,' says Jemima in annoyance. 'What is your *problem*, Lissy? Do you think you should just let men walk all over you and get away with it? Great blow for feminism.'

'I'm not saying that,' says Lissy. 'I just wouldn't get my revenge with . . . chilli oil!'

'Well, what would you do then, clever clogs?' says Jemima, putting her hands on her hips.

'OK,' says Lissy. '*If* I was going to stoop so low as get my revenge, which I never would because personally I think it's a huge mistake . . .' She pauses for breath. 'I'd do exactly what he did. I'd expose one of *his* secrets.'

'Actually . . . that's rather good,' says Jemima grudgingly.

'Humiliate *him*,' says Lissy, with a tiny air of vindication. 'Embarrass *him*. See how he likes it.'

They both turn and look at me expectantly.

'But I don't know any of his secrets,' I say.

'You must do!' says Jemima.

'Of course you do!'

'I don't,' I say, feeling a fresh humiliation. 'Lissy, you had it right all along. Our relationship was completely one-sided. I shared all my secrets with him – but he didn't share any of his with me. He didn't tell me anything. We weren't soulmates. I was a completely deluded moron.'

'Emma, you weren't a moron,' says Lissy, putting a sympathetic hand on mine. 'You were just trusting.'

'Trusting – moron – it's the same thing.'

'You must know *something*!' says Jemima. 'You slept with him, for goodness sake! He must have some secret. Some weak point.'

'An Achilles' heel,' puts in Lissy, and Jemima gives her an odd look.

'It doesn't have to be to do with his feet,' she says, and turns to me, pulling a 'Lissy's lost it' face. 'It could be anything. Anything at all. Think back!'

I close my eyes obediently and cast my mind back. But my mind's swirling a bit, from all that schnapps. Secrets . . . Jack's secrets . . . think back . . .

Scotland. Suddenly a coherent thought passes through my mind. I open my eyes, feeling a tingle of exhilaration. I do know one of his secrets. I do!

'What?' says Jemima avidly. 'Have you remembered something?'

'He . . .' I stop, feeling torn.

I did make a promise to Jack. I did promise.

But then, so what? So bloody what? My chest swells in emotion again. Why on earth am I keeping any stupid promise to him? It's not like he kept my secrets to *himself*, is it?

'He was in Scotland!' I say triumphantly. 'The first time we met after the plane, he asked me to keep it a secret that he was in Scotland.'

'Why did he do that?' says Lissy.

'I dunno.'

'What was he doing in Scotland?' puts in Jemima.

'I dunno.'

There's a pause.

'Hmm,' says Jemima kindly. 'It's not the *most* embarrassing secret in the world, is it? I mean, plenty of smart people live in Scotland. Haven't you got anything better? Like . . . does he wear a chest wig?'

'A chest wig!' Lissy gives an explosive snort of laughter. 'Or a toupee!'

'Of course he doesn't wear a chest wig. *Or* a toupee,' I retort indignantly. Do they honestly think I'd go out with a man who wore a *toupee*?

'Well then, you'll have to make something up,' says Jemima. 'You know, before the affair with the scientist, Mummy was treated very badly by some politician chap. So she made up a rumour that he was taking bribes from the Communist party, and passed it round the House of Commons. She always says, that taught Dennis a lesson!'

'Not . . . Dennis Llewellyn?' Lissy says.

'Er, yes, I think that was him.'

'The disgraced Home Secretary?' Lissy looks aghast.

'The one who spent his whole life fighting to clear his name and ended up in a mental institution?'

'Well, he shouldn't have messed Mummy around, should he?' says Jemima, sticking out her chin. A bleeper goes off in her pocket. 'Time for my footbath!'

As she disappears back into the house, Lissy rolls her eyes.

'She's nuts,' she says. 'Totally nuts. Emma, you are *not* making anything up about Jack Harper.'

'I won't make anything up!' I say indignantly. 'Who do you think I am? Anyway.' I stare into my schnapps, feeling my exhilaration fade away. 'Who am I kidding? I could never get my revenge on Jack. I could never hurt him. He doesn't *have* any weak points. He's a huge, powerful millionaire.' I take a miserable slug of my drink. 'And I'm a nothing-special . . . crappy . . . ordinary . . . nothing.'

TWENTY-ONE

The next morning I wake up full of sick dread. I feel exactly like a five-year-old who doesn't want to go to school. A five-year-old with a severe hangover, that is.

'I can't go,' I say, as 8.30 arrives. 'I can't face them.'

'Yes you can,' says Lissy reassuringly, doing up my jacket buttons. 'It'll be fine. Just keep your chin up.'

'What if they're horrid to me?'

'They won't be horrid to you. They're your friends. Anyway, they'll probably all have forgotten about it by now.'

'They won't! Can't I just stay at home with you?' I grab her hand beseechingly. 'I'll be really good, I promise.'

'Emma, I've explained to you,' says Lissy patiently. 'I've got to go to court today.'

She prises my hand out of hers. 'But I'll be here when you get home. And we'll have something really nice for supper. OK?'

'OK,' I say in a small voice. 'Can we have chocolate ice-cream?'

'Of course we can,' says Lissy, opening the front door of our flat. 'Now, go on. You'll be fine!'

Feeling like a dog being shooed out, I go down the stairs and open the front door. I'm just stepping out of the house when a van pulls up at the side of the road. A man gets out in a blue uniform, holding the biggest bunch of flowers I've ever seen, all tied up

284

with dark green ribbon, and squints at the number on our house.

'Hello,' he says. 'I'm looking for an Emma Corrigan.'

'That's me!' I say in surprise.

'Aha!' He smiles, and holds out a pen and clipboard. 'Well, this is your lucky day. If you could just sign here . . .'

I stare at the bouquet in disbelief. Roses, freesias, amazing big purple flowers . . . fantastic dark red pompom things . . . dark green frondy bits . . . pale green ones which look just like asparagus . . .

OK, I may not know what they're all called. But I do know one thing. These flowers are expensive.

There's only one person who could have sent them.

'Wait,' I say, without taking the pen. 'I want to check who they're from.'

I grab the card, rip it open, and scan down the long message, not reading any of it until I come to the name at the bottom.

Jack.

I feel a huge dart of emotion. After all he did, Jack thinks he can fob me off with some manky bunch of flowers?

All right, huge, deluxe bunch of flowers.

But that's not the point.

'I don't want them, thank you,' I say, lifting my chin.

'You don't *want* them?' The delivery man stares at me.

'No. Tell the person who sent them that thanks, but no thanks.'

'What's going on?' comes a breathless voice beside me, and I look up to see Lissy gawping at the bouquet. 'Oh my God. Are they from Jack?'

'Yes. But I don't want them,' I say. 'Please take them away.'

'Wait!' exclaims Lissy, grabbing the cellophane. 'Let me just smell them.' She buries her face in the blooms and inhales deeply. 'Wow! That's absolutely incredible! Emma, have you smelt them?'

'No!' I say, crossly. 'I don't want to smell them.'

'I've never *seen* flowers as amazing as this.' She looks at the man. 'So what will happen to them?'

'Dunno.' He shrugs. 'They'll get chucked away, I suppose.'

'Gosh.' She glances at me. 'That seems like an awful waste . . .'

Hang on. She's not—

'Lissy, I can't *accept* them!' I exclaim. 'I can't! He'll think I'm saying everything's OK between us.'

'No, you're quite right,' says Lissy reluctantly. 'You have to send them back.' She touches a pink velvety rose petal. 'It is a shame, though . . .'

'Send what back?' comes a sharp voice behind me. 'You are joking, aren't you?'

Oh, for God's sake. Now Jemima has arrived in the street, still in her white dressing gown. 'You're not sending those back!' she cries. 'I'm giving a dinner party tomorrow night. They'll be perfect.' She grabs the label. 'Smythe and Foxe! Do you know how much these must have cost?'

'I don't care how much they cost!' I exclaim. 'They're from Jack! I can't possibly keep them.'

'Why not?'

She is unbelievable.

'Because . . . because it's a matter of principle. If I keep them, I'm basically saying, "I forgive you." '

'Not necessarily,' retorts Jemima. 'You could be saying "I *don't* forgive you." Or you could be saying "I can't be bothered to return your stupid flowers, that's how little you mean to me." '

There's silence as we all consider this.

The thing is, they *are* pretty amazing flowers.

'So do you want them or not?' says the delivery guy.

'I . . .' Oh God, now I'm all confused.

'Emma, if you send them back you look weak,' says Jemima firmly. 'You look like you can't bear to have any reminder of him in the house. But if you keep them, then you're saying, "I don't care about you!" You're standing firm! You're being strong. You're being—'

'Oh, God, OK!' I say, and grab the pen from the delivery guy. 'I'll sign for them. But could you please tell him that this does *not* mean I forgive him, nor that he isn't a cynical, heartless, despicable user and furthermore, if Jemima wasn't having a dinner party, these would be straight in the bin.' As I finish signing I'm red-faced and breathing hard, and I stamp a full stop so hard it tears the page. 'Can you remember all that?'

The delivery guy looks at me blankly.

'Love, I just work at the depot.'

'I know!' says Lissy suddenly. She grabs the clipboard back and prints WITHOUT PREJUDICE clearly under my name.

'What does that mean?' I say.

'It means "I'll never forgive you, you complete bastard . . . but I'll keep the flowers anyway."'

'And you're still going to get even,' adds Jemima determinedly.

It's one of those amazingly bright, crisp mornings that make you feel that London really is the best city in the world. As I'm walking from the tube station to work, my spirits can't help rising a little.

Maybe Lissy's right. Maybe everyone at work will already have forgotten about the whole thing. I mean, let's get a bit of proportion here. It wasn't *that* big a deal. It wasn't *that* interesting. Surely some other piece of gossip will have come along in the meantime. Surely everyone will be talking about . . . the football. Or politics or something. Exactly.

I push open the glass door to the foyer with a small spurt of optimism, and walk in, my head held high.

'. . . a Barbie bedspread!' I immediately hear from across the marble. A guy from Accounts is talking to a woman with a 'Visitor' badge, who is listening avidly.

'. . . shagging Jack Harper all along?' comes a voice from above me, and I look up to see a group of girls walking up the stairs.

'It's Connor I feel sorry for,' one replies. 'That poor guy . . .'

'. . . pretended she loved jazz,' someone else is saying as they get out of the lift. 'I mean, why on earth would you do that?'

OK. So . . . they haven't forgotten.

All my crisp optimism dies away, and for an instant I consider running away and spending the rest of my life under the duvet.

But I can't do that.

For a start, I'd probably get bored after about a week.

And secondly . . . I have to face them. I have to do this.

Clenching my fists at my sides, I slowly make my way up the stairs and along the corridor. Everyone I pass either blatantly stares at me, or pretends they're not looking when they are, and at least five conversations are hastily broken off as I approach.

As I reach the door to the marketing department, I take a deep breath, then walk in, trying to look as unconcerned as possible.

'Hi everyone,' I say, taking off my jacket and hanging it on my chair.

'Emma!' exclaims Artemis in tones of sarcastic delight. 'Well I never!'

'Good morning, Emma,' says Paul, coming out of his office and giving me an appraising look. 'You OK?'

'Fine, thanks.'

'Anything you'd like to . . . talk about?' To my surprise he looks as if he genuinely means it.

But honestly. What does he think? That I'm going to go in there and sob on his shoulder, 'That bastard Jack Harper used me'?

I'll only do that if I get really, *really* desperate.

'No,' I say, my face prickling. 'Thanks, but I'm OK.'

'Good.' He pauses, then adopts a more businesslike tone. 'Now, I'm assuming that when you disappeared yesterday, it was because you'd decided to work from home.'

'Er . . . yes.' I clear my throat. 'That's right.'

'No doubt you got lots of useful tasks done?'

'Er . . . yes. Loads.'

'Excellent. Just what I thought. All right, then, carry on. And the rest of you.' Paul looks around the office warningly. 'Remember what I said.'

'Of course,' says Artemis at once. 'We all remember!'

Paul disappears into his office again, and I stare rigidly at my computer as it warms up. It'll be fine, I tell myself. I'll just concentrate on my work, completely immerse myself . . .

Suddenly I become aware that someone's humming a tune, quite loudly. It's something I recognize. It's . . .

It's the Carpenters.

And now a few others around the room are joining in on the chorus.

'Close to yoooou . . .'

'All right, Emma?' says Nick, as my head jerks up suspiciously. 'D'you want a hanky?'

'Close to yoooou . . .' everybody trills in unison again, and I hear muffled laughter.

I'm not going to react. I'm not going to give them the pleasure.

As calmly as possible I click onto my emails, and give a small gasp of shock. I normally get about ten emails every morning, if that. Today I have ninety-five.

Dad: I'd really like to talk . . .

Carol: I've already got two more people for our Barbie Club!

Moira: I know where you can get really comfy G-strings . . .

Sharon: So how long has this been going on?!!

Fiona: Re: the body awareness workshop . . .

I scroll down the endless list and suddenly feel a stabbing in my heart.

There are three from Jack.

What should I do?

Should I read them?

My hand hovers uncertainly over my mouse. Does he deserve at least a chance to explain?

'Oh Emma,' says Artemis innocently, coming over to my desk with a carrier bag. 'I've got this jumper I wondered if you'd like. It's a bit too small for me, but it's very nice. And it should fit you, because —' she pauses, and catches Caroline's eye — 'it's a size eight.'

Immediately both of them erupt into hysterical giggles.

'Thanks, Artemis,' I say shortly. 'That's really sweet of you.'

'I'm off for a coffee,' says Fergus, standing up. 'Anybody want anything?'

290

'Make mine a Harvey's Bristol Cream,' says Nick brightly.

'Ha ha,' I mutter under my breath.

'Oh Emma, I meant to say,' Nick adds, sauntering over to my desk. 'That new secretary in Admin. Have you seen her? She's quite something, isn't she?'

He winks at me and I stare at him blankly for a moment, not understanding.

'Nice spiky haircut,' he adds. 'Nice dungarees.'

'Shut up!' I cry furiously, my face flaming red. 'I'm not a . . . I'm not . . . Just fuck off, all of you!'

My hand trembling with anger, I swiftly delete each and every one of Jack's emails. He doesn't deserve anything. No chance. Nothing.

I rise to my feet and stride out of the room, breathing hard. I head for the ladies' room, slam the door behind me, and rest my hot forehead on the mirror. Hatred for Jack Harper is bubbling through me like lava. Does he have any idea what I'm going through? Does he have any idea what he's done to me?

'Emma!' A voice interrupts my thoughts and I give a start. Immediately I feel a jolt of apprehension.

Katie has come into the Ladies without me hearing. She's standing right behind me, holding her makeup bag. Her face is reflected in the mirror next to mine . . . and she isn't smiling. It's just like *Fatal Attraction*.

'So,' she says in a strange voice. 'You don't like crochet.'

Oh God. Oh God. What have I done? I've unleashed the bunny-boiler side of Katie that no-one's ever seen before. Maybe she'll impale me with a crochet needle, I find myself thinking wildly.

'Katie,' I say, my heart thumping hard. 'Katie, please listen. I never meant . . . I never said . . .'

'Emma, don't even try.' She lifts her hand. 'There's no point. We both know the truth.'

291

'He was wrong!' I say quickly. 'He got confused! I meant I don't like . . . um . . . *crèches*. You know, all those babies everywhere—'

'You know, I was pretty upset yesterday,' Katie cuts me off with an eerie smile. 'But after work I went straight home, and I called my mum. And do you know what she said to me?'

'What?' I say apprehensively.

'She said . . . she doesn't like crochet either.'

'*What?*' I wheel round and gape at her.

'And neither does my granny.' Her face flushes, and now she looks like the old Katie again. 'Or any of my relatives. They've all been pretending for years, just like you. It all makes sense now!' Her voice rises in agitation. 'You know, I made my granny a whole sofa cover last Christmas, and she told me that burglars had stolen it. But I mean, what kind of burglars steal a crochet sofa cover?'

'Katie, I don't know what to say . . .'

'Emma, why couldn't you have told me before? All that time. Making stupid presents that people didn't want.'

'Oh God, Katie, I'm sorry!' I say, filled with remorse. 'I'm so sorry. I just . . . didn't want to hurt you.'

'I know you were trying to be kind. But I feel really stupid now.'

'Yes, well. That makes two of us,' I say, a little morosely.

The door opens, and Wendy from Accounts comes in. There's a pause as she stares at us both, opens her mouth, closes it again, then disappears into one of the cubicles.

'So, are you OK?' says Katie in a lower voice.

'I'm fine,' I say with a tiny shrug. 'You know . . .'

Yeah. I'm so fine, I'm hiding in the loos rather than face my colleagues.

'Have you spoken to Jack?' she says tentatively.

'No. He sent me some stupid flowers. Like, Oh, that's OK, then. He probably didn't even order them himself, he probably got Sven to do it.'

There's the sound of flushing, and Wendy comes out of the cubicle again.

'Well . . . this is the mascara I was talking about,' Katie says quickly, handing me a tube.

'Thanks,' I say. 'You say it . . . um . . . volumizes *and* lengthens?'

Wendy rolls her eyes.

'It's OK,' she says. 'I'm not listening!' She washes her hands, dries them, then gives me an avid look. 'So Emma, are you going out with Jack Harper?'

'No,' I say curtly. 'He used me and he betrayed me, and to be honest, I'd be happy if I never saw him again in my whole life.'

'Oh right!' she says brightly. 'It's just, I was wondering. If you're speaking to him again, could you just mention that I'd really like to move to the PR department?'

'What?' I stare at her blankly.

'If you could just casually drop it in. That I have good communication skills and I think I'd be really suited to PR.'

Casually drop it in? What, like, 'I never want to see you again, Jack, and by the way, Wendy thinks she'd be good at PR'?

'I'm not sure,' I say at last. 'I just . . . don't think it's something I could do.'

'Well, I think that's really selfish of you, Emma,' says Wendy, looking offended. 'All I'm asking you is, if the subject comes up, to mention that I'd like to move to PR. Just mention it. I mean, how hard is that?'

'Wendy, piss off!' says Katie. 'Leave Emma alone.'

'I was only *asking*!' says Wendy. 'I suppose you think you're above us now, do you?'

'No!' I exclaim in shock. 'It's not that—' But Wendy's already flounced out.

'Great,' I say, a sudden wobble to my voice. 'Just great! Now everyone's going to hate me, as well as everything else.'

I exhale sharply and stare at my reflection. I still can't quite believe how everything has turned upside down, just like that. Everything I believed in has turned out to be false. My perfect man is a cynical user. My dreamy romance was all a fabrication. I was happier than I'd ever been in my life. And now I'm just a stupid, humiliated laughing stock.

Oh God. My eyes are pricking again.

'Are you OK, Emma?' says Katie, gazing at me in dismay. 'Here, have a tissue.' She rummages in her makeup bag. 'And some eye gel.'

'Thanks,' I say, swallowing hard. I dab the eye gel on my eyes and force myself to breathe deeply until I'm completely calm again.

'I think you're really brave,' says Katie, watching me. 'In fact, I'm amazed you even came in today. I would have been *far* too embarrassed.'

'Katie,' I say, turning to face her. 'Yesterday I had all my most personal, private secrets broadcast on TV.' I spread my arms widely. 'How could anything possibly be more embarrassing than that?'

'Here she is!' comes a ringing voice behind us, and Caroline bursts into the Ladies. 'Emma, your parents are here to see you!'

No. I do not believe this. I do not *believe* this.

My parents are standing by my desk. Dad's wearing a smart grey suit, and Mum's all dressed up in a white jacket and navy skirt, and they're kind of holding a bunch of flowers between them. And the entire office is staring at them, as though they're some kind of rare creature.

Scratch that. The entire office has now turned their heads in order to stare at *me*.

'Hi, Mum,' I say in a voice that has suddenly gone rather husky. 'Hi, Dad.'

What are they *doing* here?

'Emma!' says Dad, making an attempt at his normal jovial voice. 'We just thought we'd . . . pop in to see you.'

'Right,' I say, nodding dazedly. As though this is a perfectly normal course of events.

'We brought you a little present,' says Mum brightly. 'Some flowers for your desk.' She puts the bouquet down awkwardly. 'Look at Emma's desk, Brian. Isn't it smart! Look at the . . . the computer!'

'Splendid!' says Dad, giving it a little pat. 'Very . . . very fine desk indeed.'

'And are these your friends?' says Mum, smiling around the office.

'Kind of,' I say, scowling as Artemis beams back winsomely at her.

'We were just saying, the other day,' continues Mum, 'how *proud* you should be of yourself, Emma. Working for a big company like this. I'm sure many girls would be very envious of your career. Don't you agree, Brian?'

'Absolutely!' says Dad. 'You've done very well for yourself, Emma.'

I'm so taken aback, I can't even open my mouth. I meet Dad's eye, and he gives a strange, awkward little smile. And Mum's hands are trembling slightly as she puts the flowers down.

They're nervous, I realize with a jolt of shock. They're both *nervous*.

I'm just trying to get my head round this as Paul appears at the door of his office.

'So Emma,' he says, raising his eyebrows. 'You have visitors, I gather?'

'Er . . . yes,' I say. 'Paul, these are . . . um . . . my parents, Brian and Rachel . . .'

'Enchanted,' says Paul politely.

'We don't want to be any bother,' says Mum hurriedly.

'No bother at all,' says Paul, and bestows a charming smile on her. 'Unfortunately, the room we *usually* use for family bonding sessions is being redecorated.'

'Oh!' says Mum, unsure as to whether he's being serious or not. 'Oh dear!'

'So perhaps, Emma, you'd like to take your parents out for – shall we call it an early lunch?'

I look up at the clock. It's a quarter to ten.

'Thanks, Paul,' I say gratefully.

This is surreal. It's completely surreal.

It's the middle of the morning. I should be at work. And instead I'm walking down the street with my parents, wondering what on earth we're going to say to each other. I can't even *remember* the last time it was just my parents and me. Just the three of us, no Grandpa, no Kerry, no Nev. It's as if we've gone back in time fifteen years, or something.

'We could go in here,' I say, as we reach an Italian coffee shop.

'Good idea!' says Dad heartily, and pushes the door open. 'We saw your friend Jack Harper on television yesterday,' he adds casually.

'He's not my friend,' I reply shortly, and he and Mum glance at each other.

We sit down at a wooden table and a waiter brings us each a menu, and there's silence.

Oh God. Now *I'm* feeling nervous.

'So . . .' I begin, then stop. What I want to say is, Why are you here? But it might sound a bit rude. 'What . . . brings you to London?' I say, instead.

'We just thought we'd like to visit you,' says Mum, looking through her reading glasses at the menu. 'Now, shall I have a cup of tea . . . or what's this? A frappelatte?'

'I want a normal cup of coffee,' says Dad, peering at the menu with a frown. 'Do they do such a thing?'

'If they don't, you'll have to have a cappuccino and spoon off the froth,' says Mum. 'Or an espresso and just ask them to add hot water.'

I don't believe this. They have driven two hundred miles. Are we just going to sit here and talk about hot beverages all day?

'Oh, and that reminds me,' adds Mum casually. 'We've bought you a little something, Emma. Haven't we, Brian?'

'Oh . . . right,' I say in surprise. 'What is it?'

'It's a car,' says Mum, and looks up at the waiter who's appeared at our table. 'Hello! I would like a cappuccino, my husband would like a filter coffee if that's possible, and Emma would like—'

'A *car*?' I echo in disbelief.

'Car,' echoes the Italian waiter, and gives me a suspicious look. 'You want coffee?'

'I'd . . . I'd like a cappuccino, please,' I say distractedly.

'And a selection of cakes,' adds Mum. '*Grazie!*'

'Mum . . .' I put a hand to my head as the waiter disappears. 'What do you mean, you've bought me a car?'

'Just a little run-around. You ought to have a car. It's not safe, you travelling on all these buses. Grandpa's quite right.'

'But . . . but I can't afford a car,' I say stupidly. 'I can't even . . . what about the money I owe you? What about—'

'Forget the money,' says Dad. 'We're going to wipe the slate clean.'

'What?' I stare at him, more bewildered than ever. 'But we can't do that! I still owe you—'

'Forget the money,' says Dad, a sudden edge to his voice. 'I want you to forget all about it, Emma. You don't owe us anything. Nothing at all.'

I honestly cannot take all this in. I look confusedly from Dad to Mum. Then back to Dad. Then, very slowly, back to Mum again.

And it's really strange. But it almost feels as though we're seeing each other properly for the first time in years. As though we're seeing each other and saying hello and kind of . . . starting again.

'We were wondering what you thought about taking a little holiday next year,' says Mum. 'With us.'

'Just . . . us?' I say, looking around the table.

'Just the three of us, we thought.' She gives me a tentative smile. 'It might be fun! You don't have to, of course, if you've got other plans.'

'No! I'd like to!' I say quickly. 'I really would. But . . . but what about . . .'

I can't even bring myself to say Kerry's name.

There's a tiny silence, during which Mum and Dad look at each other, and then away again.

'Kerry sends her love, of course!' says Mum brightly, as though she's changing the subject completely. She clears her throat. 'You know, she thought she might visit Hong Kong next year. Visit her father. She hasn't seen him for at least five years, and maybe it's time they . . . had some time together.'

'Right,' I say dazedly. 'Good idea.'

I can't believe this. Everything's changed. It's as if

the entire family has been thrown up in the air and has fallen down in different positions, and nothing's like it was before.

'We feel, Emma,' says Dad, and stops. 'We feel . . . that perhaps we haven't been . . . that perhaps we haven't always noticed . . .' He breaks off and rubs his nose vigorously.

'Cappu-*cci*no,' says the waiter, planting a cup in front of me. 'Filter *co*-ffee, cappu-*cci*no . . . coffee *cake* . . . lemon *cake* . . . chocolate—'

'Thank you!' interrupts Mum. 'Thank you so much. I think we can manage from here.' The waiter disappears again, and she looks at me. 'Emma, what we want to say is . . . we're very proud of you.'

Oh God. Oh God, I think I'm going to cry.

'Right,' I manage.

'And we . . .' Dad begins. 'That is to say, we both – your mother and I –' He clears his throat. 'We've always . . . and always will . . . both of us . . .'

He pauses, breathing rather hard. I don't quite dare say anything.

'What I'm trying to say, Emma,' he starts again. 'As I'm sure you . . . as I'm sure we all . . . which is to say . . .'

He stops again, and wipes his perspiring face with a napkin.

'The fact of the matter is that . . . is that . . .'

'Oh, just tell your daughter you love her, Brian, for once in your bloody life!' cries Mum.

'I . . . I . . . love you, Emma!' says Dad in a choked-up voice. 'Oh Jesus.' He brushes roughly at his eye.

'I love you too, Dad,' I say, my throat tight. 'And you, Mum.'

'You see!' says Mum, dabbing at her eye. 'I knew it wasn't a mistake to come!' She clutches hold of my hand, and I clutch hold of Dad's hand, and for a moment we're in a kind of awkward group hug.

'You know . . . we're all sacred links in the eternal circle of life,' I say with a sudden swell of emotion.

'What?' Both my parents look at me blankly.

'Er, never mind. Doesn't matter.' I release my hand, take a sip of cappuccino, and look up.

And my heart nearly stops.

Jack is standing at the door of the coffee shop.

TWENTY-TWO

My heart is hammering in my chest as I stare at him through the glass doors. He puts out a hand, the door pings, and suddenly he's inside the coffee shop.

As he walks towards our table, I feel a rush of emotion. This is the man I thought I was in love with. This is the man who completely used me. Now the initial shock has faded, all the old feelings of pain and humiliation are threatening to take over and turn me to jelly again.

But I'm not going to let them. I'm going to be strong and dignified.

'Ignore him,' I say to Mum and Dad.

'Who?' says Dad, turning round in his chair. 'Oh!'

'Emma, I want to talk to you,' says Jack, his face earnest.

'Well, I don't want to talk to you.'

'I'm so sorry to interrupt.' He glances at Mum and Dad. 'If we could just have a moment . . .'

'I'm not going anywhere!' I say in outrage. 'I'm having a nice cup of coffee with my parents.'

'Please.' He sits down at an adjoining table. 'I want to explain. I want to apologize.'

'There's no explanation you could possibly give me.' I look fiercely at Mum and Dad. 'Pretend he isn't there. Just carry on.'

There's silence. Mum and Dad are giving each other surreptitious looks, and I can see Mum mouthing something. She stops abruptly as she sees me looking at her, and takes a sip of coffee.

'Let's just . . . have a conversation!' I say desperately. 'So, Mum.'

'Yes?' she says hopefully.

My mind is blank. I can't think of anything. All I can think is that Jack is sitting four feet away.

'How's the golf?' I say at last.

'It's . . . er . . . fine, thanks.' Mum shoots a glance at Jack.

'Don't look at him!' I mutter. 'And . . . and Dad?' I persevere, loudly. 'How's your golf?'

'It's . . . also fine,' says Dad stiltedly.

'Where do you play?' asks Jack politely.

'You're not in the conversation!' I cry, turning furiously on my chair.

There's silence.

'Dear me!' says Mum suddenly in a stagy voice. 'Just look at the time! We're due at the . . . the . . . sculpture exhibition.'

What?

'Lovely to see you, Emma—'

'You can't go!' I say in panic. But Dad's already opening his wallet and placing a £20 note on the table, while Mum stands up and puts on her white jacket.

'Just listen to him,' she whispers, bending down to give me a kiss.

'Bye, Emma,' says Dad, and squeezes my hand awkwardly. And within the space of about thirty seconds, they're gone.

I cannot believe they have done this to me.

'So,' says Jack, as the door pings shut.

Determinedly I shift my chair round, so I can't see him.

'Emma, please.'

Even more determinedly I shift my chair round

again, until I'm staring straight at the wall. That'll show him.

The only thing is, now I can't reach my cappuccino.

'Here.' I look round to see Jack has moved his chair right up next to mine, and is holding out my cup to me.

'Leave me alone!' I say angrily, leaping to my feet. 'We have nothing to talk about. Nothing.'

I grab my bag and stalk out of the coffee shop, into the busy street. A moment later, I feel a hand on my shoulder.

'We could at least discuss what happened . . .'

'Discuss what?' I wheel round. 'How you used me? How you betrayed me?'

'OK, Emma. I appreciate I embarrassed you. But . . . is it really such a big deal?'

'Such a big *deal*?' I cry in disbelief, nearly knocking over a lady with a shopping trolley. 'You came into my life. You fed me this huge amazing romance. You made me fall in lo—' I halt myself abruptly, panting slightly. 'You said you were gripped by me. You made me . . . care for you . . . and I believed every single word!' My voice is starting to wobble treacherously. 'I believed it all, Jack. But all the way along, you had an ulterior motive. You were just using me for your stupid research. All the time, you were just . . . *using* me.'

Jack stares at me.

'No,' he says. 'No, wait. You have this wrong.' He grabs my arm. 'That's not the way it was. I didn't set out to use you.'

How does he have the *nerve* to say that?

'Of course you did!' I say, wrenching my arm out of his grasp, jabbing the button at a pedestrian crossing. 'Of course you did! Don't deny it was me you were talking about in that interview. Don't deny you had me in mind.' I feel a fresh spasm of humiliation. 'Every detail was me. Every bloody detail!'

'OK.' Jack is clasping his head. 'OK. Listen. I don't deny I had you in mind. I don't deny you filtered into . . . But that doesn't mean . . .' He looks up. 'I have you on my mind most of the time. That's the truth, I have you on my mind.'

The pedestrian crossing starts bleeping, telling us to cross. This is my cue to storm off and him to come running after me – but neither of us moves. I *want* to storm off, but somehow my body isn't doing it. Somehow my body wants to hear more.

'Emma, when Pete and I started the Panther Corporation, you know how we worked?' Jack's dark eyes are burning into mine. 'You know how we made our decisions?'

I give a minuscule, tell-me-if-you-like shrug.

'Gut instinct. Would *we* buy this? Would *we* like this? Would *we* go for this? That's what we asked each other. Every day, over and over.' He hesitates. 'During the past few weeks, I've been immersed in this new women's line. And all I've found myself asking myself is . . . would Emma like it? Would Emma drink it? Would Emma buy it?' Jack closes his eyes for a moment, then opens them. 'Yes, you got into my thoughts. Yes, you fed into my work. Emma, my life and my business have always gotten confused. That's the way I've always been. But that doesn't mean my life isn't real.' He hesitates. 'It doesn't mean that what we had . . . we have . . . is any less real.'

He takes a deep breath and shoves his hands in his pockets.

'Emma, I didn't lie to you. I didn't *feed* you anything. I was gripped by you the minute I met you on that plane. The minute you looked up at me and said, "I don't even *know* if I've got a G spot!" I was hooked. Not because of business . . . because of *you*. Because of who you are. Every single tiny detail.' The flicker of a smile passes over his face. 'From the way you pick out your favourite horoscope every morning to the way you wrote the letter from Ernest P. Leopold. To your exercise plan on the wall. All of it.'

His gaze is fixed on mine, and my throat feels tight, and my head is all confused. And for an instant I feel myself wavering.

Just for an instant.

'That's all very well,' I say, my voice shaking. 'But you embarrassed me. You *humiliated* me!' I turn on my heel and start striding across the road again.

'I didn't mean to say so much,' says Jack, following me. 'I didn't mean to say anything. Believe me, Emma, I regret it as much as you do. The minute we stopped, I asked them to cut out that part. They promised me they would. I was . . .' He shakes his head. 'I don't know, goaded, I got carried away . . .'

'You got carried *away*?' I feel a renewed surge of outrage. 'Jack, you exposed every single detail about me!'

'I know, and I'm sorry . . .'

'You told the world about my underwear . . . and my sex life . . . and my Barbie bedcover and you *didn't* tell them it was ironic . . .'

'Emma, I'm sorry—'

'You told them how much I weigh!' My voice rises to a shriek. 'And you got it *wrong*!'

'Emma, really, I'm sorry—'

'Sorry isn't good enough!' I wheel round furiously round to face him. 'You ruined my life!'

'I ruined your life?' He gives me a strange look. 'Is your life ruined? Is it such a disaster for people to know the truth about you?'

'I . . . I . . .' For a moment I flounder. 'You don't know

305

what it was like for me,' I say, on firmer ground. 'Everyone was laughing at me. Everyone was teasing me, in the whole office. Artemis was teasing me—'

'I'll fire her,' Jack cuts me off firmly.

I'm so shocked, I give a half-giggle, then turn it into a cough.

'And Nick was teasing me—'

'I'll fire him too.' Jack thinks for a moment. 'How about this: anyone who teased you, I'll fire.'

This time I can't help giggling out loud.

'You won't have a company left.'

'So be it. That'll teach me. That'll teach me to be so thoughtless.'

For a moment we stare at each other in the sunshine. My heart's beating quickly. I'm not quite sure what to think.

'Would you like to buy some lucky heather?' A woman in a pink sweatshirt suddenly thrusts a foil-wrapped sprig in my face, and I shake my head irritably.

'Lucky heather, sir?'

'I'll take the whole basket,' says Jack. 'I think I need it.' He reaches into his wallet, gives the woman two £50 notes, and takes the basket from her. All the time, his eyes are fixed on mine.

'Emma, I want to make this up to you,' he says, as the woman hurries away. 'Could we have lunch? A drink? A . . . a smoothie?' His face crinkles into a tiny smile, but I don't smile back. I'm too confused to smile. I can feel part of me starting to unbend; I can feel part of me starting to believe him. Wanting to forgive him. But my mind is still jumbled up. Things are still wrong somewhere.

'I don't know,' I say, rubbing my nose.

'Things were going so well, before I had to go and fuck it up.'

'Were they?' I say.

'Weren't they?' Jack hesitates, gazing at me over the heather. 'I kind of thought they were.'

My mind is buzzing. There are things I need to say. There are things I need to get into the open. A thought crystallizes in my head.

'Jack . . . what were you doing in Scotland? When we first met.'

At once, Jack's expression changes. His face closes up and he looks away.

'Emma, I'm afraid I can't tell you that.'

'Why not?' I say, trying to sound light.

'It's . . . complicated.'

'OK, then.' I think for a moment. 'Where did you go rushing off to that night with Sven? When you had to cut our date short.'

Jack sighs.

'Emma—'

'How about the night you had all those calls? What were those about?'

This time, Jack doesn't even bother answering.

'I see.' I push my hair back, trying to stay calm. 'Jack, did it ever occur to you that in all our time together, you hardly told me anything about yourself?'

'I . . . guess I'm a private person,' says Jack. 'Is it such a big deal?'

'It's quite a big deal to me. I shared everything with you. Like you said. All my thoughts, all my worries, everything. And you shared nothing with me.'

'That's not true—' He steps forward, still holding the cumbersome basket, and several sprigs of heather fall to the ground.

'Practically nothing, then.' I close my eyes briefly, trying to sort my thoughts. 'Jack, relationships are all about trust and equality. If one person shares, then the other person should share, too. I mean, you didn't

307

even tell me you were going to be on television.'

'It was just a dumb interview, for Chrissakes!' A girl with six shopping bags knocks yet more heather out of Jack's basket, and in frustration he dumps it on a passing motorcycle courier's pannier. 'Emma, you're over-reacting.'

'I told you all my secrets,' I say stubbornly. 'You didn't tell me any of yours.'

Jack gives a sigh.

'With all due respect, Emma, I think it's a little different—'

'What?' I stare at him in shock. 'Why . . . why should it be any different?'

'You have to understand. I have things in my life which are very sensitive . . . complicated . . . very important . . .'

'And I *don't*?' My voice bursts from me like a rocket. 'You think my secrets are less important than yours? You think I'm less hurt by you blurting them out on television?' I'm shaking all over, with fury, with disappointment. 'I suppose that's because you're so huge and important and I'm – what am I, again, Jack?' I can feel my eyes glittering with tears. 'A nothing-special girl? An "ordinary, nothing-special girl"?'

Jack winces, and I can see I've hit home. He closes his eyes and for a long time I think he isn't going to speak.

'I didn't mean to use those words,' he says, rubbing his forehead. 'The minute I said them, I wished I could take them back. I was . . . I was trying to evoke something very different from that . . . a kind of image . . .' He looks up. 'Emma, you *have* to know I didn't mean—'

'I'm going to ask you again!' I say, my heart pounding. 'What were you doing in Scotland?'

There's silence. As I meet Jack's eyes, I know he's

308

not going to tell me. He knows this is important to me and he's still not going to tell me.

'Fine,' I say, my voice lurching slightly. 'That's fine. I'm obviously not as important as you. I'm just some amusing girl who provides you with entertainment on flights and gives you ideas for your business.'

'Emma—'

'The thing is, Jack, that's not a real relationship. A real relationship is two-way. A real relationship is based on equality. And trust.' I swallow the lump in my throat. 'So why don't you just go and be with someone on your level, who you can share your precious secrets with? Because you obviously can't share them with me.'

I turn sharply before he can say anything else, and stalk away, two tears rolling down my cheeks, trampling the lucky heather underfoot.

I don't get home until much later that evening. But I'm still smarting from our argument. I have a throbbing headache, and I feel on the verge of tears.

I open the door of the flat to find Lissy and Jemima in a full-scale argument about animal rights.

'The mink *like* being made into coats—' Jemima is saying as I push open the door to the living room. She breaks off and looks up. 'Emma! Are you all right?'

'No.' I sink down onto the sofa and wrap myself up in the chenille throw which Lissy's mum gave her for Christmas. 'I had a huge row with Jack.'

'With *Jack*?'

'You saw him?'

'He came to . . . well, to apologize, I guess.'

Lissy and Jemima exchange looks.

'What happened?' says Lissy, hugging her knees. 'What did he say?'

I'm silent for a few seconds, trying to remember

exactly what he did say. It's all a bit jumbled up in my head now.

'He said . . . he didn't ever mean to use me,' I say at last. 'He said I got in his thoughts. He said he'd fire everyone in the company who teased me.' I can't help giving a half-giggle.

'Really?' says Lissy. 'Gosh. That's quite romant—' She coughs, and pulls an apologetic face. 'Sorry.'

'He said he was really sorry for what happened, and he didn't mean to say all that stuff on the TV, and that our romance was . . . Anyway. He said a lot of things. But *then* he said . . .' My heart beats with fresh indignation. 'He said his secrets were more important than mine.'

There's a huge gasp of outrage.

'No!' says Lissy.

'Bastard!' says Jemima. 'What secrets?'

'I asked him about Scotland. And rushing off from the date.' I meet Lissy's eyes. 'And all those things he would never talk to me about.'

'And what did he say?' says Lissy.

'He wouldn't tell me.' I feel another sting of humiliation. 'He said it was too "sensitive and complicated".'

'Sensitive and *complicated*?' Jemima is staring at me, galvanized. 'Jack has a sensitive and complicated secret? You never mentioned this before! Emma, this is totally perfect. You find out what it is – and then you expose it!'

I stare at her, my heart beating hard. God, she's right. I could do it. I could get back at Jack. I could make him hurt like I've been hurt.

'But I have no idea what it is,' I say at last.

'You can find out!' says Jemima. 'That's easy enough. The point is, you know he's hiding something.'

'There's definitely some kind of mystery,' says Lissy thoughtfully. 'He has all these phone calls he won't

310

talk about, he rushes off mysteriously from your date—'

'He rushed off mysteriously?' says Jemima avidly. 'Where? Did he say anything? Did you overhear anything?'

'No!' I say, flushing slightly. 'Of course not. I don't . . . I would never *eavesdrop* on people!'

Jemima gives me a close look.

'Don't give me that. Yes you did. You did hear something. Come on, Emma. What was it?'

My mind flashes back to that evening. Sitting on the bench, sipping the pink cocktail. The breeze is blowing on my face, Jack and Sven are talking behind me in low voices . . .

'It was nothing much,' I say reluctantly. 'I just heard him say something about having to transfer something . . . and Plan B . . . and something being urgent . . .'

'Transfer what?' says Lissy suspiciously. 'Funds?'

'I dunno. And they said something about flying back up to Glasgow.'

Jemima looks beside herself.

'Emma, I do not believe this. You've had this information all this time? This has to be something juicy. It *has* to be. If only we knew more.' She exhales in frustration. 'You didn't have a Dictaphone or anything with you?'

'Of course I didn't!' I say with a little laugh. 'It was a date! Do *you* normally take a Dictaphone on a . . .' I tail off incredulously at her expression. 'Jemima. You don't.'

'Not *always*,' she says, with a defensive shrug. 'Just if I think it might come in . . . Anyway. That's irrelevant. The point is, you have information, Emma. You have power. You find out what this is all about – and then you expose him. That'll show Jack Harper who's boss. That'll get your revenge!'

I stare back at her determined face, and for a moment I feel a sheer, powerful exhilaration bubbling through me. That would pay Jack back. That would show him. Then he'd be sorry! Then he'd see I'm not just some nothing, nobody girl. Then he'd see. *Then* he'd see.

'So . . .' I lick my lips. 'So how would I do it?'

'First we try to work out as much as we can ourselves,' says Jemima. 'Then, I've got access to various . . . people who can help get more information.' She gives me a tiny wink. 'Discreetly.'

'Private detectives?' says Lissy in disbelief. 'Are you for real?'

'And then we expose him! Mummy's got contacts at *all* the papers . . .'

My head is thumping. Am I really talking about doing this? Am I really talking about getting revenge on Jack?

'A very good place to start is rubbish bins,' adds Jemima knowledgeably. 'You can find *all* sorts of things just by looking through somebody's trash.'

And all of a sudden sanity comes flying in through the window.

'Rubbish bins?' I say in horror. 'I'm not looking in any rubbish bins! In fact, I'm not doing this, full stop. It's a crazy idea.'

'You can't get all precious now, Emma!' says Jemima tartly, flicking back her hair. 'How else are you going to find out what his secret is?'

'Maybe I don't *want* to find out what his secret is,' I retort, feeling a sting of pride. 'Maybe I'm not interested.'

I wrap the chenille throw around me even more tightly, and stare at my toes miserably.

So Jack's got some huge secret he can't trust me with. Well, fine. Let him keep it. I'm not going to demean myself by grubbing after it. I'm not going to start poking around rubbish bins. I don't care what it is. I don't care about him.

'I want to forget about it,' I say, my face closing up. 'I want to move on.'

'No you don't!' retorts Jemima. 'Don't be stupid, Emma. This is your big chance for revenge. We are *so* going to get him.' I have never seen Jemima look so animated in my life. She reaches for her bag and gets out a tiny lilac Smythson notebook, together with a Tiffany pen. 'Right, so what do we know? Glasgow . . . Plan B . . . transfer . . .'

'The Panther Corporation doesn't have offices in Scotland, does it?' says Lissy thoughtfully.

I turn my head, and stare at her in disbelief. She's scribbling on a pad of legal paper, with exactly the same preoccupied look she gets when she's solving one of her geeky puzzles. I can see the words 'Glasgow', 'transfer' and 'Plan B', and a place where she's jumbled up all the letters in 'Scotland' and tried to make a new word out of them.

For God's sake.

'Lissy, what are you doing?'

'I'm just . . . fiddling around,' she says, and blushes. 'I might go and look some stuff up on the Internet, just out of interest.'

'Look, just stop it, both of you!' I say. 'If Jack doesn't want to tell me what his secret is . . . then I don't want to know.'

Suddenly I feel completely drained by the day. And kind of bruised. I'm not interested in Jack's mysterious secret life. I don't want to think about it any more. I want to have a long hot bath and go to bed and just forget I ever met him.

TWENTY-THREE

Except of course I can't.

I can't forget about Jack. I can't forget about our argument.

His face keeps appearing in my head when I don't want it to. The way he stared at me in the sunlight, his face all crinkled up. The way he bought the lucky heather.

I lie in bed, my heart hammering, going over it again and again. Feeling the same smart of hurt. The same disappointment.

I told him everything about myself. *Everything*. And he won't even tell me one—

Anyway. Anyway.

I don't care.

I'm not going to think about him any more. He can do what he likes. He can keep his stupid secrets.

Good luck to him. That's it. He's out of my brain. Gone for good.

I stare at the darkened ceiling for a few moments.

And what did he mean by that, anyway? *Is it such a disaster for people to know the truth about you?*

He can talk. He can *so* talk. Mr Mystery. Mr Sensitive and Complicated.

I should have said that. I should have said—

No. Stop thinking about it. Stop thinking about him. It's over.

As I pad into the kitchen the next morning to make

a cup of tea, I'm fully resolved. I'm not even going to *think* about Jack from now on. Finito. Fin. The End.

'OK. I have three theories.' Lissy arrives breathlessly at the door of the kitchen in her pyjamas, holding her legal pad.

'What?' I look up blearily.

'Jack's big secret. I have three theories.'

'Only three?' says Jemima, appearing behind her in her white robe, clutching her Smythson notebook. 'I've got eight!'

'*Eight?*' Lissy stares at her, affronted.

'I don't want to hear any theories,' I say. 'Look, both of you, this has been really painful for me. Can't you just respect my feelings and drop it?'

They both look at me blankly for a second, then turn back to each other.

'*Eight?*' says Lissy again. 'How did you get eight?'

'Easy-peasy. But I'm sure yours are very good too,' says Jemima kindly. 'Why don't you go first?'

'OK,' says Lissy with a look of annoyance, and clears her throat. 'Number one: He's relocating the whole of the Panther Corporation to Scotland. He was up there reconnoitring, and didn't want you spreading rumours. Number two: He's involved in some kind of white-collar fraud . . .'

'What?' I stare at her. 'Why do you say that?'

'I looked up the accountants who audited the last Panther Corporation accounts, and they've been involved in a few big scandals recently. Which doesn't *prove* anything, but if he's acting shadily and talking about transfers . . .' She pulls a face and I stare back, disconcerted.

Jack a fraudster? No. He couldn't be. He couldn't.

Not that I care one way or the other.

'Can I say that both of those sound highly unlikely to me?' says Jemima with raised eyebrows.

'Well, what's your theory, then?' says Lissy crossly.

'Plastic surgery, of course!' she says triumphantly. 'He has a face-lift and he doesn't want anyone to know, so he recuperates in Scotland. *And* I know what the B is in Plan B.'

'What?' I say suspiciously.

'Botox!' says Jemima with a flourish. 'That's why he rushed off from your date. To have his fine lines smoothed. The doctor suddenly had a spare appointment, his friend came to tell him—'

What planet does Jemima come from?

'Jack would never have Botox!' I say. '*Or* a face-lift!'

'You don't know that!' She gives me a telling look. 'Compare a recent photo of Jack with an old one, and I bet you see a difference—'

'OK, Miss Marple,' says Lissy, rolling her eyes. 'So what are your other seven theories?'

'Let me see . . .' Jemima turns the page of her notebook. 'OK, this one's rather good He's in the Mafia.' She pauses for effect. 'His father was shot, and he's planning to murder the heads of all the other families.'

'Jemima, that's *The Godfather*,' says Lissy.

'Oh.' She looks put out. 'I thought it seemed a bit familiar.' She crosses it out. 'Well, here's another one. He has an autistic brother . . .'

'*Rain Man.*'

'Oh. Damn.' She pulls a face and looks at her list again. 'So maybe not that after all . . . or that . . .' She start crossing entries out. 'OK. But I do have one more.' She raises her head. 'He's got another woman.'

I stare at her, feeling a jolt. Another woman. I never even thought of that.

'That was my last theory, too,' says Lissy apologetically. 'Another woman.'

'You *both* think it's another woman?' I look from face to face. 'But . . . but why?'

316

Suddenly I feel really small. And stupid. Has Jack been playing me along? Have I been even *more* naïve than I originally thought?

'It just seems quite a likely explanation,' says Jemima with a shrug. 'He's having some clandestine affair with a woman in Scotland. He was paying her a secret visit when he met you. She keeps phoning him, maybe they were having a row, then she comes to London unexpectedly, so he has to dash off from your date.'

Lissy glances at my stricken face.

'But maybe he's relocating the company,' she says encouragingly. 'Or a fraudster.'

'Well, I don't care *what* he's doing,' I say, my face burning. 'It's his business. And he's welcome to it.'

I get a pint of milk from the fridge and slam it shut, my hands trembling slightly. Sensitive and complicated. Is that code for 'I'm seeing someone else?'

Well, fine. Let him have another woman. I don't care.

'It's *your* business too!' says Jemima. 'If you're going to get revenge—'

Oh for God's sake.

'I don't *want* to get revenge, OK?' I say, turning round to face her. 'It's not healthy. I want to . . . heal my wounds and move on.'

'Yes, and shall I tell you another word for revenge?' she retorts, as though pulling a rabbit out of a hat. 'Closure!'

'Jemima, closure and revenge are not actually the same thing,' says Lissy.

'In my book they are.' She gives me an impressive look. 'Emma, you're my friend, and I'm not going to let you just sit back and allow yourself to be mistreated by some bastard man. He deserves to pay. He deserves to be punished!'

I stare at Jemima, feeling a few tiny qualms.

'Jemima, you're not actually going to *do* anything about this.'

'Of course I am,' she says. 'I'm not going to stand by and see you suffer. It's called the sisterhood, Emma!'

Oh my God. I have visions of Jemima rooting through Jack's rubbish bins in her pink Gucci suit. Or scraping his car with a nail file.

'Jemima . . . don't do anything,' I say in alarm. 'Please. I don't want you to.'

'You *think* you don't. But you'll thank me later—'

'No I won't! Jemima, you have to promise me you're not going to do anything stupid.'

She tightens her jaw mutinously.

'Promise!'

'OK,' says Jemima at last, rolling her eyes. 'I promise.'

'She's crossing her fingers behind her back,' observes Lissy.

'*What?*' I stare at Jemima in disbelief. 'Promise properly! Swear on something you really love.'

'Oh God,' says Jemima sulkily. 'All right, you win. I swear on my Miu Miu ponyskin bag, I won't do anything. But you're making a big mistake, you know.'

She saunters out of the room, and I watch her, a bit uneasily.

'That girl is a total psychopath,' says Lissy, sinking down onto a chair. 'Why did we ever let her move in here?' She takes a sip of tea. 'Actually, I remember why. It was because her dad gave us a whole year's rent in advance—' She catches my expression. 'Are you OK?'

'You don't think she'll actually do anything to Jack, do you?'

'Of course not,' says Lissy reassuringly. 'She's all talk. She'll probably bump into one of her ditzy friends and forget all about it.'

'You're right.' I give myself a little shake. 'You're

right.' I pick up my cup and look at it silently for a few moments. 'Lissy, do you really think Jack's secret is another woman?'

Lissy opens her mouth.

'Anyway, I don't care,' I add defiantly, before she can answer. 'I don't care what it is.'

'Sure,' says Lissy, and gives me a sympathetic smile.

As I arrive at the office, Artemis looks up from her desk with a bright-eyed glance.

'Morning Emma!' She smirks at Catherine. 'Read any intellectual books lately?'

Oh, ha ha-di-ha. So, so funny. Everyone else at work has got bored with teasing me. Only Artemis still thinks it's completely hilarious.

'Actually, Artemis, I have,' I say brightly, taking off my jacket. 'I read this really good book recently, it was called "What to do if your colleague is an obnoxious cow who picks her nose when she thinks no-one's looking."'

There's a guffaw around the office, and Artemis flushes a dark red.

'I don't!' she snaps.

'I never said you did,' I reply innocently, and switch on my computer with a flourish.

'Ready to go to the meeting, Artemis?' says Paul, coming out of his office with his briefcase and a magazine in his hand. 'And by the way, Nick,' he adds ominously, 'Before I go, would you mind telling me what on earth possessed you to put a coupon ad for Panther Bars in –' he consults the front cover '– *Bowling Monthly* magazine? I'm assuming it was you, as this is your product?'

My heart gives a little swoop, and I lift my head. Shit. Double shit. I didn't think Paul would ever find out about that.

Nick shoots me a dirty look and I pull an agonized face back.

'Well,' he begins truculently. 'Yes, Paul. Panther Bars are my product. But as it happens—'

Oh God. I can't let him take the blame.

'Paul,' I say in a trembling voice, half raising my hand. 'Actually, it was—'

'Because I want to tell you,' Paul grins at Nick. 'It was bloody inspired! I've just had the feedback figures, and bearing in mind the pitiful circulation . . . they're extraordinary!'

I stare at him in astonishment. The ad worked?

'Really?' says Nick, obviously trying to sound not too amazed. 'I mean – excellent!'

'What the *fuck* compelled you to advertise a teenage bar to a load of old codgers?'

'Well!' Nick adjusts his cufflinks, not looking anywhere near me. 'Obviously it was a *bit* of a gamble. But I simply felt that maybe it was time to . . . to fly a few kites . . . experiment with a new demographic . . .'

Hang on a minute. *What's* he saying?

'Well, your experiment paid off.' Paul gives Nick an approving look. 'And very interestingly, it coincides with some Scandinavian market research we've just had in. If you'd like to see me later, to discuss it—'

'Sure!' says Nick with a pleased smile. 'What sort of time?'

No! How can he? He is such a *bastard*.

'Wait!' To my own astonishment, I leap to my feet in outrage. 'Wait a minute! That was *my* idea!'

'What?' Paul frowns.

'The *Bowling Monthly* ad. It was my idea. *Wasn't* it, Nick?' I look directly at him.

'Maybe we discussed it,' he says, not meeting my eye. 'I don't really remember. But you know, something you'll have to learn, Emma, is that marketing's all about team-work . . .'

'Don't patronize me! This wasn't team-work. It was totally my idea. I put it in for my grandpa!'

Damn. I didn't quite mean to let that slip out.

'First your parents. Now your grandpa,' says Paul, turning to look at me. 'Emma, remind me, is this Bring Your Entire Family To Work week?'

'No! It's just . . .' I begin, a little hot under his gaze. 'You said you were going to axe Panther Bars, so I . . . I thought I'd give him and his friends some money off, and they could all stock up. I tried to tell you at that big meeting, my grandfather loves Panther Bars! And so do all his friends. If you ask me, you should be marketing Panther Bars at *them*, not teenagers.'

There's silence. Paul looks astonished.

'You know, in Scandinavia, they're coming to the same conclusion,' he says. 'That's what this new research shows.'

'Oh,' I say. 'Well . . . there you go.'

'So why does this older generation like Panther Bars so much, Emma? Do you know?' He sounds genuinely fascinated.

'Yes, of course I know.'

'It's the grey pound,' puts in Nick wisely. 'Demographic shifts in the pensionable population are accounting for—'

'No it's not!' I say impatiently. 'It's because . . . because . . .' Oh God, Grandpa will absolutely kill me for saying this. 'It's because . . . they don't pull out their false teeth.'

There's a staggered pause. Then Paul throws back his head and roars with laughter. 'False teeth,' he says, wiping his eyes. 'That is sheer bloody genius, Emma. False teeth!'

He chuckles again and I stare back at him, feeling the

blood beating in my head. I've got the strangest feeling. Like something's building up inside me, as though I'm about to—

'So can I have a promotion?'

'What?' Paul looks up.

Did I really just say that? Out loud?

'Can I have a promotion?' My voice is trembling slightly, but I hold firm. 'You said if I created my own opportunities I could have a promotion. That's what you said. Isn't this creating my own opportunities?'

Paul looks at me for a few moments, blinking, saying nothing.

'You know, Emma Corrigan,' he says at last. 'You are one of the most . . . one of the most *surprising* people I've ever known.'

'Is that a yes?' I persist.

There's silence in the entire office. Everyone's waiting to see what he'll say.

'Oh, for God's sake,' he says, rolling his eyes. 'All right! You can have a promotion. Is that it?'

'No,' I hear myself saying, my heart beating even more furiously. 'There's more. Paul, I broke your World Cup mug.'

'What?' He looks gobsmacked.

'I'm really sorry. I'll buy you another one.' I look around the silent, gawping office. 'And it was me who jammed the copier that time. In fact . . . all the times. And that bottom . . .' Amid agog faces, I walk to the pin-board and rip down the photocopied, G-stringed bottom. 'That's mine, and I don't want it up there any more.' I swivel round. 'And Artemis, about your spider plant . . .'

'What?' she says suspiciously.

I stare at her, in her Burberry raincoat and her designer spectacles, and her smug, I'm-better-than-you face.

OK, let's not get carried away.

'I . . . I can't think what's wrong with it.' I smile at her. 'Have a good meeting.'

For the rest of the day, I am totally exhilarated. Kind of shocked and exhilarated, all at the same time. I can't believe I'm getting a promotion. I'm actually going to be a Marketing Executive!

But it's not just that. I don't quite know what's happened to me. I feel like a whole new person. So what if I broke Paul's mug? Who cares? So what if everyone knows how much I weigh? Who cares? Goodbye old, crap Emma, who hides her Oxfam bags under her desk. Hello new, confident Emma, who proudly hangs them on her chair.

I rang Mum and Dad to tell them I was getting promoted, and they were so impressed! They said at once they'd come up to London and take me out to celebrate. And then I had a really nice long chat with Mum about Jack. She said some relationships were supposed to last for ever and some were only supposed to last a few days, and that was just the way life was. Then she told me all about some chap in Paris who she'd had some amazing forty-eight hour fling with. She said she'd never experienced physical pleasure like it, and she knew it could never last, but that made it all the more poignant.

Then she added I needn't mention any of this to Dad.

Gosh. I'm actually quite shocked. I always thought Mum and Dad . . . at least, I never . . .

Well. It just goes to show.

But she is right. Some relationships are meant to be short-lived. Jack and I were obviously never going to get anywhere. And actually, I'm very sorted out about it. In fact, I'm pretty much over him. My heart only went into spasm once today, when I thought I saw him in the corridor, and I recovered really quickly.

My whole new life begins today. In fact, I expect I'll meet someone new tonight at Lissy's dancing show. Some really tall, dashing lawyer. Yes. And he'll come and pick me up from work in his amazingly fab sports car. And I'll trip happily down the steps, tossing my hair back, not even *looking* at Jack, who will be standing at his office window, glowering . . .

No. No. Jack won't be anywhere. I am over Jack. I have to remember this.

Maybe I'll write it on my hand.

TWENTY-FOUR

Lissy's dancing show is being held in a theatre in Bloomsbury set in a small gravelled courtyard, and when I arrive I find the entire place crammed with lawyers in expensive suits using their mobile phones.

'. . . client unwilling to accept the terms of agreement . . .'

'. . . attention to clause four, comma, notwithstanding . . .'

No-one is making the slightest attempt to go into the auditorium yet, so I head backstage, to give Lissy the bouquet I've bought for her. (I was originally planning to throw it onto the stage at the end, but it's roses, and I'm a bit worried it might ladder her tights.)

As I walk down the shabby corridors, music is being piped through the sound system and people keep brushing past me in glittery costumes. A man with blue feathers in his hair is stretching his leg against the wall and talking to someone in a dressing room at the same time. 'So then I pointed out to that *idiot* of a prosecuting counsel that the precedent set in 1983 by Miller v. Davy means . . .' He suddenly stops. 'Shit. I've forgotten my first steps.' His face drains of colour. 'I can't remember a fucking thing. I'm not joking! I jeté on – then what?' He looks at me as though expecting me to supply him with an answer.

'Er . . . a pirouette?' I hazard, and awkwardly hurry on, nearly tripping over a girl doing the splits. Then I catch sight of Lissy sitting on a stool in one of the dressing rooms. Her face is heavily made up and her eyes are all huge and glittery, and she's got blue feathers in her hair too.

'Oh my God, Lissy!' I say, halting in the doorway. 'You look amazing! I completely love your—'

'I can't do it.'

'What?'

'I can't do it!' she repeats desperately, and pulls her cotton robe around her. 'I can't remember anything. My mind is blank!'

'Everyone thinks that,' I say reassuringly. 'There was a guy outside saying exactly the same thing—'

'No. I *really* can't remember anything.' Lissy stares at me with wild eyes. 'My legs feel like cotton wool, I can't breathe . . .' She picks up a blusher brush, looks at it bleakly, then puts it down. 'Why did I ever agree to do this? Why?'

'Er . . . because it would be fun?'

'Fun?' Her voice rises in disbelief. 'You think this is *fun*? Oh God.' Suddenly her face changes expression, and she breaks off and rushes through an adjoining door. The next moment I can hear her retching.

OK, there's something wrong here. I thought dancing was suppose to be *good* for your health.

She appears at the door again, pale and trembling, and I peer at her anxiously.

'Liss, are you all right?'

'I can't do it,' she says. 'I can't.' She seems to come to a sudden decision. 'OK, I'm going home.' She starts reaching for her clothes. 'Tell them I was suddenly taken ill, it was an emergency . . .'

'You can't go home!' I say in horror, and try to grab the clothes out of her hands. 'Lissy, you'll be fine! I mean, think about it. How many times have you had to stand up in a big court and make some really long

326

speech in front of loads of people, and if you get it wrong an innocent man might go to jail?'

Lissy stares at me as though I'm crazy.

'Yes, but that's *easy*!'

'Well . . .' I cast around desperately. 'Well, if you pull out now, you'll always regret it. You'll always look back and wish you'd gone through with it.'

There's silence. I can practically see Lissy's brain working underneath all the feathers and stuff.

'You're right,' she says at last, and relinquishes her hold of the clothes. 'OK. I'll do it. But I don't want you to watch. Just . . . meet me afterwards. No, don't even do that. Just stay away. Stay right away.'

'OK,' I say hesitantly. 'I'll go if you really want me to—'

'No!' She swivels round. 'You can't go! I've changed my mind. I need you there!'

'OK,' I say, even more hesitantly, just as a Tannoy in the wall blares out 'This is your fifteen minute call!'

'I'll go then,' I say. 'Let you warm up.'

'Emma.' Lissy grabs hold of my arm and fixes me with an intense gaze. She's holding me so tight, she's hurting my flesh. 'Emma, if I ever say I want to do anything like this again, you have to stop me. Whatever I say. Promise you'll stop me.'

'I promise,' I say hastily. 'I promise.'

Bloody hell. I have never seen Lissy like that before in my life. As I walk back out into the courtyard, which is now swarming with even more well-dressed people, I'm thudding with nerves myself. She didn't look capable of standing up, let alone dancing.

Please don't let her mess up. Please.

A horrible image comes to me of Lissy standing like a startled rabbit, unable to remember her steps. And the audience just staring at her. The thought of it makes my stomach curdle.

OK. I am not going to let that happen. If anything goes wrong I'll cause a distraction. I'll pretend to have a heart attack. Yes. I'll collapse on the floor, and everyone will look at me for a few seconds, but the performance won't stop or anything because we're British, and by the time everyone turns back to the stage again, Lissy will have remembered her steps.

And if they rush me to hospital or anything, I'll just say, 'I had these terrible chest pains!' No-one will be able to prove that I didn't.

And even if they *can* prove it, with some special machine, I'll just say—

'Emma.'

'What?' I say absently. And then my heart stops.

Jack is standing ten feet away. He's dressed in his usual uniform of jeans and jersey, and he stands out a mile amongst all the corporate suited lawyers. As his dark eyes meet mine I feel all the old hurt rushing back into my chest.

Don't react, I tell myself quickly. Closure. New life.

'What are you doing here?' I ask, with a little I'm-not-actually-interested shrug.

'I found the flyer for this on your desk.' He lifts a piece of paper, not taking his eyes off mine. 'Emma, I really wanted to talk.'

I feel a sudden smarting inside. He thinks he can just pitch up and I'll drop everything to talk to him? Well, maybe I'm busy. Maybe I've moved on. Did he think of that?

'Actually . . . I'm here with someone,' I say in polite, slightly pitying tones.

'Really?'

'Yes. I am. So . . .' I give a little shrug and wait for Jack to walk away. But he doesn't.

'Who?' he says.

OK, he wasn't supposed to ask who. For a moment I'm not entirely sure what to do.

'Er . . . him,' I say at last, and point at a tall guy in shirt-sleeves, who's standing in the corner of the courtyard, facing away from us. 'In fact, I'd better join him.'

My head high, I swivel on my heel and start walking towards the shirt-sleeved guy. What I'll do is just ask him the time, and somehow engage him in conversation until Jack's gone. (And maybe laugh gaily once or twice to show what a good time we're having.)

I'm within a few feet of him, when the shirt-sleeved guy turns round, talking on a mobile.

'Hi!' I begin brightly, but he doesn't even hear me. He gives me a blank glance, then walks off, still talking, into the crowd.

I'm left all alone in the corner.

Fuck.

After what seems like several eternities, I turn round, as nonchalantly as I can.

Jack is still standing there, watching.

I stare at him furiously, my whole body pulsing with embarrassment. If he laughs at me—

But he's not laughing.

'Emma . . .' He walks forward until he's only a couple of feet away, his face frank. 'What you said. It stayed with me. I should have shared more with you. I shouldn't have shut you out.'

I feel a dart of surprise, followed by wounded pride. So he wants to share with me now, does he? Well maybe it's too late. Maybe I'm not interested any more.

'You don't need to share anything with me. Your affairs are your affairs, Jack.' I give him a distancing smile. 'They're nothing to do with me. And I probably wouldn't understand them, anyway, bearing in mind they're so complicated and I'm such a total thickie . . .'

I swivel determinedly, and start to walk away, over the gravel.

'I owe you an explanation, at least,' Jack's dry voice follows me.

'You owe me nothing!' I lift my chin proudly. 'It's over, Jack. And we might as well both just . . . Aargh! Let go!'

Jack has grabbed my arm, and now he pulls me round to face him.

'I came here tonight for a reason, Emma,' he says gravely. 'I came to tell you what I was doing in Scotland.'

I feel the most almighty bound of shock, which I hide as best I can.

'I'm not interested in what you were doing in Scotland!' I manage. I wrench my arm away and start striding away as best I can through the thicket of mobile-phone-gabbing lawyers.

'Emma, I want to tell you.' He's coming after me. 'I really want to tell you.'

'Well, maybe I don't want to know!' I reply defiantly, swivelling round on the gravel with a scatter of pebbles.

We're facing each other like a pair of duellers. My ribcage is rising and falling quickly.

Of course I want to know.

He knows I want to know.

'Go on then,' I say at last, and give a grudging shrug. 'You can tell me if you like.'

In silence, Jack leads me over to a quiet spot, away from all the crowds. As we walk, my bravado ebbs away. In fact, I'm a bit apprehensive. Scared, even.

Do I really want to know his secret, after all?

What if it's fraud, like Lissy said? What if he's doing something dodgy and he wants me to join in?

What if he's had some really embarrassing operation and I start laughing by mistake?

What if it *is* another woman and he's come to tell me he's getting married or something?

I feel a tiny pang of pain, which I quell. Well, if it is . . . I'll just act cool, like I knew all along. In fact I'll pretend *I've* got another lover, too. Yes. I'll give him a wry smile, and say, 'You know, Jack, I never assumed we were exclusive—'

'OK.' Jack turns to face me, and I instantaneously decide that if he's committed a murder I will turn him in, promise or no promise.

'Here it is.' He takes a deep breath. 'I was in Scotland to visit someone.'

My heart plummets.

'A woman,' I say before I can stop myself.

'No, not a woman!' His expression changes, and he stares at me. 'Is that what you thought? That I was two-timing you?'

'I . . . didn't know what to think.'

'Emma, I do not have another woman. I was visiting . . .' He hesitates. 'You could call it . . . family.'

My brain gives a huge swivel.

Family?

Oh my God, Jemima was right, I've got involved with a mobster.

OK. Don't panic. I can escape. I can go in the witness protection scheme. My new name can be Megan.

No, Chloe. Chloe de Souza.

'To be more precise . . . a child.'

A child? My brain lurches again. He has a child?

'Her name is Alice.' He gives a tiny smile. 'She's four years old.'

He has a wife and a whole family I don't know

about, and that's his secret. I knew it, I knew it.

'You . . .' I lick my dry lips. 'You have a child?'

'No, I don't have a child.' Jack stares at the ground for a few seconds, then looks up. 'Pete had a child. He had a daughter. Alice is Pete Laidler's child.'

'But . . . but . . .' I stare at him in confusion. 'But . . . I never knew Pete Laidler had a child.'

'Nobody knows.' He gives me a long look. 'That's the whole idea.'

This is so completely and utterly not what I was expecting.

A child. Pete Laidler's secret child.

'But . . . but how can nobody know about her?' I say stupidly. We've moved even further away from the crowds and are sitting on a bench under a tree. 'I mean surely they'd *see* her.'

'Pete was a great guy.' Jack sighs. 'But commitment was never his strong suit. By the time Marie – that's Alice's mom – found out she was pregnant, they weren't even together any more. Marie's one of those proud, defensive types. She was determined to do everything on her own. Pete supported her financially – but he wasn't interested in the child. He didn't even tell anybody he'd become a father.'

'Even you?' I stare at him. 'You didn't know he had a child?'

'Not until after he died.' His face closes up slightly. 'I loved Pete. But that, I find very hard to forgive. So a few months after he died, Marie turns up with this baby.' Jack exhales sharply. 'Well. You can imagine how we all felt. Shocked is an understatement. But Marie was positive she didn't want anyone to know. She wanted to bring Alice up just like a normal kid, not as Pete Laidler's love child. Not as the heiress to some huge fortune.'

My mind is boggling. A four-year-old getting Pete Laidler's share of the Panther Corporation. Bloody hell.

'So she gets everything?' I say hesitantly.

'Not everything, no. But a lot. Pete's family have been more than generous. And that's why Marie's keeping her away from the public eye.' He spreads his hands. 'I know we can't shield her for ever. It'll come out sooner or later. But when they find out about her, the press will go nuts. She'll shoot to the top of the rich lists . . . the other kids will give her a hard time . . . she won't be normal any more. Some kids could cope. But Alice . . . she's not one of them. She has asthma, she's kind of frail.'

As he's speaking, my mind is filled with memories of the papers after Pete Laidler died. Every single one had a picture of him on the front page.

'I'm overprotective of this child.' Jack gives a rueful smile. 'I know it. Even Marie tells me I am. But . . . she's precious to me.' He stares ahead for a moment. 'She's all we've got left of Pete.'

I gaze at him, suddenly feeling moved.

'So, is that what the phone calls were about?' I say tentatively. 'Is that why you had to leave the other night?'

Jack sighs. 'They were both in a road accident a few days ago. It wasn't serious. But . . . we're extra-sensitive, after Pete. We just wanted to make sure they got the right treatment.'

'Right,' I give a little wince. 'I can understand that.'

There's silence for a while. My brain is trying to slot all the pieces together. Trying to work it all out.

'But I don't understand,' I say. 'Why did you make me keep it a secret that you'd been in Scotland? Nobody would know, surely.'

Jack rolls his eyes ruefully.

'That was my own dumb stupid fault. I'd told some people I was going across to Paris that day, just as an extra precaution. I took an anonymous flight. I thought no-one would ever know. Then I walk into the office . . . and there you are.'

'Your heart sank.'

'Not exactly.' He meets my eyes. 'It didn't quite know which way to go.'

I feel a sudden colour coming to my cheeks and awkwardly clear my throat.

'So . . . er . . .' I say, looking away. 'So that's why . . .'

'All I wanted was to avoid you piping up, "Hey, he wasn't in Paris, he was in Scotland!" and start some huge intrigue going.' Jack shakes his head. 'You'd be amazed at the ludicrous theories people will put together when they don't have anything better to do. You know, I've heard it all. I'm planning to sell the company . . . I'm gay . . . I'm in the Mafia . . .'

'Er . . . really?' I say, and smooth down a strand of hair. 'Gosh. How stupid of people!'

A couple of girls wander nearby, and we both fall silent for a while.

'Emma, I'm sorry I couldn't tell you this before,' Jack says in a low voice. 'I know you were hurt. I know it felt like I was shutting you out. But . . . it's just not something you share lightly.'

'No!' I say immediately. 'Of course you couldn't have done. I was stupid.'

I scuff my toe awkwardly on the gravel, feeling a bit shamefaced. I should have known it would be something important. When he said it was complicated and sensitive, he was just telling the truth.

'Only a handful of people know about this.' Jack meets my eyes gravely. 'A handful of special, trusted people.'

There's something in his gaze which makes my throat feel a bit tight. I stare back at him, feeling blood rising in my cheeks.

'Are you going in?' comes a bright voice. We jump, and look up to see a woman in black jeans approaching. 'The performance is about to start!' she says with a beam.

I feel like she's slapped me awake from a dream.

'I . . . I have to go and watch Lissy dancing,' I say dazedly.

'Right. Well, I'll leave you then. That was really all I had to say.' Slowly Jack gets to his feet, then turns back. 'There's one more thing.' He looks at me for a few silent moments. 'Emma, I realize these last few days can't have been easy for you. You have been the model of discretion throughout, whereas I . . . have not. And I just wanted to apologize. Again.'

'That's . . . that's OK,' I manage.

Jack turns again, and I watch him walking slowly away over the gravel, feeling completely torn.

He came all the way here to tell me his secret. His big, precious secret.

He didn't have to do that.

Oh God. Oh God . . .

'Wait!' I hear myself calling out, and Jack immediately turns. 'Would you . . . would you like to come too?' And I feel a ripple of pleasure as his face creases into a smile.

As we crunch over the gravel together, I pluck up the courage to speak.

'Jack, I've got something to say too. About . . . about what you were just saying. I know I said you ruined my life the other day.'

'I remember,' says Jack wryly.

'Well, I may *possibly* have been wrong about that.' I

clear my throat awkwardly. 'In fact . . . I was wrong.'
I look at him frankly. 'Jack, you didn't ruin my life.'

'I didn't?' says Jack. 'Do I get another shot?'

In spite of myself, a giggle rises inside me.

'No!'

'No? Is that your final answer?'

As he looks at me there's a bigger question in his eyes, and I feel a little shaft, half hope, half apprehension. For a long while neither of us says anything. I'm breathing rather fast.

Suddenly Jack's gaze falls with interest on my hand. 'I am over Jack,' he reads aloud.

Fuck.

My entire face flames with colour.

I am never writing anything on my hand again. Ever.

'That's just . . .' I clear my throat again. 'That was just a doodle . . . it didn't mean . . .'

A shrill ring from my mobile interrupts me. Thank God. Whoever this is, I love them. I hastily pull it out and press green.

'Emma, you're going to love me for ever!' come Jemima's piercing tones.

'What?' I stare at the phone.

'I've sorted everything out for you!' she says triumphantly. 'I know, I'm a total star, you don't know what you'd do without me—'

'*What?*' I feel a twinge of alarm. 'Jemima, what are you talking about?'

'Getting your revenge on Jack Harper, silly! Since you were just sitting there like a total wimp, I've taken matters into my own hands.'

For moment I can't quite move.

'Er, Jack . . . excuse me a minute.' I shoot him a bright smile. 'I just need to . . . take this call.'

With trembling legs I hurry to the corner of the courtyard, well away from earshot.

'Jemima, you promised you wouldn't do anything!' I hiss. 'You swore on your Miu Miu ponyskin bag, remember?'

'I haven't *got* a Miu Miu ponyskin bag!' she crows triumphantly. 'I've got a *Fendi* ponyskin bag!'

She's mad. She's completely mad.

'Jemima, what have you done?' I manage. 'Tell me what you've done.'

My heart is thudding in apprehension. Please don't say she's scraped his car. Please.

'An eye for an eye, Emma! That man totally betrayed you, and we're going to do the same to him. Now, I'm sitting here with a very nice chap called Mick. He's a journalist, he writes for the *Daily World* . . .'

My blood runs cold.

'A tabloid journalist?' I manage at last. 'Jemima, are you *insane*?'

'Don't be so narrow-minded and suburban,' retorts Jemima reprovingly. 'Emma, tabloid journalists are our *friends*. They're just like private detectives . . . but for free! Mick's done loads of work for Mummy before. He's marvellous at tracking things down. And he's *very* interested in finding out Jack Harper's little secret. I've told him all we know, but he'd like to have a word with you.'

I feel quite faint. This cannot be happening.

'Jemima, listen to me,' I say in quick, low tones, as though trying to persuade a lunatic down off the roof. 'I don't want to find out Jack's secret, OK? I just want to forget it. You have to stop this guy.'

'I won't!' she says like a petulant six-year-old. 'Emma, don't be so pathetic! You can't just let men walk all over you and do nothing in return. You have to show them. Mummy always says—' There's the sudden screeching of tyres. 'Oops! Tiny prang. I'll call you back.'

The phone goes dead.

I am numb with horror.

Frantically I jab her number into my phone, but it clicks straight on to messages.

'Jemima,' I say as soon as it beeps. 'Jemima, you have to stop this! You have to—' I stop abruptly as Jack appears in front of me, with a warm smile.

'It's about to start,' he says, and gives me a curious look. 'Everything all right?'

'Fine,' I say in a strangled voice, and put my phone away. 'Everything's . . . fine.'

TWENTY-FIVE

As I walk into the auditorium I'm almost lightheaded with panic.

What have I done? What have I done?

I have given away Jack's most precious secret in the world to a morally warped, revenge-wreaking, Prada-wearing nutcase.

OK. Just calm down, I tell myself for the zillionth time. She doesn't actually know anything. This journalist probably won't find out anything. I mean, what facts does he actually have?

But what if he does find out? What if he somehow stumbles on the truth? And Jack discovers it was me who pointed them in the right direction?

I feel ill at the thought. My stomach is curdling. *Why* did I ever mention Scotland to Jemima? *Why?*

New resolution: I am never giving away a secret again. Never, ever, ever. Even if it doesn't seem important. Even if I am feeling angry.

In fact . . . I am never talking again, full stop. All talking ever seems to do is get me into trouble. If I hadn't opened my mouth on that stupid plane in the first place, I wouldn't be in this mess now.

I will become a mute. A silent enigma. When people ask me questions I will simply nod, or scribble cryptic notes on pieces of paper. People will take them away and puzzle over them, searching them for hidden meanings—

339

'Is this Lissy?' says Jack, pointing to a name in the programme, and I jump in fright. I follow his gaze, then give a silent nod, my mouth clamped shut.

'Do you know anyone else in the show?' he asks.

I give a mute 'who knows?' shrug.

'So . . . how long has Lissy been practising?'

I hesitate, then hold up three fingers.

'Three?' Jack peers at me uncertainly. 'Three what?'

I make a little gesture with my hands which is supposed to indicate 'months'. Then I make it again. Jack looks totally baffled.

'Emma, is something wrong?'

I feel in my pocket for a pen – but I haven't got one.

OK, forget not talking.

'About three months,' I say out loud.

'Right.' Jack nods, and turns back to the programme. His face is calm and unsuspecting, and I can feel guilty nerves rising through me again.

Maybe I should just tell him.

No. I can't. I can't. How would I put it? 'By the way, Jack. You know that really important secret you asked me to keep? Well, guess what . . .'

Containment is what I need. Like in those military films where they bump off the person who knows too much. But how do I contain Jemima? I've launched some crazed human Exocet missile, fizzing around London, bent on causing as much devastation as she can, and now I want to call her back, but the button doesn't work any more.

OK. Just think rationally. There's no need to panic. Nothing's going to happen tonight. I'll just keep trying her mobile and as soon as I get through I'll explain in words of one syllable that she has to call this guy off and if she doesn't I will break her legs.

A low, insistent drumbeat starts playing over the loudspeakers, and I give a start of fright. I'm so

340

distracted, I'd actually forgotten what we were here for. The auditorium is becoming completely dark, and around us the audience falls silent with anticipation. The beating increases in volume, but nothing happens on stage; it's still pitch black.

The drumming becomes even louder, and I'm starting to feel tense. This is all a bit spooky. When are they going to start dancing? When are they going to open the curtains? When are they going to—

Pow! Suddenly there's a gasp as a dazzling light fills the auditorium, nearly blinding me. Thumping music fills the air, and a single figure appears on stage in a black, glittering costume, twirling and leaping. Gosh, whoever it is, they're amazing. I'm blinking dazedly against the bright light, trying to see. I can hardly tell if it's a man or a woman or a—

Oh my God. It's Lissy.

I am pinioned to my seat by shock. Everything else has been swept away from my mind. I cannot keep my eyes off Lissy.

I had no idea she could do this. No idea! I mean, we did a bit of ballet together. And a bit of tap. But we never . . . I never . . . How can I have known someone for over twenty years and have no idea they could dance?

She just did this amazing slow, sinewy dance with a guy in a mask who I guess is Jean-Paul, and now she's leaping and spinning around with this ribbon thing, and the whole audience is staring at her, agog, and she looks so completely radiant. I haven't seen her look so happy for months. I'm *so* proud of her.

To my horror, tears start to prick my eyes. And now my nose is starting to run. I don't even have a tissue. This is so embarrassing. I'm going to have to sniff, like a mother at a Nativity play. Next I'll be standing up and running to the front with my camcorder, going, 'Hello darling, wave to Daddy!'

OK. I need to get a hold of myself, otherwise it'll be like the time I took my little god-daughter Amy to see the Disney cartoon *Tarzan*, and when the lights went up, she was fast asleep and I was in floods, being gawped at by a load of stony-eyed four-year-olds. (Just in my defence, it *was* pretty romantic. And Tarzan *was* pretty sexy.)

I feel something nudging my hand. I look up, and Jack's offering me a hanky. As I take it from him, his fingers curl briefly round mine.

When the performance comes to an end, I'm on a total high. Lissy takes a star bow, and both Jack and I applaud madly, grinning at each other.

'Don't tell anyone I cried,' I say, above the sound of applause.

'I won't,' says Jack, and gives me a rueful smile. 'I promise.'

The curtain comes down for the last time, and people start getting out of their seats, reaching for jackets and bags. And now we're coming back down to normality again, I feel my exhilaration seeping away and anxiety returning. I have to try to contact Jemima again.

At the exit, people are streaming across the court-yard to a lit-up room on the other side.

'Lissy said I should meet her at the party,' I say to Jack. 'So er . . . why don't you go on? I just need to make a quick call.'

'Are you OK?' says Jack, giving me a curious look. 'You seem jumpy.'

'I'm fine!' I say. 'Just excited!' I give him as convincing a beam as I can manage, then wait until he's safely out of earshot. Immediately I dial Jemima's number. Straight on to messages.

I dial it again. Messages again.

I want to scream with frustration. Where is she? What's she doing? How can I contain her if I don't know where she is?

I stand perfectly still, trying to ignore my thrusting panic, trying to work out what to do.

OK. I'll just have to go to the party and act normally, keep trying her on the phone and if all else fails, wait until I see her later. There's nothing else I can do. It'll be fine. It'll be fine.

The party is huge and bright and noisy. All the dancers are there, still in costume, and all the audience, and a fair number of people who seem to have come along just for the ride. Waiters are carrying drinks around and the noise of chatter is tremendous. As I walk in, I can't see anyone I know. I take a glass of wine and start edging into the crowd, overhearing conversations all around.

'. . . wonderful costumes . . .'

'. . . find time for rehearsals?'

'. . . judge was *totally* intransigent . . .'

Suddenly I spot Lissy, looking flushed and shiny and surrounded by a load of good-looking lawyer-type guys, one of whom is blatantly staring at her legs.

'Lissy!' I cry. She turns around and I give her a huge hug. 'I had no idea you could dance like that! You were amazing!'

'Oh no. I wasn't,' she says at once, and pulls a typical Lissy-face. 'I completely messed up—'

'Stop!' I interrupt. 'Lissy, it was utterly fantastic. *You* were fantastic.'

'But I was completely crap in the—'

'*Don't* say you were crap!' I practically yell. 'You were fantastic. Say it. *Say* it, Lissy.'

'Well . . . OK.' Her face reluctantly creases into a

smile. 'OK. I was . . . fantastic!' She gives an elated laugh. 'Emma, I've never felt so good in my life! And guess what, we're already planning to go on tour next year.'

'But . . .' I stare at her. 'You said you never wanted to do this again, ever, and if you mentioned it again, I had to stop you.'

'Oh, that was just stage fright,' she says with an airy wave of her hand. Then she lowers her voice. 'I saw Jack, by the way.' She gives me an avid look. 'What's going on?'

My heart gives a huge thump. Should I tell her about Jemima?

No. She'll only get all hassled. And anyway, there's nothing either of us can do right now.

'Jack came here to talk to me.' I hesitate. 'To . . . tell me his secret.'

'You're joking!' breathes Lissy, hand to her mouth. 'So – what is it?'

'I can't tell you.'

'You can't *tell* me?' Lissy stares at me in incredulity. 'After all that, you're not even going to *tell* me?'

'Lissy, I really can't.' I pull an agonized face. 'It's . . . complicated.'

God, I sound just like Jack.

'Well, all right,' says Lissy a bit grumpily. 'I suppose I can live without knowing. So . . . are you two together again?'

'I dunno,' I say, flushing. 'Maybe.'

'Lissy! That was fabulous!' A couple of girls in suits appear at her side. I give her a smile and move away slightly as she greets them.

Jack is nowhere to be seen. Should I try Jemima again?

Surreptitiously I start getting out my phone, then

hastily put it away again as I hear a voice behind me calling 'Emma!'

I look round, and give a huge start of surprise. Connor's standing there in a suit, holding a glass of wine, his hair all shiny and blond under the spotlights. He has a new tie on, I notice instantly. Big yellow polka dots on blue. I don't like it.

'Connor! What are you doing here?' I say in astonishment.

'Lissy sent me a flyer,' he replies, a little defensively. 'I've always been fond of Lissy. I thought I'd come along. And I'm glad I've run into you,' he adds awkwardly. 'I'd like to talk to you, if I may.'

He draws me towards the door, away from the main crowd, and I follow, a tad nervously. I haven't had a proper chat with Connor since Jack was on television. Which could possibly be because every time I've glimpsed him, I've quickly hurried the other way.

'Yes?' I say, turning to face him. 'What did you want to talk about?'

'Emma.' Connor clears his throat as though he's about to start a formal speech. 'I get the feeling that you weren't always . . . totally honest with me in our relationship.'

This could be the understatement of the year.

'You're right,' I admit, shamefacedly. 'Oh God, Connor, I'm really, really sorry about everything that happened—' He lifts a hand with a look of dignity.

'It doesn't matter. That's water under the bridge. But I'd be grateful if you were totally honest with me now.'

'Absolutely,' I say, nodding earnestly. 'Of course.'

'I've recently . . . started a new relationship,' he says, a little stiffly.

'Wow!' I say in surprise. 'Good for you! Connor, I'm really pleased. What's her name?'

'Her name's Francesca.'

'And where did you—'

'I wanted to ask you about sex,' Connor says, cutting me off in a rush of embarrassment.

'Oh! Right.' I feel a twinge of dismay, which I conceal by taking a sip of wine. 'Of course!'

'Were you honest with me in that . . . area?'

'Er . . . what do you mean?' I say lightly, playing for time.

'Were you honest with me in bed?' His face is growing pillar-box red. 'Or were you faking it?'

Oh no. Is that what he thinks?

'Connor, I never ever faked an orgasm with you,' I say, lowering my voice. 'Hand on heart. I never did.'

'Well . . . OK.' He rubs his nose awkwardly. 'But did you fake anything else?'

I look at him uncertainly. 'I'm not sure I know what you—'

'Were there any —' he clears his throat '— any particular techniques I used which you only pretended to enjoy?'

Oh God. *Please* don't ask me that question.

'You know, I really . . . can't remember!' I hedge. 'Actually, I ought to be going . . .'

'Emma, tell me!' he says, with sudden passion. 'I'm starting a new relationship. It's only fair that I should be able to . . . to learn from past mistakes.'

I gaze back at his shiny face and suddenly feel a huge pang of guilt. He's right. I should be honest. I should finally be honest with him.

'OK,' I say at last, and move closer to him. 'You remember that one thing you used to do with your tongue?' I lower my voice still further. 'That . . . *slidey* thing? Well, sometimes that kind of made me want to . . . laugh. So if I had one tip with your new girlfriend, it would be don't do . . .'

I tail off at his expression.

Fuck. He's already done it.

'Francesca said . . .' Connor says in a voice as stiff as a board. 'Francesca told me that really turned her on.'

'Well, I'm sure it did!' I backtrack madly. 'Women are all different. Our bodies are all different . . . everybody likes . . . different things.'

Connor is staring me in consternation.

'She said she loved jazz, too.'

'Well, I expect she does! Loads of people *do* like jazz.'

'She said she loved the way I could quote Woody Allen line for line.' He rubs his flushed face. 'Was she *lying*?'

'No, I'm sure she wasn't . . .' I tail off helplessly.

'Emma . . .' He stares at me bewilderedly. 'Do *all* women have secrets?'

Oh no. Have I ruined Connor's trust in all of womankind for ever?

'No!' I exclaim. 'Of course they don't! Honestly, Connor, I'm *sure* it's only me.'

My words wither on my lips as I glimpse a flash of familiar-looking blond hair at the entrance to the hall. My heart stops.

That can't be—

That's not—

'Connor, I have to go,' I say, and start hurrying towards the entrance.

'She told me she's size ten!' Connor calls helplessly after me. 'What does that mean? What size should I really buy?'

'Twelve!' I shoot back over my shoulder.

It is. It's Jemima. Standing in the foyer. What's she doing here?

The door opens again and I experience such a shock, I feel faint. She's got a guy with her. In jeans, with cropped hair and squirrelly eyes. He's got a camera slung over his shoulder and is looking around interestedly.

No.

She can't have done.

'Emma,' comes a voice in my ear.

'Jack!' I wheel round, to see him smiling down at me, his dark eyes full of affection.

'You OK?' he says, and gently touches my nose.

'Fine!' I say a little shrilly. 'I'm great!'

I have to manage this situation. I have to.

'Jack – could you get me some water?' I hear myself saying. 'I'll just stay here. I'm feeling a bit dizzy.' Jack looks alarmed.

'You know, I thought there was something wrong. Let me take you home. I'll call the car.'

'No. It's . . . it's fine. I want to stay. Just get me some water. Please,' I add as an afterthought.

As soon as he's gone I tear into the foyer, almost tripping up in my haste.

'Emma!' Jemima looks up brightly. 'Excellent! I was just about to look for you. Now, this is Mick, and he wants to ask you some questions. We thought we'd use this little room here.' She heads into a small, empty office which leads off from the foyer.

'No!' I say, grabbing her arm. 'Jemima, you have to go. Now. Go!'

'I'm not going anywhere!' Jemima jerks her arm out of my grasp and rolls her eyes at Mick, who's closing the door of the office behind me. 'I told you she was being all hissy about it.'

'Mick Collins,' Mick thrusts a business card into my hand. 'Delighted to meet you, Emma. Now, there's no need to get worried, is there?' He gives me a soothing smile, as though he's completely used to dealing with hysterical women telling him to go. Which he probably is. 'Let's just sit down quietly, have a nice chat . . .'

He's chewing gum as he speaks, and as I smell the spearmint wafting towards me, I almost want to throw up.

'Look, there's been a misunderstanding,' I say, forcing myself to sound polite. 'I'm afraid there's no story.'

'Well, let's see about that, shall we?' says Mick with a friendly smile. 'You tell me the facts . . .'

'No! I mean, there's nothing.' I turn to Jemima. 'I told you I didn't want you to do anything. You promised me!'

'Emma, you are such a wimp.' She gives Mick an exasperated look. 'Do you see why I've been forced to take action? I told you what a bastard Jack Harper was to her. He needs to learn his lesson.'

'Absolutely right,' agrees Mick and puts his head on one side as though measuring me up. 'Very attractive,' he says to Jemima. 'You know, we could think about an accompanying interview feature. My romp with top boss. You could make some serious money,' he adds to me.

'*No!*' I say in horror.

'Emma, stop being so coy!' snaps Jemima. 'You want to do it really. This could be a whole new career for you, you realize.'

'I don't want a new career!'

'Well then you should! Do you *know* how much Monica Lewinsky makes a year?'

'You're sick,' I say in disbelief. 'You're a totally sick, warped—'

'Emma, I'm just acting in your best interests.'

'You're not!' I cry, feeling my face flame red. 'I . . . I might be getting back together with Jack!'

There's a thirty-second silence. I stare at her, holding my breath. Then it's as if the killer robot jerks into action again, shooting yet more rays.

'Even *more* reason to do it!' says Jemima. 'This'll keep him on his toes. This'll show him who's boss. Go on, Mick.'

'Interview with Emma Corrigan. Tuesday, 15th July, 9.40 p.m.' I look up, and stiffen in horror. Mick has produced a small tape recorder and is holding it towards me.

'You first met Jack Harper on a plane. Can you confirm where this was flying from and to?' He gives me a smile. 'Just speak naturally, like you would to a mate on the phone.'

'Stop it!' I yell. 'Just leave! Leave!'

'Emma, grow up,' says Jemima impatiently. 'Mick's going to find out what this secret is whether you help him or not, so you might as well be—' She stops abruptly as the door handle rattles, then turns.

The room seems to swim around me.

Please don't say – please—

As the door slowly opens, I can't breathe. I can't move.

I have never felt so frightened in my entire life.

'Emma?' says Jack, coming in, holding two glasses of water in one hand. 'Are you feeling OK? I got you both still and sparkling, because I wasn't quite . . .'

He tails off, his eyes running confusedly over Jemima and Mick. With a flicker of bewilderment, he takes in Mick's card, still in my hand. Then his gaze falls on the turning tape recorder and something slides out of his face.

'I think I'll just make myself scarce,' murmurs Mick, raising his eyebrows at Jemima. He slips the tape recording into his pocket, picks up his rucksack and sidles out of the room. Nobody speaks for a few moments. All I can hear is the throbbing in my head.

'Who was that?' says Jack at last. 'A journalist?'

All the light has gone from his eyes. He looks as though someone just stamped on his garden.

'I . . . Jack . . .' I say huskily. 'It's not . . . it's not . . .'

'Why . . .' He rubs his brow, as though trying to make sense of the situation. 'Why were you talking to a journalist?'

'Why do you *think* she was talking to a journalist?' chimes in Jemima proudly.

'What?' Jack's gaze swivels to her with dislike.

'You think you're such a bigshot millionaire! You think you can use little people. You think you can give away someone's private secrets and completely humiliate them and get away with it. Well, you can't!'

She takes a few steps towards him, folding her arms and lifting her chin with satisfaction. 'Emma's been waiting for a chance to get her revenge on you, and now she's found it! That *was* a journalist, if you want to know. And he's on your case. And when you find your little Scottish secret plastered all over the papers, then maybe *you'll* know what it feel like to be betrayed! And maybe you'll be sorry. Tell him, Emma! Tell him!'

But I'm paralysed.

The minute she said the word Scottish I saw Jack's face change. It kind of snapped. He almost seemed winded with shock. He looked straight at me and I could see the growing disbelief in his eyes.

'You might think you know Emma, but you don't,' Jemima is continuing delightedly, like a cat tearing apart its prey. 'You underestimated her, Jack Harper. You underestimated what she's capable of.'

Shut up! I'm screaming internally. *It's not true! Jack, I would never, I would never . . .*

But nothing in my body will move. I can't even swallow. I'm pinioned, staring helplessly at him with a face I know is covered with guilt.

Jack opens his mouth, then closes it again. Then he turns on his heel, pushes the door open and walks out.

For a moment there's silence in the tiny room.

'Well!' says Jemima, smacking her hands triumphantly, 'That showed him!'

It's as though she breaks the spell. Suddenly I can move again. I can draw breath.

'You . . .' I'm almost shaking too much to speak. 'You stupid . . . stupid . . . thoughtless . . . bitch!'

The door bursts open and Lissy appears, wide-eyed.

'What the hell happened here?' she demands. 'I just saw Jack storming out. He looked absolutely like thunder!'

'She brought a journalist here!' I say in anguish, gesturing at Jemima. 'A bloody tabloid journalist. And Jack found us all closeted here, and he thinks . . . God know what he thinks . . .'

'You stupid cow!' Lissy slaps Jemima across the face. 'What were you thinking.'

'Ow! I was helping Emma get vengeance on her enemy.'

'He's not my *enemy*, you stupid . . .' I'm on the verge of tears. 'Lissy . . . what am I going to do? What?'

'Go,' she says, and looks at me with anxious eyes. 'You can still catch him. Go.'

I pelt out of the door and through the courtyard, my chest rising and falling rapidly, my lungs burning. When I reach the road I look frantically left and right. Then I spot him, down the road.

'Jack, wait.'

He's striding along with his mobile phone to his ear, and at my voice he turns round with a taut face.

'So that's why you were so interested in Scotland.'

'No!' I say, aghast. 'No! Listen, Jack, they don't know. They don't know anything, I promise. I didn't tell them about—' I stop myself. 'All Jemima knows is that you were there. Nothing more. She was bluffing. I haven't said anything.'

Jack doesn't answer. He gives me a long look, then starts striding again.

'It was Jemima who called that guy, not me!' I cry desperately, running after him. 'I was trying to stop her . . . Jack, you know me! You *know* I would never do this to you. Yes, I told Jemima about you being in Scotland. I was hurt, and I was angry, and it . . . came out. And that was a mistake. But . . . but you made a mistake too, and I forgave you.'

He's not even looking at me. He's not even giving me a chance. His silver car pulls up at the pavement, and he opens the passenger door.

I feel a stab of panic.

'Jack, this wasn't me,' I say frantically. 'It wasn't. You have to believe me. That's not why I asked about Scotland! I didn't want to . . . to *sell* your secret!' Tears are streaming down my face, and I brush them away roughly. 'I didn't even want to *know* such a big secret. I just wanted to know your little secrets! Your little stupid secrets! I just wanted to know you . . . like you know me.'

But he doesn't look round. The car door closes with a heavy clunk, and the car moves away down the road. And I'm left on the pavement, all alone.

TWENTY-SIX

For a while I can't move. I stand there, dazed, with the breeze blowing on my face, staring at the point at the end of the road where Jack's car disappeared. I can still hear his voice in my mind. I can still see his face. The way he looked at me as though he didn't know me, after all.

A spasm of pain runs through my body and I close my eyes, almost unable to bear it. If I could just turn back time . . . if I'd been more forceful . . . if I'd marched Jemima and her friend off the premises . . . if I'd spoken up more quickly when Jack appeared . . .

But I didn't. And it's too late.

A group of party guests comes out of the courtyard onto the pavement, laughing and discussing taxis.

'Are you all right?' says one curiously to me, and I give a start.

'Yes,' I say. 'Thanks.' I look one more time at where Jack's car disappeared, then force myself to turn around and make my way slowly back up to the party.

I find Lissy and Jemima still in the little office, Jemima cowering in terror as Lissy lays into her.

'. . . selfish immature little bitch! You make me sick, you know that?'

I once heard someone say Lissy was a Rottweiler in court, and I could never understand it. But now, as I watch her striding up and down, her eyes blazing in fury, I'm actually pretty scared myself.

'Emma, make her stop!' pleads Jemima. 'Make her stop shouting at me.'

'So . . . what happened?' Lissy looks at me, her face alight with hope. Mutely, I shake my head.

'Is he—'

'He's gone.' I swallow. 'I don't really want to talk about it.'

'Oh, Emma.' She bites her lip.

'Don't,' I say in a wobbly voice. 'I'll cry.' I lean against the wall and take a couple of deep breaths, trying to get back to normal. 'Where's her friend?' I say at last, and jerk my thumb at Jemima.

'He got thrown out,' says Lissy with satisfaction. 'He was trying to take a picture of Justice Hugh Morris in his tights, and a bunch of lawyers surrounded him and bundled him out.'

'Jemima, listen to me.' I force myself to meet her unrepentant blue gaze. 'You cannot let him find out any more. You *cannot*.'

'It's OK,' she says sulkily. 'I've already spoken to him. Lissy made me. He won't pursue it.'

'How do you know?'

'He won't do anything that would piss Mummy off. He has a pretty lucrative arrangement with her.'

I shoot Lissy a 'can we trust her?' look, and she gives a doubtful shrug.

'Jemima, this is a warning.' I walk to the door, then turn round with a stern face. 'If anything of this gets out – *anything* at all – I will make it public that you snore.'

'I don't snore!' says Jemima tartly.

'Yes you do,' says Lissy. 'When you've had too much to drink you snore really loudly. *And* we'll tell everyone you got your Donna Karan coat from a discount warehouse shop.'

Jemima gasps in horror.

'I didn't!' she says, colour suffusing her cheeks.

'You did. I saw the carrier bag,' I chime in. '*And* we'll make it public that you once asked for a serviette, not a napkin.'

Jemima claps a hand over her mouth.

'. . . and your pearls are cultured, not real . . .'

'. . . and you never really cook the food at your dinner parties . . .'

'. . . and that photo of you meeting Prince William is faked . . .'

'. . . and we'll tell every single man you ever date from now on that all you're after is a rock on your finger!' I finish, and glance gratefully at Lissy.

'OK!' says Jemima, practically in tears. 'OK! I promise I'll forget all about it. I promise. Just please don't mention the discount warehouse shop. Please. Can I go now?' She looks imploringly at Lissy.

'Yes, you can go,' says Lissy contemptuously, and Jemima scuttles out of the room. As the door closes, I stare at Lissy.

'Is that photo of Jemima and Prince William really faked?'

'Yes! Didn't I tell you? I once did some stuff for her on her computer, and I opened the file by mistake – and there it was. She just pasted her head onto some other girl's body!'

I can't help giving a giggle.

'That girl is unbelievable.'

I sink into a chair, feeling suddenly weak, and for a while there's silence. In the distance there's a roar of laughter from the party, and somebody walks past the door of the office, talking about the trouble with the judiciary system as it *stands* . . .

'Wouldn't he even listen?' says Lissy at last.

'No. He just left.'

'Isn't that a bit extreme? I mean, he gave away *all*

your secrets. You only gave away one of his—'

'You don't understand.' I stare at the drab brown office carpet. 'What Jack told me, it's not just anything. It's something really precious to him. He came all the way here to tell me. To show me that he trusted me with it.' I swallow hard. 'And the next moment he finds me spilling it to a journalist.'

'But you weren't!' says Lissy loyally. 'Emma, this wasn't your fault!'

'It was!' Tears are welling up in my eyes. 'If I'd just kept my mouth closed, if I'd never told Jemima anything in the first place . . .'

'She would have got him anyway,' says Lissy. 'He'd be suing you for a scraped car instead. Or damaged genitals.'

I give a shaky laugh.

The door bursts open, and the feathered guy I saw backstage looks in. 'Lissy! There you are. They're serving food. It looks rather good, actually.'

'OK,' she says. 'Thanks, Colin. I'll be along in a minute.'

He leaves and Lissy turns to me.

'Do you want something to eat?'

'I'm not really hungry. But you go,' I add quickly. 'You must be starving after your performance.'

'I am rather ravenous,' she admits. Then she gives me an anxious look. 'But what will you do?'

'I'll . . . just go home,' I say, and try to smile as cheerfully as I can. 'Don't worry, Lissy, I'll be fine.'

And I am planning to go home. But when I get outside I find I can't bring myself to. I'm wound up with tension like a metal coil. I can't face going into the party and having to make small talk – but I can't face the four silent walls of my bedroom either. Not quite yet.

Instead, I head across the gravel, towards the empty auditorium. The door is unlocked and I walk straight in. I make my way through the darkness to a seat in the middle, and wearily sit down on the cushiony purple plush.

And as I stare at the silent blackness of the empty stage, two fat tears make their way out of my eyes and trickle slowly down my face. I cannot believe I've fucked up so monumentally. I can't believe Jack really thinks I . . . that he thinks I would . . .

I keep seeing the shock on his face. I keep reliving that trapped powerlessness, that desperation to speak; to explain myself.

If I could just replay it . . .

Suddenly there's a creaking sound. The door is slowly opening.

I peer uncertainly through the gloom as a figure comes into the auditorium and stops. In spite of myself, my heart starts to thud with unbearable hope.

It's Jack. It has to be Jack. He's come to find me.

There's a long, agonizing silence. I'm taut with apprehension. Why won't he say anything? Why won't he speak?

Is he punishing me? Is he expecting me to apologize again? Oh God, this is torture. Just say something, I plead silently. Just say *something*.

'Oh Francesca . . .'

'Connor . . .'

What? I peer again, more sharply, and feel a crash of disappointment. I am such a moron. It's not Jack. It's not one figure, it's two. It's Connor and what must be his new girlfriend – and they're snogging.

Miserably, I shrink right down in my seat, trying to block my ears. But it's no good, I can hear everything.

'Do you like this?' I hear Connor murmuring.

'Mmm . . .'

'Do you really like it?'

'Of course I do! Stop quizzing me!'

'Sorry,' says Connor, and there's silence, apart from the odd 'Mmmm'.

'Do you like *this*?' his voice suddenly comes again.

'I already told you I did.'

'Francesca, be honest, OK?' Connor's voice rises in agitation. 'Because if that means no, then—'

'It doesn't mean no! Connor, what's your problem?'

'My problem is, I don't believe you.'

'You don't *believe* me?' She sounds furious. 'Why the hell don't you believe me?'

Suddenly I'm filled with remorse. This is all my fault. Not only have I wrecked my own relationship, now I've wrecked theirs too. I have to do something. I have to try to build bridges.

I clear my throat. 'Er . . . excuse me?'

'Who the fuck's that?' says Francesca sharply. 'Is someone there?'

'It's me. Emma. Connor's ex-girlfriend.'

A row of lights goes on, and I see a girl with red hair staring at me belligerently, with her hand on the light switch.

'What the hell are you doing? *Spying* on us?'

'No!' I say. 'Look, I'm sorry. I didn't mean to . . . I couldn't help overhearing . . .' I swallow. 'The thing is, Connor isn't being difficult. He just wants you to be honest. He wants to know what you want.' I summon up my most understanding, womanly expression. 'Francesca . . . tell him what you want.'

Francesca stares at me incredulously, then looks at Connor.

'I want her to piss off.' She points at me.

'Oh,' I say, taken aback. 'Er, OK. Sorry.'

'And switch the lights off when you go,' adds Francesca, leading Connor up the aisle towards the back of the auditorium.

Are they going to have *sex*?

OK, I really do not want to be around for this.

Hastily I pick up my bag and hurry along the row of seats towards the exit. I push my way through the double doors into the foyer, flicking the light switch as I pass, then step out into the courtyard. I close the door behind me, and look up.

And then I freeze.

I don't believe it. It's Jack.

It's Jack, coming towards me, striding fast across the courtyard, determination on his face. I haven't got time to think, or prepare.

My heart really is racing. I want to speak or cry or . . . do *something*, but I can't.

He reaches me with a crunch of gravel, takes me by the shoulders, and gives me a long, intense look.

'I'm afraid of the dark.'

'What?' I falter.

'I'm afraid of the dark. Always have been. I keep a baseball bat under the bed, just in case.'

I stare at him in utter bewilderment.

'Jack—'

'I've never liked caviar.' He casts around. 'I . . . I'm embarrassed by my French accent.'

'Jack, what are you—'

'I got the scar on my wrist by cracking open a bottle of beer when I was fourteen. When I was a kid I used to stick gum under my Aunt Francine's dining table. I lost my virginity to a girl named Lisa Greenwood in her uncle's barn, and afterwards I asked if I could keep her bra to show my friends.'

I can't help giving a snuffle of laughter, but Jack

360

carries on regardless, his gaze fixed on mine.

'I've never worn any of the ties my mother has given me for Christmas. I've always wanted to be an inch or two taller than I am. I . . . I don't know what co-dependent means. I have a recurring dream in which I'm Superman, falling from the sky. I sometimes sit in board meetings and look around and think "Who the hell *are* these guys?"'

He draws breath and gazes at me. His eyes are darker than I've ever seen them.

'I met a girl on a plane. And . . . my whole life changed as a result.'

Something hot is welling up inside me. My throat is tight, my whole head aching. I'm trying so hard not to cry, but my face is contorting all by itself.

'Jack,' I swallow desperately. 'I didn't . . . I really didn't . . .'

'I know,' he cuts me off with a nod. 'I know you didn't.'

'I would never—'

'I know you wouldn't,' he says gently. 'I know you wouldn't.'

And now I can't help it, tears start flooding out of my eyes in sheer relief. He knows. It's OK.

'So . . .' I wipe my face, trying to gain control of myself. 'So does this . . . does this mean . . . that we . . .' I can't bring myself to say the words.

There's a long, unbearable silence.

If he says no, I don't know what I'll do.

'Well, you might want to hold back on your decision,' says Jack at last, and gives me a deadpan look. 'Because I have a lot more to tell you. And it isn't all pretty.'

I give a shaky laugh.

'You don't have to tell me anything.'

361

'Oh, I do,' says Jack firmly. 'I think I do. Shall we walk?' He gestures to the courtyard. 'Because this could take some time.'

'OK,' I say, my voice still wobbling a bit. Jack holds out an arm, and after a pause, I take it.

'So . . . where was I?' he says, as we step down into the courtyard. 'Oh, OK. Now this you really *can't* tell anybody.' He leans close and lowers his voice. 'I don't actually like Panther Cola. I prefer Pepsi.'

'No!' I say, shocked.

'In fact, sometimes I decant Pepsi *into* a Panther can—'

'No!' I give a snort of laughter.

'It's true. I told you it wasn't pretty . . .'

Slowly we start to walk around the edge of the dark, empty courtyard together. The only sound is the crunching of our feet on the gravel, and the breeze in the trees and Jack's dry voice, talking. Telling me everything.

TWENTY-SEVEN

It's amazing what a different person I am these days. It's as if I've been transformed. I'm a new Emma. Far more open than I used to be. Far more honest. Because what I've really learned is, if you can't be honest with your friends and colleagues and loved ones, then what is life all about?

The *only* secrets I have nowadays are tiny little essential ones. And I hardly have any of those. I could probably count them on the fingers of one hand. I mean, just off the top of my head:

1. I'm really not sure about Mum's new highlights.
2. That Greek-style cake Lissy made for my birthday was the most disgusting thing I've ever tasted.
3. I borrowed Jemima's Ralph Lauren swimsuit to go on holiday with Mum and Dad, and I bust one of the straps.
4. The other day when I was navigating in the car, I nearly said 'What's this big river all round London?' Then I realized it was the M25.
5. I had this really weird dream last week, about Lissy and Sven.
6. I've secretly starting feeding Artemis's spider plant 'Rebuild' plant food.
7. I'm *sure* Sammy the goldfish has changed again. Where did that extra fin come from?
8. I know I have to stop giving out my 'Emma

Corrigan, Marketing Executive' card to complete strangers, but I just can't help it.

9.   I don't know what advanced pro-ceramides are. (I don't even know what backward pro-ceramides are.)

10. Last night, when Jack said 'What are you thinking about?' and I said 'Oh nothing . . .' that wasn't quite true. I was actually planning the names of all our children.

But the thing is, it's completely normal to have the odd little secret from your boyfriend.

Everyone knows that.

THE END

THE SECRET DREAMWORLD OF A SHOPAHOLIC

Sophie Kinsella

*When the going gets tough – the tough go
shopping . . .*

Meet Rebecca Bloomwood.

She's a journalist. She spends her working life
telling others how to manage their money. She
spends her leisure time . . . shopping.

Retail therapy is the answer to all her problems. She
knows she should stop, but she can't. She tries
Cutting Back, she tries Making More Money. But
neither seems to work. The stories she concocts
become more and more fantastic as she tries to
untangle her increasingly dire financial difficulties.
Her only comfort is to buy herself something – just a
little something . . .

Can Becky ever escape from this dream world, find
true love, and regain the use of her Switch card?

The Secret Dreamworld of a Shopaholic . . . the
perfect pick me up for when it's all hanging in the
(bank) balance.

'I ALMOST CRIED WITH LAUGHTER'
Daily Mail

0 552 99887 7

BLACK SWAN

SHOPAHOLIC ABROAD

Sophie Kinsella

. . . Because there just aren't enough shops in Britain

Will travel broaden the mind . . . or loosen the purse strings?

For Rebecca Bloomwood, life is peachy. She has a job on morning TV, her bank manager is actually being *nice* to her, and when it comes to spending money, her new motto is Buy Only What You Need – and she's really (sort of) sticking to it. The icing on the brioche is that she's been offered a chance to work in New York.

New York! The Museum of Modern Art! The Guggenheim! The Metropolitan Opera House! And Becky does mean to go to them all. Honestly. It's just that it seems silly not to check out a few other famous places first. Like Saks. And Bloomingdales. And Barneys. And one of those fantastic sample sales where you can get a Prada dress for $10. Or was it $100? Anyway, it's full of *amazing* bargains.

Shopaholic Abroad – for the biggest culture shop of your life.

'A LAUGH-A-MINUTE READ THAT'S GUARANTEED TO ENTERTAIN YOU'
Glamour

0 552 99940 7

BLACK SWAN

SHOPAHOLIC TIES THE KNOT

Sophie Kinsella

For once in Becky Bloomwood's life, things are going
smoothly. She's got the dream job as a personal shopper
(spending other people's money – *and* getting paid for
it). She's got a fabulous Manhattan apartment with her
boyfriend Luke. They've even opened a joint bank
account together (although they can't quite agree
on whether a Miu Miu skirt counts as a
household expense).

Then Luke proposes – and all of a sudden life gets
hectic. From the first meeting of the in-laws, Becky's
Mum and Luke's mother Elinor don't hit it off. Mum
wants Becky to get married in Oxshott and wear her old
frilly wedding dress. Elinor wants to host a grand
extravaganza at the New York Plaza, complete with
woodland glade and the New York Philharmonic.

Becky knows she has to sit down and decide – but to be
honest, it's a lot more fun tasting cake, trying on dresses
and registering wedding presents. Time's ticking by,
plans are being made both sides of the Atlantic and
soon she realises she's in trouble . . .

Is the answer to come clean? Or simply register some
more silverware at Tiffany's?

Shopaholic Ties The Knot . . . because you only do it
once. Don't you?

'BRILLIANT . . . FUNNY, ROMANTIC AND
BELIEVABLE'
Heat

0 552 99957 1

BLACK SWAN

SHOPAHOLIC & SISTER

Sophie Kinsella

Becky Bloomwood is back!

Becky thought being married to Luke Brandon would be one big Tiffany box of happiness. But to be honest, it's not quite as dreamy as she'd hoped.

The trouble started on honeymoon, when she told Luke the tiniest little fib, about the teeniest little purchase. Now she's on a strict budget, she doesn't have a job — and worst of all her beloved Suze has a new best friend. Then she receives some incredible news. She has a long-lost sister!

Becky has never been more excited. Finally, a real sister! They'll have so much in common! They can go shopping together . . . choose shoes together . . . have manicures together . . .

Until she meets her — and gets the shock of her life. It can't be true. Surely Becky Bloomwood's long-lost sister can't . . . hate shopping?

A sister. A soulmate. A *skinflint*?

'THE FUNNIEST SO FAR'
Sunday Express

0 552 77111 2

BLACK SWAN